THE MOREVA OF ASTORETH

Roxanne Bland

Other Books by Roxanne Bland

The Underground (The Underground Series, Book 1)
Invasion (The Underground Series, Book 2)

To
Ann Coluzzi

GLOSSARY

All terms Devian except where noted.

Time
    Arhu = 40 days = 1 month
    Marun = 10 days = 1 week
Distance
    Da-na = 7 miles
    Nindan = 20 feet
    Šīzu = 1 foot
Volume
    Gur = 79 U.S. gallons
Weight
    Manû = 1 pound
Expletives
    Dicknut = asshole
    Foutéz = bullshit
    Merda = shit (Devian)
    Puta = bitch
    Skit = shit (Syrenese)
    Tik = bitch (Syrenese)
    Voi bastardi = you bastards
Religion
    Dingir = Heaven
    É = Temple
    Ohra-Namtar = the holiest rite of the Devian Gods
    Ohra-Sin = the holiest Astorethian rite
Other
    Albaitari = veterinarian
    Belye mouton = battering ram
    Gnut = a hornet-like insect
    Hakoi = a person without Devi blood
    Köldskador = frostbite (Syrenese)
    Krelo = a monkey-like animal
    Perritory = of the planet Peris
    Pettula mi = piss me off
    Skratz = a rat-like, artificial animal
    Skyrin = a hawk-like bird
    Terk = a cat-like, eight-legged animal
    Varsi = a contagious, non-lethal viral infection

Chapter One

"I could have you executed for this, Moreva Tehi," Astoreth said. My Devi grandmother, the Goddess of Love, scowled at me from Her golden throne in the massive Great Hall of Her equally massive É. Today, Her long, white hair had been woven into slender braids entwined with multicolored strands of tiny jewels. They sparkled in the candescent light radiating from the ceiling and the bulbous, wall-height fixtures. Her golden eyes burned with fury.

Sitting on my heels, I bowed my head, not wanting to see Her anger. I stared at the black and gold polished floor, trying to ignore the trickle of sweat snaking down my spine. My unbound hair, white like Hers, hung over my face. "Yes, Most Holy One," I said, trying to keep my voice steady.

"You blaspheme by not celebrating Ohra-Namtar, the holiest rite of the Gods. You are well aware that this was not Ohra-Sin praising my role in creating Peris but extolling all the deeds of the Great Pantheon in bringing this planet to life. Ohra-Namtar celebrates our creation of the hakoi, and the worthiest, handpicked by me and my brothers and sisters, celebrated with us. Marduc asked me of your whereabouts. Your absence sorely disappointed Him."

I shuddered in fear and loathing. Marduc, Lord of the Skies, was Astoreth's twin brother, and my grand-uncle. I'd been scared of Him since childhood and always made sure I was never alone with Him. I hated the way He'd stare at me when no one was looking, licking His lips as if I were a juicy piece of meat just waiting to be devoured. I had been too young to participate in the last Ohra-Namtar and knew He would have been only too eager to get His hands on me during this one.

"Moreva Tehi," Astoreth's hard tone brought me back to the

moment. "You are my acolyte. Your participation was not an option. By your absence, you did not share your body with Us, your brother and sister morevs, and Our worthy hakoi. You sullied the sacredness of Ohra-Namtar. What do you have to say for yourself?"

"I can only offer my most abject apologies, Most Holy One."

"Your apologies are not accepted."

"Yes, Most Holy One."

"Where were you?"

"I was in the laboratory, working on a cure for red fever. Our four-year cycle will end this summer, and thousands of hakoi in the Gods' cities and towns could die, so—"

"I know that," my grandmother snapped. "But why did you miss Ohra-Namtar? Did you not hear the bells?"

"Yes, Most Holy One. I heard them. I was about to lay aside my work when I noticed an anomaly in one of my pareon solutions, so I decided to take a minute to investigate. What I found...I-I just lost track of time."

"You lost track of time?" She repeated, sounding incredulous. "Do you expect me to believe *that?*"

"Yes, Most Holy One. It is the truth."

My head and hearts began throbbing, my grandmother probing me for signs I had lied. But She wouldn't find any. Lying to Her was pointless, and Her punishment for lying was harsh. Swaying under the onslaught, I endured the pain without making a sound. After what seemed like forever the throbbing eased, leaving me sick and dizzy.

"Very well. I accept what you say is true. I still do not accept your apology."

"Yes, Most Holy One," I said, panting a little.

A minute passed in uncomfortable silence. Uncomfortable for me, anyway. Another minute passed. And another. *Is...is She finished with me?* I prayed to be dimissed. But I wasn't.

"What do you have against my hakoi, Moreva?"

I frowned. "I don't understand, Most Holy One."

"I have watched you. You give them no respect. You heal them because you must, but you treat them like animals. Why is that?"

The trickle of sweat reached the small of my back and pooled there. "But my work—"

"Your work is a game between you and the red fever. It has nothing to do with my hakoi."

I didn't reply. It was true. Discovering the cure was a challenge I'd taken on because no one since the dawn of Peris had been able to find one. It was a war, me assaulting the virus's defenses, and the virus fending off my attacks. Our war was my obsession, and one I meant to win. And I *didn't* care about the hakoi. I despised them. They were docile enough—the Devi's spawning and breeding program saw to that—but they were slow-witted, not unlike the pirsu the É raised for meat and hide. They stank of makira, the pungent cabbage that was their dietary staple. From what I'd seen traveling through Kherah to Astoreth's and to the És of other Gods, all the hakoi were stupid and smelly, and I wanted nothing to do with them.

But I wouldn't—couldn't—admit that She was right. I wracked my brain, trying to think of something that wasn't an outright lie. Then it came to me. "Most Holy One, I treat Your hakoi the way I do because it is the Hierarchy of Being as the Devi created it. You taught us the Great Pantheon of Twelve is Supreme. The minor Devi are beneath You, the morev are beneath the minor gods, and Your hakoi are beneath the morev. Beneath the hakoi are the plants and animals of Peris. But sometimes Your hakoi forget their place and must be reminded."

The Great Hall was silent. I held my breath, praying She wouldn't probe me again.

"A pretty explanation, Moreva Tehi. But my hakoi know their place. It is you who does not know yours. You are the only morev in Kherah to have more Devi blood in your veins than hakoi, but that does not change your station, nor can you rise above it. Your privileges—to freely move about Uruk without É authorization, to participate in the Gods' festivals and games, to travel most anywhere in Kherah—are the same as any of your brothers and sisters. And it is the morev who attend my hakoi. As a healer, you are not too good to minister to their needs, and you are surely not too good to celebrate Ohra-Namtar with them."

I swallowed. "Yes, Most Holy One."

"Look at me."

I raised my head. My grandmother's expression was fierce.

"And that is why you let the time get away from you, as you say. *You,* Moreva Tehi, my acolyte of Love, are a bigot. I might understand if you were still a child, but you are not. You have done nothing to better yourself since then. Your bigotry is the reason you did not celebrate Ohra-Namtar. You did not want to share your body with Our hakoi." She glared, as if daring me to contradict her.

I stared into Her golden eyes, wanting to deny Her accusation, but that would be a lie. I kept quiet.

She leaned forward. "I have overlooked many of your transgressions while in my service. I know you use your psi power to harass other morevs for what you perceive as slights. But I cannot overlook your bigotry, or your missing Ohra-Namtar. However, I will not execute you because you are too dear to my heart. The stewardship for Astoreth-69 in the Syren Perritory ends in two days. You will take the next rotation."

My hearts froze. This was my punishment? Getting exiled to Syren? Everyone knew the Syren Perritory in Peris's far northern hemisphere was the worst place in the world to steward a landing beacon. Cold and dark, with dense woods full of wild animals, the Syren was no place for me. My place was in Kherah, a sunny desert south of the planet's equator where the fauna was kept in special habitats for learning and entertainment. As for the Syrenese, they were the descendants of one of the Devi's earliest and failed hakoi spawning and breeding experiments and were as untamed as the perritory where they lived.

My throat tightened, and a tear formed in the corner of my eye. *Eresh…he's in the Syren Perritory now. I'll be taking his place. It's already been a year since I've seen him, and now I won't see him again for another year. Two years without my best friend…my only friend. What am I to do?*

I managed to get up the gumption to protest but didn't. Challenging my grandmother was disrespectful, and my punishment for that would be even worse than exile. It would also be futile. Astoreth's word was law, and it had just come down on my head. "Yes, Most Holy One," I said, my voice meek.

She leaned back on Her throne. "Mehmed will come to your room after breakfast tomorrow so you can be fitted for your uniform."

"My uniform, Most Holy One? I will not be taking my clothes?"

"No. As overseer of the landing beacon, you are the liaison between the Mjor village as well as the commander of the garrison. Your subordinate, Kepten Yose, will report to you once a marun, and you are to relay the garrison's needs to Laerd Teger, the Mjoran village chief."

"Yes, Most Holy One."

"I will make allowance for your healer's kit and a portable laboratory, but you are not to take your red fever research. I am sure you have other projects you can work on while you are there."

"But—"

"No, Moreva Tehi. It is too dangerous."

"I can take precautions—"

"No. I will not allow you to endanger the Mjorans. That is my final word." She gazed at me for a long moment. "You should also know that they, like all Syrenese, are not a forgiving people. They do not take transgressions—of any kind—lightly."

I swallowed. "I understand, Most Holy One."

"Good." Her eyes narrowed. "One more thing. As the garrison's moreva, you will lead the services in worship of me, and that includes Ohra-Sin. Go now."

"Thank you, Most Holy One." I stood on shaky legs, bowed, and backed out of the Great Hall. Fleeing to my room, I fell on the bed and sobbed. It was bad enough to be exiled to the Syren Perritory and to spend another year without Eresh, but Ohra-Sin with the garrison? Only the hakoi served in Astoreth's military. I felt dirty already. And not allowing me to work on my red fever project was punishment by itself.

A hand touched my shoulder. "Tehi, what's wrong?" a worried voice said. It was Moreva Jaleta, one of my friendlier morev sisters.

"I-I'm being sent to the Syren Perritory to steward Astoreth-69," I wailed.

"But why?"

I sat up. "I missed Ohra-Namtar yesterday, and n-now Astoreth is punishing me."

She gave me an unsympathetic look. "You're lucky She didn't have your head. Be thankful you're Her favorite."

I sniffed, but said nothing.

Jaleta patted my shoulder. "It won't be so bad, Tehi. The year will be over before you know it. Come on, it's time to eat."

◎⫘⫘⫘⫘◎

That night, I stood in line with fifty-nine of my brother and sister morevs in a hallway covered in colorful mosaics of the wildlife that lived in the Kamala River's estuaries, waiting for the doors to open. In a similar hallway on the opposite side of the É, another sixty morevs stood in line, waiting for the same. Tonight was Ktana, and I couldn't wait.

I loved all the Astorethian rituals—except for the Ohras—but Ktana was my favorite. Held four times a year, it was a renewal of sorts, bestowing on us the gift of witnessing Her vast power, to bask in Her glory, and giving us a taste of Dingir. Yet Ktana had another purpose. Tiny implants in our earlobes fed our visions to Ginzu, an artificial intelligence that interpreted what we saw, and based on our psychological profiles, decided whether any one of us needed counseling. After a Ktana, Ginzu always counseled me about something or other, but I paid it no mind. I was fine the way I was.

Thinking about the upcoming ritual, it occurred to me my implant would be removed before I left for Syren. *No Ktana for a whole year.* My mood started to plummet. *Never mind. Ktana's not going anywhere, and it's not like I'll be stuck in the Syren Perritory forever.* That cheered me.

"About time she was punished for something," someone behind me said in a low voice. Several morevs snickered. "The Syrenese'll put her in her place," someone else said. More twittering.

Holding my head high, I ignored them. Jaleta could be kind, but she had a big mouth, and by the time we'd finished dinner, everyone knew about my punishment. I knew by their voices who'd said what and could've zapped them with a knifelike bolt of pain that would linger for a good while. But I didn't. Zapping them would delay Ktana until they recovered, and I was in no mood to wait.

I endured a few more jibes before the doors whispered open. We filed into the majestic, semi-circular sanctorium, its unadorned walls emitting a soft, gently pulsing blue glow. We found our assigned places, and after making ourselves comfortable on large, thick, square pillows, assumed the sacred lutos—our legs folded so that each foot nestled in the crevasses created by our bent knees, our palms pressed together, and fingers pointing upward before our chests. I closed my eyes and with my brothers and sisters, began singing in a low, wordless monotone.

The air vibrated from our song, evoking a feeling of being lightly stroked with feathers. The singing and the sensation lulled me into a light trance.

The Moreva of Astoreth

A mild pressure on my brain signaled Astoreth's power flowing into me. When we entered the sanctorium, She'd been seated in sacred lutos on a dais, separated from us by a rippling ribbon of shimmering, liquid silver.

Breathless, I waited for the swirling colors, the bright golden lights streaking across my vision like falling stars, the sense of flying through Dingir, and so much more. In a moment, a small, round ball of white light appeared and rushed forward. Just before it would have enveloped me, it exploded into a mass of spinning, kaleidoscopic colors. My clothes melted away. I laughed, the sound reverberating. This was how my visions always started, and I eagerly stepped into the rotating mass, ready to be lifted and tossed about by gentle, invisible forces.

Except I wasn't. As soon as I stepped through, the bright colors vanished. Zigzagging shades of gray surrounded me, thunder assaulted my ears, and a fierce wind howled. Something slammed me against what felt like a rough, rock wall, and my breath whooshed out. I tried to take another, but couldn't. The unseen force pressed harder and harder against my chest. It hurt. Struggling against it proved useless.

Whatever had pinned me disappeared, and in the next second, I was tumbling down a great, black hole. I screamed as hard and loud as I could. Silence.

After falling for an eternity, I landed hard on something wet and squishy. It smelled awful. Horrified and disgusted, I sprang to my feet, slipped, and fell on my butt. Then I noticed the blackness surrounding me had lightened the tiniest bit. Straining my eyes, I could make out a faint, green glow to my left. It brightened, even as I stared. Head swiveling, I saw the glow came from all directions, but couldn't see its source. Moments later, it was bright enough for me to see clearly. I looked down and screamed again. This time, it echoed.

I was sitting in a pile of rotting entrails, streaked with old, black blood.

My fear ramped into hysteria. Whimpering, I crawled through the mess until I reached dry ground. I jumped to my feet and ran as fast as I could, not caring where I was headed. I ran until I could run no more. I squeezed my eyes shut and gasped for air, fell to my knees, and let my head drop to my chest.

When I finally opened my eyes, fresh terror made my skin pucker.

I was kneeling in a wriggling mass of...something. The glow was coming from them. I leapt to my feet and started running again, my screams echoing.

The vision abruptly disappeared, and my eyes popped open. Panting, my head swiveled left and right. I was back in the sanctorium. Astoreth had withdrawn Her power. Shaking, I watched my brothers and sisters wake from their trances.

The hairs on the back of my neck stood up. Someone was watching me. I turned. It was my grandmother. Her golden stare bored into mine for a full minute. Then She closed Her eyes.

Ktana was over, and I filed out of the sanctorium with the others. In the hallway, I forced myself to keep pace instead of elbowing them out of my way and running for the elevators. I kept my head down, not wanting anyone to see the fear I knew still showed in my eyes.

I rushed out of the cab and ran to my room. Falling against the door, I closed my eyes and blew a heavy breath, willing my quivering to stop and my heartsbeat to slow. After gaining control over myself, I let out another breath. *What...that's never happened to me before.* For me, Ktana had always been a beautiful, joyous experience. But this... *I've never been so scared in my life.* I swallowed and tried to blot out images of the rotting entrails and the green wriggling things from my mind's eye. Then I remembered Astoreth. *Why was Grandmother staring at me like that? Did She know?*

Blowing a final breath, I opened my eyes and saw two blinking lights on my console. I had messages. I knew the pink one was from Ginzu, wanting to talk to me about my vision. The purple one could have been from anybody.

I needed to talk to Ginzu. I settled in the float chair, lay my index finger on a small dark panel to my right and held it there. Once my identity had been confirmed, I tapped the flashing pink panel. Ginzu's' avatar appeared on my left.

She wore her usual white robe over a pale yellow gown with a jeweled clasp at her left shoulder. Long, curly black hair cascaded over her chest, and her black eyes were like deep, unfathomable pools. Her rendering was so precise she could pass for a living being. The only difference between her and the living was that she wore her shoulder clasp on the left, whereas the living wore theirs on the right. She pressed her palms and gave a deep bow. "Greetings, Moreva Tehi. May the Most Holy One turn Her face to you."

I repeated the gesture and bowed my head. "And to you, Ginzu." As always, it felt strange to engage in formal greetings with a machine. I pointed to the float chair next to the console. "Please, sit."

She made herself comfortable and then looked up, face grave. I frowned. *What? Is it that bad?*

Ginzu seemed to take a breath. "Tehi, you had a difficult Ktana."

I snorted. "That's an understatement. What does it mean?"

Her lips tightened. "You are in great danger."

My jaw dropped. *In Astoreth's name, has she blown a circuit?* "From what? Ginzu, this is the É. What could possibly hurt—"

She held up a hand. "From yourself. I have been telling you for years that there are dark elements in your Ktana visions that signal you need cleansing. You have never taken my counsel seriously. You are in danger of..."

"Of what?"

Ginzu looked at me for a long moment. "Of losing your soul."

I rolled my eyes. "Ginzu, come on. That's ridiculous. Why am I in danger of losing my soul? I mean, what specifically—"

"That is a question only you can answer. I am but a machine."

"But—"

"There is nothing more I can tell you. I will leave now." Ginzu paused. "Please take my counsel this time, Tehi. Before it is too late." She disappeared.

I stared at the chair Ginzu had vacated for a long time, my thoughts churning. *Losing my soul over what? I've always obeyed Astoreth's tenets. I believe. I worship. I sing hymns. Astoreth, I write some of them. What's Ginzu talking about?*

I threw up my hands. "I'll think about this later," I muttered and changed into my nightgown. Lifting the hem, I sniffed, and then smiled. I loved the smell of freshly laundered clothes. Crawling into bed, its arms draped a blanket over me. I sniffed again. The blanket was clean, too.

I rolled over and a wave of annoyance rippled through me. The purple message light was still blinking. I let out a sigh. I was so warm and cozy now. Did I really want to get up and find out what the message was about? *No. I'll look at it tomorrow before breakfast.*

I closed my eyes and went to sleep.

A chime sounded, loud enough to wake the dead.

Bolting upright, I shook my head hard, trying to clear the sleep-fog from my brain. Fully awake now, my eyes widened. That chime was the last of four calling us for breakfast. If I didn't hurry, I'd be late. If I was, I wouldn't be fed until lunchtime.

I scrambled out of bed, shedding my nightgown as I ran to the closet. No time for a shower. Throwing on my day-gown and robe, I fumbled the jeweled clasp that held my robe together. I burst out of my room and sprinted toward the elevators. When the doors opened at ground level, I charged out of the cab and ran through the hallway to the dining room. A small knot of my brothers and sisters were walking inside. Relief washed over me. *Made it just in time.*

Outside the doorway, I leaned against the wall to calm myself. I took a deep breath and slowly let it out until my lungs were empty. Then I took another breath. *Wonder why didn't I hear the first chime?* I rarely slept well and often didn't sleep at all. The first chime, soft as it was, normally woke me in a second. *Guess after that vision, my body needed the rest.* I took one last breath.

I walked into the dining room and tightened my lips. Moreva Quora, my archenemy, was sitting in my chair. Quora detested me because, until my birth, she'd been Astoreth's favorite.

No you don't, puta. I marched to the table and stood with hand on hip. "Out of my chair, Quora."

She looked up and smiled. "Why, Tehi! We thought you'd be in the Syren Perritory by now."

"The supply airship doesn't leave until tomorrow, and you know it. Out of my chair."

"No. I don't see your name on it. What are you going to do, run to our Most Holy One and complain?"

I thought to give her a good zap but decided there was a better way. I rested my hands on the table's edge and gave her a mirthless grin. "If you don't, I'll put a simi in your bed. Maybe two." Simis were long, thin, harmless snakes that made their homes in crevasses. A bed, with its sheets, mattress, and pillows, was an ideal place for them. And Quora was afraid of snakes.

Her face paled. She knew I'd do it, too.

Without another word, she got up and left. I plopped into my chair and looked around. Everyone was staring. "What?"

"You didn't have to do that," Morevi Sabo said. Sabo worked in the lab with me.

"She was in my chair."

Our food arrived, cutting off further talk. I didn't realize how hungry I was until the delicious aromas made my mouth water. I wanted to dive in, but we had to wait for the blessing. *Hm. Who's going to give it?* Morevi Prian got up, and I let out a little groan. He was one of the older morevs, well-respected for his work in cosmology. The problem was that he tended to ramble.

After what seemed like an hour, the blessing had been given and we could eat. Prian had talked for so long, my food had cooled until it was just warm. I would have sent it back to the kitchen for reheating, but I was hungry enough not to care. I finished first. Etiquette demanded I should wait until at least two of my tablemates had finished before leaving but I didn't feel like being polite and took my plate to the cart at the far end of the dining room.

I needed to get to the lab to pack my portable.

I walked to a different elevator bank and rode one to the basement. Traversing the last hallway, I thought again about what reason Astoreth could possibly have had for sticking the life sciences section down here. Unlike the other sections, ours had no windows. Getting the rooms to a decent temperature was hopeless; it was either too warm or too cold. And it was hard to get to; our section could be reached only after tramping through what seemed like an endless maze of hallways.

I entered the lab, turned right, and walked through the third doorway on my left into the storage room. Grabbing the handle of a big, white trunk, I wheeled it to my workstation. I'd probably need two but wanted to wait until I'd figured out what equipment should go into which trunk. I didn't want to block my workstation with them and make my life any harder than it already was.

I set the trunk as far out of my way as possible, picked up my tablet, and wandered about my station, dictating what I thought I'd need. All Astoreth's life scientists were healers, so we had extensive medical knowledge. Each of us also has two sub-specialties, sometimes more. Mine were virology and bacteriology.

The more I dictated, the more annoyed I became. The portable lab I'd put together would be primitive, to say the least. I could take a 3-D microscope, but I couldn't take a 3-D modeler. It was too big to fit inside a trunk. I could take plenty of isolate and whole plant extracts, but I preferred making my extracts from living plants, and I was sure that wherever I'd be working in Mjor, there wouldn't be enough room for a habitat. It didn't matter. I couldn't take a centrifuge with me, anyway. Like the 3-D modeler, it was too big to go into a trunk.

The lab's door opened, and then the sound of shuffling feet. I spoke louder so to hear myself over the noise. After all was quiet, I didn't lower my voice. I knew I was disturbing my labmates. I didn't care.

A minute later, I stopped dictating and tightened my jaw. *What difference does it make what I take if I can't work on my project? I'm sure morevs in the other Gods' És are trying to find a cure too, and I want to find it first. If I lose a year's worth of research, it could ruin my chance.* My eyes widened a fraction. *Wait. I can still work. I can take a portable sterile environment. It's small enough, and then the lab will have everything I need. Most of what I need, anyway. And it'll be easy to sneak the red fever vials out of here, just mix their box in with extracts that have to be kept frozen. One will do. Well, maybe two. And I need a lot of hairless skratzes for one of the other projects I'm taking with me. A couple of extra boxes...no one will suspect.*

I thought about Astoreth's order not to take my project to Mjor. *If I find the cure while I'm gone, I doubt She'll punish me. And if I find it soon enough, imagine the glory the* É *will get for saving thousands of hakoi lives this summer. And selling it to the other* És *will pull in so many talents, She'll be up to Her ears in them.* Then I remembered what She'd said about the Mjorans, that they don't take transgressions lightly. *Bringing my red fever project...I'm sure they'd see it as a transgression.* I gave a minute shrug. *Well...who says they have to know?* Staring at tablet's screen, my lips stretched into a small, tight smile of satisfaction.

Looking over my list, I decided I had enough for the first trunk. I had pulled up its lid when the jeweled clasp at my shoulder holding my robe together beeped. I tapped it. "Moreva Tehi."

"Moreva, this is Mehmed. Please come to your room. I am ready for your fitting."

"Can't we do this later? I'm packing my lab."

"No, Moreva. I must have enough time to make your uniforms. Any later than now, and you will not be ready to leave on the airship tomorrow. Our Most Holy One would not be pleased."

"Oh...*fine*." Astoreth was already angry with me, and it wouldn't do to anger Her even more. I closed the trunk and headed for the door. Giving it a shove, it almost smacked Morevi Sabo in the face. I didn't apologize.

I rode the elevator to the É's main floor, then walked to the dormitory elevators. I waved my hand over the call panel and waited, growing more irritated by the second. The dormitory elevators, unlike the ones in every other part of the É, were notoriously slow. A cab arrived two minutes later, and I stepped inside. "Three."

Stopping at the third floor, the doors whispered open. An oblong patch of sunslight lit the hallway's carpet about eighty šīzu away. My eyes narrowed. Mehmed was already inside my room. There was precious little privacy in the dormitory. The doors had no locks, and anyone could walk in at any time. Everyone knew better than to enter my room without being invited, though. My power let me sense that not only someone had been in there, but their identity, too. If anyone did, that morev might walk inside their room next to find clothes strewn over the floor or the mirror smashed. As it was, I barely tolerated the hakoi who cleaned it. But Mehmed was a special case. He made all our clothes, and could easily alter a garment so it didn't fit perfectly, as Astoreth demanded. A morev in ill-fitting clothes was subject to punishment in whichever way suited Her whim. Which might include torture—the kind that left no marks.

In the hallway, the makira's stench hit me like a wall. Steeling myself, I entered my room to find Mehmed and a fitting robot standing before a three-way mirror. He handed me a dark red blouse and a matching pair of trousers. "Here is your uniform. Please put it on."

For the next hour or so, I stood on a little box he'd brought with him, not moving unless I was told, listening to him mutter to his robot, and trying to breathe as little as possible. When he'd finished, I took off the uniform and inspected it. Mehmed gave me a lot of instructions about it that mostly went in one ear and out the other. I handed him the garment. "Thank you, Mehmed. May the Most Holy One turn Her face to you."

"And to you, Moreva Tehi." He nodded once, and with his fitting robot carrying the mirror, left my room. His stench faded, and I took in a great gulp of air.

After dressing, I stepped over to the console and its blinking purple light. I accessed the message. It read "Protocol and Manual. Astoreth-69." *Guess I'm supposed to read this.* I looked at the page count at the screen's bottom, and my brows shot up. *One hundred and seventy pages? I don't have time for this.* I shook my head. *Never mind. I'll just download it and read it on the way there.*

I'd turned to leave my room when despair overwhelmed me. *This is really happening…I'm leaving Uruk for the Syren Perritory tomorrow.* In the back of my mind, I'd been hoping Astoreth would change Hers, but I now knew that wasn't going to happen. I collapsed on the bed and tears ran down my cheeks. Soon I was sobbing again, except this time there was no one around to hear it.

Eventually, my tears dried, and my determination returned. If I was to be sent into exile, I needed to finish getting my portable packed. I returned to my workstation, opened the trunk, and picked up my tablet. Glancing over the notes I'd made, I continued packing. By dinnertime, I'd almost finished. Just a few more pieces and the vials of red fever, and everything would be ready to go.

But would I?

Chapter Two

The airship landed on its pad. After the pilot, a minor Devi, gave the "all clear," I stepped out of the machine onto a stone slab.

The trip had been awful. I'd never flown before and almost as soon as we'd lifted off, my breakfast rose into my throat. I'd tapped the pilot's shoulder and told him. He handed me a bag. I promptly threw up into it. When I stopped retching, he'd turned in his seat and peered at me, then handed over a stack of bags. I'd immediately torn one open. Two bags later, I thought I'd be all right. Then we'd flown into something he called turbulence. Despite its leviathan size, the airship was tossed around like a toy, repeatedly throwing me hard against the harness straps. It hurt, even through the thick material of my winter uniform. Sure we were about to die, I'd grabbed another, umpteenth bag.

After what seemed like an eternity, we finally reached Mjor. My stomach calm—at least for the moment—I looked out the airship's window as we made our descent. The landing beacon made for a riveting sight. Its colossal stationary dish, blazing like silver fire in the twin sunslight, was perched on an even more colossal tower of white kyrolite at least a thousand šīzu high. Two tanks had been parked alongside the tower's base. Dwarfed by its size, they looked insignificant.

I waved to the pilot and headed toward a large knot of people in the distance, taking in the place where I would stay for the next year. It looked dour. A featureless, mirror-smooth wall of grayish-black stone rose about a hundred šīzu high, with two huge stone doors set in its middle. At its top, the wall was crenelated with deep, narrow slits and partially covered by a steep-pitched roof. Two thick towers, far smaller and shorter than the beacon, anchored the wall at each end. A short, tube-like kyrolite bridge connected the top of the right-hand tower to the beacon. On the ground, the beacon tower had been cemented to the shorter tower. Next to the fortress, the beacon looked monstrously out of place.

A walled village...Astoreth, I'll be claustrophobic before the end of this marun.

I stopped before the first of three people standing in front of the garrison. Joy filled me at seeing Eresh. It had only been a year, but it seemed like forever. A moment later, a pang of sadness soured my happy mood. *It's not fair he can't stay at least until tomorrow. We have only a few hours.*

Half-Devi, half-hakoi, his skin was three shades lighter than my medium-hued, blue-violet. Tall and slender, long, black curls fell around his face and shoulders, and his eyes were darker than the night. In contrast, I looked like a Devi goddess—white curls, hourglass curves, and golden eyes—but that was where the resemblance ended. A Devi would have towered over Eresh. I had to crane my neck just to look into his face.

Behind us, the forty-one person garrison stood at attention. Wearing a solemn expression, he pressed his palms, and I did the same. We gave each other a deep bow. "Moreva Tehi, may the Most Holy One turn Her face to you."

"And to you, Morevi Eresh."

He smiled. "Welcome to the Syren Perritory and the Mjor village." He turned to a blue-uniformed hakoi standing a step behind him. "This is your second in command, Kepten Yose."

I nodded once. "Kepten." It was disconcerting, acknowledging a hakoi as if he was my equal.

"Moreva Tehi." He inclined his head and clicked his heels, a proper military salute to a superior officer. "Garrison ready for inspection, Moreva."

I looked sideways at Eresh, who gave me a nod. "Very well, Kepten. Lead the way."

It was too cold out for my taste, but at least the suns warmed me a little. Birds sang as we walked along the ten orderly rows of four troops each. They all looked straight ahead, their eyes never veering from whatever it was they were looking at. I peered into their faces. They were blank, yet there was something in the eyes I couldn't place, a look the

É hakoi didn't have. I wondered for a moment, then dismissed it. *My imagination. At least they don't stink.*

Inspection completed, I turned to meet who I presumed to be Mjor's chief. Barely standing at his waist, my gaze traveled up, then up some more. He was the biggest hakoi I'd ever seen. His muscular shoulders looked as broad as the mountains that surrounded us, and his deep bronze skin was far darker than the pale hakoi back home. Long, thick golden hair, the same shade as the third, summer sun, ruffled in the breeze. His light-colored brows—almost white—matched his short beard. But it was his eyes that intrigued me most. All the hakoi I'd ever known had brown eyes. His eyes were blue, like the stars, and just as cold.

I didn't like him. Judging by his scowl, he didn't like me, either.

"I am Laerd Teger, Chief of Mjor," he said in a deep, gravelly voice. His heavily accented Devian was barely intelligible.

"Laerd. I am Moreva Tehi."

"I heard." He turned and strode toward the stone doors.

My jaw dropped. "How...how dare he disrespect...who does this dicknut think he is?" I narrowed my eyes. *Well, I know how to fix him.* Aiming to zap his spine, I was about to let fly when a hand settled on my shoulder.

"Tehi, don't," Eresh said, his voice quiet. "Let it go."

I jerked my head around. "But—"

"Let it go."

The Laerd reached the village gate. He pushed on a door and it swung open as if oiled. I looked at Eresh in surprise. "Perfectly balanced," he said. "Otherwise, it'd take one of those tanks over there to move them." Eresh glanced at the garrison, still standing in orderly rows. "You need to dismiss the troops," he whispered.

"How do I do that?" I whispered back.

"Tell Kepten Yose the garrison is dismissed."

I turned. "Kepten Yose, the garrison is dismissed."

"Yes, Moreva." He barked an order to the troops and gave instructions to two of them. I watched the garrison enter the beacon tower through double doors, except for the two who marched toward the airship.

"That's where they live? In the tower?"

"Yes."

"Why?"

"The better to protect it, silly. Besides, they can't live anywhere else." Eresh frowned. "Didn't you read the Protocol?"

"No."

He gave me an exasperated look. "What were you doing when you were getting ready to come up here? You should have read—"

"Eresh, I barely had time to pack. I tried to download it this morning to read on the way here but couldn't. I kept getting error messages. And there wasn't time to call the techs before I had to leave." I paused. "So what's the Protocol, anyway?"

He sighed. "The Protocol is the agreement between Astoreth and Mjor about the beacon. It's like a contract. She pays Mjor for allowing it to be here. There's a lot of other stuff too, like relations between the garrison and the Mjorans, but the most important is that, except for us, no military presence—that's personnel or equipment—is allowed inside the village walls without the Laerd's permission."

Relations? What kind of relations? I gave my head a minute shake. *Doesn't matter.* I'm *certainly not going to have any relations with them.* "All right. Got any advice on how I'm supposed to survive the year?"

"Keep busy. There's really nothing here, and it's deadly once you get used to the routine." He shrugged. "You've got your lab, so you should be fine."

"What about the Mjorans?"

"They'll ignore you."

My eyes widened. "You didn't talk to anybody for a whole *year?*"

"Well, there's Hyme. He's Mjor's healer. Nice man, but he'll talk your ear off if given half a chance." His brow quirked. "But then you're both healers, so I guess you'll have lots to talk about."

"Healer, huh? Bet I could teach him a few things."

Eresh smiled as if he knew something I didn't.

"So when do I get to meet him?"

"He's been away for a few days. He goes on these...errands, I guess, every now and then. He'll be back soon."

Walking to the gate, he gave me a sidelong look. "What'd you do to get sent up to this place?"

I bristled. "What makes you think I'm being punished for something?"

He chuckled. "Tehi, no one comes here because they want to. I was unlucky enough to have my name pulled for the rotation. Besides, I was expecting Morevi Nareet from Erdu. So what are you doing here?"

My lips twisted. "I missed Ohra-Namtar."

His eyes popped, and he let out a low whistle. "You don't know how lucky you are. Anybody else, She would have executed."

"I know."

We walked through the gate's portal and stepped into the village. He gave me another sidelong look. "So...what do you think?"

My brows rose. The entire village had been painted in just about every hue imaginable, a riot of color dazzling in its intensity. There wasn't a speck of gray stone anywhere. But the centerpiece was the rectangular plaza. Made of varicolored stone blocks aligned in a spiral pattern, in its middle lay a square pool covered with ice. "It's beautiful."

"It is, isn't it? There's a gorgeous fountain in the pool, too. They'll turn it on later in the spring. Come on. I'll show you where you'll be staying." He headed for the tower on the right. On this side, it was painted bright red with even brighter green diagonal stripes. "You'll understand the reason for all these colors come winter."

I took in the Mjorans milling about on the plaza. The men were all tall like the Laerd. Some looked taller. Even the women were tall. Watching them made me self-conscious about being short. I pushed the feeling away.

A gust of wind knocked me off balance, the cold slicing through my heavy uniform as if I wore one of my lightest gowns. I shivered. "Eresh, I thought you said it was spring."

He didn't seem bothered. "It is, though it's still early. This is balmy compared to winter."

At the tower, Eresh stepped up to a stone door nestled under a curved arch. A loud click sounded, and then he pushed it open. "A bioscan," he said as we stepped through. "Right now, it only recognizes me, but once I reprogram it, it'll only recognize you." He pressed a button above the scanner twice. "All right, I've deleted myself. Put your thumb here," he said, pointing to a small, shallow cavity.

I did, and the scanner began vibrating. It stopped about ten seconds later. The machine emitted a low beep.

Eresh nodded once. "It's done. Let's go in."

We crossed the threshold. Lights flickered, illuminating a vestibule. He smiled. "Give me a hug."

I leapt, almost knocking him over. Holding him in a tight lock, my tears threatened to spill. It felt so good being in his arms again, and it had been so long. Close contact wasn't forbidden among morevs, but Astoreth frowned upon it, so back home, our hugs were rare and secret. "Astoreth, I missed you so much," I murmured into his uniform.

"Me, too."

After a few minutes, we let go of each other and turned to a short flight of stairs leading to a spacious landing. Another flight of stairs, steeper than the ones before us, ran straight. Further on, they curved around the tower. I shivered again. Our hug had warmed me, but now it seemed just as cold as outside.

Eresh began my tour. He showed me the É, a huge, round, and windowless room as wide as the tower. In its center was a water-filled pool about ten šīzu deep. He pointed. "For Ohra-Sin. By the way, we're on the same schedule as back home, so your first one's tomorrow night."

A picture blossomed in my mind's eye. The garrison and I in the pool, naked. They grabbed at me, eager to consummate the rite. I shuddered. *Ugh. I can't wait.* Mercifully, the vision disappeared.

Eyeing the pool again, I frowned. "There isn't enough room for forty-one."

"Right. There'll be twenty and twenty-one of the garrison here at a time. It'll take two arhu to serve them all. They also rotate for morning and evening services."

He showed me where the ritual supplies were kept. I shivered a third time. "Why's it so cold in here?"

"The Mjorans are pretty frugal. They heat rooms only as they need them." He cranked the handle on a floor-to-ceiling grate. "Now you'll have some heat for tonight's service." He paused. "Any questions?"

"No."

"All right. Let's go to your apartment."

We climbed the stairs. *I'll set up the lab in there. Nice and private.*

At the top, Eresh reprogrammed the door's bioscan lock. We stepped inside. The round room was just a little smaller than the É and almost as bare. Closest to me was a rectangular table and four uncomfortable-looking chairs with straight backs and no padding. My lips tightened. *I can't set up the lab in here. That table's not big enough. I took a quick look around the rest of the room. And there's nothing in here to keep anything cold. Well, the trunk's got battery-powered cooling and freezing, so the skratz and the virus will keep for a little while. But I can't wait too long. I've got to get the virus into a real freezer before it becomes active. I let out a quiet hiss. I'll figure out something. I didn't bring my project all the way up here for nothing.*

A clanking sound caught my attention. Eresh cranked the handle on another floor-to-ceiling grate. "Like downstairs, it'll warm up in here in a couple of hours."

I eyed the mound of furs draped over two generously padded chairs in front of an enormous fireplace and a bed big enough for three people. "Are you sure? It looks like someone skinned an entire zoo."

"The heat gets turned off at night."

"What if I want to leave it on?"

"You can't. They have a central system. The heat is turned off at five Durm and isn't switched on until two Gor. If you get cold at night, that's what the fireplace is for."

"Durm? Gor?"

"It was in the manual, Tehi."

"I told you I couldn't download it."

Eresh sighed. "Time. The Syrenese tell time differently than we do. Instead of dividing the day into two periods of fourteen hours, they divide the day into four periods of seven hours. The names of the periods are Ekban—that's the earliest—Gor, Tryn, and Durm, which is the latest."

"Sounds complicated."

"Not really, once you get used to it. Besides, your uniform timepiece is programmed for it. You won't have a problem."

"Oh, that's right." Then, "let's get back to the heating. Suppose I want to bathe after five Durm?"

He grinned. "You don't." He pointed to a narrow door hard by a large vanity. "And speaking of bathing…that's the bath. It's tiny, and it's got a low ceiling. I had to crouch to keep from bumping my head." He gave me a sly look. "But you shouldn't have a problem."

I ran over and punched his arm.

"Ow. The closet's over there." He nodded toward an open dark space. "And over there," he pointed to a narrow door in the wall on the other side of the room, "is the larder. Tinned food is kept in there in case the dining hall is closed for some reason."

"Dining hall?"

"Yes. Mealtimes are communal, like home." Eresh opened the three windows in the room, then the stone shutters, and the overhead lights winked out. Sunslight streamed in, and the room was just as bright as it had been before.

I frowned. "Why'd you do that?"

"Less wear on the generators," he explained. "Keep the shutters open during the day and close them at night. It'll stay warmer in here after they turn the heat off."

Behind me, something scraped against stone. I looked over my shoulder in time to see the end of one of my trunks fall to the floor with a heavy thump. "Be careful with that, you idiot," I snapped. "You'd better hope my lab equipment isn't in there. If anything's broken, I'll hold you responsible."

The look on the soldier's face turned frightened. "A thousand pardons, Moreva," he said, panting. "Moreva, where shall we put your luggage?"

"Put them over there." I pointed to the wall across from the bed.

Eresh tugged on my sleeve. "This door leads outside." I followed and watched him pull back the deadbolt's metal bar. It slid through the collars easily enough, even though the lock looked ancient. He opened the door, revealing the battlement I'd seen from outside the village walls. On one side was the stone wall with slits I'd noticed. The wall across from it was solid. The two sides created a walkway about eight šīzu across and connected my tower to the other one. Most of the walkway was covered by the steep roof. I nodded at the other tower. "What's that over there?"

"That's the Laerd's apartment. By the way, if you need to see him, it's easiest to get to him this way. Both doors—his and yours—have a bell." He shut the door and bolted it, then stepped over to the nightstand next to the bed. "And here's the intercom."

I peered at the simple, square box with two buttons and a knob. Decorating its face was a lighted series of what I guessed were Syrenese letters or numbers. I'd never seen anything like it.

He touched the yellow button. "When it chimes, press this to answer. The red one is for messages. The knob controls the volume. The timepiece you won't need because of the one on your uniform."

"Is that what that is? A timepiece?" I inspected the machine further. Two slim cables, one black and the other blue, sprouted from the intercom's rear. I looked up with wide eyes. "Are those what I think they are?"

"Believe it or not."

I shook my head. "Astoreth. How primitive can you get?"

Eresh grinned. "It's not just them. Wait'll you see the converter."

"The what?"

"Never mind. I'll show you. Anyway, you might like to know only three people can call you—the Laerd, Hyme, and Kepten Yose." Pulling the nightstand's top drawer open, he took out a sheet of nupaper and handed it to me. "These are the rules of the village. Read them carefully. No one is exempt, especially not us."

"Nupaper? They don't have tablets?"

"Not that I've seen."

"Unbelievable," I muttered. At least it was written in Devian. I glanced over it and rolled my eyes. "Rules, schmules."

"Stop it, Tehi." Eresh's voice was stern. "The Mjorans barely put up with us as it is. You break those rules, it'll only make it worse."

My lip curled. "What are they going to do—kick us out?"

He glared. "In a heartsbeat. We'd lose the beacon, leaving a hole in the Devi's spaceship flight path. And wouldn't Astoreth be happy about *that*."

I let out an exasperated sigh. "All right, all right." Walking to the fireplace, I sat in one of the fur-covered chairs and scanned the sheet. As Eresh had said, dining was communal. The villagers ate in shifts. My dining shift was at six Gor for breakfast, three Tryn for lunch, and seven Tryn for dinner, sharp. Tardiness was not tolerated. If I missed my shift, I couldn't eat until the next one. *Well, that's no different from home.* No one was to venture into the woods alone. And on, and on, and on. I looked up. "Lot of rules."

He shrugged. "Not much different from the É. You'll get used to it. Come on, let's go to the tower."

I dropped the sheet and followed him to the door. After reprogramming its lock, we walked through the tunnel-like bridge I'd seen from the outside and emerged into the tower. In its center stood a thick pole. I looked up. *Thing looks like it goes all the way to Dingir.*

"Here are the lifts," Eresh said when we'd reached it. "Hop on."

The lifts were two kidney-shaped platforms with curved railings for handholds. He stepped on one, and I stepped on the other. A low buzzing sounded beneath my feet. The platform vibrated.

"All right, look. This governs your speed." I turned. Facing backward, Eresh's finger rested at the bottom of a black strip centered in a vertical white wall panel. To the left was an identical panel. I placed my finger on the strip.

"Right now it's in the stop position. Pull your finger up to go faster, down to go slower. Be careful, though. These things can fly. I pushed it to full speed once and was almost thrown off at the top. Midway is about right." He traced his finger along the black line.

I did the same. The strip turned bright blue. I dropped my finger at the halfway point, and the lift rose.

On the long ride up, I filled him in on É gossip and other goings on during the year he'd been in Mjor. "Astoreth kicked Morevi Ying out of Uruk and put him in Gapar."

Eresh frowned. "Gapar? Whew. What a dump. A tiny town in the middle of nowhere. What'd he do?"

"Monitor caught him in Morevi Santi's room after hours."

He shook his head. "Idiot. A child could figure out how to get around that thing. Who'd She bring in?"

"A Morevi Barut."

"He from Gapar?"

"Yes."

Eresh whooped. "I know he was glad as all Dingir to get out of *that* place."

I let out a giggle. "You should have seen him when he arrived. As usual, we were all there to greet him, and I swear I thought he was going to get on his knees and kiss Astoreth's feet."

"What's he like?"

"Kind of annoying at first. I mean, he was so happy to be in Uruk, he was fawning over everybody like a baby krelo. He calmed down after a while, and he's nice enough. Pleasant. He's in biosciences. And from what I hear from the morevs in that section, he's very, very, smart."

"Pleasant and smart. Good combination." Eresh chuckled. "Poor Ying. Couldn't have happened to a nicer pirsu's ass." He cocked his head. "What happened to Santi?"

"Astoreth locked him in one of the underground cells for a marun. All he got to eat was makira."

Eresh's face twisted. "Eewww."

On the second level, we stepped off the lifts into beacon control room. The motors' buzzing faded into silence. "So weight turns them on and off?"

He nodded. "Real handy when you have to get something heavy up here."

"Huh?"

"No one's allowed up here but you. The garrison's allowed up here only in emergencies."

"What kind of emergency? And why is there a garrison, anyway? From what I've seen, this place is pretty isolated. Nothing but mountains. What could happen here?"

"Morevi Opuku—I took over from him—told me the Devi had insisted on it while negotiating the Protocol. Said at the time the tower was built, tensions between the Syrenese and the Devi were much worse than they are now. Mjor might be isolated, but that wouldn't have stopped hotheads from doing something stupid, like attacking it."

"Oh." I looked around the control room. Windows lined most of it, and light from Peris's twin suns poured inside. "Do those windows open?"

"Some of them. Here, let me show you." Eresh pressed his palm against a black panel, and four of the screened windows opened. Cold air whooshed in. He pressed the panel a second time, and the windows closed with a soft click.

"What are those for?" I pointed to two huge fans set in the far wall.

"Exhaust. In case there's a fire. That and the siren have their own power source so if there *is* a fire, they'll still work. The controls for the windows, fans, and siren are labeled so you can finger read them in the dark if you have to."

Eresh stepped over to a bank of computers. "Here's the main terminal. The brains of the lot. It pretty much runs everything." He rested his hand on the console to the right. Most of its top was taken up by a black screen with a fat cylinder nearly as wide floating above it. Multicolored and translucent, the cylinder slowly rotated, its colors sparkling. "As long as the cylinder looks like that, you're fine. If it turns white, put your thumb here," he pointed to a small indentation to the far right, "until it looks like it does now."

He crossed the room to an oversized door and opened it. Inside was a bulky tower covered with red and yellow lights. It was almost as tall as me. We stepped into the closet and edged around to the back of the machine. The first thing I noticed were the cables. Of varying sizes, they looked like black vines sprouting from the sockets that peppered the tower's rear. I thought my eyes would pop. "Don't tell me this is—"

"The converter," he said with a nod. "It's ancient. To be honest, I'm not sure why it's still being used, or why it was installed in the first place. It's not like the Devi didn't have wireless when the tower was built. Maybe there was some kind of shortage and this was the only one available." He shook his head. "Anyway, the cables have a tendency to slip, so you have to make sure all the connections are intact."

"Well, if this one has problems, why didn't you ask for a wireless?"

"I did. Central ignored me."

We stepped out of the closet. I looked around, then back at him. "What else?"

"What else, what?"

"What else do I have to do?"

He raised his brows. "Nothing."

My jaw dropped. "You mean this is it? This is the big job that's so important somebody has to come up here for a year?" I looked around again. "I can't...why do they need a person? A robot could do it just as well. Better yet, put in an AI."

Eresh laughed. "That was my reaction, too. Opuku said most of the Gods' beacons have been fully automated. Why Astoreth hasn't done it to this one..." He shrugged. "I guess you'd have to ask Her."

I shook my head but said nothing.

Leaving the control room, he stopped and pointed to an electronic reader on a nearby shelf. "That's the manual. The Protocol's downloaded on there, too." He gave me a sly look. "So now you don't have an excuse *not* to read it."

I stuck my tongue out. He did, too.

We stepped on the lifts and rode to the main floor. Eresh took my hand. "Come on. I'll give you a tour of the village. Not that there's much to see."

Outside, we strolled along a sidewalk lined with canopied shops. While Eresh pointed out some of the larger buildings and their uses, I peeked at the wares displayed in the windows. Some I recognized, most not. "Where's that go?" I nodded at a long, narrow space between two buildings.

He turned his head. "They call it an alley. From what I can tell, it's where the stores take deliveries." He pointed to a building painted bright aqua. "That's where they make cloth. The looms are huge. You might want to go see them sometime." He pointed to another building. "And here's where they—"

"Tell me about the Laerd. Is he always that way?"

Eresh frowned. "Well, like everybody else, he doesn't like us. Still, he was always civil to me. But I saw the look on his face when you introduced yourself. It's almost as if he hates you."

"Maybe he doesn't like women."

"Maybe. I've never seen him with one."

Great. "So what are the Mjorans like? Are they stupid like the hakoi back home?"

"Not at all. Don't forget, their ancestors were rejects from the Devi's first spawning and breeding experiments twenty-five hundred years ago. When they were brought here, they weren't expected to survive, but they did. That took the kind of intelligence and ingenuity the Kherah hakoi don't have because it was bred out of them."

I smirked. "I'm sure we're smarter than they are."

"Probably. But I never had a chance to compare wits."

We walked on, and then it occurred to me. In Uruk, morevs were required to exercise every day. Yet I saw no exercise equipment of any kind in the tower. "How did you get your exercise?" I frowned. *"Where* did you get your exercise?"

"The É. I either danced or swam in the pool."

"But isn't that—"

"It's your É, Tehi. You can do what you want, within reason. Besides, it's the only place you *can* exercise."

By then, we'd toured the central plaza, its prettiness enhanced by tall streetlamps with teardrop globes lining the sidewalks. We stopped at a corner on the plaza's far side. "Is this it?"

"No, but we're not supposed to leave the plaza."

"Why?"

"It's not safe."

"I want to see it. Besides, you said the Mjorans will ignore us."

Eresh shook his head. "Not a good idea."

"Come on. There are two of us, and it's the middle of the day. What can happen?" I tugged on his hand. "Let's go."

"Tehi—"

"You scared? I'll protect you. Just act natural." I giggled and gave his hand another tug.

"No, Tehi."

I twisted my lips in annoyance.

"Listen. The Laerd warned me not go past the plaza, and I *don't* think it was because he didn't want me to see the rest of the village. Yes, the Mjorans ignore me, but that's here. They might not if you go wandering the streets."

I rolled my eyes. "Eresh, nothing's going to happen. Let's go."

He blew out an explosive breath. "Tehi, that's exactly your problem. You don't listen. You just do whatever you want, and damn if anybody tells you different. Why do you think you're here instead of Uruk? You broke Astoreth's canon. Like I said, if any of the rest of us did that, we'd be dead by now. You? You only got exiled for a year. This is your punishment for doing it, instead of death. Can't you see that?"

My eyes narrowed. "You're just jealous."

Eresh threw up his hands. "I'm trying to keep you from getting hurt," he said, his voice rising. "You're ready to go off somewhere in a place you know *nothing* about, except that the people don't want you here. Think about the consequences, for once. You head off, something bad might happen to you. Might not. Do you want to take that chance? I sure don't."

We glared at each other. Then I closed my eyes. "Fine, then. We won't." I opened them and looked into his face. "Happy?" I snapped.

He gave me a small smile. "For you...yes."

I closed my eyes again. He was right. About everything. *Sometimes I think I don't deserve a friend like him.* I opened them and nodded. "So what do you want to do now?"

"Let's go this way." He lifted his chin, angling it toward the far end of the plaza's other side.

"All right."

We started walking, Eresh next to the street. Crossing the alley's mouth, a high-pitched whistling sound stopped me in my tracks. I whipped around and lashed out with my arm. A rock a little smaller than my hand smacked against my palm with a hard *thwap*. If I hadn't heard it coming, it would have hit me in the head.

A boy I thought old enough to know better stood in the alley. Legs planted and hands on hips, he glared, obviously daring me to retaliate. I glared back, then dropped the rock. The plaza was deserted just now, and in the silence, its *thunk* when it hit the pavement sounded like a cannon shot. Turning, Eresh and I continued on our way.

He gave me a sidelong look. "See what I mean?"

I sighed. "Point taken."

At the plaza's end, a delicious aroma tickled my nose. He tapped the bar on his uniform. "Time."

"Second hour, fifty-eight minutes, Tryn," an androgynous voice said.

He sucked in a breath. "Astoreth! It's almost three. You'd better get to the dining hall."

I hesitated. I really needed to set up my lab. The table was too small, but I was sure I could find something in the apartment to make it work. "No, I'll just go back. I've some stuff to do."

"Don't do that. Not on your first day."

"What difference does it make?"

"We're ambassadors. Not going—the Laerd might take it as some kind of slight. We have to keep Astoreth in his good graces."

"Why? He hates us."

He closed his eyes for a beat, then opened them. "Tehi, don't argue with me. Missing lunch might seem like a small thing, but we have to do everything we can to keep good relations."

I tightened my lips, then let out a sigh. "All right. Where's the dining hall?"

"I showed you. That big blue building right over there."

I started walking, but stopped when I realized he wasn't following. "Aren't you coming?"

He shook his head. "You're the steward now. I'm eating with the garrison. Meet me at the landing pad after lunch."

I nodded once and turned away.

I was two minutes late. The people on the dais had already been served. I slipped into the last of two empty chairs at its end, hoping no one noticed me.

The Laerd noticed me. "Moreva Tehi," he growled, "when we say lunch is at three Tryn, we mean it. Don't be late again." He signaled a server, and then fixed me with his cold stare. "Give her a plate. This time."

My anger flared. "Just touring your lovely village," I said, keeping my tone light.

He grunted. "Make sure you stay in the plaza."

"Oh, I did. But someone threw a rock at me, anyway."

His head jerked up. "You get hurt?"

"No, but thank you for your concern." *Like you even care, dicknut.*

A woman placed a vegetarian plate and a small, hard roll before me. My mouth watered. I hadn't realized it while out with Eresh, but I was ravenous. Considering I'd lost my breakfast in the airship, I really hadn't eaten since dinner the night before. I picked up my fork and dug in. The vegetables, done to perfection, tasted like Dingir. I shoveled the food into my mouth, heedless of my manners. Finishing my plate, I looked around, wondering who I could ask for more. I noticed most people were getting up, and some were leaving. Puzzled, I watched for a few seconds, then realized. *Oh, the next meal shift is coming in soon. Kitchen staff has to clean up.*

I pushed my chair under the table and headed for the hallway. "Moreva Tehi," the Laerd growled behind me. I turned. A moment later, I was looking into his cold, star-colored eyes. He was scowling, too. "I suppose you're going to report the rock throwing incident to Kepten Yose?"

I raised my brow. "Why? I wasn't hurt."

He opened his mouth, but I beat him to it. Taking a step, I stood just inches away, giving him a hard stare. "Laerd Teger, what's your problem with me?"

His jaw tightened. "I have no use for your kind."

"That's not what I asked you."

The look in his eyes turned surprised. His scowl disappeared for a second. "I have—"

"Tell you what. I might be your liaison, but I don't want to be here any more than you want me here. So let's just stay out of each other's way. Deal?"

He didn't answer for what seemed like a long time. "Deal." Then he brushed past me and strode away.

I arrived at the landing pad as Eresh and the pilot were almost ready to leave. Two of the garrison stowed the last of his trunks in the airship floating over tarmac. Spotting me, he walked over and put a hand on my shoulder.

He leaned down until his mouth was at my ear. "Be careful of Kepten Yose," he said in a low voice. "He's not like the hakoi back home. He may not be as smart as we are, but he's smarter than you think. He's cunning, too. One of his jobs is to make sure we're doing ours, and he reports to Astoreth once a marun. And he takes it very seriously. If you miss a service or do anything against É rules, She'll find out about it and punish you."

I grimaced. "Couldn't be any worse than being here."

"One more thing. Don't let anyone know you're psi. You already know how the Mjorans feel about us. Knowing you're psi will only make it worse. And I want you to come home next year."

He straightened and smiled. "You'll be all right, Tehi. I've shown you everything there is to show, you've got the manuals...you're all set. I'll see you in Uruk." He looked around, then at me. "Good luck." He walked to the airship and climbed inside.

The machine's engines revved. The glow beneath its belly brightened until it was almost blinding. The airship lifted off with an ear-shattering roar, banked, and headed south. Tears spilled down my cheeks. *Come back, Eresh...please come back. I need...can't...* Shivering in the spring chill, I watched until it was out of sight.

My tears eventually dried. Blowing a heavy sigh, I headed for the village gate, trying not to think about the upcoming year. Between the Laerd and the Mjorans' contempt, it was going to be a long one.

I sighed again. *A very* long *one.*

Chapter Three

The night I'd been dreading since before leaving Uruk had arrived. Tonight, I would deliver the Ohra-Sin with twenty of the garrison.

I'd done most of the set up earlier. After purifying the air with a bonbon stick, made from the dried leaves of a plant native to Kherah, I fitted water absorbent mats around the perimeter of the pool. Behind the mats, I arranged twenty-one pillows covered in waterproof fabric and on each pillow, I placed a nose filter to allow for breathing underwater. Finally, I wheeled four, bowl-shaped braziers from the closet, and positioned them around the pool. Into each, I dropped a brick of rasen, a fuel that gave off flames but no smoke.

Right now, I was setting up the altar. I lit the candles first. "Kir Astoreth, mer Tia Hela Om," I whispered as I lit each one. "For Astoreth, the Most Holy One." Then I lit the incense—a relaxing, libidinous, and mildly hallucinogenic blend designed to enhance the ritual experience. After that, I walked around the pool, lighting the braziers.

My role was to serve as Astoreth's avatar. The rite required special makeup. I'd painted my face and body with sacred symbols describing Her part in creating the world, especially the hakoi and the morevs. Applying the paint was difficult. Sometimes a plaster strip didn't smooth out properly, leaving a gap in the design. If that happened, the paint had to be cleaned off and a new strip applied. Only the most experienced morevs could work with the body plaster as easily as plastering their faces. I was an experienced moreva, but not that experienced. So I'd taken my time.

My mood had grown darker with each strip I used. If there'd been a way I could get out of Ohra-Sin, I'd have taken it in a heartsbeat. But there wasn't. By the time I'd finished, I was angry enough to throw a bottle of makeup remover against the wall.

Then I had an idea. I couldn't get out of the ritual, but there *was* a way I could make it more bearable. I dug around in my healer's kit and pulled out a jar of basi gel. Clear and odorless, the gel wasn't an immediate need for routine healing, yet there were times when it was necessary. The best part was that it was waterproof and would make my skin slick as a tamper, an eel-like fish that lived in Kherah's Ven River. I'd smeared on gobs of it.

I looked around the É. All was ready. Tonight's ritual would last three hours, a far cry from the half-hour daily morning and evening services I'd be giving until the next Ohra-Sin. Three hours would give all a chance to commune with Astoreth. Or rather, with me. Bile rose in my throat. I barely managed to swallow it back.

I turned off the lights, but the braziers' orange-white flames lit up the É, bright enough to read by. My bare feet whispering on the polished stone, I crossed to the seero and chose the music written especially for Ohra-Sin. The sounds of pipes, flutes, and strings filled the air. Drums provided an incessant, hypnotic beat.

At the pool's far end, I sat on the center pillow in sacred lutos. I let my body relax and with upturned hands on knees, closed my eyes, and waited for the garrison. The heady aroma from the incense made me slightly dizzy, and my muscles slackened until they felt rubber-like. I didn't feel sexually aroused, though. That wasn't surprising.

I heard the twenty make their way up the stairs. After what sounded like a scuffle, I heard the padding of bare feet and then fabric rustling. When all was quiet, I opened my eyes. To me, the hallucinogenic incense gave each of the naked men and women kneeling on the mats a multicolored aura. The music had assumed colors, too. I saw the red beats of the drums, yellow streaks of the strings, and green dots of the winds.

I waited, allowing time for the incense to take effect. When I'd judged it had been long enough, I stood and closed my eyes. I had to perform Ohra-Sin with them, but that didn't mean I had to look at them.

"You may stand." More rustling as the penitents got to their feet. Spreading my arms chest-high, I recited the opening prayer. "Astoreth, our Most Holy One, welcomes you to Her House to celebrate the holy rite of Ohra-Sin. We celebrate Ohra-Sin to remember that it was She who gave life to the morev, the hakoi, and our world. We immerse ourselves in Her Holy Womb, from which all life came." I opened my eyes, but kept them lowered as I let my arms down. Picking up the filters, I fitted them into my nostrils and stepped to the pool's edge. "Let Ohra-Sin begin."

I dove into the water. As usual, it was icy. As usual, hard prickles rose on my skin. As usual, all I wanted to do was hop out and shiver at the pool's rim. I kept swimming. Soon I'd warmed enough to feel comfortable.

The twenty joined me, and I swam through the mass of writhing bodies. The basi gel was doing its job. Hands reached for me, caught me, but I slipped through their grasps like...well, water. Every so often, I'd swim to the surface and take a deep breath of incense-laden air. On and on I swam.

I was swimming for the surface when someone grabbed my hair and yanked hard. It hadn't occurred to me to gel it. I jerked my head around, ready to zap whoever it was that had hold of me.

It was Kepten Yose.

My eyes widened a fraction. *What's he doing here?* According to the schedule Eresh had left for me, he was one of the evening penitents. Tonight was for the morning ones. I stared. From the stern look on his face, I knew he knew what I'd done, and if I didn't do what the rite required, he would report me to Astoreth. She must have told him about me. And She would not be pleased.

I nodded. He let go.

Now when hands clawed at me, I didn't try to break away. I let them have me, penetrated in every orifice so many times I lost count. I didn't swim to the surface for breaths of incensed air. Underwater, no one could see my tears of rage and humiliation.

Not soon enough, the vibrations from a giant gong rippled through the water. The penitents climbed out of the pool. I was the last one out. Dripping wet, I stood at the pool's edge, spread my arms, and then intoned the benediction. After dismissing them, I sat on my pillow and closed my eyes. Before I'd closed them completely, I saw Yose's smile. I knew what it meant. He wouldn't report me to Astoreth. I was safe.

I think.

At last, the É was silent. I opened my eyes. The braziers still glowed, giving off enough light to see the pool and a little beyond, but the room's far reaches were drenched in gloom. I got up and switched on the lights, their harsh glare searing my eyes.

I wiped down the pillows, doused the braziers, and returned them to their closet. Inside the main closet, I opened the sink's tap. Upending the incense holders, I poured the ashes into the sink and watched them swirl down the drain. After the last ash had disappeared, I washed the rest of the ritual paraphernalia, then stowed them.

Now I had to clean the pool. I filled a bucket and hauled it to the edge. I stared at the water, trying not to think about what had happened in it a half-hour ago. It was no use. My thoughts were riveted on the ritual, and all the anger and shame I'd felt during flooded through me again. Gritting my teeth, I dumped in the enzymes and threw the bucket back into the closet.

I returned to the pool. *Thank Astoreth there won't be a morning service, just the evening one.* Standing on a mat, I looked around and let out a weary sigh. My exhaustion was catching up to me. *I should put the mats away and robo-mop the floor, but I'm too tired. I just want to go to bed.* Throwing on my cloak, I trudged up the stairs to my apartment.

I smeared on makeup remover and stepped into the shower. It was after five Durm, but the hot water hadn't yet cooled. I scrubbed hard, trying to rid my skin of the garrison's imagined fingerprints. It didn't work. I left the bath still feeling dirty. Rummaging through my kit, I found my herbal suppositories and inserted one into my vaginal canal and one in my rectum. In a few seconds, my soreness disappeared.

Crawling beneath the furs on my bed, I curled into a fetal position and tried to go to sleep. But sleep didn't come. I couldn't get rid of the feel of their hands on me. Tossing and turning, I tried every trick I knew to put myself to sleep. The more I tried, the more awake I became.

Giving up, I rolled onto my back and stared at the ceiling. *A whole year of this. Astoreth.* My thoughts wandered from what Eresh might be doing now, whether my room in the dormitory would be kept clean while I was away, to what the morevs back home had eaten for dinner tonight. They finally settled on my talk with Ginzu after Ktana. *I'm in danger of losing my soul...but why? How? What am I doing wrong?* Several possibilities ran through my mind, but I dismissed them. None of them made sense. I thought about the hakoi and my feelings for them. Was that it? I shook my head. *So what? They are what they are, but that doesn't mean I have to like them.*

The Moreva of Astoreth

Unable to figure out this soul business and unable to sleep, I got up. Plucking my speech tablet off the low table between the fireplace chairs, I plopped into one and switched it on. *Might as well look over my sermons.* I made it a habit to have several ready, in case I was called on to give one with little notice. And I needed to choose a homily for the evening service, anyway. As I flipped through the electronic pages, memories of the Ohra-Sin ritual threatened my concentration, but I managed to beat them back. I chose the sermon for that night, then flipped through a few more pages. *Hm. Getting low on inventory…need to fatten my reserves. Give me something to do until I go down and finish cleaning up.*

I memorized my next sermon and wrote three more before leaving for the É. Heading to the dining hall for breakfast, it was just as cold as it had been the day I arrived. I couldn't stop shivering. *Eresh said it's spring. Right. Astoreth, I'd give anything to be in Uruk right now. Grandmother could punish me any way She likes, but at least I'd be warm.*

I walked into the dining room. The Laerd was already seated. He glared at me with star-cold eyes, face twisted into a scowl. Pulling my chair up to the table, I let out a little sigh, barely resisting the urge to say something rude. Things were bad enough between us, and if I said something, whatever I said would only make it worse.

A whole year. Astoreth, if You can find it in Your heart, please, please, please *give me the strength to survive.*

⊙ ⊐⊐⊏⊏⊐⊏⊐ ⊙

That aftermidday, I sat in inside Kepten Yose's office while he delivered the first of his marunly reports. When I walked in, I'd been astonished to see his computer. Everything the Devi built was built to last, but this machine had to be a hundred years old. Maybe older. Machines like this, I'd only seen in pictures. *Astoreth. Would anybody even know how to fix this thing?*

"I've put in a requisition for our rations and thalin gas for the generator. Here's the requisition form." He swiveled the monitor so I could see it. "We need two hundred manû of pirsu meat, a hundred manû of assorted vegetables, and sixty gur of thalin gas."

"Seems like a lot for the forty-one of you."

37

"It isn't. This will last us ten days. More would be better, but that's all our freezers and the generator tank will hold." He pushed the keyboard toward me and pointed to a small box at the bottom of the screen. "Initial here."

I did so. Inserting a small disc into the drive, he downloaded the form. The disc popped from the slot. He pulled it out and slid it into a nupaper envelope.

Unbelievable. It uses discs. Then I frowned. "Wait. They don't have electronic messaging?"

"Not that I know of. Even if they are networked, we wouldn't be on it. Communications are limited, too. I can only call you, the Laerd, or the healer on the intercom." He proffered the envelope. "Please give this to the Laerd."

"All right. Is there anything else?"

Yose shook his head. "Under the Protocol, this is all we're allowed to request."

"Why?"

He shrugged. "From what I understand, the Mjorans drove a hard bargain when hashing out the Protocol with our Most Holy One. The beacon couldn't be located anywhere else, so She had no choice but to agree to almost anything they asked." He paused. "The only other request I can make is for the services of the village healer when we need it. But we won't need him now that we have you. For the next year, at least." He swiveled the monitor back to face him. "As for personnel, we had five troops rotate out this marun, and we'll have five new ones coming in on the next supply run."

"How long does a trooper serve? Do they rotate on every supply run?"

"No. Each trooper serves a year. The rotations are staggered so I don't end up with a garrison of inexperienced recruits."

I nodded, then frowned again. "Kepten, what do you and your people do all day? I know you protect the tower, but it's not like the Mjorans have a habit of storming the place."

He stiffened. "We train daily, Moreva. Come. I'll show you." He held the office door open for me.

"This way."

Following him through the barracks, the troops snapped to

attention at the sight of me and stayed that way. "As you were," I said in a loud voice. Yose had told me what to say when I'd entered the barracks.

The soldiers went back to whatever it was they were doing. We came to a darkened room, and I peeked inside. Fifteen of the garrison was standing before an equal number of black screens larger and taller than they were. Each soldier wore a thin black strip covering their eyes and black gloves that fit like a second skin. A profusion of electrode dots decorated each bald head. All were in motion, ducking and jumping as if trying to avoid something. "What are they doing?" I whispered.

"No need to whisper. They can't see or hear us. What they're doing is fighting virtual battles. They train in all kinds of perrain, in all kinds of weather, against all kinds of enemies. Best equipment the military has to offer. Keeps them in top fighting shape." He sounded proud. "We also conduct field exercises just in case. The perrain around here can be tricky."

"In case of what?"

He gave me a blank look that I knew would be withering if I weren't his superior officer.

I put it together a few seconds later. A sting of annoyance pricked me. *Why would I have known? There isn't a reason for anybody to attack this place anymore.* "Oh. I see. Well, this is all very interesting. I'll be going now. And I'll make sure your requisition gets to the Laerd today. Thank you for your report."

"No need to thank me. It's my job."

"Very well, then." We walked to the barracks door. He opened it, and I stepped onto the landing. "I'll see you at services tonight."

He saluted, and I started up the stairs. I'd just picked up my tablet to go over a sermon when I realized I hadn't heard the barracks door close.

⊙᠆᠆᠆᠆᠆⊙

One-thirty Durm found me getting dressed for the evening service at second hour. I was still full from dinner and knew I'd be uncomfortable in my tight-fitting vestments. *That's easy to fix. I'll just change the time for service. Two-thirty. I'll let Yose know tomorrow morning.*

Tonight was Moro, which meant I had to wear purple. All the daily services had different names, depending on the day of the marun. They didn't refer to a particular type of service, like Ohra-Sin, but were a memory aid for morevs.

I shucked my uniform and stood before the vanity to remove my secular makeup. Outside the É, morevs were never seen without makeup. The paint was a badge of our status, the different patterns and colors indicating which É a morev served.

Picking up a bottle of special makeup remover—the only way the makeup could be cleaned off—I squeezed a dollop onto my fingers and spread it over my face. After showering, I pulled out the vestments I'd wear tonight. I shimmied into my short, tight dress, rolled a pair of black stockings over my legs, and fastened them to the garters sewn into the dress. When a little girl, I'd asked my grandmother why Her morevs wore such clothes for services. Astoreth had stroked my curls and chuckled. "Because I like them, child."

I slid my feet into a pair of flimsy slippers and returned to the vanity. Opening a drawer, I retrieved a makeup mask designed to fit me alone and plastered it on my face. Thirty seconds later, I peeled it off and inspected myself in the mirror. Perfect, as always. I drew on a pair of black, elbow length gloves, and then threw over my shoulders a collarless cloak lavishly embroidered with iridescent thread. Last, I retrieved a black crop and a pair of purple, spike-heeled shoes from the closet. I left for the É.

Sliding out of my slippers, I stepped into the sacred space, and dimmed the lights. After hanging my cloak in the supply closet, I grabbed the bonbon stick and purified the air. I pulled out three bowls—glass, wood, and brass—from a cabinet beneath the closet's sink. The glass bowl, I filled with water, wooden one with salt, and the brass bowl with herizab, a plant known for its libidinous effect when its leaves were chewed. These I arranged on the altar. Back in the closet, I gathered several candles, incense sticks, and their holders. Finally, I tucked a large statuette of Astoreth under my arm. As I struggled to pull the lighter from its holster, the paraphernalia shifted and threatened to spill. I caught them just in time. "Next time, just leave the thing on the altar," I muttered.

Carefully setting everything onto the altar's polished wood, I fixed the statuette in place, arranged the candles and incense, and then lit them. I retrieved three bells—glass, wood, and brass—and their matching sticks, and placed them just so on the altar. Selecting the music for the service, the soft sound of flutes filled the air. I closed my eyes while the sweet melodies washed over me.

I slipped on my sacred shoes. Heels clicking on the polished stone floor, I bowed before the altar and sank to my knees onto a padded cushion. A minute later, the sound of booted feet clumped on the stone steps, followed by the whisper of sock-clad feet. When all was quiet, I got up and turned. Twenty-one of the garrison's soldiers, including Yose, were topless and knelt with foreheads on the floor around the circular pool.

I picked up the glass bell and tapped it with the rod. "Astoreth, Most Holy One, we, the unworthy, beg forgiveness for our sins," I intoned.

"Astoreth, Most Holy One, we, the unworthy, beg forgiveness for our sins," they repeated.

I picked up the brass bell and tapped it. "Astoreth, Most Holy One..."

After the litany, I gave the sermon I'd written and memorized, about Astoreth's deep love for Her followers. By strictly following Her tenets, they would gain Her favor and be showered with Her blessings. Then I circled the pool, giving each soldier one slash on the back from my crop. The slashes raised a welt, the sign of Astoreth's punishment for their sins and Her forgiveness. The service concluded, and I dismissed them.

I still felt tired from Ohra-Sin. I thought about leaving the cleaning until the morning, but decided against it. *If I do it now, I'll be able to sleep a little longer before I have to get up.* My lips twisted. *Assuming I sleep at all.* Sighing, I went about my chores, and was grateful it didn't take long. I turned out the lights and headed to my apartment.

Chapter Four

For the next four days, I stayed in my apartment except for mealtimes and É services.

By that point, I was on the verge of biting my fingernails. The battery in the trunk with the skratz and red fever vials would last only two more days. I'd used one with a short life because I'd assumed I could set up in the apartment. But nothing I'd tried worked.

Lengthening the table by stacking the boxes I'd found in the larder on each end was a failure. Two boxes weren't tall enough to reach the table's edge, and three boxes were too high. The same for the low table between the two fireplace chairs. One box, too short; two boxes, too high.

I'd rummaged through the É's supply closets, looking for anything I could use to build a makeshift table. Nothing. I'd considered the vanity, but its surface was too narrow. I'd even thought about figuring a way to set up in the tower or the control room. I'd been so desperate, it took me ten minutes to give up those ideas as ludicrous.

Swiveling my chair before the communications console in the control room, I stared at it, trying to get up the nerve to call home. Beacon stewards were forbidden from doing so except in emergencies. My situation was definitely an emergency, but if I had to tell anyone why, I would end up in a whole lot more trouble than I already was. And there was no way for me to know who was on the Uruk É's communications board right now. If it was Eresh, I'd be fine. If it were someone else, I'd be in double trouble— one for calling home, and two, for my emergency.

I've got to call. The virus box doesn't have an all-temperature seal. It'll last indefinitely if the box is kept frozen. If it gets warm it'll disintegrate, and the virus will come out of dormancy. The vials might keep it from escaping, but there's no way to guarantee that.

I smacked the console's stand. *I can't wait anymore.* My nerves thrumming and holding my breath, I covered the transmit panel with my palm. An outsized holographic of Eresh's head appeared to float before my eyes. "Astoreth-69, what's your emergency?" he said, face alarmed.

I blew a sigh of relief. "Eresh, I need a huge favor."

His expression melted into concern. "If I can. What's going on?"

"I need a heavy-duty battery for my cooler-freezer trunk. I've got some...stuff that has to be kept cold and frozen. The one I have is going to last only two more days, and if I don't get one, everything will be ruined."

"You haven't set up your lab?"

"There's no place to do it. Nothing's big enough. Even if there was, there's nothing to keep what I need cold."

He was silent for a moment. "But the next supply run isn't for another five marun. How—"

"Yose told me there's one tomorrow. Some kind of troop exchange."

"Hold on."

His head disappeared and returned a minute later. "All right. I can do it. I'll send two. That should last you a while. What's the model number?"

"205-GYV."

"Got it. I'll mark it for you so no one'll open it."

I nearly cried. "Thanks, Eresh. I owe you a big one."

He smiled. "What're friends for?" His eyes darted to the right. "Someone's coming. Gotta go." He cut the transmission, and his head disappeared.

Slumping, the last of my nervousness drained away. A short while later, I tapped the bar on my uniform. "Time."

"Second hour, fifty minutes Tryn."

Lunch would be served soon. I let out a sigh. I didn't want to go. Eresh had said the Mjorans would ignore me, but they didn't. More than once, I'd had one spit at my feet. *Well, I am hungry.*

Through the dining room's doorway, I saw a bald, older man sitting in the seat next to mine. I walked inside, braced for more hostility.

He turned as I pulled my chair back. "You must be Moreva Tehi," he said in heavily accented Devian. His tone was welcoming. "I'm Hyme."

I smiled. "Hello, Hyme. May the Most Holy One turn Her face to you."

"And to you, Moreva."

In my peripheral vision, I saw the Laerd's frown but he said nothing.

"I'm Mjor's healer," Hyme said while our soup was served.

"Yes, I know. Eresh told me."

"How is he these days?"

"He's fine." I drank spoonful of soup. "If you don't mind my asking, where've you been?"

"I've been visiting other villages, trading knowledge with their healers." He sighed. "Trading knowledge is the best part of being a healer." He cocked his head. "What do you do at the É?"

"I'm a healer, too."

He grinned. "Marvelous! Perhaps we can—"

"We don't need another healer," the Laerd growled, loud enough for some sitting closest to the dais to turn their heads.

"Who said anything about another healer?" I snapped. "All we're talking about is trading knowledge. Are you saying Hyme can't do that?"

His faced reddened. "No."

"I didn't think so."

Hyme leaned in close. "Not many would have stood up to him like that, Moreva," he whispered.

"He had no business butting into our conversation," I whispered back.

The old healer smiled.

After lunch, we headed to his apothecary. I peered through the outsized paned window. It was a charming little space chock-full of jars lined up in neat rows on shelves stretching almost to the ceiling. There was a counter in front of the shelves and two, comfortable-looking chairs hard by the window. I turned. "I like it. So cozy."

"Thank you."

I waited for him to open the door, but he didn't. Instead, he started walking along a colorful stone wall. I followed. We turned left at the corner, and about a quarter of the way down the block, we came to another door. Hyme unlocked and held it open for me.

I crossed the threshold. My brows shot up. The room was far larger than the apothecary. And it was a full-fledged lab. It even had a centrifuge. All the equipment was old but serviceable. *Astoreth. This is incredible. They aren't as primitive as I thought. At least* he *isn't.*

I turned to see him looking at me with a twinkle in his eye. "Not what you expected, eh?" He chuckled.

"Not at *all.*"

"This is a big building, and the apothecary takes up little space. There's what I like to call the hospital wing on the other side. Come. I'll show you around."

The hospital held five beds, each connected to a wall panel that measured energy flow and kept track of vital signs. Two hyperbaric chambers were pushed up against the far wall. He took me to the operating theater, a medium-sized room with two surgical tables and monitoring equipment. The technology wasn't as advanced as what we had in Uruk, but it was more than adequate for what it was intended to do. My estimation of the Mjorans went up a tiny notch.

I traced my finger along one table's raised edge. "How often do you use the hospital?"

"Not often. Mjorans are a sturdy lot. Usually, I'm setting broken bones and things like that, mainly for the thalin miners."

Returning the lab, I swiveled my head left and right. "This is impressive. Do all healers have labs like this?"

"No. But of those that do, some even have assistants." A wistful look passed across his face. "I wish I had an assistant, but I can't seem to get anyone in the village interested in healing. I don't know what they'll do when I'm gone." He gave a little shrug. "No need to talk about that. I've plenty of years left in me."

"So what do you do when you're off on one of your trading trips?"

He smiled a little. "I pray." Then he waved his hand. "Anyway, when I'm not busy, I come back here and work on cures. I've discovered lots of them. Like Birk's foot—one treatment, and it's gone. We've saved many a pirsu with it."

My eyes widened. Even we didn't have a cure for Birk's foot. The scourge of single-hoofed livestock, the disease was an inflammation between the outer and inner wall of the hoof. If left untreated, it eventually separated from the foot and the pirsu had to be put down, if only to end its terrible pain. In Uruk, the animals were shot at the first sign of Birk's foot because the treatments we had only prolonged the inevitable.

The albaitari would love this. "Would you be willing to share the formula with me? For a price, of course. The É will be happy to pay."

"No need for money. We'll take it out in trade for knowledge. But as far as I know, the ingredients only grow here."

"Once our albaitari know the formula, maybe they can find an equivalent in Kherah."

"Maybe. Or…perhaps you could take some cuttings when you leave and grow them down there? Here—this is skagwort." He pointed to a glass tub filled with dark powder. "It's the base for my formula. Good for burns, cuts, and a host of other things, too."

"What a wonderful idea. Our engineers could build a habitat. It'd be perfect."

"Excellent." We crossed the lab and stood before a large door. "And this," he waved his hand theatrically, "is a closet." He opened it, and we stepped inside. The overhead lights flickered.

Swiveling my head, my eyes widened again. The space was huge and practically empty. "A closet? This is another room."

"Well, really, it is. I only call it a closet."

"What do you use it for?"

"Mostly for storing worn-out equipment or things I don't need anymore. I usually have the equipment refurbished to trade for knowledge. I just did a cleaning for my trip. That's why the closet is as empty as it is. The rest of it is stuff I couldn't bear to part with."

Back in the main room, a flash of bright red caught my eye. I turned to look. What I'd glimpsed was peeking from between heavy coats hanging on a rack near the lab's street door. Walking over, I lifted it off its peg and turned it over in my hands. It was a full-body suit, its shell made of a smooth, stiff material that didn't look like cloth. The inside was plush, criss-crossed by narrow, clear bands of what looked like flexible plaztik embedded in the material.

Looking up, I spotted something in the same color lying on a shelf above the pegs. Standing on my toes, I took it down. It was an over-the-head skullcap, made of the same material as the suit, with clear, bulbous lenses over the eyeholes and a slit for the nose and mouth.

"Hyme, what's this? There's one like it in my closet."

"A quiltsuit."

"Where do you wear it?"

"Not where. When. We get an arhu or so in winter when temperature dips below zero Calerian, and it's so cold you'll freeze to death if you're not wearing it. Any warmer than that, the heat won't turn on."

"Heat?" I inspected the suit more closely. "Where's the battery?"

"You are. It works off the body's electrical impulses."

I raised my brows. *Really? That's pretty sophisticated. I wouldn't have thought they'd have* this *level of technology.* "Why's it so bright?"

"So you can be seen in the snow." He paused. "I should put it away now that the weather's warming, but I haven't gotten around to it."

I returned the suit and skullcap to the rack. We were in the midst of a conversation about the ups and downs of healing when I spied a long, wide table against one wall. There was nothing on it. "Um, Hyme? What do you use that table over there for?"

"That? Nothing, really. It usually just catches debris from my experiments. Why?"

I told him about my portable lab and how there wasn't room in my apartment to set it up. "I also have a sterile environment I use for testing. That closet would be perfect. Do you think...I mean, once you've gotten settled...will you let me to set up in the closet and on that table?"

"Of course, Moreva, of course. When would you like to do it?"

"How about now? If you're not too tired from your trip."

"Oh no, that's a splendid idea."

I grinned. "Let me check the beacon first, and then it's as good as done." I turned to leave, but stopped. "And Hyme?"

"Yes, Moreva?"

"Call me Tehi."

He beamed. "Wonderful, Tehi. Now we're friends."

I beamed back at him. "Friends."

On my way to what I'd come to think of as my tower, I thought about how I'd just become friends with a hakoi. The irony wasn't lost on me. *Hakoi or not, he's Astoreth-sent. The batteries from home would've lasted the year, but I'd have gotten zero work done. Grandmother has given me great good fortune, and I'm not about to question where it came from.*

As I expected, all was well in the control room. The cylinder rotated, its sparkling colors glowing steady. I checked the converter. The red lights for the power output gave off a bright glow. So did the yellow lights, which meant the transformer was doing its job. The wires were snug in their sockets. I called Central, reported no problems, endured a rude response by the minor god who answered, and ended the transmission. My stewardship duty had taken all of five minutes.

In my apartment, I opened the nine remaining trunks until I found the two holding my equipment. I picked up the first trunk and carried it to the door, then down the stairs with relative ease. Being three-quarters Devi came in handy. If I was hakoi, I wouldn't have been able to move the trunk by myself. Outside, I unlocked the retractable wheels and handle, then started for the lab. I was almost there when I saw the Laerd hurrying toward me. I groaned.

"Where are you going with that?" he snapped.

"To Hyme's."

"I thought I told you we didn't need two healers."

"I'm not healing anything. This is my lab. I'm setting up so I can continue some work I was doing in Uruk. Or did you expect me to sit around and do nothing for a year?"

"I expect—"

My temper flared. "Laerd Teger, I don't care what you expect. I'm your advisor in Mjoran-Devian affairs. Instead of doing that, I have tried my best to stay out of your way. But you seem more than ready to get into mine, and I won't have it."

His eyes narrowed. "I expect you at a Council meeting in the sessions hall at five-thirty Tryn. Be there." He strode away.

My jaw dropped. *Did that dicknut just...* "I don't take orders from you, either," I yelled.

He ignored me.

Fuming, I grabbed the trunk's handle and continued to the lab. I had just under an hour before the Council meeting. The lab's street door was open. I stepped through, pushing my trunk ahead of me.

Hyme looked astonished. "My goodness, did you get that trunk here all by yourself?"

"Yes. I'm a lot stronger than I look."

"You must be. I'm impressed." He paused. "I heard you yelling out there."

"Oh, there's a Council meeting at five-thirty Tryn." I shook my head. "That hakoi is so infuriating."

"I take it you mean the Laerd."

"Who else?" I blew an explosive breath. "Hyme, what's his problem?

Every time I turn around, he's either growling or snapping at me for something. I haven't been here a marun. What in Astoreth's name have I done to him?"

He sighed. "The Laerd—he wasn't Laerd then—hasn't been quite the same since his heartsbound died in the last red fever epidemic."

"When was that?"

"Going on two years, now. Her name was Urla. She was a village girl, a lovely girl. So sweet, with a kind word for everyone. She was pregnant when she died. He never got over it."

I said nothing for a moment. "I'm sorry for his loss, but what does that have to do with me?"

"Maybe nothing." He paused a beat. "Maybe everything."

"What does that mean?"

He smiled. "Come, come. Don't listen to the prattling of foolish old man. You haven't much time. Let's get your lab set up."

"I've got one more trunk of equipment. Why don't you start on this one while I fetch the other?"

"Splendid idea."

I brought the other trunk. While Hyme set up the contents of the first, I worked on the second. A bit later, I touched the bar. "Time."

"Fifth hour, twenty-six minutes Tryn."

I don't have time for this. I'll just skip... Then I remembered what Eresh had said about stewards being ambassadors to the village. I sighed and looked up. "I'd better go. I'll see you after the meeting."

"Come to the apothecary when it's over."

"All right." I left and jogged across the plaza. Hardly anyone was out here. "Must all be at the meeting," I murmured.

I stepped into the hall, a room as big as the building. Up front was a dais like the one in the dining hall. I started along a narrow aisle between the wall and benches for the attendees.

"Sssss. Sssss," I heard from several mouths as I made my way. I also heard a lot of unintelligible muttering.

Reaching the dais, I climbed the stairs and slipped into a seat at the closest end. The eight council members were already seated. The Laerd sat in the center.

He glared. "Glad you could join us, Moreva. Next time use the side entrance."

My jaw tightened, then relaxed. "Glad to be here, Laerd," I said, keeping my tone light. "And I will certainly remember that."

He narrowed his eyes but said nothing. Banging a gavel twice, he called out the names of the council members, each name followed by a "Ja." He didn't call my name.

I stared. He didn't look my way but that was a jab, and we both knew it. *You dicknut.*

Lips tight, I looked out over the sessions hall. Men, women, and even children filled every bench. For so many people, the big room was quiet.

The meeting was conducted in Syrenese. As the meeting went on, the angrier I became. The Laerd knew I had no clue what was being said. At least he could have translated the Council reports into Devian. Then, after what seemed like forever but was really less than an hour, it was over.

I cornered him in the hallway. "Laerd, was there a reason why I had to be here? You know I didn't understand a thing. If this is part of my job as liaison, if I'm supposed to give my opinion—"

"I will tell you what you need to know, Moreva. And if I want your opinion, I'll ask for it." His cold, star-colored stare bored into mine. Then he pushed past me and headed for the entrance.

I gaped at his retreating back. In all my time as a Moreva of Astoreth, no one had *ever* shown me such disrespect. I was tempted to zap him but then remembered what Eresh had said about not letting anyone know I was psi. Clenching my hands into fists, I stalked out of the hall to the apothecary. Reaching it, I stepped inside.

Hyme looked up. "How was the meeting?"

"I don't want to talk about it."

"That bad?"

Instead of answering, I pretended to study the powders and pills on the shelves.

"I did some more set up while you were gone. I hope you don't mind."

I turned. "No, not at all. Saved me from having to do it."

"By the way, I was surprised to see you back so soon after you left to tend your beacon. I thought it would take a while."

"The beacon really runs itself. I only check it once a day to make sure everything's running as it should."

He shook his head. "Poor Eresh. I wonder what he did all day."

"He told me he read."

"That's a lot of reading."

"Well, Eresh was always a great reader. A wide range, too. Sometimes I think he's an expert on just about everything."

The chime rang, and a Mjoran walked through the doorway, her toddler in tow. She gave me a hard stare. I stared back, just as hard. "Hyme, I'll be in the lab."

I walked to my table and picked up a medium-sized insulated box Hyme hadn't opened. I dipped my hand inside. It was still cold, but it had been out of the cooler trunk long enough to have warmed some. *Need to get these hydrated.* Looking around, I spotted the box I thought I wanted. Walking over to it, I squatted and pulled off the lid. It was the right one, filled with a jumble of clear lysite pieces. I carried it to the far end of my table and fit the pieces together. After making sure the joints were tight, I poured about an inch of jabb tree scrapings into the cage.

Hyme walked up behind me. "What's that? I opened it but didn't know what it was, so I decided to leave it to you."

"A cage," I said over my shoulder. "For the skratz."

"The what?"

"Skratz. The Devi make them. They're for my research. I've got two kinds. The hairy kind has the same genetic makeup as the mysi. The hairless ones have the same genetic makeup as the hakoi, so I don't—" I bit off the rest.

"Don't what?"

I scrambled for an answer. I didn't think he would appreciate that until the Devi decided to have mercy, morevs experimented on the hakoi themselves. Then it came to me. "Well, before the Devi started making these, we grew our subjects from hakoi stem cells. For some reason, the results were always inconclusive. No one could figure out why, so—"

"But—"

"Anyway, let me show you," I said hastily. I knew my answer was lame, and I also knew that as a healer, he'd see through it.

I picked up the box. "You have to keep them cold until you're ready to use them. Otherwise, they won't quicken." I spotted a large bowl on a countertop across the room. "Could I use that bowl over there?"

"Of course. What do you need it for?"

"Just fill it halfway with warm water and bring it here."

Returning with the bowl, he set it next to the box of skratz. I picked up a packet of pink, viscous goo and tore off the top. "This is the quickener. You dump it into the bowl of water and," I grabbed a large spoon, "mix it together," I plucked a hairy and hairless skratz from the box and dropped them into the mixture, "and ho! Look what we have here." The skratz's little bodies plumped out. In a moment, they were swimming around the bowl. Sticking my hands into the goopy water, I caught one in each palm. I put them into the cage and watched them shake the liquid, one from its skin and the other from its hair. Whiskers twitching, they explored their new home. I smiled. "See? Aren't they cute?"

"Indeed they are."

I looked up. "I've got more skratz, but the boxes need to be kept cold. May I put them in your refrigerator?"

"Certainly."

I put the dehydrated skratzes away and returned to the cage.

"You said the hairless ones have the same genetic makeup as the hakoi," Hyme said. "Why?"

I bit my lip, and my hearts skipped a couple of beats. What was I going to tell him? *Astoreth, we just met. If he knows I have red fever with me, he could get me kicked out of Mjor, and then I'd have to answer to Her. And I can't lie. If we're working in here together, he's bound to find out. Can I trust him? I...no. I don't have a choice.*

"Um...well, I'm trying to find a cure for red fever. That's why I've got a sterile environment." I held my breath.

His look turned incredulous. "Red fever? Are you..." He gaped, but said nothing. The seconds ticked by.

Oh, no...

Then he grinned. "Oh, that'd be marvelous! How far along have you gotten?"

Thank you, Astoreth! My heartsbeat returned to normal. "Not far enough. What I know, you probably already know. Like, it's a virus, it's airborne, and it can't live under extreme conditions—cold or heat or acidic. From watching the hakoi back home, I don't have proof, but I think once you've had it—if you survive—your chances of contracting it again are small. I suspect it's because the virus goes dormant."

"So, you're living with red fever, but it's not affecting you."

"As far as I can tell. There may be a trigger of some sort that'll make it flare up again, except I don't know what that might be."

The chimes rang in the apothecary, and Hyme hurried off. Picking up the hairy skratz, I petted it for a while and then set it on top of my head. I winced when the little beast's tiny claws dug into my scalp. Once it had a firm hold, I danced around the lab. One step, twirl, two steps, twirl, one step, twirl...

The apothecary door opened. "You should try this, Hyme. The skratz love it."

He laughed. "I'm afraid I don't have enough hair for that. But you look cute with the skratz on your head. Anyway, it's almost time for dinner. We should go."

I put the skratz back in its cage. Hyme locked up, and we started across the plaza. "I take it you have the virus with you?"

I smiled. "It was the first thing I put in the deep freezer."

"Good." His looked turned grave. "We have to be careful, Tehi. If my people find out you brought red fever into our midst, there's no telling what will happen. Mostly to you."

Astoreth's warning echoed in my head. *The Mjorans are an unforgiving people...* "Like what?"

"You could be hanged from the battlement. Or worse."

My throat tightened. "What could be worse than that?"

"You could be dropped into a played out section of one of the thalin mines, sealed inside, and left to starve or until you run out of air."

"But the garrison—"

"The garrison be damned. They're outside the walls. All we have to do is shut and lock the gates. By the time the garrison finds out what's going on, it'll be over."

"What about the Protocol?"

"The Protocol doesn't cover this. Besides, it was you who brought the virus to Mjor, so we'd claim we were within our rights to punish you as we saw fit."

"What about you?"

"I might be in the mine with you."

I let out a breath. "So I guess we'd better keep it as our little secret."

"We'd better. We must never speak of your project outside the lab, even in Devian. No precaution we take can ever be too much."

Outside the hall after dinner, I lay my hand on Hyme's arm. "I have a few things to do before evening services. Maybe I'll stop by later."

"That's fine. I hope I'll see you then."

We parted ways. I didn't have anything to do—not really—but I wanted to be alone for a while. Walking, I eyed the colorfully painted battlement and imagined myself hanging from there. *Or worse.*

I stepped inside my tower and climbed the stairs to my apartment, shivering all the way.

Chapter Five

The following night, Hyme and I were crossing the plaza when the Laerd caught up to us. "Moreva."

I looked over my shoulder.

"I'll see you at the lab, Tehi," Hyme said.

"All right."

I turned. *Shocking surprise—he's not scowling.* Yet he didn't look happy to see me, either. I kept my expression neutral. "What is it, Laerd?"

"I need your help."

I frowned the tiniest bit. "With what?"

"I have to get these quarterly reports to the Council tomorrow. None of them can help, so you'll have to do. Come to my apartment after your services."

Anger zipped through me. "Laerd, are you ordering—"

"Yes." He looked away, eyes darting as if searching for someone. "Gar! Vänta!" A man on the street stopped. He strode toward a hakoi I recognized as a Council member. Reaching him, I watched his lips move. The other man replied, and they walked away.

Fuming, I stalked to the lab. "I can't believe that dicknut," I muttered. "Ordering me around like that. Me!" I flung the door open, but didn't see Hyme. "Hyme? Where are you?"

The apothecary door opened, and he stepped inside. "Hello, Tehi." His expression turned puzzled. "What's wrong?"

"Your Laerd has gotten into a bad habit of giving me orders."

"I'm sure he didn't mean—"

"He did. He said so. Astoreth damn him, I'm his liaison, not his minion." I slapped the bar. "Time to services."

"One hour, five minutes."

I grabbed my tablet. "Well, I know how I'm going to fix your Laerd Teger." I headed for the street.

"What are you going to do?"

"I'll see you tomorrow."

I stomped up the stairs to my apartment, threw the tablet on a fireplace chair, and then plopped into the other. Hands clenched, black thoughts about the Laerd crowded my mind. But I couldn't sit here and brood. I had get ready for the service.

When it concluded, I dismissed the penitents and began cleaning up. I took my time. I washed the three bowls twice before putting them away. I polished the already-polished bells while the robo-mop glided over the stone floor. On inspection, the floor was pristine. I decided it could use another mopping. Then another. And another. After the fourth mopping, I thought about a fifth, but the robo-mop's power supply was getting low. I purified the air twice, then leisurely set up for the morning. I looked around. *Nothing more to do here.* Draping my cloak over my shoulders, I headed for the apartment.

At the vanity, I wiped off my sacred makeup and then showered, spending far more time than was necessary. I dressed with all deliberate slowness. By the time I slipped on my boots, almost two hours had passed since the service had ended. Opening my healer's kit, I took out three vials and dropped them into my pocket. Then I unbolted the battlement door. The intercom's chimes signaled an incoming call, but I ignored it.

I settled into a fireplace chair. Picking up my tablet, I started reading today's lab notes. A buzz sounded, but I didn't move. The bell rang again. I waited a minute or two, then opened the battlement door. The Laerd stood behind the threshold, glaring and scowling harder than ever. "I told you to come to my apartment after your evening service."

I matched his glare. "And I told *you* I don't take orders from you."

Neither of us spoke. Then he took a breath. "Moreva."

I said nothing.

"Moreva, would you come to my apartment and help me finish these quarterly reports?" His tone was polite, but I could hear the tightness beneath his words.

I raised my brow. "Please?"

His jaw clenched. "Please?" he said through his teeth.

I gave him a sweet smile. "Of course." I stepped through the doorway, forcing him back. "Ready when you are."

He strode along the battlement, me trotting behind. Light from his partially open door spilled onto the stone walkway. He pushed the door further open and held it for me. My eyes widened in surprise. With a desk in front of the window, a plain table with three chairs, a bed, two fur-covered chairs before the fireplace and a formidable-looking set of weights on the far side of the room, his apartment was as bare as mine.

"Something wrong?"

"Ah...no. I'd expected something a bit more luxurious for the village chief."

"All I do is sleep here. What difference does it make?" He pointed to a hard table chair next to the desk. "Sit there."

I stayed where I was.

He sighed. "Please."

I sat, a small smile on my lips.

"Do you want some ale?"

"That'd be nice."

The Laerd fetched a mugful of the village's best. Then he rolled his chair up to the desk. I sipped my drink and set it down. "So what do you want me to do?"

He handed me a sheaf of nupapers. "I want you to read off the numbers, and I'll enter them into the computer."

I barely stopped my jaw from hitting my chest. *What? They don't have voice-to-text? Astoreth, I can't* believe *this.* Letting out a small hiss, I scanned the top sheet. My brows shot to the ceiling.

"Is there a problem?"

I looked up. The Laerd's face was twisted into something just short of a scowl. "Yes, there's a problem. I can't read this. It's in Syrenese."

His almost-scowl melted, and he stared for a few long moments. "Well, you're about to learn." Closing the screen's window, he brought up a blank page and typed a string of characters. "Come here." He gave me a sideways look. "Please." Then he stepped behind his chair. "Sit."

I blinked.

"Please."

I sat. "Now what?"

He pointed to the first character on the screen's left-hand side.

"Noll," he said in Syrenese. "Zero," he translated into Devian. Then he pointed to the second. "En. One. Två. Two. Tre. Three..." and so on until he'd reached the end of the string. "Say it with me."

I did, without mistake.

"Again."

I didn't make a mistake this time, either.

He frowned. "Let's see you do it by yourself."

I did, again without error. He had me repeat the string four more times, then gave me an appraising look. "You learn fast."

I smiled. "Always did." I retook my seat and picked up the nupapers. "Ready."

He brought up the previous screen. "So, I need you to read off the numbers in their groups, left to right."

"All right." The writing was uncomfortably small. Squinting, I read the first string. Then the second. And the third. It was slow going, mainly because the Laerd wasn't much of typist. We often had to stop because of a mistake he'd made, and start over.

After three hours, he called a halt. We'd gone through only a quarter of the pile. "Ugh," he growled, fixing it with a baleful stare. "My eyes are burning and gods, my back hurts. How are we ever going to get through this tonight?"

"I have something for that." I fished through my pocket. Pulling out a flexible, nubby-sided vial, I uncapped it. Then I stepped behind his chair. "Here. Tilt your head back and look at me."

"What is it?"

"Eye drops." I squeezed the vial twice, one drop for each eye.

Straightening his neck, he looked around the room. "Hey, this is great."

"I know." I tipped my head back and squeezed. The tiredness from squinting at the nupaper's cramped writing disappeared.

He let out a small sigh. "I could use a massage. Where's Hyme when you need him?"

I said nothing. I was an expert masseuse, but did I really want to touch this hakoi without gloves? I swallowed, thinking about the second Ohra-Sin ritual I'd conduct next arhu. I'd have to endure more than enough touching then. On the other hand, I was a healer. My job was to ease suffering. And the Laerd was definitely suffering; I could see it in the way he slumped in the chair. Distaste and duty warred in me until duty won out. I bit my lip. "Well, I'm not Hyme, but maybe I can help."

He looked up with wide eyes. "You can give massages?"

"It's standard practice for healers."

He got up, swung the chair around, and sat with his back facing me. "Go ahead."

Resting my fingers under his jaw, I frowned. Little sparks of what felt like static electricity crackled through my hands and traveled up my arms. It didn't hurt, so I kept going. I gently rotated his head, moving it up and down, then left to right. I kneaded his thick neck muscles. It was like massaging wood. I kept kneading, increasing the pressure little by little. His muscles finally relaxed.

I went to work on the hard muscles in his shoulders and back. They too were like wood, but with the heavier sinews, I could use greater pressure. I massaged him for several minutes, my fingers digging deep. I noticed the static electricity feeling had stopped.

"Ahhh," he groaned. "You're much better than Hyme."

"Maybe I'll teach him a few things."

The apartment was quiet. "All right," he said after a minute or two. "That's good."

I let go of his broad shoulders. "Feel better?"

"Wonderful. But there's just one problem."

"What?"

"I'm sleepy."

"I have something for that, too."

"You came prepared."

I nodded. "For the past few days, I've seen the light in here burning way into the night. When you, ahem, asked me to help, I figured it'd be a long one, so I thought it best to bring a few things to make it go more smoothly."

"So what have you got?"

I fumbled in my pocket and held up another vial. "This."

"What's that?"

I handed it to him. "A stimulant. It's made from coca berries and a few other herbs."

"Wait. I've heard of coca berries. Don't they make you—"

"Not in these doses." I waved my hand. "Go ahead. Drink it. Make sure you've plenty of ale to chase it."

"Why?"

"Just drink it. Please."

The Laerd popped off the top and upended it. His eyes widened. Then his face screwed as if trying to knot itself. Grabbing his ale, he took a long draught and wiped his mouth on the back of his hand. He grimaced. "That's the nastiest stuff I've ever tasted."

I had already popped open my vial. "I know." Upending it, I squeezed my eyes shut, grabbed my drink, and took a hefty swig.

He peered. "Now what?"

"We wait. It'll only take a minute."

The apartment fell silent again. His look turned thoughtful. "Moreva, listen. I'm—" He sat up and grinned. "This stuff's great. I'm wide awake now. Let's get back to work." His smile broadened. "Please."

I blinked, realizing this was the first time I'd seen him smile since my arrival. He had a nice one, and it made him look younger. An odd, warm feeling flooded my belly. I blinked a few more times.

"Moreva? Are you all right?"

The sound of his gravelly voice jerked me into the present. "Oh... yes. But—"

"But what?"

I hesitated. "Let me type instead of you. I've been watching, so I'm pretty sure I know which numbers go where."

"Why?"

I took a breath. "Because you're a terrible typist. If we go on the way we've been doing it, we'll be here well into tomorrow morning."

He narrowed his eyes. "Let's see you do it."

We switched places. The Laerd rattled off the first string of numbers. I typed them into the boxes. After we'd finished the sheet, he stepped behind me. I twisted my neck to see his face. He studied the computer screen, consulted the nupaper, and looked back at the screen. "It's perfect," he said, as I knew it would be. He clapped me on the back, nearly slamming me into the desk. Barely managing not to recoil at his touch, I gave him a weak smile.

After that, the work went fast. We finished long before the first sun rose. I gathered the vials and got ready to leave.

He held up his hand. "Wait. How long is this stuff supposed to last?"

"Only a half-hour or so longer. You'll have plenty of time to sleep before breakfast."

"What about you? Don't you have to get up for your service?"

"I've time to sleep, too. Besides, I can always take a nap later or after midday." Walking me to the door, he opened it and gazed down. "Thank you, Moreva. I couldn't have done this without you." A small smile appeared on his lips. "And thank you especially for the massage."

I smiled back. "You're welcome, Laerd." Stepping onto the battlement, I headed to my apartment.

Inside, I tossed the eye drops into my kit, then threw the empty vials in the trash. Taking off my blouse, I set the alarm and draped it over the back of a fireplace chair, then sank into its cushion. After removing my boots, I settled back, luxuriating in the feel of the thick fur rug through my thin stockings. I closed my eyes and thought about the massage I'd given the Laerd, remembering the feel of his thick neck and back muscles beneath my fingers. *He'd be a great subject for the massage classes at the É. Maybe for the more advanced students. They have stronger hands.*

Then I remembered the static-like sensation while I'd massaged him. *What was that about? He obviously didn't feel it.* My shoulders twitched. *Probably nothing. The air was pretty dry in there, and he was wearing that wool sweater. That must have been it.*

Picturing his smile, I wondered if it meant our little war was over. *Be nice if it was.* I wasn't looking to be his bosom friend, but I'd had enough hostility from the villagers. If even one person—besides Hyme— was on my side, it would make this tour a lot more bearable, especially if that person was the village chief.

I dozed off. It seemed only minutes before the alarm woke me. Yawning, I rose to get ready for the service.

Chapter Six

After I helped him with the reports, the Laerd ignored me as if I'd become invisible. I didn't mind.

Late one morning, I slowly walked across the plaza's colorful stones, trying to figure out why one of my skratzes had dropped dead. The autopsy had shown nothing amiss. I had plenty more skratz, but not so many that I could afford to lose them like that.

I'd taken another step when a shadow crossed my path. My head snapped up.

The Laerd was only five šīzu away and moving fast. I skipped to the side moments before being knocked to the ground.

"You could have at least warned me," I yelled.

He kept walking.

"Du kan åtminstone titta på där du ska," a man's voice called in Syrenese. I turned my head. A small knot of villagers strolled along the sidewalk, packages in hand. They didn't look my way. I'd no idea who'd spoken or what was said, but I suspected it was along the lines of "watch where you're going." Hyme had suggested I learn Syrenese. I declined. I had no intention of becoming even remotely familiar with the Mjorans. Being familiar with one hakoi was enough.

Tightening my lips, I marched to my tower and walked into the É, setting the lights for continuous burn. Five days ago, I'd fashioned a service for myself. It helped me deal with the villagers' hostility, or at least I liked to believe. After setting up the altar, I knelt and bowed my head. "Most Holy One..."

That was as far as I got. Tears rolled down my cheeks, carrying all my fears and doubts of whether I could get through my tour. I cried for what seemed like hours.

When my crying finally stopped, I stared at the altar in misery. *I should do something. Take my mind off all this.* I blinked. *All right… what?* I didn't want to go back to the lab, and I didn't have to check the beacon until later. I didn't feel like taking a nap, either.

Dance, a small voice echoed in my brain. I nodded. *It's been a while. Be good for me.*

Shedding my clothes, I made my selection on the seero. In a moment, the sound of drumming filled the room. I turned up the volume and closed my eyes, swaying to the heady beat.

I took a few steps and was then swept away. Time meant nothing as I leapt and gyrated around the É until exhaustion forced me to stop. Dripping with sweat, I staggered to the seero on trembling legs and switched it off. But my mind was clear. I knelt at the altar and bowed my head in silent prayer. When I looked up, I knew the answer to my problem—dancing. The power of dance would see me through this tour. Resolving to dance once a day, I thanked Astoreth for her guidance.

After dressing, I decided to leave the cleaning for later. Passing through the portal, a quick movement from below caught my eye. The door to the barracks had just closed. I frowned. It had to be Yose, which meant he'd been spying on me. My frown deepened. After all, this was my É and I could do almost whatever I wanted in here. Uneasy, I climbed the stairs to my apartment.

I showered and decided to check the beacon. Central had given me a specific time to call in, but today they were going to get it early. In the control room, the cylinder was glowing white. Covering the small cavity with my thumb, I held it there until the cylinder had regained its normal, multicolored hues. The converter needed no adjustment. I called Central and made my report. The minor goddess's response was curt to the point of rudeness. I noticed she said nothing about my calling early.

Returning to my room, I realized my dancing had left me spent. I climbed on the bed without taking off my boots and without meaning to, fell asleep. When I woke, I tapped the bar. "Time."

"Seventh hour, two minutes Tryn."

Late for dinner. I decided to try an experiment. My depression returned as soon as I'd stepped outside. *Maybe I'll dance again after the evening service.*

I slipped into my seat, and the Laerd didn't even look up. To my surprise, a server placed a bowl of sprouts and maizur before me. I picked up my fork, but couldn't eat. I stared at the food, pushing it around.

Hyme nudged me. "Everything all right?"

I shook my head.

"Do you want to talk about it?"

"Not here."

"All right. But you must eat."

I shoved a forkful of vegetables in my mouth and tasted ashes. We ate the rest of our meal in silence.

Afterward, I sat in a comfortable, fur-covered chair next to the unlit fireplace in Hyme's apartment over the lab. During dinner, I had started to feel better and didn't want to confess my loneliness and isolation, not even to my friend. "Honestly, there isn't a problem, really. I was just feeling sorry for myself. You know, being so far from home, the villagers' hostility..." I let out a light snort. "And the Laerd—either barking at me or treating me like a ghost. It wears me down, that's all." I cocked my head. "How come you don't treat me like they do?"

He chuckled. "I like talking to people, especially those from far away. It gives me new perspectives. Besides, I always learn something whether it has to do with healing or not." He sat back in an identical chair opposite mine. "I just wish the rest of my people would get over their grudge against the Devi. Maybe they'd treat you better."

Happy to be off the subject of my personal life, I settled back. "What grudge are you talking about?"

He gave me an enigmatic smile. "Oh, something that happened a long time ago."

He said nothing more, and I didn't push. I would have, but whatever had happened might be something he didn't want to talk about. The last thing I wanted to do was alienate my only friend. After a moment's reflection, I thought I knew the answer, anyway. Astoreth had said the Syrenese were not a forgiving people.

Neither of us said anything for a long while. "Hyme, what's the Protocol for? I know things were tense between Mjor and Astoreth when it was negotiated. I guess that's why She thought the tower needed protection. But times have changed, haven't they? Who's going to raise an army and attack the tower now?"

"Tell me, how would you feel if there was an armed garrison and a couple of tanks camped right outside your door?"

"I'd feel safe."

"From what? We're not lawless here. Your É is paying us and we're not going to jeopardize that. Even if that wasn't the case, it would be foolish of us to try anything. Mjor has a robust trade in thalin with the Devi, and we'd like to keep it that way." He paused. "The Protocol is protection for us."

"I see." I stared at my hands. *There's more to it than that. He told me everybody in the village has at least one gun. No way the garrison could take Mjor with forty-one soldiers and two tanks. The Mjorans don't need protection from the garrison. The garrison needs protection from* them. My shoulders twitched. *Guess I'll never know.* I tapped the bar. "Time to service."

"One hour, two minutes."

"I'd better be going," I said, getting to my feet.

"Of course. Here, let me see you to the door."

Hyme opened the street door for me. "I'll see you tomorrow, Tehi."

"Good night."

"And a good night to you."

Entering my tower, I climbed the stairs and thought about tonight's service. *Hm. It's Ulum, so I need the red.* After a shower, I pulled out my strapless red corset and collar, a symbol of service to the Most Holy One. While waiting for my makeup to dry, I shoved my feet into slippers, then dug my red crop and shoes out of the closet. I checked my makeup in the mirror and left.

Kneeling before the altar, I soon heard booted feet on stone. Once everyone had settled, I began the service, and at its end, I cropped the penitents' backs. I cropped Yose extra hard for spying on me. He flinched. I smiled in satisfaction.

I cleaned the É, and decided against another dance session. Returning to my apartment, I shed my cloak. My skin prickled. It was still cold in here, even though I'd turned on the heat earlier. Grabbing my robe, I was about to slip into it when I looked at the bed. *That nap I took wasn't enough.*

I draped the robe over a chair, hurried to the bed, and climbed in. Arms behind my head, I stared at the ceiling, pondering the Laerd's behavior. *Why is he such a dicknut to me? For whatever reason, he doesn't like me, and that's fine. He didn't like Eresh either, but he didn't treat* him *like merda*. I thought about it for another minute or so. *Well, whatever*. I rolled onto my side and fell into a fitful sleep.

⊙⊒⊒⊒⊒⊙

After the morning service, I filled the bucket with enzyme crystals and paced the pool's perimeter, pouring the mixture into it.

The hairs on the back of my neck stood up, and I looked over my shoulder. Yose stood in the doorway, staring. *Is he spying on me again?* A second later, I decided he wasn't. There was nothing to keep him from seeing me while I was here, and besides, he was standing in the open.

I straightened. "Yes, Kepten? What can I do for you?"

"One of Pavet Dal's marks broke open and is infected. Please come to the barracks."

"Of course. Let me finish here and get my bag. I'll be down in about fifteen minutes."

"Thank you." He left.

I ran to my apartment, dressed, and then grabbed my healer's kit. The garrison snapped to attention as I walked into the barracks. "As you were."

Yose met me and pointed to a shirtless woman lying face down on her bunk. Sitting on its edge, I inspected her broken skin. It was an arryia infection, painful and alarming to look at but not dangerous. I dug into my kit and pulled out a bottle of bactericide and a pair of nuskin gloves. Snapping on the gloves, I then poured the liquid into her wound. She gasped. From past experience, I knew the antiseptic stung like a gnut. Reaching into my bag again, I pulled out a roll of treated nuskin, cut a length, and dressed her injury.

I turned to call Yose over and startled. He'd been standing right behind me. "Dal's back should be kept bare for the next couple of days. She can get up and move around, but no uniform." I touched the pavet's shoulder. "Sleep on your stomach to cut down on irritation."

Yose nodded once. "Dal, you're on sick leave as of now." He looked up. "Can she come to service?"

"Of course." I repacked my bag. "Anything else, Kepten?"

"No. Thank you." His eyes were like stones.

I matched his stare. "All right. I'll be at the lab. Call Hyme if you need me."

Inside my apartment, I set my healer's kit on the table went back out. Walking across the plaza, I wondered if skagwort, Hyme's miracle plant, would have had an effect on Dal's infection. "Should have taken a sample," I muttered, thinking of the arriya. "Well, maybe I'll get a chance some other time."

I opened the lab's street door and stopped in my tracks. My jaw dropped. Shattered glass lay everywhere I looked, sparkling in the overhead candescent light. Liquids dripped from the counters, powders flung had turned the floor into a colorful abstract. Most of the drawers had been pulled off their tracks, their contents scattered. The cage had been overturned and the skratzes stomped, their crushed bodies in pools of silvery blue blood. I still had plenty of skratz so this wasn't a real setback, but that their lives had been snuffed out so cruelly made my hearts hurt.

I looked up. Hyme stood in the middle of the mess, clearly dumbfounded. "Wh-what happened?"

"Someone picked the lock last night and did," he swept his arm, "this."

Our eyes widened at the same time. "The virus," we said as one. Feet crunching on broken glass, we ran to the freezer. I threw up the lid, grabbed the box with the vials, and opened it. It hadn't been touched.

"Whew," we breathed at the same time. I returned the box to the freezer. "Thank Astoreth."

Stepping back into the wreckage, I blew a heavy breath. "Why would someone want to vandalize the lab? I mean, you're the healer. Why would somebody—"

"I suspect they were trying to get at you."

My hand flew to my chest. "Me? I haven't done—"

"Because you're here. If you haven't noticed, the main damage has been done to your work, not mine."

Taking a second look, I saw he was right. "How did they know it was my equipment they were destroying, and not yours?"

"Easy enough to figure out. It was half-sized. Plus, it was new."

"So...what if they decide to come after me next?"

"I don't think you're in any danger. Bringing the virus here is one thing, but if you turn up missing or dead for no reason, Astoreth would be perfectly within her rights to retaliate. And who knows what form that might take? I'm sure no one wants to find out." He shook his head.

"Come on. Let's see how much of this we can get cleaned up before breakfast. We have to let the Laerd know what happened, too."

We picked up the overturned table and shoved it back against the wall. Inspecting the drawers, we set the damaged ones aside. The others we slid into their spaces. Hyme picked up the more durable equipment that hadn't been broken and set them on the counter. While he sorted the rest, I gathered the pieces from the skratz cage, giving Astoreth silent thanks that lysite was unbreakable. "I'm going to wash these, and then—"

"Hyme, I...great gods, what happened in here?"

Both our heads snapped up.

Eyes wide, the Laerd stood in the doorway, staring at the ruin.

I picked up another cage panel and crossed to the sink. "We were vandalized."

"Wait a minute, wait a minute. Stop."

I set the panels in the sink and turned.

The Laerd looked at Hyme. "When did you discover this?"

"This morning. Tehi arrived a few minutes after I got here."

"How'd the vandals get in?"

I pointed to the door. "They picked the lock. Look at it. It's not damaged."

The Laerd inspected it, then looked at Hyme again. "You didn't hear anything?"

He shook his head. "My bedroom is in the back."

"Hm." The Laerd consulted a dark brown wristband. "Come on. It's almost time for breakfast. We'll talk about what to do then."

I turned back to the sink. "You two go on," I said over my shoulder. "I'll work on cleaning up this mess." I wanted them out of the lab so I could use my psi power to discover the vandal's identity. Then I'd figure out a way to tell them without letting them know how I knew.

The Laerd's face settled into an expressionless mask. "I'd rather you went with us, Moreva."

"I'll be all right. I don't think they're coming back. They've made their point."

"I don't want you in here alone."

Something in his tone told me he'd brook no argument. He didn't know I was perfectly capable of defending myself, but I saw no reason to press the point. "All right. I'm coming."

Crossing the plaza, we talked about what had happened and what to do about it. "Get a new lock, obviously," the Laerd said. "Then we'll put our energy into finding who did this."

We entered the dining hall, the Laerd abandoning his usual seat in the center to sit closer to Hyme and me. The two men started a conversation about locks. The Laerd suggested a thumb lock while Hyme argued the old lock be replaced. "Like the Moreva said, I don't think they'll be back."

I cleared my throat. "May I speak?"

The Laerd's eyes narrowed. "Moreva—"

"Look, I know my opinion isn't valued around here, but since it was mostly my equipment that was destroyed, I think I have a right to join this conversation."

His lips tightened. "Go on."

I looked at Hyme, then the Laerd. "Do you know what a keyless lock is?"

"Of course we do," the Laerd snapped. "We're not—"

"All right, all right," I said, holding up a hand. "I was just asking." I looked from one man to the other again. "So how about one of those? It can't be picked, it's easy to use, and no headaches over lost keys. Hyme can set the combination, maybe change it every other arhu for added security."

No one spoke for a moment. "Well..." the Laerd said.

I sat back, irritated. It was a good idea, even if the big dicknut couldn't recognize it.

He pursed his lips. "All right. We'll have Drost put in a keyless lock for the lab door."

I leaned forward. "Three locks. One for the apothecary and one for the hospital."

"Why?"

"Because someone can get into the lab through those doors, too."

He blinked a few times, and then gave a short nod. "All right. Three locks. Hyme, the Moreva, and I will have access. I'll speak to Drost after we leave."

I cocked my head. "Can you trust him?"

"Of course we can trust him. Why?" He looked annoyed.

"Does he sell lock picking tools?"

"No."

"Then where did whoever did this get the tools?"

Hyme rested a hand on my arm. "It wouldn't have taken much to pick the lock. It's pretty flimsy. Probably should have had it changed years ago, but I never thought I'd get vandalized."

"Until I came," I muttered.

"What was that?" the Laerd said.

"Um, nothing. Come on, Hyme. We need to get the lab cleaned up."

"And I'll go talk to Drost."

We headed for the hallway. "Moreva," the Laerd said from behind. I turned.

His face was impassive. "Thank you for the suggestion. It was a good one."

I blinked, surprised by the compliment. "You're welcome, Laerd."

Inside the lab, Hyme and I continued cleaning up. While I washed the cage and glassware we managed to save, he vacuumed, the machine gobbling up the pooled liquids and powders strewn over the floor.

I'd just finished putting the cage together when I heard a tiny squeal. I looked at Hyme. "Well, at least one's still alive," he said.

Instead of answering, I walked along the floor close to the baseboards, making clucking sounds. "Tsk-tsk. Tsk-tsk." Another squeal, this time much closer. "Tsk-tsk, tsk-tsk." About to cluck again, a hairless skratz darted from under a cabinet. I bent and held out my cupped hand. The little beast jumped into it, ran along my arm, grabbed onto my hair with its hand-like paws. It pulled itself up until it was sitting on top of my head. Quaking, its tiny claws dug into my scalp.

"Do you think that's the only one?" Hyme said.

"Well, let's see." I walked around the lab, clucking. No other skratzes appeared. "Guess this little one is the only survivor."

He sighed. "Too bad it can't talk. It could tell us who did this."

"It can't, but maybe I can," I blurted without thinking. My eyes widened a fraction. *Oh, no...I can't believe I just said that!*

Hyme frowned. "What do you mean?"

"Well, I..." *Astoreth, I've gotten too comfortable with him. I trust him as far as my project goes, but this...* I bit my lip. Except for Eresh, the morevs back home feared my power because they knew I'd use it if they crossed me. As far as I knew, there were no psi hakoi on Peris. That didn't mean they didn't know what it was and what it could do, though. If they feared it, I knew how they'd react. I closed my eyes. *You idiot. No way out of it now.*

I opened them. Hyme looked concerned. "Tehi, is something wrong?"

"Ah...no. I mean..." I let out a heavy sigh. "I'm not sure how to tell you."

"Tell me what? Out with it."

I sighed again. "I'm psi. That's how I might be able to tell who the vandal is." I stared, holding my breath.

Hyme stared back, but said nothing.

I bowed my head. His silence made me nervous.

I waited. He still didn't speak. My nervousness spiked. *Astoreth, why couldn't I have kept my big mouth shut?*

"So it's true," he said, his voice quiet.

I looked up. "What?"

He still stared. "We have a legend that the Devi have this power. I thought that's all it was...until now."

I bowed my head again. "What will you do?"

More silence. "Nothing," he finally said.

My head snapped up. "You're...not afraid?"

Hyme laughed. "Oh my, no. I think it's marvelous. Come on. Show me what you can do."

Relief swept through me. "All right." Closing my eyes, I centered myself and opened my senses. Two sets of vibrations belonging to two people who were not here now flowed through me. I opened my third eye. The first person was the Laerd. Another person appeared, but the image was indistinct. I concentrated, trying to bring it into focus. The image remained fuzzy. I concentrated harder and harder still. It didn't work. Sighing, I gave up and opened my eyes.

Hyme gave me an intent look. "What did you see?"

"I saw the Laerd and a shadow. That's our vandal, but I couldn't get anymore. Too much time has passed between then and now."

The apothecary's bell rang, and Hyme jumped to his feet. "Be right back."

The street door opened a second later. The Laerd and an old man with a long white beard stepped inside. The Laerd nodded once.

"Where's Hyme?"

"Out front. Can I help with anything?"

"No. Moreva, this is Drost, Mjor's locksmith."

The dismissal stung, but I smiled at the newcomer and gave a deep bow. "May the Most Holy One turn Her face to you."

The locksmith gave me an odd look. I knew he hadn't understood what I'd said, but... *Oh. The skratz is still on my head.*

He gave a single nod. "Moreva."

"Drost is here to put new locks on the doors," the Laerd said.

My lips twisted into a smirk. "I figured."

He narrowed his eyes, but said nothing.

We pulled up the swivel chairs, and Drost got to work.

"Whoever did this is in a lot of trouble."

The Laerd gave me a sideways look. "Of course they are. Mjor has laws against this kind of thing, you know."

"It's more than that. This is about the destruction of É property. When I ask for new equipment, they're bound to ask what happened. And I'll have to tell them."

"So?"

"So they'll probably send investigators to work with you. Or, if you've already caught them, they'll assume jurisdiction. And Astoreth is not known for leniency when it comes to Her property."

He grunted. "Assume jurisdiction? Not if I have anything to say about it."

Silent, we watched Drost drill out the old lock.

"You look funny with that thing on your head."

"This thing is called a skratz. And I'm sure I do, but this little one is the only survivor." I leaned toward him. "Would you like to pet it? They like that."

He reached for my head. The skratz shivered; they always did that when pleased.

"It's so soft."

"Scratch between its ears. They like that, too." I looked up from beneath my lashes. The Laerd was grinning. Our gazes met, and he stopped his petting. His grin faded. "It's cute once you get used to it."

Hyme walked into the lab. "Åh, hej, Drost. Tack för att du kom så kort varsel."

Drost grunted.

We watched him for a while longer. Then he turned and walked over to us. "Klart. Jag fixar apotekare dörr, och sedan sjukhusets. Installationen kommer att—"

"Rådet kommer att ta hand om det," the Laerd said.

Drost nodded and left.

I looked from one man to the other. Hyme took a breath to say something, but I beat him to it. "What'd he say?"

The Laerd turned. "He'll do the apothecary door next, and then the hospital. He was going to give you a price, but I told him the Council would take care of it."

"Thank you, Laerd," Hyme and I said as one.

"You're welcome. It's the least we can do after someone destroyed most of your equipment." He paused. "Speaking of equipment, when do you plan to notify your É?"

"Soon as I can."

"All right." He gave a nod to each of us, then left.

Hyme held out a nupaper pad and stylus. "Make a list of everything you lost so you don't miss anything."

"That's all right. I know what I brought with me." I put the skratz into its cage and watched it sniff at the fresh jabb shavings. My jaw clenched. *This foutéz is going to set me* way *back, and I don't have time for it. Damn the dicknut who did this.*

"Tehi."

I turned.

Hyme's face was somber. "What happens now?"

"I call home. There won't be a problem getting new equipment." I gazed at my feet. *If this isn't an emergency, I don't know what is.* I blew a heavy sigh and then looked up. "Well, I'd better be going. See you at lunch."

"See you then."

Crossing the plaza, I thought about what I'd tell whoever was on the board about what had happened. *I can't tell them about the vandalism. I don't want the investigators here any more than the Laerd does.* The É investigators were a hard-nosed, thorough lot, and would leave no stone unturned until they found the perpetrator. There was every chance they'd dig up secrets best left buried. *Can't imagine what the Mjorans have to hide, but if there is anything, I don't want to be the reason anybody finds out.* I bit my lip. I had to find a way to keep them from coming here.

Standing before my door, I was about to push it open when I had an idea. I ran back to the lab.

⊙⊐⊐⊐⊐⊙

The Laerd and I stood outside his tower. "You and Hyme set fire to the lab?" he said, expression horrified and incredulous.

"Shh! Of course not," I snapped. "We set fire to a trash can in the back. Some herbs and plants when burned produce a lot of smoke but not much flame. The point was to make it look like a real fire."

"Why?"

"Because that's what I told the investigators when I asked for new equipment."

"So that's what the fire siren was about." He cocked his head. "Are they going to do it? Replace your equipment?"

I grinned. "Yes. Kepten Yose was outside, and he saw and smelled the smoke. He heard the siren, too. He said he'd be glad to talk to them."

"Are they going to send investigators?"

"No. As far as they're concerned, there's nothing to investigate. Lab fires aren't unheard of. Besides, Mjor is one of the last posts on the landing strip. Too expensive to fly up to some backwater village to investigate something that has a plausible explanation."

His face darkened. "Is that how you think of Mjor? As some backwater village?"

Oh, wonderful. I've insulted him. "No, no...but you have to admit we're awfully far from Uruk."

"Hmph." He still looked annoyed. "So when do you get your new equipment?"

"Well, the garrison's due for a supply run, so I'll have my new equipment in about three marun."

"What do you plan on doing in the meantime?"

I shrugged. "I'll figure something out."

"All right." He walked to his door, then looked over his shoulder. "Oh, and Moreva? Thanks for keeping the investigators out. We'll catch whoever did it. Mjor may be a backwater village, but we're not wanting."

I ducked my head. I thought he'd let the matter drop. "Of course, Laerd. Happy to help."

He disappeared into his tower, and I headed for my own. *Three whole marun. What in Astoreth's name am I going to do in Mjor for the next thirty days?*

Chapter Seven

Amarun after the vandalism, I was at loose ends. Hyme had tried his best to keep me busy, but there wasn't enough work for the two of us. I'd studied the pictures in the herb manuals he'd given me, but tired of it after a day or so since I couldn't read the text. Flipping through the pages, I'd been tempted to take him up on his offer to teach me the language. But I didn't. I didn't want to know any more about the Syrenese than I already did, and that was nothing. I'd been so bored, I even went to the small factory and watched the village men and women make cloth.

One morning, while prowling through Hyme's herb and plant stocks, I noticed he was low on masich berries. He'd told me the masich bush blooms only during winter, and the berries appear late in the season. Though winter's cold lingered in the springtime air, the weather was definitely turning. If he wanted to replenish what he had, he'd better do it soon. "Hyme, you need more masich berries. Want to get some?"

"Not right now. I have to fill these orders before lunch."

"All right." I returned to my chair and spun it a few times. "This is ridiculous," I muttered. "I've got to *do* something." Spying Hyme's collection bag in the corner, I walked over to it and peered inside. The cutters were lying at its bottom. *I'll just go by myself.* The village rule—*always in pairs, one with a gun*—ran through my head. I dismissed it. *It's not far. I'll be fine.* I picked up the bag and slipped out the door.

I walked about forty šīzu along the paved road outside the gates, then stepped onto the dirt path leading into the forest. Being alone didn't bother me. Hyme had shown me the masich bushes on our first trip into the woods, and I knew exactly where they were. I turned right at the path's first fork, bypassed the second, and turned right again at the third. Under the trees, the air was chilly, but not cold. *Warmer out here than I thought.* I quickened my step. What berries were left might have already rotted.

The sights and sounds of life awakening after a long winter's sleep surrounded me. I caught glimpses of drab hens building nests while their brilliantly-colored mates perched nearby, their sweet melodies warning off intruders. Every so often, striped mice darted across the path. The trees and bushes crowding each other had started to bud. In my mind's eye, I could see the forest's wild lushness in the marun to come. Soon it would be hard to believe a village lay just a bit more than twelve nindan away.

So different from home. Kherah was a desert, and Uruk's water source, the wide and deep Ven River to the east, had allowed Astoreth to turn Her capital into a lavish garden. Exotic, hanging flowers in all colors cascaded down many a courtyard wall. The streets were lined with stands of qal, water-loving trees with delicate, willowy trunks and long, pointed red leaves. Sprawling tracts of box farms surrounded most of the city. Other urban areas had their own rivers or underground sources and were decorated with foliage as colorful as Uruk's. The cities and towns were like islands, for outside their boundaries there was only sand, jagged rockscapes, and the occasional stand of succulents.

A moment later, I spotted the masich bushes, looking like big, fat balls with their shiny, dark blue leaves. Stepping off the path, I forged my way through the underbrush and trees, pushing the skeletal branches out of my way. Reaching the bushes, I parted a few branches with my fingers. I was just in time. Many of the round, orange berries had started to dimple. "A sure sign of rot," Hyme had told me. I fished for the cutter and started clipping twigs sporting the best-looking berries, then dropped them into the bag.

After about an hour, the bag was half full. I smiled, thinking about the happy reception I'd get on returning with even this much.

I headed for the path, pushing branches out of my way. I'd walked about ten šīzu when I heard something crashing through the forest. It sounded close by. I stopped to listen. Whatever it was, it was a lot bigger than a mouse.

I swiveled my head, but saw nothing that could make that kind of noise. Curious and uneasy, I kept going. I reached the path, then stepped out from the underbrush.

And froze.

Standing on the packed dirt was a great, shaggy beast. A curved horn, narrowing to a lethal point, grew out of its snout. It had feet the size of dinner plates, ringed by wicked-looking claws. And it was staring at me.

It bellowed, reared onto its hind legs, and then charged.

My world slowed to a crawl. Paralyzed by fright, I didn't even think to zap it. I screamed, hurled my bag into the underbrush, and ran. Even at Devi speed, I sensed it gaining on me. I could almost feel its hot breath on my neck. Unless I did something and fast, I wasn't going to make it out of the forest alive.

Up ahead, I spied a tree that looked sturdy enough to hold me. I put on a burst of speed, leapt into its branches, and started climbing. Higher and higher I climbed. When I dared look down, the beast was snarling and clawing at the trunk as if to tear it apart. I squeezed my eyes shut. *Astoreth, deliver me!* Then the tree started shaking so hard I nearly lost my grip. Hanging on for dear life, I screamed again and again.

CRACK!

A roar of pain. The shaking stopped. The beast smashed through the forest, the sound growing ever fainter.

I opened my eyes. The Laerd stood about twenty šīzu from my tree, wearing his usual scowl. "Moreva, come down from there!"

I shook my head.

He moved closer, and his dark expression melted into concern. "Moreva," he said, his deep, gravelly voice gentle. "Come down, Moreva."

I stared in the direction where the beast had gone. It was still out there, and as long as it was, I wasn't going anywhere. I shook my head a second time.

"It's not coming back, Moreva. It's all right to come down now. Besides, I've got my gun so if it does come back, I'll just shoot it again."

Well, that made sense.

I heard the sound of many running feet. Peering from my tree, it turned out to be seven men, all armed with rifles and carrying nets. They stopped on seeing us. Pointing, the Laerd told them something in Syrenese. The men ran off.

He looked up. "Please, Moreva," he said, switching back to Devian. "Come down."

I nodded, then started picking my way through the branches. Twelve šīzu off the ground, I shuddered at the deep gouges the beast had made in the trunk. I jumped from the last branch onto the forest floor. I didn't move after that.

The Laerd leaned his rifle against a nearby tree and spread his arms wide. "Come here, Moreva."

Too terrified to care he was hakoi, I flew into his waiting arms. Gasping and shaking, I wrapped my arms tight around him, digging my fingers into his back. I burst into tears. The ground seemed to shift beneath my feet, but I paid it scant attention.

While I sobbed, the Laerd made rumbling, cooing noises while stroking my hair. An eternity seemed to pass before my trembling and crying stopped. I looked up, a stray tear trickling along my cheek. "Wh-what was that?"

He brushed my tear away. An electric spark zinged through my flesh. I didn't pay that any attention, either.

"An ura. It's rutting season, so they'll charge anything they see. Or anything that moves."

"Oh."

He gave my hair another stroke. "What were you doing out here alone, Moreva? You know the rule."

"I-I was getting some masich berries for Hyme. He couldn't come with me and I knew nobody else would, so I thought it'd be all right if I went by myself. I mean, it wasn't far and—"

His face turned alarmed. "You and Hyme come out here together? No one else?"

"Hyme carries the gun."

"Great gods. Hyme couldn't hit a tree from three šīzu."

I giggled.

He smiled. "Feeling better now?"

"I-I think so."

"Let's get back to Mjor, then."

Letting go, he picked up his gun and headed for the path. Walking along the packed dirt, he regaled me with stories of his youth, the miscreant that he was. I don't know how much of it was true—how much trouble can one boy get into?—but I knew what he was doing and was grateful.

My step faltered when we reached the spot where the ura had attacked me. I steeled myself to go on. Then I stopped. "Wait." I backtracked and peered into the undergrowth. Spotting my bag, I pulled it out. No berries had been lost. Even the cutter was still inside. I straightened and smiled. "It's all right. I'd have hated to think all that work had been for nothing."

We started walking again.

"How come you're not angry with me? I broke one of your rules."

He looked down from the corner of his eye. "Oh, I'm angry with you. And if they had a mind to, the Council could send you back to Uruk. But I'll talk to them. I think you've learned your lesson."

I ducked my head but said nothing.

We stepped onto the road. The village beckoned. He quickened his pace and so did I, never so glad to see it. Marching through the gates, we headed straight for the apothecary. Mjorans stared at us, silent.

Hyme turned when the Laerd opened the door. "Come in, you two. Come in." He ushered us into the lab. I leaned against the long counter.

The old healer frowned. "What's wrong, Tehi? You look as if you've been crying."

I opened my mouth, but the Laerd beat me to it. He related my adventure with the ura. Hyme's expression turned horrified. He ran into the apothecary and returned with a small bottle, poured two fingers' worth into a beaker, then handed it to me. "Here. Drink this."

"What is it?"

"A mild sedative. You've had quite a scare."

"Hyme, I don't need—"

"Drink it."

I obeyed, then gave him the beaker.

The Laerd eyed us. "Now listen to me, both of you. The next time you plan to go flower hunting, you tell me and I'll go with you. If I can't, I'll send somebody along. Understand?"

We nodded.

"Good." He walked toward the street door.

I pushed myself off the counter. "Laerd, wait."

He looked over his shoulder.

I hurried over to him. Pressing my palms, I gave a deep bow, then gazed into his star-colored eyes. "Kea leboha. Thank you."

He nodded once and left.

"I think you embarrassed him," Hyme said.

I yawned. "Are you sure this is a mild sedative?"

"I'm sure. Why don't you lie down? I'll wake you in time for lunch."

I tried to protest, but only managed to yawn again. "All right."

He led me into the hospital. In the patient's room, I sat on the nearest bed while he switched on the positive flow. After I'd made myself comfortable, he turned down the lights and left me alone.

In the near-darkness, I thought about the Laerd holding me and stroking my hair. How ironic—me, taking refuge in a hakoi's arms. It would have been laughable if it hadn't happened.

Falling asleep, I wondered about the ground shift I'd felt. *Do they have periquakes up here? I wonder if he felt...*

Then, I knew nothing.

⊙ ⊟ ⊟ ⊟ ⊟ ⊙

In my sedative-induced fog, I sensed someone standing over me and opened my eyes. It was the Laerd. He was smiling.

"Are you awake?"

I smiled back. "Not really."

"Then I'll leave you be."

He bent and kissed my forehead. That electric crackling flooded through me. Still smiling, I closed my eyes. When I opened them again, he was gone.

I went back to sleep.

⊙ ⊟ ⊟ ⊟ ⊟ ⊙

Hyme woke me just before lunch. "How do you feel?"

I sat up. "Groggy."

"You'll feel more like yourself in a few minutes. The sedative I gave you lasts exactly two hours."

"What's in it?"

"Olarian is the base. It's a soporific herb. I add in a few more herbs to strengthen it. Works well, doesn't it?"

I yawned. "It sure does." I swung my legs over the side and looked at my feet. True to his word, the grogginess disappeared within minutes. Straightening my back, I swiveled my head left and right to stretch the muscles in my neck.

84

"Ready for lunch?"

"Very." I slipped on my boots. "You'll have to show me how to make that. I have sedatives too, but nothing that wears off that fast. Or that completely."

"Be glad to."

Crossing the plaza, I saw the Laerd enter the dining hall through the side entrance. I pursed my lips. "Hyme, did anyone come sit with me while I was out?"

"No, not that I know of. Why?"

I shook my head. "No reason."

After eating, Hyme and I had gone outside when I spotted the Laerd in the hall's corridor. I lay a hand on the old healer's arm. "Just a minute."

I stepped back inside and planted myself in the Laerd's way. "May I speak to you for a moment?"

He frowned. "What is it?"

"Did you come back to the hospital this morning after Hyme gave me that sedative?"

His expression turned unreadable. "No."

I nodded. "All right. It must have been a dream."

"I'm sure it was. Now, if you'll excuse me." He brushed past.

I watched him leave. I didn't believe him. His kiss, that feeling of crackling electricity, was no dream. My brows rose. Or was it? I couldn't imagine him coming to see me for any reason outside Mjoran/Devian affairs. *And I'd* never *let a hakoi kiss me, except during Ohra-Sin when I don't have a choice. Even the thought makes my stomach turn.* I frowned a little. *But it had felt so real.* Shaking my head, I rejoined Hyme outside.

"All finished?"

"Yes. Let's get back. I'm anxious to learn more about that sedative."

In the lab, Hyme took out one large bag and two smaller bags of herbs from a tall, narrow closet set into one wall. As many times as I'd been here, I'd never noticed it.

"These are the sedative's ingredients." He held up the largest bag filled with dried, dark green leaves. "This is olarian. It grows just about everywhere and is easy to get. This," he held up the next largest bag, "is lujan. It's plentiful too, but only grows further up in the mountains. And this," he held up the smallest bag, "is helly. It grows on the mountain-tops, and only experienced climbers can get to it. It's expensive and a healer has to trade a lot of knowledge to get some."

For the rest of the after midday—with me taking a break to check the beacon and dance—he explained the properties of each herb and the sedative's formula. By the time he'd finished, I knew I could make it myself. He had enough, so I didn't ask. Then it occurred to me. "Hyme, when you say you 'trade for knowledge' what do you mean?"

"Just that. Some healers are more experienced than others, espe-cially those just starting out. Trading knowledge enriches our healing practices. Sometimes we trade other things, too." He held up the bag of helly. "I got this for one of my old microscopes. The healer's scope had broken and was irreparable. So, I came along and offered her an upgrade from her old one in exchange for the helly. She was so grateful, she gave me two bags."

"What else do you trade?"

"Formulas, books, things like that. I've several editions you can't get anymore, and some healers would die to get their hands on them. So I have copies made, bind them like the original, and trade them for plants and knowledge." He grinned. "I'm considered a rich man around these parts."

I smiled back, but it soon died. "Hyme, you're giving me all this knowledge, but I don't feel I'm giving you anything in return. I mean—"

"Nonsense. You've been teaching me about your desert plants. All herbal and plant lore, of whatever kind, is useful knowledge. Most of all, even though you're not swimming in them, you've shared your skratz with me for my own work. That alone is worth all the knowledge I've shared with you." He paused. "You say the Devi make the skratz. We have nothing like it. If you lived here, you'd be a very rich woman, indeed."

I laughed. "Well, skratz are easy to come by. I just put in an order with Kepten Yose, and poof! they're here on the next supply run. But don't tell anybody. They really belong to the É, not me."

"Well, you can always tell them you traded them for knowledge."

"Somehow, I don't think they'd appreciate that."

Hyme looked at the timepiece on the wall. "It's time for dinner, already. I can't believe we've been at this all after midday. The time just flies, doesn't it?"

"Sure does. But you've stuffed me with so much knowledge I'm not sure I can eat."

He laughed.

We headed for the dining hall. The Laerd was headed the same way. He spotted and walked our way. Reaching us, the Laerd looked down, face composed in that expressionless mask it always had when he wasn't scowling at me. "I should have asked earlier, Moreva—how are you feeling after your morning scare?"

"I'm fine, Laerd. Thank you for asking."

"Good." He strode away.

"I thought he'd walk with us," Hyme said.

"Maybe it's me. I told you, when I got here, he took every opportunity to confront me about something or other. Now he avoids me as much as he can."

Leaving the dining hall after dinner, Hyme said, "Are you coming back to the lab tonight?"

"I can. Why?"

"Because I have to do inventory and could use the company."

"All right. I'll be there."

Walking across the plaza after leaving the apothecary, I breathed in the crisp, night air. This was my favorite time, which was why I often stayed late at Hyme's. No villagers spitting at me, no Laerd and his scowling face. The night was my favorite time in Uruk, too. Sometimes, after everyone was asleep, I'd sneak out of the É and visit the gardens or play with the animals in their cages. Astoreth forbade us from being outside after bedtime, so I always made sure to return before daybreak.

My mood was light as I stepped inside my tower. Despite my scare, it had been a good day. For once, I was looking forward to seeing what tomorrow would bring.

Chapter Eight

The next day didn't start out so well.

I almost missed the morning service. During the rite, I couldn't find my center and had trouble keeping focused. After cleaning the É, I went back to bed, not caring I would miss breakfast.

Lying under the furs, I stared at the ceiling. I'd had a rough night. Full of vivid, harrowing nightmares, leaving me with pounding hearts and covered in sweat. One dream stood out in particular. It replayed in horrifying detail in mind's eye...

I'm hiding inside a cubbyhole in back of one of the imposing columns in the Grand Hall, straining my ears for sounds of my Devi classmates. It's hot in here. This is where the electronics for the column's lighting are, and except for the twinkling green, yellow, and blue orbs, it's dark. Gasping, my hearts pounded in fear. My classmates have been chasing me for hours. They caught me a few times, but I managed to break away. I know what they want. They want to hurt me, like they have so many times before. But they'll find me eventually. I know it. My power to hide myself isn't that strong. They'll sense me with their hyper keen Devi senses. I can hide from the hakoi, but not from them.

The door to the cubbyhole is flung open. I squeeze my eyes shut. Someone grabs my arm and yanks hard, dragging me from the cubbyhole. I open them. It's Jangi, the boy who hates me the most. "There's the dirty hakoi," he snarls, face contorted with evil glee. I chomp on his forearm, tasting blood. Yowling, he snatches his arm away.

In the next second, excruciating pain explodes at the top of my head. Jangi has seized hold of my hair. Eyes squeezed shut again, I scream as he hauls me into the corridor. I reach up with both hands and grab his arm. Twisting and kicking, I try to escape. The whooping of myriad high-pitched voices echo through the hallway. "Dirty hakoi! It's the dirty hakoi! Dirty hakoi!"

Jangi lets go of my hair and thrusts me into the arms of my classmates. I struggle but can't get free. They carry me, thrashing and screeching, into the vast Ohra-Namtar sacrarium to the giant, sacred pool. Its deep waters can hold scores of writhing bodies. Still screaming "dirty hakoi," they throw me in, then jump in after me. I swim as fast as I can, but they are faster. Catching me, they push me under. I claw my way to the surface.

"No," I shout. "I'm one of you!"

Someone yells, "You're not! You're just a dirty hakoi!"

I fight my way to the surface again and again, shrieking, "I'm not hakoi!" They push me under every time. By now, my lungs are filling with water. I battle on, fighting until I can fight no more. The last thing I see before drowning are their faces, full of mad exultation.

When I woke, I'd bolted upright. Gasping and sweating, my hearts beat a wild staccato while my head swiveled, trying to figure out where I was and how I'd managed to survive. When fully awake, I'd lain back down, knowing there'd be no more sleep for me.

Astoreth had taught us to put great stock in dreams as messages from the subconscious and, less often, messages from other dimensions. I tried to figure out what my dream meant, but soon gave up. Nothing made sense.

My thoughts drifted, eventually settling on my childhood. It had been a disaster. Mostly, anyway. From the day of my birth until I was school age, the only person I could remember seeing was Astoreth. Unlike other newborn morevs and the hakoi, the neonatal androids didn't see to my baby needs. She'd mothered me Herself, changing my diapers, comforting me when I cried, and feeding me until I could feed myself. I'd traveled with Her through Kherah, to Her És in Her cities and towns. During rituals like Ktana, She'd hold me on Her lap instead of leaving me with an android. After discovering I was psi, She'd taught me how to control my power.

When I'd been of age, Astoreth told me I'd attend the Devi school. "You are not like other morev children. Being more Devi than hakoi, I think you will be happier with children who are closer to your heritage."

Tears had welled in my eyes. "Why? Why can't you teach me?"

She'd smiled. "Because the domines can teach you what I cannot. And you need other children to play with."

A week after starting school, I found out Astoreth wasn't my mother. Jangi had told me. "She isn't your mother," he'd shouted. "Your mother's hakoi. A dirty hakoi!" My classmates had crowded around me, jeering. That night, while tucking me into bed, I'd stared into Her eyes. "A boy at school told me You aren't my mother. Is it true?"

Astoreth had let out a little sigh. "Yes, child. I am your grandmother."

"Where's my mother?"

She'd stroked my hair while giving me a sad smile. "I will tell you when you are old enough to understand." She'd kissed my forehead. "Sleep, now. You must be up early for school."

As for school, Grandmother had been wrong. The Devi children didn't play with me. I wasn't as big as they were, and my size made me a target. During breaks, the children beat me, always in enough numbers I couldn't fight back. I never told Her. She'd taught me self-defense, and I hadn't wanted Her to think I didn't measure up. My bruises had been easy to hide under the long sleeves and trousers of my school attire. At night, I'd insisted on wearing long-sleeved gowns.

One after midday, I'd returned to the É with a black eye.

Astoreth had looked horrified. "What happened, child?"

I'd burst into tears. "They h-hurt me, Grandmother," I hiccupped. "Almost every day, they gang up on me."

Her look had turned incredulous. "Where are your domines when this happens? What do they do?"

"Nothing, Grandmother. They watch. Sometimes they laugh."

Her face had darkened. I had never seen Her angry before, and it frightened me.

Astoreth had taken me to school the next day and called all the domines into the school's conference room. Gripping my hand, She'd said,

"This child is of my line. You and the children serve me. No one will lay a hand on her again. If you allow it, you will answer to me, and you will not leave my É alive."

After that, the beatings had stopped, but not the cruel taunts. It didn't last long because I'd turned Astoreth into my weapon. When the children bashed me, I'd give a sweet smile and tell them, "Say that again, and Grandmother will know tonight." The fear in their eyes had delighted me.

I rolled onto my side and closed my eyes. My morevic apprenticeship had begun as a repeat of prep school, though not for long.

The first day I walked into music class, the room had filled with twittering. I looked around.

The apprentices had stared, faces twisted into sneers. They'd known who I was because Astoreth had never kept me secret. "Run along, little one," one boy had said. "You must be lost. You don't belong with us." More giggling.

Standing well over five šīzu tall at that age, the apprentices—like all morev—were remarkably similar in looks. And, like all morev, they considered themselves an elite club. With my looks, I obviously didn't fit in. But I knew something about me they didn't.

I'd given the boy who'd spoken a sweet smile. Then I'd zapped him. He'd screamed and crumpled to the floor, writhing and whimpering for a good five minutes while I watched. When he'd stilled, I looked up and stared at the other apprentices' pale faces one by one. After that, they'd needled me about my looks behind my back, but long as no one said anything to my face, I let it go.

Over time, I'd filled out and my Devic traits manifested. I got stronger, faster, nimbler, and had greater endurance than every morev in the É. My senses had honed to razor sharpness. Though I would never match the Gods, my psi power had continued to ripen, and I'd taken every opportunity to let the others know I wasn't shy about using it. No longer ignoring their biting comments, they soon learned I had no qualms about zapping anyone stupid enough to tempt me. The apprentices had complained to the elder morevs, and they'd taken it up with Astoreth. But She never disciplined me.

Rolling onto my back again, I wondered about the time. I got up and tapped the bar on my uniform's blouse slung over the chair. "Time."

"Second hour, forty-seven minutes Tryn."

Almost lunchtime. If I hurried, I could make it. The Laerd would probably give me dirty looks, but Hyme and I could have a nice chat.

I went back to bed instead.

Curled under the blanket, my thoughts drifted again, settling on my conversation with Ginzu. *Losing my soul. What does that even mean? I'm not a bad person. I don't wish evil on anyone, not even on dicknut. I don't hurt people. Well, not unless they deserve it. Does that make me evil? Am I supposed to let people hurt me and just take it, instead of fighting back?*

I fell asleep for a couple of hours. Mercifully, I had no dreams. On waking, I dressed, and checked the beacon. Once back in my apartment, I looked at the bed. *I've had enough sleep.* After straightening the furs, I plopped into a fireplace chair. *What to do now?* My new lab equipment wouldn't arrive for another two marun or so. There wasn't a reason to go to the lab unless I wanted to talk with Hyme, and I didn't want to do that. I didn't want to talk to anyone. I also didn't feel like composing a sermon, and the one I'd give tonight—the same one I'd given this morning—was locked in my memory.

I let out a small sigh. *I could always go over my lab notes.* They were old, but it wouldn't hurt to read them. Before the vandalism, I'd mapped out several serum formulas to attack the virus. Mapping out more would get me that much further.

I picked up my tablet. The formulas I'd developed earlier gave me several ideas for new ones. While doing my calculations, I couldn't help thinking how I wished I could work with live plants instead of extracts. Some morevs believed serums made from extracts were just as powerful and effective as those made from live or dried plants, but I didn't. What we did agree on was that serums made from extracts or plants were far superior to those made from synthetics.

I'd created seven new candidates when my stomach rumbled. I tapped the bar. "Time."

"Sixth hour, twenty-five minutes Tryn."

I sat back. *Should I skip dinner?* I wanted to keep working, but I hadn't eaten today. Judging by the noises my stomach was making, I needed food. *It's early, but if I start on another formula, I won't finish it before I have to leave.* So what to do?

My gaze roamed about the room, fixing on the battlement door. *I've been in here all day. Could use some air.* Walking over, I pulled back the bolt. I opened the door a crack and saw the Laerd standing in the corridor near his apartment. Elbows resting against the stone and hands clasped behind his head, he seemed to be staring through one of the slits in the wall. I frowned a little. Something about his stance…

I sent a tendril of power. When it reached him, the force of his sadness and despair hit me so hard I had to step back. My eyes widened. *Astoreth. I've never… He still grieves for her.* My hearts went out to him. I understood all too well what it was like to suffer under a terrible burden, alone. *I should…* I started to open the door wider but stopped. Would he accept comfort from someone he hated? I thought about how he'd comforted me after being treed by the ura yesterday. He hated me, but he'd done it. And right now, did it really matter if he was hakoi? My lips tightened a bit. *The least I can do is return the favor.*

But before I could open the door further, he bowed his head, then straightened and headed for his apartment. I watched him step inside and close the door behind him.

I closed my door and leaned against it, reflecting. He'd lost his woman. I was a woman. I looked nothing like his heartsbound, but that was beside the point. Eresh had said he'd never seen the Laerd with a woman, and Hyme had said he'd never gotten over his heartsbound's death. Was my being a woman the reason for the difference in the way he'd treated Eresh and the way he treated me? But why? Outside of handling the garrison's needs and at meals, we had little contact with each other.

Then I thought about the night he'd asked me to help with the Council reports. He hadn't acted like he hated me then. He'd smiled a lot. *You don't smile at people you hate…do you? Maybe it's a cultural thing. I'll ask Hyme about that.* I frowned. *But if it isn't cultural… No. I don't know what his problem is, but I won't let it become mine.*

My stomach rumbled again. I tapped the bar. "Time."

"Sixth hour, fifty minutes Tryn."

I'd better get going. Except for those two instances, I made it a point to be punctual for mealtimes, even if it meant arriving early. It wouldn't take me anywhere near ten minutes to get to the dining hall, but the last thing I wanted was to give the Laerd any reason to say something cutting.

I picked up my tablet and made a mental note where I'd stopped. Switching it off, I threw it on the chair and left my apartment.

Chapter Nine

Three marun to the day after the lab was vandalized, two things happened.

One, the vandal was caught. It was the same boy who'd thrown the rock at me. Since he wasn't in school and hadn't seemed inclined to find gainful employment, the Laerd sentenced him to a year of working in the thalin mines. "Let's see how you like breaking rocks instead of other people's property," Hyme had reported.

I frowned. "Isn't he a little young for the mines?"

He snorted. "He's a lot older than he looks. I know—I delivered him. And he's been in trouble before. This isn't the first time he's been hauled before the Council. Believe me, a year in the mining camp will straighten him out. The other miners won't stand for any nonsense."

Second, my new equipment arrived. There were five trunks, and three were twice the size of the other two. Puzzled, I watched five of the garrison—with the Laerd's permission—wheel the trunks to the lab. The soldiers were then escorted out of the village.

I opened the two smaller trunks first. There was my new three-dimensional microscope, all the glassware that had been broken, and everything else I'd ordered, plus a few extras. Hyme and I set up my equipment posthaste. Then we turned our attention to the first of the oversized trunks. I opened it. Inside was a nupaper box with no markings. Intrigued, I pried open the box's lid. My jaw dropped. A heap of insulated metal rods and four large rolls of black cloth. I squealed in delight.

Hyme peered into the box. "What is it?"

"It's a habitat. For my plants."

He rubbed his hands together. "Now we can really trade knowledge," he crowed. Then he sobered. "But where will we put it?"

"We can put it anywhere." I grinned. "Let's see what's in the other two trunks."

The second trunk contained square and rectangular lysite panes and more insulated metal rods, some with a strip of lysite down one side, others with holes. I picked up one with a lysite strip. "This is a lightrod. With the others, it simulates our diurnal cycle."

"What about heat?"

"The lightrods take care of that. They'll heat the habitat just like a desert day back home."

I put the lightrod down, then picked up one with tiny holes. "This is a driprod, part of the watering system. There'll be a motor around here somewhere. Hook it up to a water source, and it turns on and off by itself. No need to watch over it."

Hyme looked doubtful. "A drip system, eh? Do we use the sink? I don't think having water running all the time will go over well with the water board."

I shook my head. "We use a bucket. All I have to do is remember to keep the water fresh." Stuffing the packing back into the box, I closed it. "Now for the third trunk." I pulled up its lid and then pried open the box inside. Unlike the others, this one had been divided into compartments. I pointed to the larger compartment on the bottom left. "That's the motor for the drip system." Then I pointed to the one on the right. "Here's the fan. It pulls out excess moisture, so the air is dry, like in the desert. It also cools down the habitat to simulate night. Since there's little to hold the suns's heat, the desert sometimes gets pretty cold." I looked over the bags nestled in the box's large middle section. "And there we have the dirt and gravel and the trays."

I picked up a smallish bag from the topmost compartment. "These are the seeds." Hyme looked over my shoulder as I pulled the top open and took out a small packet. "This is alis. It's like your skagwort—the base for just about everything I make." I dropped it back into the bag. "Funny thing about alis sap. It's dark yellow, but if you put some on a piece of nupaper, it disappears after it dries. Hold it over a burner—being careful not to burn the nupaper—and it reappears as black."

"How did you figure this out?"

"I discovered it after accidentally spilling some on a piece of packing."

"Did you tell anyone else?"

"Why? I did it on a whim. It doesn't mean anything." I clapped once. "Let's put the habitat together. It's easy. We'll be finished before lunch."

"Well, that brings me back to my original question. Where do we put it?"

"The only place it'll fit is in the closet."

"Then that's where it'll go."

I took the box with the habitat's frame into the closet, then fetched the box with the lysite panes and the rods. True to my word, we finished setting up within three hours. Since we then had only fifteen minutes until lunch, we decided to quit. I picked up the bags of dirt and gravel from the third trunk. Bringing my load to the closet, I set them against the wall. Hyme lay the bag of seeds on top. "We can start planting these next," I said.

A happy grin spread across his face. "Can't wait." Then he frowned. "Did you order the habitat when you asked for replacements?"

"No."

"Then—"

"Eresh." I smiled. "He's the only person who would do something like this for me."

"I hope he doesn't get in trouble for it."

"Not him. He knows how to cover his tracks."

Hyme's frown didn't go away. "How did he know which seeds to send?"

"He's been in my lab any number of times, and I showed him the plants I work with most often." I paused. "Maybe he included some of the more exotic ones, too. That'd be nice. If not..." I shrugged. "I'm happy with what I have."

Back in the lab after lunch, I picked up the seed trays and a bag of soil, then handed both to Hyme. "Now comes the fun part. Fill those trays until they're three-quarters full. Then give them back to me."

He did so. "Now what?"

"Now we start planting." Working in silence, we poked small, shallow holes in the soil. I handed him a pack of alis seeds. "Drop a seed into each of the holes in that section. Then take this," I handed him an undersized spoon, "and fill the holes with more soil. Don't pack it, though."

We worked the entire after midday. I took a break to check the beacon but decided against dancing. Now it was almost dinnertime. Hyme wiped his brow with the back of his hand. "Whew. I never knew planting was such hard work."

I frowned. "You don't grow your own plants?"

"I'm a terrible farmer. I get everything from the woods or in trade with other healers."

We hurried through dinner, then hustled to the lab. I picked up a tray. "This is the last one."

Hyme's brow creased. "But I didn't see any more seeds."

"Well, there's got to be a packet around here somewhere." I rooted in the seed bag but found nothing. Then my fingers poked through a rip in its wadding. "Ah-hah."

"What?"

Instead of answering, I pulled out a piece of plaztik and turned it over. I let out a happy squeal.

"What's that?"

"It's cooli. A hybrid I developed. I was working with it before I came here." I planted the seeds in the last tray. "There. All done. Now all I need is a bucket of water."

"I can help with that." He left the closet, returning with a good-sized bucket filled with water moments later. "Will this do?"

"It'll do fine." I took the bucket and set up the drip system. When finished, I tapped the bar. "Time to services."

"Thirty-five minutes."

I clapped my hands to my head. "I'm late!" I ran for the door, with Hyme right behind me. "I'll be back later," I shouted over my shoulder. Sprinting across the plaza, I burst into my tower and rushed to my apartment. Throwing on my garb, I hurried to the É. The penitents would arrive in about ten minutes, so I worked furiously. By the time I heard their boots on the stairs, everything was ready.

It took all my willpower not to hurry through the service. This was especially important since Yose was in the evening group. I didn't know if he'd report it—it seemed trivial to me—but it might not seem so to Astoreth.

After the garrison had gone, I gave the É a quick cleaning and ran to my apartment. Fifteen minutes later, I was on my way to the lab.

Entering, I found Hyme writing in a well-used book of nupaper. "What are you doing?"

"I'm writing down what we talked about today."

"Why don't you use the computer?"

"Oh, I'll transcribe these notes later. Writing by hand forces me to think about whatever it is I'm writing. Right now, it's helping me to remember our conversations." He peered. "Do you know how to write?"

"Not like that."

"You should learn. It really is a useful exercise." He put his stylus down. "Now. Show me how your habitat works."

We stepped inside the closet. Eresh had somehow managed to find an adapter and electric cords since Mjor didn't have wireless. After making sure all the connections were tight, I plugged the array into the wall. "I'll program this for a short day so you can see how it works." I played my fingers over the control panel and switched on the power. "All right, let's see what we've got."

Crossing the habitat's threshold, we watched its western edge start to glow, the beginning of a new day. Ten minutes passed. The once-soft glow now blazed with the intensity of midday. In the next ten minutes, the blaze softened until only the habitat's eastern edge was aglow. Then darkness fell. I turned off the habitat.

Hyme sighed as we stepped outside. "That was marvelous. I wish I could have something like that."

I winked. "Astoreth giveth but sometimes She doesn't taketh away."

"What do you mean?"

"If I know Eresh and the way he operates, nobody back home knows I have this. When my tour is over, I can't take it with me. So it stays here."

Hyme's grin said it all.

After reprogramming the habitat for the start of the growing season, I picked up a small remote. Tapping it, I watched the black covers roll down. "Now comes the hard part."

"What's that?"

"Waiting for the plants to grow."

In the main room, Hyme walked to his desk chair, and I pulled mine up next to him. Neither of us spoke for a while.

I turned. "You know, this habitat might be just what I needed.

You've watched me work, I've explained the properties of the extracts I brought with me, and you've given me suggestions on revising serum formulas I'd already worked out and helped me calculate new ones. And I've told you I think working with whole plants is more valuable than working with extracts. Maybe I've already discovered the red fever cure, but the extracts—"

"What's this about red fever?" the Laerd's gravelly voice sounded behind us. As one, we jumped in our seats and spun our chairs around. He looked at Hyme, then me. "What's this about?"

"I, uh…" Hyme stammered.

I glanced at him, then looked at the Laerd. "We were talking about the virus and possible cures. Like which plants from here or back home have properties that might cure it or at least have an effect." I shrugged. "Just a brain exercise."

The Laerd said nothing for a few moments. Then his eyes narrowed. "I think this was a bit more than a brain exercise. I heard you say maybe you'd already discovered the cure."

My eyes widened a fraction. *Astoreth! How do I get out of this?* "Well…yes. I was saying—"

"No, Moreva. I heard what you said. I—"

"Laerd. I was working on finding a cure before I came here. I've told Hyme about it, and we were just having a discussion. That's all."

He didn't say anything. His star-colored stare pierced me. I opened my mouth to explain further, but he beat me to it.

"The truth, Moreva."

My jaws snapped shut. *No way out of it, now.* I took a breath. "I brought a lab so I could continue my work."

His face darkened. Jerking his head around, he glared at Hyme. "And you *knew?*"

Hyme nodded. "Yes, Laerd," he said, his voice quiet.

"How could you?" the Laerd shouted. "The last time we had the fever, almost a quarter of us *died!*"

Hyme jumped to his feet. "I'm well aware of that," he snapped. "But what Tehi's doing is necessary. It's vital. If she can find the cure, we can *all* rest easier."

"No. That's not good enough. You two are endangering this entire village. I won't allow it." He turned to me. "Get rid of it. Now."

I shot from my chair. "I will *not,*" I shouted. "I've taken every precaution I know so the virus doesn't get loose. I'm going to find the cure, and you are not going to stop me!"

The Laerd's furious look melted into incredulousness. "Are you defying—"

"Yes. I. Am."

His look turned furious again. "If I tell the Council about this, they'll—"

"Either hang me from the battlement or drop me in the mine. I know. Hyme told me."

The Laerd glanced at Hyme. "I was going to say they'd demand your recall to Uruk."

"If that happens, all my research comes to a halt. I'll either have my project taken away, or I'll be kicked out of the É. Or worse."

He frowned. "Why?"

I took a breath. "Because I disobeyed Astoreth's direct order not to bring my research with me."

"Then why—"

"I couldn't afford to lose a year's worth of work. And if my project is stopped, it would all have been for nothing."

"Why would She order you not to bring your research with you?"

"Everything I do is confined to my lab at the É. It's—"

"Why?"

I squared my shoulders. "Because the morev are immune to red fever."

His eyes seemed to burn. "What?" he shouted. "You would...no. You will get rid of it *now!*"

"No," I shouted back. "I told you, I've taken every precaution. The virus is not leaving this lab!"

We glared at each other. After a few long minutes, his fierce look faded into resignation. Then he sighed. "All right. I'll keep your secret."

Relief washed through me, followed by puzzlement. "Why?"

"Because if this gets out, the Council will either hang me from the battlement or drop me in the mine."

"Why? It's not your fault."

"The Council won't see it that way. All they'll see is that because of your work, Mjor could be done for. As Laerd, my job is to protect the village, and it's my job to know anything and everything about anything and everything that could do that. To them, my ignorance would be no excuse. They'd say I should have had you vetted before you came here. And I didn't." He fell silent for a few moments, then sighed again. "So, we're agreed. Your research stays between the three of us."

"Yes," Hyme and I said at the same time.

"On one condition."

I frowned. "What?"

"That you report to me your findings each marun."

"Deal."

He sighed a third time. "I'd better go. I've still got a lot of work to do before going to bed."

Hyme cocked his head. "Why did you come by, Laerd?"

He gave us a small smile. "I don't remember. When I do, I'll let you know." Giving us a long look, he left the lab.

I fell into my chair. "Whew. That was close."

Hyme's brow quirked. "I don't think so."

"Why?"

"You heard him. If he says anything to anybody, he's not only putting us in danger, but himself, too."

"Then why did he—"

"He was angry. And rightfully so." He stood. "Would you like a cup of olarian tea? After all that excitement, I could use one."

"Me, too."

Hyme unlocked the door to his apartment and started up the stairs. While he busied himself making tea, I settled in one of the chairs by the unlit fireplace. I looked around. Books lined the walls. More books were piled on the tables and floor. On the low table, I reached for one I hadn't seen before and flipped through its pages. It was yet another book on medicinal botany. One particular entry caught my eye, and I studied the exquisitely rendered drawings. I had no doubt I'd have any trouble recognizing the plant if I saw one.

I closed it and smiled, thinking about how I'd told Eresh I could teach Hyme a thing or two. It had been the other way around. I'd learned so much about northern botany and herbology since meeting him. The knowledge I traded for his seemed meager by comparison. He had the kind of wisdom and humility that came only with age and experience.

I was morev and he was hakoi, but I considered him my equal—if not more so—in every way. I was happy and proud to call him my friend. My smile broadened. *Never in my life would I have thought I'd be friends—real friends—with a hakoi.*

I set the book on the table just as Hyme came bustling out of the kitchen. "Here you are," he said, handing me a steaming mug. He set his mug on the table and sat in the matching chair. Picking it up, he sipped and made a face. "Too hot. Let it cool a little."

Neither of us said anything for a while. Then he leaned forward. "What were you going to tell me when the Laerd came in?"

"Well, now that I have my plants, I have more to work with. I can do different combinations. Some of the more exotic ones I haven't used before."

He nodded. "I can see where that might work."

"Too bad I have to wait for my plants to grow."

"How long will you have to wait?"

"About three marun. There's special fertilizer and other chemicals mixed with the soil that speeds growth. Otherwise, it would take twice as long."

Hyme picked up his mug and sipped. "Nice and cool, now." He set the mug in his lap and peered at me. "What will you do in the meantime?"

I took a draught. "I have four more calculations for serums I want to try. I'm not expecting much, but it might give me a few clues. And I still have plenty of skratz, so if they don't work, killing a few more won't make a difference." I paused. "I also have a couple of small projects I brought with me. I can work on those, too."

We traded knowledge for about an hour. After finishing my tea, I set the mug on the table. "I should be going. I'll see you tomorrow."

Hyme walked me to the street door. "Do you want me to come with you? It's pretty late."

"That's all right. I'll be fine."

"All right, then. Good night, Tehi."

"Good night."

I stepped outside. It was a clear night if a little chilly. Peris's three moons shone with a lovely bluish-lavender light. *So beautiful.* Enjoying the moonslight, I turned the corner and walked onto the plaza. The streetlights' harsh glare overpowered the moons' glow, and my peaceful mood dropped a bit. The moonslight was so much prettier.

Heels thumping on the pavement, I hadn't gone far when I heard someone behind me. There was no one else about. *Guess someone's out for a late-night stroll.*

The footsteps came closer. "What are you doing out here this late?" a familiar voice rumbled.

I turned. Planting my feet and with hands on hips, I gave the Laerd a defiant stare. "Do I need a permit to walk at night?"

"That's not what I meant, and you know it."

"If you must know, I'm going back to my apartment. What are you doing out so late?"

"Getting some air."

"Why didn't you just open a window?"

"I like to walk. Clears my head." He paused. "Come on. I'll walk with you."

"Why?"

"Because I want to."

We continued across the plaza. "Do you think anyone would bother me?" I said after we'd taken a few steps.

"I don't know. They might."

"What about the Protocol?"

"A lot of my people don't care about the Protocol."

"Hyme says if anything happens to me, Astoreth would be within her rights to retaliate, and no one wants to see what that might look like."

"Hyme doesn't know everything."

"And you do?"

He didn't answer.

I thought about the young man who'd thrown the rock at me my first day. He was obviously one who didn't care about the Protocol. "All right. I'll be more careful."

"Good."

We walked the rest of the way in silence. At the door to my tower, I looked into his face. Out of the glare of the streetlights, his star-colored eyes seemed to glow. The effect was striking, and I couldn't resist the urge to stare. "Thank you for walking with me, Laerd. I appreciate it." He nodded once. "You're welcome. Good night, Moreva." He headed for his tower.

"Good night," I whispered. Climbing the stairs, I let out a mighty yawn. The olarian tea was doing its work. In my apartment, I shucked my uniform and threw it over the chair. *Should I take a shower?* I shook my head. It was long after five Durm and the water would be ice cold. After wiping off my makeup, I stepped into the bath. Rinsing my face, I was glad I'd hadn't showered.

Back in the big room, I shivered. I hadn't turned on the heat earlier. Even so, I walked to the window and opened the stone shutters. Light from Peris's triple moons flooded inside, throwing shadows against the walls. Yawning a second time, I got into bed and burrowed beneath the furs, anticipating the warmth. I closed my eyes, expecting to fall asleep at any moment.

But I didn't. I kept thinking about the Laerd and his glowing eyes. I'd seen anger in them, but at least he hadn't looked at me like something the terk had dragged through the door. I wondered if it meant our relationship had reached the point where we could be civil instead of snapping at each other. I hoped it was true. I was tired of fighting.

By now the bed was toasty warm and carrying me toward slumber. I rolled onto my side and in the next minute, was sound asleep.

All my dreams were about the Laerd.

Chapter Ten

Three days after the Laerd learned about my red fever project, it was time to make another supply run. Hyme was busy with children's day at the apothecary, so I'd have to go alone. Well, not alone. I'd have one of the armed village men with me.

I went looking and found the Laerd outside the sessions hall surrounded by a knot of Mjorans. They fired questions at him right and left, and I admired the way he answered their questions with clear, calm conviction. Some in the crowd began nodding, obviously reassured by what he'd told them.

I stood at a respectful distance with my collection bag slung over my shoulder. After the villagers had left, he closed his eyes and let out a little sigh. His facial muscles drooped. Over the past several marun, I'd learned that being Laerd was hard work. Many a night I'd gone to bed, noticing the lights in his apartment burning, only to see the lights burning again when I rose to get ready for the morning service.

He opened his eyes and spotted me. I knew he was still angry but wouldn't show it—at least not in public. His face settled into an expressionless mask, and his stare just as bland. "May I help you, Moreva?"

I stepped forward. "Yes, Laerd. Hyme asked me to gather supplies for him, and I need protection. Would you assign someone to go with me, please?"

He looked around, then back at me. "I'll go. You need someone who speaks Devian." He stepped off the stair and started across the plaza. I followed and had to practically run to keep up with him. We reached his tower. "Wait here," he said over his shoulder.

While waiting, I wondered what our outing would be like. Would we be as carefully dispassionate as we were now? Or would he let his anger show once we were outside the village? I was tempted to ask him to assign someone else. Even if they didn't speak Devian, we could always communicate by sign. But if he wanted to go, then he wanted to go, and there was nothing I could do about it.

The Laerd reappeared, cradling his rifle. "I'm ready." He strode away.

Running to keep up, my keen hearing picked up the villagers' snickering. It was embarrassing, but I was not about to give them the satisfaction of seeing me beg him to slow down. I'd had endurance training. At our current pace, I could run ten da-na without getting tired.

He stopped outside the gates and looked down. "Where to?"

"This way." I led him along the road and then stepped off onto a dirt path, the same one I'd taken the day the ura treed me. "I need praeslip, makilroy, mellolly, and skagwort." We started along the trail. By now it was truly spring, and the growing season had begun. The trees had budded with vari-colored leaves and the undergrowth, though mostly brown, showed patches of blue and green. Some of the faster-growing plants had already bloomed.

We'd walked about three nindan when I spotted a patch of makilroy growing about six šīzu from the path. Unslinging my bag, I dug around for my small shovel, then waded through the undergrowth to the small clump of orange. I squatted and dug up the plants, roots and all. I only took the mature ones. On the path again, about thirty šīzu further, I saw another patch of makilroy. I left the trail, dug up samples, and then spotted a clump of mellolly bushes deeper in the woods. Trading the shovel for a set of clippers, I made my way over to them. I clipped its leaves and branches, once again leaving behind the immature growths. Then I spied praeslip growing not far away. I cut six handfuls of flowers. Wading through the undergrowth a second time, I rejoined the Laerd on the path.

He hadn't said a word since we'd left the village. His steps made no noise as he followed me. Mine did. I tromped along, my feet crackling last year's leaves and crashing through the undergrowth. I sensed his disapproval but didn't care.We'd walked several nindan further when I spotted skagwort vines wrapped around the branches of several trees. There were plenty of flowers with their seed pods, but they weren't mature enough for harvesting. And it was skagwort Hyme needed most of all. I clucked in disappointment.

"What's wrong?"

I explained the problem. "Hyme should have enough to see him through the next marun, but these won't have ripened by then."

He gave me a speculative look. "I know where there are some."

My eyes widened. "Where?"

"Further up the mountain. Come on."

We started walking. A hundred šīzu further, I glanced to my right and saw the ripped up bark where the ura had treed me. I shuddered at the memory.

Without warning, he stopped, and I nearly ran into him. He peered through the foliage as if looking for something. Then he gave a grunt and plunged into the forest.

I hesitated. This wasn't my idea of a walk through the woods. Who knew what kinds of dangerous animals lurked among the trees? *That's why he's got a gun,* a little voice echoed in my head.

"Are you coming? We've not got all day."

I looked up. He was scowling. My lips tightened, and I followed him into the trees.

The going was as bad as I'd feared. There was a path, but it obviously hadn't been used for some time. Branches from the taller bushes and other plants had grown across it, in some places almost like a screen. The lower branches and vines constantly snagged my legs and ankles, threatening to topple me face down into the dirt. It didn't help that the branches the Laerd pushed out of his way snapped backward, sometimes hitting me in the face if I wasn't careful. The only good thing was that the foliage slowed him down, and I could keep up without effort.

We walked for about an hour and came to a creek. I eyed its rushing waters. It didn't look deep, but I didn't fancy getting my feet wet. I looked to my right. The Laerd stood about ten šīzu away, one foot on a large rock. Then I noticed three more stones strategically placed across the creek. He crossed and stood on the far bank, waiting for me.

Seems easy enough. I walked to the rocks, placed one foot on the first and slipped. Righting myself, I realized the soles of his boots must have grips instead of being smooth like mine, and the reason he'd been able to cross with such confidence. I pursed my lips, trying to decide what to do next.

A chuckle made me look up. He bent and scooped a handful of water, then drank. "Delicious. But cold. Very cold."

My jaw set. That was a straight on dare if I'd ever heard one. So what if I fell in? I might be uncomfortable for a while, but my uniform would dry and be none the worse for wear.

I put my foot on the first stone, testing my balance. Then I pushed off, planting my other foot squarely in the center of the second stone.

I stared at the third. This might be a problem. The gap between the second and third stones was much wider than the gap between the first two. The Laerd, with his long legs, had spanned the distance easily, but my legs were much shorter. I grimaced. There was no way around it. I'd have to jump. Crouching, I tensed and sprang.

My timing and release were perfect. My feet touched stone, and I stood on the third rock. I smirked at him, then stepped off the third rock onto the fourth. Sure of myself now, I stepped up onto the embankment...and immediately slipped. Falling backward, I windmilled to right myself, but it did no good. I was going down.

Oh, no—my plants! Something tugged at my left arm, throwing me further off balance. I fell hard onto the creek bed. The impact stunned me, but the ice-cold water brought me to my senses. I leapt to my feet. The water came to my knees, yet I was wet to the chest.

"I saved your pack," the Laerd's deep, gravelly voice sounded from above. I looked up. He held my dry collecting bag aloft. "I didn't think you'd want your plants to get wet."

I realized it was his tugging on my arm that had helped tip me into the water. Anger surged through me. *You...you dicknut!* I opened my mouth to let loose with all sorts of invective but didn't. After all, he *did* save my plants. "Thank you," I said instead, my teeth chattering.

He held out his arm. "Give me your hand." I eyed his palm. Did I want to touch him? *If I want to get out of this creek, yes.*

Reaching up, I clasped him, and with a gentle tug, he pulled me from the water. My spine tingled, and I held on to his hand for a few seconds longer than necessary. He was so warm, and I was so cold. I stared into his star-colored eyes. He gazed down, inscrutable.

We pressed on. Under the budding canopy, the day was shaping up to be on the cool side. My still-wet uniform chilled me, and I couldn't stop shivering. We came to a rocky outcropping, and the Laerd started climbing. I sized up the pile, then started after him. To my relief, it was easier than crossing the creek. With plenty of hand and footholds, I had no problem finding my way.

After that, the going was pretty easy. We'd left the denser forest behind, and the foliage had thinned out. I was wondering how much further we had to walk when the forest abruptly ended. Before us lay a meadow carpeted with small yellow flowers.

"We're here. What you want is over there." The Laerd pointed to a stand of medium-sized trees that were practically choked with skagwort vines. Being in the suns had matured them much faster than the ones below.

Delighted, my lips stretched into a big smile. "Exactly what I want." I turned to thank him, but he'd already walked away. He settled in the purple grass, hands behind his head and the rifle at his side.

The skagwort flowers here were much larger than the ones below. There were more colors, too. I'd seen the yellow, pink, and white ones. Here there were deep red, dark blue, greens, and a color that was almost silver. I snipped with enthusiasm. I'd thought I'd clipped enough—my bag was full—when I spotted three particularly fine specimens near the top of the tree. No way could I reach it. I parted the branches and peered within. That wouldn't work, either. They were too thin to hold my weight.

Maybe the Laerd can reach them. I turned. Lying in the flowers, he looked like he hadn't moved since we'd arrived. Annoyed, I walked over to him. "I thought you were supposed to be protecting me," I said, keeping my voice neutral.

He opened one eye. "I am."

"You don't look like it. What if some predator had tried to snatch me while I was clipping?"

"Unlikely."

"Why?"

"No prey up here. There's nothing for them to eat." He closed his eye.

I said nothing. Looming over him, I cast a shadow over his face.

He opened his eye again. "Finished?"

My annoyance vanished, replaced by uncertainty. "Actually, er, no. I have only a few more flowers to get but, um, I need your help. Please."

He opened his other eye. "Why?"

"The flowers are too high for me to reach. Would you...?"

"All right." In one fluid motion, he seemed to flow to his feet. "Where are they?"

"Over here." I led him to the tree and pointed up.

"Um. I'm not sure I can reach them, either." He stretched his arm and fell short about half a šīzu. He stood on his toes, but his fingers merely brushed the branch.

I winced, discouraged. Big as they were, just three of those bulbs would have kept Hyme in plenty of base for his medicines. "Well, I guess that's that."

"I have an idea." He squatted. "Sit on my shoulders."

This time I didn't hesitate. I climbed on, and he shot to his feet. Now the skagwort was within easy reach. I clipped five of the ripest ones, then tapped him. "Done."

"What about those over there?"

"Not ripe enough."

"Mm. Ready?"

"Ready." I expected him to squat again. Instead, he lifted me off his shoulders and set me on the ground. I turned to find him standing close enough for me to catch his scent. I looked up. My eyes widened, and my hearts started pounding. Stone-faced, his star-colored gaze held me in an unyielding grip. A dream-like haze clouded my mind. I tried to step back, but my feet seemed to have grown roots.

"You must be tired. Have a lie-down in the suns."

The spell broke at the sound of his voice. I nodded, unable to speak. I wasn't the least bit tired but my heavy uniform was still damp, so it sounded like a good idea.

We ambled over to where he'd been lying. He settled in the grass next to his rifle, and I settled beside him. Closing my eyes, I waited for my heartsbeat to return to normal. The warm rays from the twin suns caressed my face. I barely noticed.

My thoughts churned. *What happened back there? Why was he staring at me? It was like I was caught in a web or something. I've never—*

"How does someone get to be a morev?" he rumbled.

I snapped out of my reverie. "Huh?"

"How do you get to be a morev?"

I smiled a little. "You don't. You don't become morev, you're *born* morev, to serve the God and the É you were born into."

Except for the birds, the meadow was silent. Watching the clouds float past, I thought again about what had happened under the tree.

"So what's your story?" he said before I'd gotten too deep into my musing.

I frowned. "What do you mean?"

"What's your story? Besides that you like to break rules and disobey orders."

My brow quirked. "There's not much to tell. I grew up in the É, the elder morevs educated us, taught us the ways—"

"No. Tell me about you."

While I tried to think of something to say, my mouth blurted, "I'm lonely." My mind reeled in embarrassment. *What in Astoreth's name made me say* that? I tried to cover it over. "I mean, I'm the only morev here, and though being with Hyme has helped—"

"I don't think that's what you meant."

I said nothing for a long time, fighting a strange compulsion to confess all. I lost. "I'm not supposed to be here," I said in a low voice.

"Why?"

I swallowed. "My mother was a moreva and my father is Devi, one of the Gods in the Great Pantheon. I'm mostly Devi. I inherited many of his traits—superior hearing, sight, strength..." I bit my lip. *Should I tell him? I don't know why, but...*

I took a deep breath. "I'm psi, too."

"You're psi?" he echoed, sounding shocked. "I thought—"

"It was a myth?" I rolled my head toward him. His eyes looked as if they'd pop out at any moment.

"Well, yes."

"Hyme said that, too."

"What else does Hyme know about you that I don't?"

I smiled. "You know more than he does, now." My smile died. "Are you—"

"Am I what?"

"Most people who aren't psi are scared of us." I thought about all the morevs I'd zapped back home. "And not without reason."

He fell silent for a few moments. "No, I'm not." He paused. "Are there any other psi morevs?"

"I'm the only one."

He nodded. "I can see why you'd be lonely. But why are you the only one?"

"There's a strict rule against the morev and the Supreme Devi mating. Otherwise, they end up with morevs like me. My power is nowhere near as great as theirs, but the next morev's might be. And if enough of us are..."

"The lot of you could mount a rebellion, or something."

"Right. By myself, I'm no threat."

He said nothing for a few moments. "So, your mother broke the rule."

"She broke two rules."

"What's the other one?"

"She fell in love."

"Why is there a rule against falling in love?"

"Astoreth demands complete devotion from Her morevs. Hearts divided cannot serve because it forces us to make a choice."

"So your mother chose her Devi lover over Astoreth."

"Right again."

"What happened to her?"

"I was told she was stripped of her morevic status and left to die in the desert."

He frowned. "Kind of harsh, isn't it?"

"To the Devi, they're life-or-death rules."

"What about your father?"

I shrugged. "She never told anyone who he was."

"Well, if the Supreme Gods are all psi, wouldn't one of Them have been able to figure out who your father is?"

"Their powers don't work on each other. They can block one another out."

The meadow was quiet for a while. "Tell me about Astoreth."

"She's my grandmother."

"And She killed her own daughter?" he said, his tone incredulous.

My lips tightened. "Before you start thinking terrible things about Her, Astoreth can be cruel, but She's not evil. The others in the Great Pantheon—including my father, I guess—forced Her to do it. Make an example of my mother."

"How do you know that?"

"I overheard two Gods visiting Astoreth's É talking about how hard She'd fought for my mother's life and how I should have been aborted as soon as they found out she was pregnant. But Astoreth fought for me, too. In the end, that was the choice She had to make. My life or my mother's. At my mother's insistence, so I'm told, She chose mine." I paused. "The only thing I have left of my mother is her harp. Astoreth gave it to me when my apprenticeship ended. My music teacher told me she'd been the best harpist and singer in the É."

The Laerd said nothing. I turned my face to the sky, trying not to think about his mesmerizing stare under the tree.

"What's it like, being a moreva?"

I rolled my head a second time. "What do—"

"What do you do all day?"

"Hyme and I—"

"No. Back home."

"Well, being a healer, I spend a lot of my time in the lab or attending to sick hakoi. I teach classes to the apprentices. I write sermons and—"

"What about sex?"

"What about it?"

"I've heard Astoreth and Her morevs are all about sex."

I gave him a half-smile. "We have sex but not for the sake of sex. It's a sacrament. Morevs take a sacred vow that we will lie only with each other, except by Astoreth's special dispensation for the hakoi. Which rarely happens." I thought about the Ohra-Sin I'd conducted almost an arhu ago. "At least back home."

"How many morevs serve Astoreth's É in Uruk?"

"One hundred and twenty. Not including the apprentices."

Neither of us spoke.

A few minutes later, he sat up. "Come on. We'd better get back else we'll miss lunch." He got to his feet and picked up the gun.

Walking, I noticed we headed in the opposite direction from the way we came. Reaching the forest, we started along a clearly defined path. The going much easier. "Why didn't we come up this way?"

"I didn't know how long you'd be, so I took the shortcut."

We made the trip back in silence. This time I didn't crunch over the dead leaves but stepped as quietly as he did. We reached the open village gates and walked through. After a split-second hesitation, I lay a hand on his arm. "Thank you for coming with me today, Laerd."

His star-colored eyes had turned cold. "You're welcome," he said in a voice as cold as the look in his eyes. Brushing my hand off his arm, he strode toward his tower.

Stung, I headed for the apothecary, wondering about his sudden change in attitude. He'd been so friendly. His coldness made me uneasy, and I regretted having told him I was psi. *Should have kept that to myself. Should have kept* everything *to myself.* At the shop's door, I shook my head and entered.

Hyme looked up. "Any luck?"

I pushed my thoughts about the Laerd aside. Grinning, I reached into the bag and pulled out a huge, deep red skagwort flower. "What does this tell you?"

His eyed widened. "The gods' mercy! You two must have gone up to the ridge."

"We did."

"Nice of the Laerd to take you all that way. I used to go up there all the time before I got too old." He cocked his head. "Did he talk to you?"

"Some." I wasn't going to admit I'd done most of the talking, and about things I'd never told anyone.

"That's good to hear. Maybe he's not angry with you anymore."

I thought about the Laerd's sudden change in behavior. "Maybe." I stowed the bag in the lab and would sort the plants when I came back. Returning to the apothecary, Hyme stood by the door, waiting for me. "Let's go," I said. "I'm starved."

After lunch, Hyme went into the apothecary while I slipped into the lab to begin sorting. Some—like the skagwort—I hung on the drying rope he'd strung across far wall. Others I laid out on a round, perforated drying table. By the time I had to leave for my stewardship duty, I'd finished except for the plants that needed heat to dry properly. Hyme would take care of that. By special dispensation, he had an oven in his apartment.

I stuck my head through the apothecary door. "Hyme, the plants are all sorted, and I need to go. I'll see you later."

"Are you coming back?"

"No, I've got sermons to write. I'm behind on that."

He smiled. "I'd like to hear one of your sermons, sometime."

"You have to become one of Astoreth's penitents, first."

We laughed, knowing that would never happen.

Jogging across the plaza, I thought about the Laerd but pushed it away. I didn't want to think about him. I forced my thoughts elsewhere, like on the plants I'd gathered, the ones in the habitat, and my upcoming red fever experiments. In the control room, the colorful cylinder was rotating as it should. The old coverter hadn't had any problems. I called Central and made my report.

Returning to my room, I shucked my uniform and draped it over the chair. It was still a little damp. Shoving my feet into slippers, I headed for the É. I chose my music, setting the recording for loop. The sound of flutes and a barely discernible drumbeat filled the air.

I closed my eyes, letting the notes and the beat fill my mind. Then I started my dance. My hair flew as I twirled and leapt around the pool. My feet slid across the highly polished stone floor as if it were made of ice. After I'd had enough, I switched off the music. Instead of leaving, I pulled a pillow from the closet and sat by the pool.

I tried to think of a topic for my sermon, but my mind crowded with thoughts about the Laerd. That strange ground shift when I held him after the ura had treed me, the way I was mesmerized by his stare today. His behavior was strange, too—on again, off again. Like this morning, when we were alone, it was almost as if we were friends. But when we got back, it was as if a switch had been thrown, and he was as cold as the first day we'd met. It was confusing. And to my surprise, it hurt.

My lips tightened. *Why should I care? If he wants to behave that way, let him. It's nothing to me.*

I tried to concentrate on my sermon again, but it wasn't working. I couldn't stop thinking about him. Disgusted, I got up and began cleaning the É. While the robo-mop did its work, I chose the musical selection for that night's service, then purified the air. I was putting the bonbon stick away when I heard someone coming up the stairs.

I stepped out of the closet. Yose stood at the entrance and saluted. "Moreva. I'm sorry to bother you, but it is past time I gave you my marunly report."

I blinked. I'd forgotten about it. "My apologies, Kepten. I'll be down in a few minutes." His expression didn't change, but there was a disapproving look in his eyes. He saluted again and left.

I finished with the É and raced to my apartment. Throwing on my now-dry uniform, I leapt through the doorway and almost slipped running down the stairs. Yose had left the door open. Barreling over the threshold, the troops jumped to attention. "As you were," I all but yelled.

I slowed as I approached Yose's office. It wouldn't befit his superior officer to run inside or to be out of breath. I walked in, sat in my usual chair, and folded my hands on my lap. "I'm ready for your report Kepten, whenever you are."

He turned the monitor so I could see it. "Our field maneuvers were successful. The green team captured all the blue team, with no casualties to the green team. No disciplinary actions were taken this marun."

"Very good." I looked over his food requisition, the same as last marun and the marun before that. "Don't you get tired of eating pirsu meat all the time? The Mjorans raise other kinds of livestock for meat, you know."

He stiffened. "Of all the meats the Mjorans raise, pirsu is the leanest and most nutritious. Our cook prepares it in many different ways, so the troops don't get bored. And whatever the shortcomings of eating pirsu all the time, it's better than field rations."

I nodded once. "All right, Kepten. I'll give this to the Laerd." He pushed the keyboard over, and I initialed the form.

"Thank you, Moreva." He downloaded the request onto a disc and handed it to me. Then he escorted me to the door, saluting just before I walked through. On my way upstairs, I thought about the Laerd. *I should call him first, but I won't. I want to catch him off-guard. See how he treats me after I show up.*

Marching across the battlement, I reconsidered my decision not to call. He might not be in. I shook my head. If he wasn't, I'd come back later. Besides, I was curious to see how he'd behave. Standing at his door, I pressed the bell.

"What is it, Moreva?" he snapped.

So it's going to be like this, huh? "I have the requisition from Kepten Yose."

I heard a sigh. The door opened. "Come in," he said, stepping to the side.

Walking into his apartment, I saw why he'd been so curt. His desk was piled with stacks of folders. One lay open. Whatever he was doing, it looked like tedious work. My eyes narrowed. *That's no excuse.*

He returned to his desk, lay down his stylus, and gave me an expectant look.

I handed him the disc without a word. He slipped it into the computer's slot, brought up the requisition form, and nodded. "All right. I'll take care of this."

I started for the door.

"Um, Moreva?"

I looked over my shoulder.

His expression was cautiously hopeful. "May I have a massage, please?"

I stared for a second. "No." Without waiting for his reply, I walked out.

Striding to my apartment, my healer's duty kicked in. For a few long moments, I was tempted to go back. He'd asked for a massage, and after looking at that pile on his desk, I knew he needed one. But anger overrode duty. *If he wants anything from me, he will learn to treat me with respect.*

Letting myself into my room, I half-expected the intercom to be ringing. It wasn't. I checked for a message. There was none.

Good. Now I can work on my sermon.

I sat in a fireplace chair, reached for my tablet, and set it on my lap. Switching it on, I stared at the glowing blank screen. Several ideas later, I had a topic. I would talk about the different kinds of love relationships, both sexual and nonsexual, and how all reflect Astoreth's divinity. I started dictating. After finishing my sermon, I touched the bar on my uniform. "Time."

"Sixth hour, fifty-four minutes Tryn."

I blinked. *I was working that long?* It didn't seem like it. I only had a few minutes to get to the dining hall. I dropped the tablet on the seat and hurried out of my apartment.

I made it with about a minute to spare. As I pulled out my chair, Hyme turned and smiled. "Did you finish your sermon?"

"Just the first draft."

"What's it about?"

I told him.

"Sounds interesting." He cocked his head. "Have you ever been in love, Tehi?"

"I love Astoreth."

"Yes, but that's not quite what I mean."

I frowned.

His look grew far away. "Being in love is like soaring through the heavens. You see, for the first time, the beauty of the world around you. With her by your side, you feel invincible. You strive to be a source of comfort and a safe haven when she hurts. Nothing matters but her and all you want is for her to be happy." He smiled. "Or something like that. There really are no words for it."

"You sound like you speak from experience."

"I do. We were heartsbonded for almost ninety years."

"Well, going by your description, no, I've never been in love. I have Astoreth. She gives me all the love I could ever need or want."

In my peripheral vision, I saw the Laerd put down his fork and stare into space, looking wistful. Then he started eating again.

I knew he'd been listening to us. *Thinking about his heartsbound, I guess.* He was a dicknut, but after what I'd witnessed on the battlement, I felt sorry for him.

"Coming to the lab tonight?" Hyme said as we walked out of the dining hall.

"Yes. I want to see how those cultures are coming along."

"Splendid. I'll see you after your evening service."

I started for my tower, and the hairs on the back of my neck stood up. I looked over my shoulder. The Laerd was watching me. I caught a glimpse of that same wistful look just before his expression settled into his usual inscrutable mask. He turned and walked in the opposite direction.

Climbing the stairs, I couldn't stop thinking about it. *Why would he look at me that way?* After the way he'd behaved this morning when we'd returned to Mjor, his looking at me like that was puzzling. *He goes hot, then cold. I don't get it.*

Inside my apartment, I undressed, pulled tonight's garb out of the closet, and laid it on the bed. The service wouldn't begin for at least another hour, so I went over the sermon I'd dictated. Then it was time to get ready. I dressed and walked out the door. After setting up the É, I knelt at the altar and waited for the evening penitents.

The service seemed to go slowly. Even my sermon seemed to take up a lot more time than it had when I'd practiced it in my room. Then it was over, and the garrison left. I ran to my apartment. Barely fifteen minutes after the service had ended, I was running down the steps, headed for the lab.

Leaping from the last stair, I pulled open the door and ran out into the night.

Chapter Eleven

The following evening, I turned away from the fountain in the plaza's center and began the trek to my tower. I'd been standing there for at least five mintues, trying to admire its asymmetrical beauty, its waters shooting high into the air and cascading in sinuous, ever-changing patterns. I'd hoped that watching it would help relieve my frustration and sour mood. It didn't.

Astoreth, I beg of You, shower Your love on my plants. Make them grow faster.

It had been just under a marun since Hyme and I had planted them. Their skinny stems had poked from the soil, and on a few, the seed leaves had begun to open. That was good, except it'd be another two marun before they'd be ready for harvesting. I was still experimenting with the extracts, though I knew there really wasn't a point. I needed my plants, and without them, my red fever project had come to a standstill. I'd kept going because working with the extracts and one of the other small projects I brought had kept me busy.

"Tehi," Hyme called.

I turned.

He caught up, wearing a big smile. "Come to the lab after your service. There's something you need to see."

"What?"

"Just come."

I gave a little shrug. "All right."

In my peripheral vision, I caught the Laerd staring at us with that unreadable look. I'd noticed him walking close by just before Hyme had called but hadn't realized he'd stopped.

"Good," Hyme said. "I'll see you then." He headed toward the apothecary, and I started for my tower again.

"Moreva. Wait."

I closed my eyes. *What does dicknut want now?* Opening them, I turned. The Laerd strode up to me. "I heard you were going to Hyme's after your service. Mind if I come along?"

"Why?"

"I've already told you. I don't want you walking out here alone. I don't want anything to happen to you. Not while I'm Laerd."

My eyes narrowed. "Oh. So, if you weren't Laerd, you wouldn't care what happens to me?"

"I didn't say that."

"That's what it sounded like."

"All right. I didn't mean it that way."

"I think you did."

His jaw tightened. "Fine. Do whatever you want." He stomped away.

Inside my tower, I headed up the stairs, wondering if I should have been more polite. He'd caught me in a bad mood, and even in a good mood, politeness had never been my strong point. Eresh had said we were ambassadors. The Laerd was just a hakoi, but he was still the head man in Mjor. I hadn't planned to take him up on his offer, but still, it wouldn't have hurt for me to have been polite about it. I rolled my eyes. *So what? He's a dicknut.* My conscience kept needling me until I gave in. *All right, fine. I'll be more polite.* My lips set in a line. *As long as he's polite to me.*

Inside my apartment, I shed my uniform, thinking about what Hyme wanted me to see. I let it go. Right now, I had the service to think about. Searching the closet, I pulled out my garb, and while dressing, recited the sermon I'd memorized. I checked myself in the mirror. Satisfied, I left for the É.

◎⊡⊡⊡⊡◎

"So what do you have to show me?" I said, shutting the lab's street door.

"Here, look." Hyme led me to the cage where a mysi skratz dug around in the shavings and pointed.

I peered. "All right...what?"

"Don't you see? You've discovered the cure for your keras."

Keras was one of the small projects I'd brought with me. I looked closer. I'd known the rough patch had healed, but now I could see tiny hairs growing. My oral herbal syrup had worked.

I spun around and gave Hyme a tight hug. "It works, it works," I crowed, dancing around the lab. "I've just saved the É thousands of talents. And since I found it first, we'll make even more selling the solution to the other És!"

He frowned. "Sell it? You're not going to trade it for knowledge?"

I stopped dancing. "No."

Hyme shook his head. "You should trade. That's worth far more than money."

I shrugged. "Maybe. But it's not just the money. It's a game. The Gods compete with one another on just about everything. For this, Astoreth will have a monopoly on the cure, and the other Gods have no choice but to pay."

"If you sell it, can't other É healers reproduce it?"

"We'd sell by contract with the stipulation that they can't."

He shook his head again. "All right, whatever you say. But now, I suggest we celebrate. Would you like a cup of ale?"

"I'd love one."

"Come on upstairs, then."

I settled in one of the fireplace chairs while Hyme fetched the ale. He emerged from the kitchen and handed me a mug. "Here you are."

I raised it high. "I propose a toast. To success."

"Hear, hear." We clinked mugs, and then he sat in the chair across from mine.

For the next few hours, we talked and drank. He kept bringing out more ale, and I noticed he was getting drunk. I wasn't. The Devi metabolized alcohol as fast as they could drink it, and I had enough Devi blood to metabolize it almost as fast as they could.

When Hyme began snoring, I knew it was time to go. I took a blanket from his bed and draped it over him. Then I collected the mugs and set them in the kitchen sink. Tiptoeing out of the apartment, I let myself out.

Walking along the well-lit street, I thought about my keras cure. I was happy about it, but I wished I could celebrate because I'd beaten the virus. And I was running low on hairless skratz. I'd have to ask for another couple of boxes to be delivered on the next supply run and hope no one questioned it. If they did, I had a good story prepared but I'd rather not have to lie.

Halfway to my tower, someone yanked my arm. It hurt. Then whoever it was, dragged me into an unlit alley. In the streetlamps' ambient light, I saw the man who'd grabbed me. Another waited in the near-darkness. I didn't recognize either of them.

The man who'd grabbed me pulled my arms behind my back. The other came forward. He said something in Syrenese and drew back his arm, hand balled into a fist.

I could've zapped him but didn't. I didn't need to. These dicknuts had no idea who they were dealing with. They were about to find out.

Before he could hit me, I lifted both legs and rammed my feet into his midriff. He flew backward, hit the opposite wall with a hard thump, and then fell on his butt. Leaping to his feet, he came at me again. I bent over. His fist slammed into his partner's stomach. I heard a grunt, and the man holding me let go. The one who'd tried to hit me was about to try again, so I kicked his groin. He crumpled. Spinning, I jumped straight up, then rammed the second man's face into the wall. I heard a sharp *crack*. With a cry, he fell to his knees.

I backed away, hoping they'd come at me. They did. They shot to their feet and rushed me, one on either side. When they'd gotten close enough, I jumped. Kicking out with both legs, my boots connected with the soft spot under each man's chin. Both staggered backward and crashed onto the bricks. Down for only a second, they leapt up as one, this time with murder in their eyes. They rushed me again, and the fight was on. My body became a weapon, my punches and jabs driving home, and my kicks almost always connecting with a soft belly or head. I was like a desert whirlwind, merciless to anyone foolish enough to get in my way. Our fight ended with both men unconscious.

Breathing hard, I stood over them with hands on knees. Behind me, the sound of running feet echoed. I jerked my head over my shoulder. My eyes narrowed. *A third one? He's going down, too.* I ran toward the alley's mouth. Someone appeared at its entrance, and I launched myself. Too late, I saw it was the Laerd, and it was too late to change my trajectory. I plowed into him, and we tumbled to the sidewalk. He landed on his back, letting out a loud grunt.

"I'm sorry," I panted in his face. "Did I hurt you?"

Wheezing, he managed to shake his head. I got to my feet and helped him up. Electric shocks radiated through my hand.

"Why...why'd you do that?" he said after he'd gotten his breath.

"I thought you were another one of them."

He frowned. "Them? How many were there?"

"Two."

"Where are they?"

I pointed. "Back there. They're probably still unconscious."

His look turned incredulous. "Unconscious?"

"Yes. It was the only way to stop them."

"Come on. Let's see what we've got." He started walking.

I followed. For once, he didn't take those long strides that forced me to run to keep up with him.

We reached the two fallen men. He squatted and peered at each. "I can't see. Let's get them to the street." Grabbing both men by the collar, he dragged them to the sidewalk. They didn't wake. In the better light, he squatted again, then looked up with wide eyes. "Great gods, Moreva. What did you *do* to them?"

The two's faces were covered with contusions and lacerations, some still oozing blood. I'd blacked both eyes on one man and one eye on the other. Their lips were bloodied and swollen. I'd broken both men's noses. One looked like he might have a broken jaw. Through the gaps in their torn clothing, I could see ugly bruises forming.

I shrugged. "Well, they were trying—"

"Never mind." He gave me an appraising look. "Where'd you learn to fight like this?"

"É school."

"I thought you morevs were the peaceful sort."

"We are. But sometimes the Gods war on each other, and if a city's overrun, it's our duty to defend the É."

He eyed me. "Overrun, huh? Sounds like a losing proposition to me."

I shrugged again. "So what now?"

"I call the police. I know these men. Hert and Prag Harst. They're brothers and troublemakers." He pulled a slim rectangle out of a holster on his belt, punched it seven or eight times, and then put it up to his ear.

My brows rose. It was wireless communications device. *Winter wear that uses the body as a battery for heat, and they have wireless, too. Not as backward as I'd thought. But if they have that, why do they still use cords instead of sensors?*

"Muts? Laerd här. Ta med vagnen. Jag har två till dig."

Within five minutes, a large, squarish vehicle barreled around the corner and screeched to a halt, not two šīzu from where we stood on the sidewalk. A man climbed out, even taller and broader than the Laerd. He walked up to him and gave him a hard clap on the back. The Laerd did the same. "Så, vad har vi här?" the man said.

"Muts, dessa två attackerade Morevan."

Muts bent over the two men. "De ser ganska utslågna." He looked up. "Var det somu gjörde detta, Laerd?"

The Laerd jerked a thumb toward me. "Nej—det varhon."

Muts looked over his shoulder and raising an eyebrow, eyed me.

By now, I was annoyed. I was being left out of this conversation, and I didn't like it. "What did he say?"

"He said they looked pretty beat up and asked if I did it. I said no, you did."

"Oh."

Muts turned one man face-down and pulled his arms back. He fished from his pocket what looked like a flimsy length of plaztik with tiny, serrated edges and a hole at one end. Holding the unconscious man's wrists in one big, meaty hand, he deftly looped the plaztik around the man's wrists, and with the other, inserted the piece's end into the hole, then pulled it tight.

"Doesn't look like it'll hold him," I whispered to the Laerd.

"It will. It's a lot stronger than it looks. You can't get it off unless you cut it off."

Muts bound the other man and stood. "Jo, vi borde någ få dessa två ner till stationen."

"Come on. We're going to the police station."

"Why?"

The Laerd looked impatient. "Because you have to make a statement about what happened here. We can't prosecute these knobbleheads unless you do."

"Oh...all right."

Muts unlocked the vehicle's rear door and opened it. Picking up the two men, one in each hand, he threw them into the back. Slamming it, he then unlocked the passenger side door. "Låt oss gå."

I poked the Laerd. "What did he say?"

"He said let's go."

We climbed into the truck—the Laerd by the window, Muts behind the wheel, and me in the middle. Being sandwiched between the two big men was claustrophobic. Muts started the engine and floored the accelerator, throwing me backward. Now I knew how he'd gotten to the scene so fast. He drove like a maniac.

Wide-eyed and frightened, I stared through the windshield, sure we were going to either hit one of the streetlights or ram into a building. The Laerd, either for his own comfort or for mine, wrapped his arm about my shoulders. His touch was welcome, and not just because I was frightened. It kept me from being bounced around, too.

We screeched to a halt in front of the police station, a square, squat building that had been painted bright yellow. Muts got out of the truck and walked to a door set in the middle of the station's façade. Taking out a ring of keys, he searched through them and then unlocked the door. He turned. "Gå in och vänta på mig."

We stepped out of the vehicle, and I gave the Laerd an expectant look.

"Come on. Let's go in."

We entered the station. The interior was almost empty. A large, elevated desk sat in the center of the gray room. A few tables and chairs were pushed up against one wall. The other wall was bare. No curtains hung at the barred windows. It was about as bleak as could be.

Something clanged behind a door that obviously led to the station's recesses. Muts appeared a few minutes later. He walked past us to the street door and locked it. "De vaknar."

"They're waking up," the Laerd whispered.

Muts motioned for us to follow. He opened another door, different from the one he'd come through, and held it for us. With him in the lead, we walked along a drab hallway with doors on both sides and stopped at a third door which he again opened for us. I looked around. This room appeared to be an office. A desk and padded chair sat in the room's center with two more padded chairs facing the desk. The desk held a computer and keyboard but nothing else. There were no windows, no pictures on the walls. The room was as bleak as the rest of the station.

Muts pointed to the chairs, and we each took one. He sat behind the desk. A moment later, the computer whirred. Rapid clicking sounds came from the keyboard. Then he looked up. "Jag kommer att ta ditt uttalande nu."

The Laerd turned to me. "He's going to take your statement now."

"How? He doesn't speak Devian."

"And you don't speak Syrenese. Just talk, and I'll translate. When we're done, I'll read it back to you to make sure it's what you want to say." He translated what he'd said to Muts, who nodded. He turned back to me. "Ready anytime you are."

I began my tale. Sentence by sentence, I spoke, the Laerd translated, and Muts typed it into the computer. It seemed to take hours. Muts typed something, and the room filled with a humming sound. When the hum had stopped, he reached under the desk, brought out three sheets of nupaper, and gave them to the Laerd.

The Laerd read aloud, translating as he went. When finished, he gave me an inquiring look. I nodded. It was what I'd said, almost word for word. He turned to Muts. "Ja, det stämmer."

Muts opened a desk drawer, deposited my statement inside, and then locked it. He got up, motioning for us to do the same. Inside the room with the elevated desk, he looked over his shoulder. "Jag kör er hem nu." He disappeared into the back.

I looked at the Laerd.

"He's going to take us home, now."

My eyes widened. "Can't we just walk?"

He laughed. "Why? Muts is the best driver in the village."

Tires squealed outside. After a brief moment of silence, a door slammed. Keys jingled, the lock on the front door turned, and Muts stepped inside. He motioned to us. We went out to the truck.

Muts started the vehicle, and after putting it in gear, gunned the engine. The truck leapt forward like some kind of raging ura. The Laerd wrapped his arm around me again. It was a good thing, too—I was terrified. Instead of looking through the windshield, I squeezed my eyes shut and buried my face in his chest. Above my head, the two men laughed and jabbered in Syrenese as if Muts wasn't about to kill us all in the very next second.

We screeched to a halt, throwing me forward. If the Laerd hadn't been holding me, my head would have smacked into the dashboard. Sitting up, I opened my eyes. We were in front of my tower. The Laerd got out of the truck and then helped me. My legs shook.

He turned to Muts. "Behöver vo komma till stationen i morgon?"

The policeman waved a massive hand. "Nej, nej—jag ringer dig om jag behöver dig."

I looked at the Laerd.

"I asked if he needed us to come to the station tomorrow. He said he'd call if he needs us."

I nodded.

Gripping the door's sill, he leaned through the truck's open window. "Tack för allt och ha en bra kväll." Straightening, he gave the door a firm slap. Muts waved, and with another squeal of tires, roared away. The Laerd stepped forward until he stood only inches from me, his expression stern. "We need to talk."

I craned my neck to look at his face. "About what?"

"About tonight."

I let out a small sigh. I was tired and wanted to go to bed. I opened my mouth but closed it when I realized he wasn't going to take "no" for an answer.

Entering my tower, I peered at the barracks door, looking for any sign of light. There was none. *Good.* I knew Yose was still spying on me, and the last thing I needed was for him to see the Laerd following me to my room.

We climbed the stairs in silence. Inside my apartment, I pointed to a chair, and I settled in the chair opposite. "I'd offer you some ale, but I don't have any," I said, trying to keep my tone light.

"Don't want any."

We stared at each other, saying nothing. I gave my head small shake. "So what did you want to talk about?"

His lips tightened. "Why didn't you listen to me when I told you about walking alone in the village at night?"

"I've done it lots of times. Nothing's ever happened before."

"Moreva, let me tell you something. That attack wasn't one of op-portunity. Those two were waiting for you."

My eyes widened. "How would they know I'd be going to Hyme's tonight?"

"Prag speaks Devian. I heard him boasting about it one day. He must have overheard us outside."

"Where would he have learned to speak it? I mean—"

"That's not important. What's important is you have to take more care. You told me on your first day someone threw a rock at you. You're not stupid, so why didn't you take that as a clue? In the future, if you're going to stay that late at Hyme's, let me know and I'll walk with you."

"How do you know someone won't attack the two of us?"

"They wouldn't dare attack the Laerd. Besides, I can fight as well as you can."

I nodded. "All right."

"Good." He headed for the battlement door and opened it. Looking over his shoulder, he gave me a meaningful stare. "Remember what I said."

"Wait." I hurried over to him. I pressed my palms and bowed. "Kea leboha, Laerd."

The look in his eyes softened, and he gazed at me for a full minute. "Good night, Moreva." He left.

Bolting the door, a mighty yawn escaped me. It had been a long day with too much excitement. *I should take a shower. Hm...maybe not.* Five Durm had long since passed, and by now the water would be freezing. I glanced into the vanity's mirror. *I should at least take off my makeup.* I shook my head, too tired to do even that. Undressing, I draped my uniform over the chair, then crawled beneath the furs.

Instead of falling asleep, I kept thinking about the Laerd and his insistence on accompanying me when I was out at night. Did he really care? Or was it just the Protocol? And what was he thinking about when he stared at me?

I was in the middle of another thought when my brain just stopped, and I fell into a deep sleep.

Chapter Twelve

Tonight was my second Ohra-Sin. And I was dreading it as much as I had the first.

I finished applying my body makeup and inspected myself in the mirror. All symbols were correctly positioned. There were no gaps in the paint. It disappointed me because I'd hoped to find a mistake. If there was, I'd have to re-plaster the symbol, which would have given me that much more time before heading to the É.

Descending the stairs, I barely resisted the urge to run back to my apartment. At the É's portal, I stared into the darkness. *It won't be so bad this time.* I had a plan to participate without really being there. Before the garrison arrived, I'd put myself in a trance, light enough to allow me to speak the opening prayer. After I dove into the pool, I'd fall into a deeper trance that would numb my mind and body.

Stepping inside, the lights flickered, and I looked around. I'd set everything up earlier today. All I had to do was to light the candles, incense, and the braziers. After doing that, I switched on the seero. The Ohra-Sin music filled the big room. At the far end of the pool, I sat in sacred lutos, closed my eyes and pushed my consciousness down until I floated.

The penitents' arrival sounded far away. When all was quiet, I recited the opening prayer, then fitted my nose filters. "Let Ohra begin." I dived into the pool. My world disappeared. Unknowing and uncaring, I drifted in my personal darkness.

Without warning, I popped out my trance. Disorientation held me in its grip for a few seconds, then fell away. The garrison's hands grabbing my arms, legs, and waist was sickening. I lost it. Black hate exploded through me, all the way to my core. In that moment, I hated everything about everything, including Astoreth for sending me here. And I was *not* going to stand for this. These hakoi didn't amount to skratz, and I'd be damned if I allowed them to swarm over me. I fought—punching, kicking, and zapping everyone. But nothing I did had an effect. They were too high on the incense to feel pain.

The gong finally sounded. All climbed out of the pool, including me. In a shaky voice, I intoned the benediction and dismissed them.

After they'd gone, I sank onto the pillow and dropped my head into my hands. I'd never felt like that before. I hated the hakoi, but this was different. My hate had been all-consuming, as if I'd disappeared and something else had taken my place. It terrified me. Did my hate make me unfit to be a moreva born to serve the Goddess of Love? If it did, where would I go? Where *could* I go? *And to hate Astoreth...that's the worst of all. She means* everything *to me.*

"I don't know what to do," I whispered.

I sat for a long time, thinking. Should I call home? I really needed to talk to my grandmother. I needed Her guidance. If I did call, would She think it important enough to count as an emergency? Or would she punish me for breaking the rule? *Do I even dare to call? What if She calls me home and then dismisses me from Her service? Would She do that?*

For the first time in my life, I was unsure whether I could trust Her.

I sat for a few more minutes, then let out a heavy sigh. I had to get upstairs and shower before the hot water cooled. If I slept without removing my body paint, it wouldn't damage the fur, but right now, I felt...unclean.

Throwing on my cloak, I trudged upstairs, still pondering what to do. But I knew I couldn't go on like this. It wasn't just presiding over the daily services, or even Ohra-Sin. The depth and intensity of the hate I felt during the rite, knowing it was boiling inside me... *I never listened to Ginzu because I thought there was nothing wrong with me. But she's right. There* is *something wrong with me, and whatever it is, I have to fix it.*

Stepping out of the shower, I still felt dirty. I set my alarm for four-thirty Gor and climbed into bed. But instead of sleep, I re-lived the past three hours with astonishing clarity, seeing every face, feeling every touch, feeling hate and rage while my punches, kicks, and zaps had done nothing to get them off me.

I couldn't stand it anymore. I jumped out of bed. If I couldn't sleep, the least I could do was go over my lab notes or dictate a sermon. I plopped into the fireplace chair and decided on a sermon. Writing sermons usually absorbed me, but if that didn't get my mind off Ohra-Sin, I'd look at my notes instead. Grabbing my tablet, I thought of a topic and started dictating. While I spoke, a thick fog fell over my mind, leaving me aware of nothing but the sound of my voice.

The dream-like state lifted. I looked at the tablet and gasped. Horrified, I threw it to the floor. The screen was filled with hateful invective leveled at the hakoi. "They're worthless! Merda heads! Created by the Gods—oh, yes! From merda straight out of Their asses! Why are they allowed to live? Merda is flushed down the toilet! Flush them all! Every last fucking one of them!"

It got worse. There were words and phrases I didn't know I knew. I tried to tear my gaze away but couldn't. The abuse leapt out at me, a mirror to show how I looked from the inside.

I curled in the chair and sobbed. I knew that attack applied even to Hyme. In that moment, I understood what I was—a monster, unfit to be a moreva in Astoreth's service.

I let out a wail. I didn't want to be this way. I *didn't!*

From somewhere deep in my memory, the warning Ginzu had given me before I left Uruk floated to my surface. "You are in danger... losing your soul." I cried even harder. Had I lost it already? If I had, could I get it back? How?

Embrace your hakoi-ness, a still, small voice echoed in the back of my mind.

I cried for hours. Eventually, my tears stopped, and I stared miserably into the cold, dark depths of the huge fireplace. I was lost. Everthing I had known and held on to about myself had been ripped away. *What am I to do? How do I reclaim my soul?* I closed my eyes. *I wish Ginzu was here.*

Embrace your hakoi-ness, the small voice echoed again.

"Embrace my hakoi-ness," I whispered. "But how?"

The voice was silent.

My thoughts drifted like rudderless boats on the Ven River. After a long while, visions of my childhood appeared in my mind's eye, especially the way my classmates' looked at me with loathing and contempt.

Visions of my apprenticeship paraded past, my brothers' and sisters' snickering, the fear in their eyes once they knew I was psi.

The pictures faded. *It's never been easy, being me. I've never belonged. Is that the reason I treated them the way I did? Not just because they were dicknuts, but...jealousy?* Eresh was was the only morev who'd accepted me as I was. While apprentices, he'd told me the others had needled him about our friendship, but thankfully, he'd ignored them. I'm not sure what I would have done if he hadn't.

Still staring into the fireplace, I thought about my morevic life in Uruk. Despite being short, I was the best at every physical activity we were required to know. I was the best in the arts too, except for singing. My voice was average, but I wasn't bothered. It wasn't important to me. My brothers and sisters knew my superior ability and power came from having more Devi blood than they, and all—except Eresh—resented me because they couldn't compete. I rubbed their noses in it every chance I got. For me, it was payback for every insult they'd thrown at me while growing up. Even so, there was a short period when I'd tried—at Eresh's prompting—to make friends with the others. They wouldn't have me. I returned to my old ways with a vengeance.

I remembered what Astoreth had said the day She'd sentenced me to exile—that I didn't know my place. *She's right, but not for the reason She thinks. I don't know my place because I* have *no place.* I frowned. *But what does that have to do with embracing my hakoi-ness?*

The alarm rang. I shut it off and returned to my chair. Picking up my tablet from the floor, my lips tightened as I stared at the screen. Erasing my rant, I put the tablet in sleep mode and set it on the table.

Curling again in the chair, I lay my head on its armrest. I thought about embracing my hakoi-ness. What could it mean? I came up with several possibilities but discarded them because they made no sense. I let out a sigh. *I can't think about this anymore. I should go downstairs and clean the É.* But I didn't feel like it. I didn't feel like doing anything except staying right where I was. *Besides, I have all day to do it. There isn't going to be a service until this evening.*

Closing my eyes, I let my thoughts drift. They settled on the morning the Laerd took me to the ridge to get the skagwort for Hyme. I recalled what I'd said when we'd talked about what it was like being morev. That for me, it was lonely. *If I was morev like the rest of them, I wouldn't be lonely. They would have accepted me. I would have belonged.*

A bolt of rage tore through me, and my jaw tightened. *No. I can't help being who I am. I can't help that I don't look like them. We're supposed to be acolytes of Love. We're supposed to revere all life. What love and reverence did they show me? None. Except for Eresh, no one even tried to help me feel like I belonged. If they had, maybe I wouldn't be such a puta. They treat me like merda, and I've enough self-respect not to take it. They deserve every insult, every zap I dish out.*

My anger slowly ebbed. However justified my behavior back home, it changed nothing for me. I was still alone, and lonely. And as long as nobody accepted me as I was, I would always be lonely.

I stared at the other chair without seeing it. My thoughts drifted again and settled on the Laerd. *What's it like for him, being hakoi? To be like everyone else. To know you're not the only one.* I let out a soft snort. *As if he would tell me. He talks to me only if he has to.*

I looked at the floor, thinking about that morning on the ridge. *That was nice, talking like that. Even though I did most of the talking. It was so...easy. No being on guard, waiting for him to say something rude. But then we got back to Mjor, and it was like it had never happened.* I wondered if something like that could ever happen again. Did I want it to? My brow quirked. *Doesn't matter. Even if I did, and even if he liked me, what in Astoreth's name would we talk about?*

My thoughts drifted back to embracing my hakoi-ness but I got nowhere with it. I just went round and round in circles, like a skratz chasing its tail. *It can't be nonsense, though. Could it?*

I shook my head. *Enough of this. I'm going to clean the É. By the time I finish, it'll be time for breakfast.* Rising from the chair, I readied myself for the day, then headed downstairs.

Chapter Thirteen

The next aftermidday found me walking across the battlement to the Laerd's apartment. It was gorgeous out, sunny and bright. It was also getting warmer. *Have to pull out my summer uniforms, soon.*

It had been a marun since he'd found out about my red fever project, and it was time to give him my first report. Surprisingly, I was a little nervous. Was he going to be a dicknut or was he going to be nice? I let out a small sigh. *Please, don't be a dicknut.*

Reaching his door, I rang the bell. "Moreva Tehi."

"Come," his gravelly voice boomed from the speaker.

I walked inside and stopped short. My eyes widened. The Laerd wore nothing but the shortest of short pants and fingerless gloves. His sculpted, god-like body ran with sweat, and it dripped from his hair. I watched his muscles bulge each time he lifted the barbell above his head then lower it to his waist in slow, rhythmic repetitions.

But his near-nakedness wasn't why I stood gaping. It was the weight on the barbell. Courtesy of our Devi blood, morevs partook in the strength of the Gods but I knew no other morev in the É could have lifted that kind of load. I wasn't sure *I* could. *Astoreth. That's impressive.*

He did a few more repetitions, then set the barbell on the rack. Clapping his gloved hands, the chalk dust made a pastel blue cloud around his fingers. He tugged the gloves off, dropped them on the weight bench, and grabbed a nearby towel to swipe his face and hair. He pointed to the chair next to his desk. "Have a seat."

Still staring, I sat.

"Mind if I take a quick shower first?"

"Oh, no...no. Go ahead."

He walked into the bath. Seconds later, I heard the shower. True to his word, it didn't take long. Within ten minutes he was back, fully dressed. Pulling up his desk chair, he plopped into it and smiled. "So what do you have for me?"

My lips tightened. "Nothing."

He frowned. "Nothing?"

"Nothing."

"Why? What happened?"

"The skratz all died. One skratz had smaller pustules than the others, but so what? It still died."

He gave me a thoughtful look. "Must be frustrating."

"It is."

"So what will you do now?"

I sighed. "I've gone as far as I can with the extracts I brought from Uruk. There's nothing more I can do until my plants mature."

He cocked his head. "Your plants?"

"I have a habitat set up in Hyme's closet. It arrived a marun ago, the same day you found out about my project."

"How long will it take them to mature?"

"About two more marun."

"What will you do in the meantime?"

"I've another small project I brought from home. But right now, the important one is going nowhere." I blew a hard breath, then stared through the window.

"Moreva. Look at me." His rumbling voice was soft.

I turned my head. The look in his eyes was as soft as his voice. "I believe you'll find a cure. It's just going to take time."

"Time is something I don't have. When the fever strikes, a lot of hakoi are going to die. I can prevent that if I could just find the cure."

Silence reigned in the apartment. "How often does it strike back home?" His voice was still soft.

"Every four years. We're due for a hit this summer."

"I see." He fell silent. "Our outbreaks are every four years, too. The last one was two years ago."

"I know. Hyme told me. Your heartsbound and unborn child died." I paused. "I'm sorry."

"Thank you." He took a breath. "I understand if you don't find the cure before your summer, thousands of hakoi back home will die. But if you don't, it's not your fault. You're doing the best you can."

"That's not good enough."

"Yes, it is." He shook his head. "Listen. You're too hard on yourself. Red fever is a huge problem you're trying to solve. You're doing it because you don't want to see us die. Problem is, the world usually doesn't give us what we want, when we want it. If there's an outbreak before a cure is found, yes, we'll die. I might die. But that doesn't mean you stop trying. You just keep at it. Finding the cure isn't just for the hakoi living now. It's for those who'll be living in the future, too."

I stared at the floor, remembering my vile screed from yesterday. Shame pricked me. *I wasn't doing it for you. I was doing it for me.*

"Moreva."

I looked up. A small smile played on his lips. "I'll be expecting another report next week."

"Why? I won't have anything to tell you."

His smile broadened. "Because I'm interested in whatever else you're doing."

I smiled back. "All right." I started to get up, then paused. "Wait... can I ask you something?"

"Sure."

I licked my lips. "What's...what's it like, being you?"

A small frown appeared. "Being me?"

"I told you what it's like for me. Being the only one. I...guess I want to know what it's like to be a part of something. To belong somewhere."

He fixed me with a compassionate gaze but said nothing for a long time. "I've never thought about it," he said. "But if I had to describe it, I'd say it feels safe."

I gave a slow nod. "I sort of...figured it would be like that." I got to my feet and headed for the door.

He was faster. "Here, let me get this." He opened it. "Thanks for the report."

I stepped outside and looked up. "Thank *you*, Laerd. For what you said. It...helped a lot."

He smiled again. "I'll see you at lunch." The door shut.

I started across the battlement. Walking, I thought about what had just happened between us. He'd been so likable and kind. *Why can't he always be like that?* Then it dawned on me. He was only like this when we were alone. In public, he either snapped at or ignored me. So was his being kind to me in private the act or was his callousness in public? In either case, why?

I entered my apartment and flopped onto a fireplace chair. Glancing at the bed, I wondered if I should take a nap. *Didn't sleep last night... might do me some good.* I shook my head. I was tired, but I didn't feel sleepy. *Though if don't do it now, there's a better chance I'll pass out tonight.* I raised my brows. *Could always go to the lab...* The project I'd started was still in the preliminary stage. No rush there. *And I've already checked the beacon. So I really don't have to go anywhere.*

I leaned back and closed my eyes. My inner ear played back the conversation I'd had with the Laerd. *Feeling safe...* I felt plenty safe with Astoreth, and as Her moreva. On the streets of Uruk, no one would dare lift a finger to me for any reason. It was true inside the É too, if only because my brothers and sisters knew what would happen if they tried anything with me.

But it's not the same. If I got hurt or something and Grandmother wasn't around, none of Her morevs would help me, whether inside the É or out on the street. A tear formed in the corner of my eye. *Just once, I'd like to feel I belonged somewhere. Anywhere.*

My thoughts turned to my diatribe from last night and then what the Laerd had said about my search for the cure. *He obviously doesn't know me. That they'll be free of the fever when I find the cure is just a happy side effect. To me, it'll mean I've won. I'll have defeated my enemy, that's all. Then on to the next project.*

I stared at my knees. *But...I want it to mean more than that. I want it to really* mean *something. I want to feel the satisfaction that I've helped someone to live.*

My jaw set. *I want that feeling, and I'm going after it.* And to get what I wanted, I knew what I had to do.

I had to see the hakoi as people, not less than animals. I'd studied psychology and knew my prejudice was deeply ingrained. It wasn't a matter of just changing my mind. I had to change my hearts. The question, though, was how.

Well, there's meditation and prayer. It won't get me where I need to go, but it's a start. The other part...that's going to be a problem. I needed to have a close familiarity with the hakoi. I had Hyme, but that wasn't enough. I needed a group, a community. *Guess I can count out the Mjorans.* It was more than the language barrier. They didn't want me here. I might want to be part of their community, but I was sure they wouldn't want *me* to be a part of their community. *And the garrison's out, too.* If Yose caught me or found out I was fraternizing with the lower ranks, I'd be headed to Uruk on the next supply flight. *Or sooner.*

"All right, then," I murmured. "I'll start with prayer and meditation. The rest I'll figure out later." *Hm. When would be the best time? Morning after breakfast? After the evening service?* I raised my brows. *Wait. Why don't I do it before I dance? If I do that, I can start today.*

I touched the bar. "Time."

"Fourth hour, fifty minutes Tryn."

Great. I've plenty of time before dinner.

I stripped to my underwear, shoved my feet into slippers, and went to the É.

⊙═⊐⊒⊐⊒⊙

...

You sit on the bank of the mighty Ven River, watching the water as it flows. The waters are like your thoughts, ever drifting. Just as you do not attach your attention to any of the wavelets, you do not attach yourself to any of your thoughts. You simply watch as the current takes them away...

...

For five days, Morevi Bibo's sonorous voice filled my mind, intoning the words to induce a meditative trance. Except it didn't work. My thoughts were like magnets, pulling me in every direction, clamoring for my notice. And I gave it to each one. After every meditative session, I danced to near exhaustion out of sheer frustration.

The only bright spot was when I finally caught Yose spying on me. In the middle of a pirouette, I saw his face peeking around the corner. I stopped in mid-twirl and stared. "May I do something for you Kepten?"

He looked disconcerted. "Ah, no...I mean yes. A few of my people seem to have come down with something, and I'd like you to take a look at them."

I gave him a toothy grin that I knew didn't reach my eyes. "Of course. Just let me clean up, and I'll be right down."

"Thank you, Moreva." Saluting, he clomped down the steps.

In the barracks, I examined five soldiers. All were running low-grade fevers. I handed out pills to bring the fever down and advised Yose they needed rest. "No electronic or field maneuvers for today or tomorrow."

"Yes, Moreva."

On the sixth day, after my dance session, I sat down to think. *I've been practicing for five days now, the way I was taught. What am I doing wrong?* To keep from becoming more frustrated than I already was, I lay back on the floor, spread my arms chest-high, and relaxed. I closed my eyes. In a moment, I felt as if I floated. A grayish-white, swirling fog rolled in. Then it cleared.

...

A sense of wonder creeps through me. I hover over a verdant landscape, the likes of which I've never seen. I see vibrant, green, rolling hills dotted here and there with clumps of trees. I look around. Behind me are more hills and a ribbon of a river cutting through the beautiful, alien landscape. I don't see the suns, yet the strange blue sky is bright. A light breeze ruffles my feathers—

Feathers?

I look down. My breast is covered in fine, blue-violet feathers with a small, golden jewel nestled over my hearts. It glows, seemingly from within. It's lovely.

I flap my wings fast and shoot forward. Frightened, I instinctively lower my tail feathers. I slow. I try again but don't flap my wings as fast. It works. I experiment with flying fast and slow a few more times. Satisfied with my prowess, I experiment some more. Soon I'm swooping, soaring, and diving through the air. It's exhilarating.While on a dive, I see something I hadn't noticed before—a black dot hovering over the horizon. Curious, I fly toward it. At first, it doesn't seem to grow any closer. I keep going. In the next minute or so, I can see that it's another bird, a black one. I can also see it's much larger than I am. That only piques my curiosity. Moments later, I see the flaming red jewel on its breast. The jewel is exquisite, yet somehow unnerving.

Before I know it, the other bird is upon me. Screaming, it dives, its dagger talons open. I flutter away, but not fast enough. Its beak snaps closed, severing the tips from a few of my tail feathers. It comes at me again.

I'm terrified. The big bird is trying to hurt or even kill me. I manage to evade it several times. It finally catches me and rakes my breast. Blood flows. It clips me with a wing. I spin out of control. Regaining my balance, I see it coming straight for me. I try to fly away, but it catches my wing in its beak and bears down, harder and harder. The pain is excruciating. Shrieking, I squeeze my eyes shut.

Just when I think my wing will break, the pressure disappears. My eyes pop open. Another bird, brown and white speckled with a green jewel in its breast, has knocked the black bird away. It wheels to face this new threat. The other bird, even larger than the black one, dives and crashes into it. The black bird is bowled over by the impact.

The fight is on. The black bird attacks. Its opponent holds its ground. At the last minute, it flips upright. Its talons puncture the black bird's breast. A thick, green ichor flows from the wound. Now the speckled bird attacks. It flies up and over the black bird, catching its neck in its hooked beak. The black bird screams. Tossing its head, the speckled bird throws the other to the side. The two birds dive and smash into each other again. Raking its beak down the side of the black bird's head, the speckled bird plucks out the other's eye.

The black bird flies away, its screeching growing fainter and fainter until it has again become a black spot on the horizon. Hovering on the air currents, I face the speckled bird. Will it hurt me, too?

No fear, little one. I came to help you.

You did? Then why didn't you kill it?

I cannot. The black bird is your hate. Only you can destroy it.

My eyes widened. *Me? How?*

You must pluck out the jewel that is its heart.

But I'm so much smaller. How am I supposed to do that?

That is for you to figure out.

The swirling fog enveloped me again, then disappeared. Opening my eyes, I gazed at the ceiling.

Elation filled me. Not only did I meditate, I had a vision, too. Morevi Bibo would be pleased. And that was the key, I realized—dancing before meditation. That way, my body and mind would be relaxed enough for my efforts to pay off.

I rose onto my elbows and almost collapsed from the pain in my arm, a deep ache that went to the bone. My midriff stung, too. I looked down. Three, angry-looking welts started at my chest, ending almost at my stomach. I stared, wide-eyed. "Astoreth. It was real."

In a second, I remembered the time. How long had I been out? Did I miss dinner? If I had, the service would begin soon, and I had to clean up. Jumping to my feet, I ran to the closet. Hauling out the robo-mop, I set up the altar while it skated across the floor. When finished, I threw it into the closet, then ran upstairs.

I barreled into the apartment, slapping the bar on my uniform as I ran past to my closet. "Time to service," I shouted, fishing for tonight's garb.

"Three hours, forty minutes."

I blinked. It was only two hours past lunch. My trance, which had seemed to last for hours, had lasted less than twenty minutes. I had plenty of time before the evening service.

After showering, I went to my healer's kit and dug inside until I found a jar of skin cream. The concoction would heal my welts by dinnertime. It wouldn't do for Astoreth's moreva to sport visible injuries at the service.

I should check the beacon now. In the control room, the cylinder glowed in its usual colors. No problems with the converter. I called Central and made my report. As usual, the Devi who took it was rude.

Sitting before the communications console, I leaned back, thinking about my vision. I understood two of the birds, myself and the black bird, but who or what was the brown speckled bird? Was it a person or a spirit? If it was a person, who? I knew beings from other realms sometimes kept watch over certain people. Was that what the brown bird was, my guardian? And how was I supposed to kill the black bird when it was so much bigger? If it hadn't been for the brown, who knew what might have happened? At the very least, I'd have had a broken wing.

I squeezed my arm. "Ouch." If the black bird had broken my wing did that mean I would've had a broken arm when I awoke from my trance? *And the black bird had been trying to kill me. If you die in a vision, do you die for real?* I shivered and pushed the thought aside. I didn't want to think about that.

By now, my head was spinning. *I can't deal with this anymore.* I tapped the bar. "Time."

"Sixth hour, fifty-three minutes Tryn."

My brows rose. I'd been sitting here longer than I thought. *Better go.* I took one last look around, then headed for the lift. My mind went blank on the ride down and stayed that way until I reached the dining hall.

Walking to the lab afterward, Hyme gave me a concerned look. "You were awfully quiet. Anything wrong?"

"Just trying to work out a sermon I want to write."

"Tell me about it."

I hesitated, trying to come up with something without giving myself away. "I'm working on how to counteract the negative mindset—negative thoughts, feelings, things like that."

He said nothing for a moment. "I've come to believe many times, that sort of negativity is based on fear. Fear of not getting what we want, fear of getting what we don't want, fear of what I call 'the other'—anyone or anything not like us. When we fear, we feel threatened, and that threat makes us angry. If those feelings are internalized, we become unwilling to even try accepting what or who it is, and our anger turns to hate. To conquer that hate, that fear, the first step is to figure out what it is we're afraid of."

"What's the next?"

"Facing our fear. Once we do that, we may find there was nothing to fear at all."

"And we can replace our fear with love."

"That's one way of putting it. Does that help?"

I felt more confused than ever. "Yes, it helps a lot."

We arrived at the lab, and Hyme opened the door. "Wait. I'm going back to my room and work on my sermon. This talk has given me a lot of ideas. I'll see you tomorrow."

"Very good, Tehi. Good night."

"Good night."

I started across the plaza, thinking on what was it about the hakoi that I feared. *Sounds silly. Why should I be scared of* them? *They're nothing to be afraid of. If I felt anything, it'd be pity.* Stepping inside my tower, Hyme's words echoed in my mind. I shook my head. *I just don't get it.*

I let out a small sigh. *Well, I'll let it go for now. Maybe it'll make sense in the morning.*

It didn't.

Chapter Fourteen

After breakfast, Hyme and I stopped at the fountain to watch its cascading waters sparkle in the suns.

"You didn't sleep well again last night," he said.

I laughed. "You can always tell. How?"

"Your eyes. They aren't as bright a gold as they usually are."

I raised by brows. No one, and certainly no other healer, had ever said that to me when I hadn't slept well back home. "Very observant of you."

"Healers have to be observant. Even the smallest of things can tell you a lot."

My lips tightened. How many hakoi in Uruk hadn't gotten the exact medicines they'd needed because I hadn't been observant enough? *Every single one.*

When I get home, I'm going to do better by them. That's a promise. And I can start by being more observant of the Mjorans. That'll help Hyme if I spot something before he does.

"Oh," Hyme said. "I've got a herb I want to tell you about. It's called linmen, and it has strong antiviral properties. It occurred to me this morning that maybe it's something you'd like to experiment with sometime."

"I'd like that. Let me set up the É for tonight's service, and I'll be right over. It shouldn't take more than ten, fifteen minutes."

We went our separate ways. I entered my tower and readied the É in ten minutes. Sitting on the steps, while slipping on my left boot, the door to the barracks opened. Yose appeared and saluted. "Moreva, the supply airship is coming tomorrow with three new recruits. I understand they've not been inoculated against varsi. The vaccine will be brought with the rest of the supplies. Will you be available to give them vaccinations?"

"Of course. Just let me know."

"Thank you." He saluted again and disappeared into the barracks.

I frowned. *How did he know I was here? Was he spying on me? Maybe the door was open a crack and I didn't notice?* I slipped on my other boot. *Well, it could have been a coincidence. I was here for a little over ten minutes before he showed up.* I squeezed my eyes shut. *Stop it. Yose has you spooked from one end to the other. This is just where he wants you, constantly worrying and afraid to move, much less think.*

I headed for the lab. Inside, the door to Hyme's apartment was open. I climbed the steep steps and on reaching the top, looked around. He was nowhere to be seen. "Hyme," I called. "I'm here."

He emerged from the kitchen with two steaming mugs of tea. "Just a little something to perk you up. Here you go. Be careful—it's very hot."

I set it on the low table before the fireplace, sat in the fur-covered chair, and settled back. I was looking forward to this, like I did all his lectures.

Hyme set his mug on the table and picked up an open book from the bookshelf. Sinking into his chair, he began to speak.

⊙⊒⊒⊡⊒⊒⊙

"Take this," he said, handing me the book. The page showed a plant in various stages of growth.

"This is the linmen herb. It grows in the forest about an hour's drive from here. As you can see, it has star-shaped flowers. The flowers, however, have no value to us. It—"

Fwoomp! The building shivered. I looked up. "What was that?"

Hyme's expression turned grim. "The mine. There's been an accident. They'll be bringing in the casualties soon. Come on." He jumped to his feet and clattered down the steps. Throwing the book on the table, I raced after him.

We hurried into the hospital wing. "What kind of accident?" I said.

"An explosion."

"Why?"

"No time for questions, Tehi. We have to get ready. Do you know anything about treating burn victims?"

"Yes, but I haven't had a lot of practice with it."

"Well, you're about to get some practice, now." He ran to the hospital's entrance and propped open the wide stone door.

Rushing into the patients' room, I switched on the beds, making sure the positive energy flow was circulating normally. We met in the locker room and donned an identical pair of surgical coveralls and helmets. My suit was too big, so we made do by rolling up the pant legs and sleeves. We pulled out the surgical equipment we'd need from the supply area. Laden with laser debriders and other instruments, we sped into the operating theater and set up. We leaned against the counters and waited. Neither of us spoke.

It wasn't long before the first victim arrived. The woman looked as if she'd been roasted. Third-degree burns covered half her body. I could see places where the skin had been completely burned away, revealing scorched muscle. It was a wonder she was still alive.

"Sklar," Hyme muttered. "I'll take this one."

The next victim was the young man who'd thrown the rock at me. His wounds, though serious, weren't as extensive. To prevent dehydration, I started him on an intravenous drip containing electrolytes and antibiotics. Then I debrided his wounds, lasering away the burned skin. Next, I smeared a skagwort-based cream over his burns to help with skin regeneration, then draped passim moss over the treated areas to help keep it moist. Finally, I wrapped a length of nuskin over the passim moss, just tight enough so it wouldn't slip. Lifting him onto a gurney, I rolled him into the patients' room, laid him on the nearest bed, and then returned to the operating room.

The third miner was in worse shape than the first one. I set to work on him. Reaching for the debrider, the man gripped my forearm. His hold was surprisingly strong. "Hyme," he whispered.

I held up the debrider and pointed it at him.

"Nej. Hyme."

I pantomimed his death and pointed the debrider at him again.

"Hyme."

I nodded. Turning, I found him debriding one of the other victims. "Hyme, I've got a patient who won't let me work on him. He keeps asking for you."

"How bad is he?"

"Pretty bad."

"All right. You finish up here, and I'll take care of him." We traded places. I'd just begun working when he tapped me on the shoulder. "Tehi, he's dead."

"Not surprising, but he insisted." I continued debriding.

He sighed. "I'll inform the Laerd so he can tell his widow."

I looked over my shoulder. "You know him?"

"Yes. His name was Vors Leften. I delivered him."

I finished up with my charge. Wheeling him into the patients' room, I tucked him into bed. Returning to the operating theater, the next victim was waiting for me. I patched her up and rolled her into the patients' room. Hyme wheeled in yet another victim. I bit my lip. I hoped the next patient wouldn't need a bed. There weren't any left.

The next victim entered under her own power. *Thank Astoreth.* The woman had suffered second-degree burns on her arms and chest. I treated and released her. The second and third victims were also ambulatory. We treated several miners with lesser degree burns and released them.

By now, the burn victims had either been hospitalized or treated and released. Next came those with broken bones. I was familiar with bone setting, so was able to work just as fast as Hyme. Finally, there were only two patients left. We each took one and finished up at the same time.

"Whew," he breathed after the last patient had left the hospital. "Tehi, I can't thank you enough for everything you've done. I hate to think how those miners would have suffered while waiting for me."

"You're welcome. Glad I could help."

In the locker room, we hung our suits in the vertical washer, and Hyme set the machine's cycle. He was closing the hospital's door when the Laerd walked in with a nasty gash on his right bicep. Whatever had cut him had sliced right through his jacket, and the sleeve was soaked in blood. Hyme treated and dressed his wound, then the three of us walked into the lab.

I rolled my chair up next to Hyme while the Laerd leaned against the counter. He looked as tired as I felt. So did Hyme. No one said anything for a long while. "What happened, Laerd?" Hyme said.

"The miners hit a gas pocket. And you know how flammable

thalin gas is. One little spark and all hell broke loose. Part of the mine collapsed."

"How many dead?"

"Five."

"How many were married?"

"Three. The other two were single."

"Have you informed the spouses and the parents?"

"Yes." He shook his head. "It goes with the job, but this is one part of being Laerd I hate."

Hyme's lips tightened. "There's been one more death. Vors Leften."

The Laerd closed his eyes and sighed. "All right. I'll tell his widow."

We fell silent again. The Laerd opened his eyes and looked at me. "Moreva, thank you for helping today. I'll admit, having two healers came in handy."

"You're—"

A young man burst into the lab. "Laerd," he shouted. "Kom fort! Det finns tjugo gruvarbetare instängda i gruvan och dörren går inte att öppna!"

The Laerd's expression turned horrified. "Inte ens på den manuella omställningen?"

"Nej. Vi har försökt allt. Dörren är fast."

He hurried over to the young man. "Låt oss gå." The two ran out the door.

I looked at Hyme. "What's going on?"

The old healer wrung his hands. "Twenty miners are trapped behind the blast door. It won't open, not even with the manual override. The door's stuck."

My eyes widened. "What does that mean for the trapped miners? What happens if they can't get the door to work?"

"They'll die. Thalin gas is poisonous in large amounts. If enough gas burned off in the explosion, they'll have air to breathe but eventually the air will run out. They'll suffocate."

"There's nothing we can do?"

"Unless they can get that door working again, no. If they're going to get those people out, the Laerd had better come up with an idea and fast."

I stared at the floor, biting my lip. Nodding once, I ran for the door.

"Tehi! Where are you going?"

"Which way is the mine?"

"Take the road out of the village and turn right at the first fork."

"All right. Thanks." I yanked the door open and rushed outside. Hyme was right behind me.

"What do you mean to do?" he called from the doorway.

"I'll be back," I yelled over my shoulder. I sprinted across the plaza toward the front gates. I couldn't get into the barracks from my tower, so I had to go outside, then around to the main entrance. I prayed the door wasn't locked. There was no time to lose.

My prayer was answered. I threw the door open and barreled through. The garrison leapt to attention. "As you were," I shouted.

I burst into Yose's office. He looked up, obviously annoyed at the intrusion until he saw it was me. He jumped to his feet and saluted, face composed into a blank mask.

"Kepten, there's been an explosion at one of the thalin mines," I said between breaths. "Twenty miners are trapped inside behind the blast door. I need a tank and crew to help get them out."

"What are you going to do?"

"Punch a hole through the blast door."

He stared. "Permission to speak frankly, Moreva."

"Go ahead."

"This is not a good idea, for two reasons. First, this is an internal village affair that as Moreva, doesn't concern you or this garrison. Second, the fastest way to get to the road is through the village. Driving a tank through the middle of Mjor will break the Protocol."

"Kepten, these hakoi will *die* if we don't do something."

Yose said nothing.

I tightened my lips. "Very well. Kepten, I order you to provide me with a tank and crew. I will take full responsibility for breaking the Protocol."

He looked at me for what seemed like a long time. "Yes, Moreva." He walked into the barracks. "Misa. Tovak. Gratch," he shouted. "In my office. Now!"

Three soldiers, two men and a woman, sprang from their chairs and jogged over. Yose ushered them inside. I explained what I wanted to do. They didn't bat an eye, though they must have known we were breaking the Protocol. I looked at each soldier. "Any questions?"

"No, Moreva," they said as one.

"All right. Let's go."

We left the barracks and climbed into the nearest tank. "You can sit here," the female soldier said, pointing to the tank commander's seat. She climbed down into the driver's seat, then fired up the engines. A rumbling beneath my feet escalated into a roar. The tank lifted from the ground.

The driver guided it through the gates and drove across the plaza. On the tank's topmost panoramic screen, I saw Mjorans goggle at us as we passed. After clearing the rear gates, she opened up the throttle, and then we were speeding through the countryside.

I instructed the driver to turn right at the first fork. Barreling along the road, we reached the mine an hour and a half later. I told the driver to head for the center of the three gargantuan mine entrances. Judging from the throng crowded around it, I figured this was the one that had collapsed.

Halting about two nindan from the center mine's entrance, I climbed out of the tank and jumped to the ground. Eyes like saucers, the miners stared, slack-jawed. I looked for the Laerd but didn't see him. "The Laerd," I shouted. "The Laerd!"

At that moment, he came running out of the mine. "Great gods, what are you doing?" he yelled. He stopped a few sīzu away and glared.

I glared back. "I'm here to help you."

"This is none of your business."

"I'm making it my business. Have you got that blast door open yet?"

He shook his head. "It's stuck good and tight." Then my plan must have dawned on him. His jaw dropped. "You mean to fire a round through the blast door? Are you crazy? What if there's more thalin gas behind it? You could blow up the entire mine!"

"Have you got a better idea?" I snapped. "If we don't do something, those miners are dead. Now are we going to do this thing or aren't we?"

"No, Moreva. It's too dangerous."

I pointed to the mine. "And you're willing to let those people die because there *might* be thalin gas behind the blast door? What if there isn't? How many more families do you want to visit today, Laerd?"

Instead of answering, he looked over his shoulder.

"Well?"

Turning, he gazed into my eyes for a full minute, then nodded. "We'll do it," he said, sounding tired. Looking around, he curled his hands around his mouth. "Ror," he shouted. A man standing about forty šīzu away jogged over to us. "Berätta för gruvarbetarna att de ska komma bort från dörren. Vi kommer att försöka spränga den." He looked at me. "I told him to get the miners away from the blast door. We're going to try and blow a hole through it."

Ror ran into the mine and was back out in less than a minute. At least fifty hakoi scurried after him. The large crowd clustered at its entrance scattered.

I climbed onto the tank, told the driver to choose the best vantage point for firing, and then climbed down. The Laerd and I watched the enormous vehicle float to the mine's cavernous entrance and settle into position. My hands clenched. Would this work? Or would I, as the Laerd had said, bring the entire mine down on top of the miner's heads?

The gunner fired.

Even outside, the roar from the big gun, followed almost immediately by the shell exploding, was deafening. My ears rang. But the mine was quiet. The thalin gas—if there had been any—had dissipated.

After the smoke had cleared, the Laerd and I ran into the mine with the crowd. The plasma round had carved a hole in the blast door big enough for the trapped miners to climb through. Cheers thundered as nineteen miners clambered through the breach. The twentieth had a broken leg. All were loaded on stretchers, then whisked away in ambulances to Mjor. I thought about Hyme. *I need to get back. I'm sure he can use my help.* I hurried to the entrance.

The driver guided the tank to where I stood and came to a rumbling halt. Grasping the handhold, I had set my foot on the step when a hand rested on my shoulder. I let go and turned. It was the Laerd, wearing that unreadable expression. "Moreva, you have my permission to take this tank and its personnel through Mjor," he said in a quiet voice.

"Thank you, Laerd."

"You are also under arrest for violating Protocol Article Nine. Muts will meet you at the gate and escort you to your tower, where you will stay until further notice. The other three will go to the barracks where they will be confined, also until further notice. I will notify Kepten Yose."

"Will they be allowed to attend services?"

He hesitated. "Yes."

"Thank you."

Neither of us spoke. "And I want to talk to you."

I nodded. "Figured you would."

He released me, and I climbed into the tank. On our way back, I explained to the soldiers what the Laerd had said. They didn't seem particularly worried. Then it dawned on me. *I ordered them to break the Protocol, so they'll probably just be transferred to other units. Me, they'll throw into prison.* I swallowed, hard.

We reached Mjor. As promised, Muts stood at the gates, blocking the entrance. The driver stopped, and I climbed out of the tank. Mut's piercing gaze was hard, his lips set into a line. It was as if our escapade, when he'd been so friendly, had never happened. I walked over to him. Only then did he move out of the way so the tank could proceed.

We walked in silence. Mjorans stared at us. Some pointed. Lots of excited babbling—about me, no doubt.

At my tower, the sound of the bioscan's lock disengaging seemed unnaturally loud. I started to push open the door, but Mut's meaty hand on my arm stopped me.

"Do...not...leave," he said in halting, heavily accented Devian. The Laerd must have told him what to say.

I nodded. He released me, and I walked inside. The door shut, its *thunk* sounding like a death sentence.

⊙⊒⊒⊒⊒⊙

"Are you telling me I should have let those poor miners die?"

The Laerd's jaw tightened. "Article Nine states—"

"Article Nine be damned! I couldn't just sit by and do nothing. I'm a healer. My job is to save lives, using whatever means at my disposal. And that's exactly what I did."

He threw up his hands. "There you go again, Moreva. Breaking rules whenever it suits you. Didn't you learn anything after that ura treed you? Or are you that thick-headed?" He gave me a hard stare. "The Protocol is there for a reason. It's our agreement with the Devi about your beacon and your military presence. Its rules are not made to be broken or even bent. I know you did what you thought was right—"

"No. What I did *was* right."

He said nothing for a moment. Then his eyes narrowed. "You really have no idea what you've done, do you? Moreva, did you *read* Article Nine?"

"Of course," I snapped. In truth, I'd only skimmed it, like I had the rest of the Protocol.

His eyes narrowed further. "All of it?"

I said nothing.

The Laerd tightened his lips. "I didn't think so." He took a deep breath. "When the landing beacon was built, the garrison was five times the size of this village." His tone was stern. "A small army. That was because tensions between the Syrenese and the Devi were still dangerously high. We—"

"Dangerously? Wh—"

"We insisted on Article Nine because we weren't taking any chances. Without the Laerd's permission, just one of your soldiers or vehicles inside Mjor's walls would have been taken as a hostile act. And our military had been camped right outside the rear gates, ready to defend us."

My eyes widened in shock.

"That's right, Moreva. By driving that tank through Mjor, you've declared war on the Syren Perritory."

I fell into the fireplace chair, speechless. My jaw worked. "I...I didn't mean..."

"I know you didn't. But you did, and it's up to the Council to decide what to do with you. Thank your Most Holy One it happened now, and not back then."

Staring through the window, I recalled that conversation. Two days ago, I'd testified before the Council about what I'd done, and since then, they'd been deliberating on my fate. If they found in my favor, I would be allowed to stay. If not, they'd either imprison me or demand my recall to Uruk. If imprisoned or recalled, Astoreth would have no choice but to comply. And if I was recalled to Uruk, I'd have to face Her. My fate would be in Her hands. She had several options. She might execute me. Or, She might strip me of my morevic status and throw me out on the street to fend for myself. Or, She might banish me to an É in one of Her lesser towns. Or, She might give me a reprimand. Or, She might do nothing at all.

The battlement door's bell sounded. My hearts beat faster. I ran to open it.

The Laerd stood behind the threshold, expressionless. "Moreva, I have news. May I come in?"

"Yes...yes, of course." I stepped back and pointed to one of the fireplace chairs. "Please, sit down." I perched on the edge of the other chair, hands folded in my lap.

He said nothing, just gave me that unreadable stare. Then he took a breath. "First, the Council thanks you for all your work in the hospital and in saving the lives of those twenty miners. Second, they voted to drop the Protocol Article Nine charge against you."

"And the other three?"

"They were acting under your order. Those charges were dropped, too."

I almost let out a sigh of relief. My heartsbeat returned to normal. "If I might ask, what was the vote to drop the charges?"

He didn't answer at first. "Five to four."

I bowed my head. I understood what that meant. Eight people served on the Council and if they deadlocked on whatever it was before them, the Laerd cast the deciding vote. In our case, he broke it by voting to have the charges dropped.

"Kea leboha, Laerd," I whispered.

"You're welcome. But do yourself a favor?"

"What?"

"Don't do it again."

"I can't promise that."

"If you do, I may not be able to help you next time."

"I understand."

He was silent a moment. "Then let's hope there won't be a next time."

I walked him to the door. Just before stepping out, he turned. "You are an amazing woman, Moreva Tehi." He left.

I shut the door and bolted it. With a sigh, I got ready for the evening service.

Heading for the dining hall the next morning, I took a deep breath and smiled at the air's springtime freshness. While confined, I'd opened the windows in my apartment, but it wasn't the same.

Walking inside, I was surprised to see the big room full since I was usually one of the first to arrive. Even the Council was here, and they were almost always the last. I pulled out my chair. "Good morning, Hyme. Isn't it a glorious day?"

Instead of answering, he stood and started clapping. Then the Laerd. Then the Council. In seconds, almost all the diners were on their feet, clapping, cheering, and whistling. Confused, I looked around the room. They were giving me a standing ovation, but for what?

In the next instant, I understood. It was because I'd saved the lives of those miners and had dared to break the Protocol to do it. I ducked my head, embarrassed.

After the clapping had died down, I stood behind my chair, pressed my palms, and gave a deep bow. "Kea leboha," I said, loud enough to be heard throughout the hall. I sat and turned to Hyme. "Thank you, but that really wasn't necessary."

He smiled. "Of course it was. It was a very brave thing you did, and the people recognize it. Several here testified on your behalf even though they weren't affected."

Breakfast was served and my food tasted as sweet as the smell of the springtime air. While leaving, Hyme lay a hand on my arm. "Coming to the lab? I've missed you."

"I would, but I need to get to the beacon's control room. I...I'm expecting a transmission. I'll come afterward."

He frowned and then his face relaxed. "Oh. Good luck, Tehi."

"Thanks. I'll need it."

On the walk to my tower, I didn't think about what Astoreth would have to say. I was pretty sure I knew. I pushed the door open and slowly climbed the stairs. In the control room, I pulled the chair up to the communications module. Swiveling back and forth, I wondered if anything I said would make a difference.

The module buzzed, and the green light blinked. I stared a moment, then held my hand over the panel. "Astoreth-69."

Astoreth's head floated before me. Her face held no expression. "You violated the Protocol. Explain yourself." She appeared and sounded calm. I knew better. My grandmother looked like and used that tone of voice only when She was enraged.

"Greetings, Most Holy One." Hoping my expression was just as neutral, I explained about the mine explosion, the trapped miners, and why I'd ordered Kepten Yose to give me a tank and crew. "It was the only way to get the blast door open, Most Holy One. Otherwise, those miners would have died."

Astoreth said nothing for a minute or two. "So you thought it fell upon you to save those hakoi. Moreva Tehi, you had no right to intervene."

"There were lives at stake, Most Holy One."

"Since when do you care about the lives of the hakoi?"

"I care about all life, Most Holy One."

Silence. She pursed Her lips. "You have changed, then."

I thought about my vision and medical promise but said nothing.

"What does the Council say?"

"They voted against my recall, Most Holy One."

More silence. "Very well. I will abide by their decision. But do not think this is over, Moreva Tehi. I will deal with you on your return." Her head disappeared.

I let out the breath I didn't know I'd been holding. She could have recalled me despite the Council's decision. And the last thing I wanted was to face Her wrath while it was still fresh. As for Her dealing with me when I got back, my tour had barely begun. Maybe by the time it ended Her anger would have cooled and my punishment wouldn't be too harsh.

I left the control room, trying not to think about what Astoreth might do with me when I got home.

Chapter Fifteen

I headed for the lab, still trying not to think about my grandmother.

"Moreva—wait!"

I turned. The Laerd trotted over to me and smiled.

I smiled back. "Yes, Laerd?"

"What are you doing today?"

"Right now, I'm going to the lab to check on a project and look in on the burn victims."

"What about after lunch? I mean, is there anything you need to do?"

I hesitated. Besides my stewardship duties, there was my dance and meditation session. But I was curious. "I just have to check the beacon. Why?"

"You've been invited to visit the mines. The miners want to thank you in person, and I accepted for you." He peered at me. "That was all right, wasn't it?"

"Oh...yes, of course."

His smile returned. "Good. Meet me outside your tower. I'll have a car waiting."

"See you then."

He strode off, and I continued on my way. Mjorans smiled and waved. I waved back. Going from a nonentity to a celebrity in a matter of days was a bit unsettling. I thought about the Laerd's friendliness. *He actually smiled at me in public.* Then I remembered his kindness when I'd given him my red fever report. *So maybe he isn't a dicknut? But then, it's not like I have to go. If he hadn't been so nice about it, I'd have told him to go fuck himself.*

I entered the lab, setting thoughts of the Laerd aside. Hyme looked up. Holding a conical flask with a pair of tongs, a wide grin split his face. "Tehi. How did your call go?"

"Our Most Holy One is abiding by the Council's decision. I'm staying."

His grin widened. "Splendid. Come. Let's celebrate with some tea." Hyme set the flask on a nearby ring stand and took off his lab coat.

"But," I held up a finger, "I'm not out of trouble. Astoreth said she'd punish me after my tour is over."

"Oh, that's not for fourteen or so arhu yet. Maybe Her anger will have cooled and your punishment won't be too bad."

"That's what I'm hoping."

Inside his apartment, I took a seat on the couch facing the fireplace and listened to his bustling in the kitchen. He emerged a few minutes later with two mugs of tea, handed me one, and then took his seat. He raised his mug. "To your staying in Mjor."

"To my staying in Mjor."

I set the mug on my lap. "How are our patients coming along?"

"Fine. I've put your boy—his name is Jarl, by the way—in the hyperbaric chamber, and his burns are healing nicely. It looks like there'll be very little scarring." His brows rose. "Are you sure you hadn't had experience with burn victims? You did a marvelous job."

"No. Really, I hadn't. I just did the best I could." I sipped my tea. "Is he talking yet?"

"Oh my, yes. He can't thank you enough for saving his life, especially after what he'd done."

"Throwing rocks and destroying lab equipment are hardly reasons for the death penalty."

Hyme looked over the rim of his mug. "He doesn't see it that way. He's been asking to see you. Do you mind?"

"Of course not."

"Good. Let's finish up and go to the hospital."

After drinking our tea, we headed downstairs. Walking into the patients' room, Jarl spotted me and grinned. "God morgon."

"Means good morning," Hyme whispered.

I smiled. "May the Most Holy One turn Her face to you."

Hyme translated, and the young man's grin broadened. He held out a mottled hand. I hesitated for a split-second, then took it.

"Jag är ledsen för att jag kastade de där stenent på dig och förstörde ditt lab."

"He's sorry for throwing that rock at you and destroying your lab."

I dipped my head. "Thank you. Everything turned out all right."

After Hyme had translated, I noticed Jarl's lids drooping. "Time to go," Hyme said. I gave Jarl's hand a minute squeeze, and we left the hospital.

In the lab, I made observations on the second small project I'd brought with me. I was trying to find an alternate cure for corolis, a bacterial infection. My idea was to develop something that worked faster than the standard cure. So far, I hadn't any luck. Studying the three-dimensional pictures of the hairless skratz's gut, it was time to try out my new and hopefully, miracle drug. Injecting the little beast, I'd be able to tell if it was working in a few days.

Now I needed to see about my plants. Picking up the remote, I watched the habitat's cover roll up, and began pacing its perimeter. *Astoreth. Look how much bigger they are, and in just two days! I might be able to start harvesting next marun.*

"Tehi, it's time for lunch," Hyme called.

"All right." I re-covered the habitat and stepped out of the closet. "Ready."

Crossing the plaza, he turned. "After lunch, do you want to—"

"The Laerd is taking me to the mine. Said the miners want to thank me in person."

"That'll be a nice outing for the two of you."

"Depends on how he behaves."

After monitoring the beacon, I stepped out of my tower and saw the car the Laerd had promised. Four-wheeled, it was long and low with two doors and no top. It looked almost like an air car. He opened the passenger door. I slid onto the seat, and then he got in on the driver's side.

I raised my brow. "I hope it doesn't rain."

"Not in the forecast, else I would have requested something with a roof."

"Requested?"

"Yes. Mjor has a pool of cars we can use for a fee." He gave me a sideways look. "How did you think Hyme gets around on his tours?"

I curled my lip. "How was I supposed to know?"

He chuckled. "Point taken." We pulled off.

Clearing the rear gates, the Laerd picked up speed. I closed my eyes and tipped my head back, enjoying the wind blowing in my face and whipping through my hair.

"You look peaceful," the Laerd rumbled.

I opened my eyes. He stared through the windshield and shot glances my way, a small smile playing about his lips. His long hair, usually tied with a thong, was loose and waving in the wind like a shiny, golden flag.

"I've never ridden in a car like this. One with no roof. I feel so free."

"Don't they have these where you come from?"

"No. The suns would roast you alive, especially in summer."

In less than two hours, we arrived at the mine. He pulled the car into an empty lot and shut down the engine. I stepped out. Swiveling my head, my perspective was different than the one in the tank. From this angle, I could see more of the untouched mountain. If I'd been standing at its far side, I wouldn't be able to see the mine works at all.

The Laerd tugged my sleeve. "Come on. There's the mine administrator."

A tall, broad, woman with frizzy red hair walked toward us. We met her about halfway between the parking lot and the nearest mine.

"God eftermiddag, Laerd."

"God eftermiddag, Piri. Detta är Moreva Tehi. Moreva, Piri Nyag."

Piri pressed her palms and gave a deep bow. "May the Most Holy One turn Her face to you," she said in unaccented Devian.

Astonished, my eyes popped for a second. I recovered in the next, hoping she hadn't seen it. I returned her bow. "And to you, Piri Nyag."

She grinned. "Surprised? Don't be. I deal with the Devi's hakoi buyers when they come shopping. Come on. My people are anxious to meet you."

My brows raised a fraction. *Hakoi buyers? Shopping?* That was news. The only hakoi I knew were farmworkers and menials. They weren't nearly smart enough to go around buying thalin. *The Devi have a spawning and breeding program for this kind of work? Where do they keep them? I've been all over Kherah, and I've never seen* any *of them.*

Piri and the Laerd started toward the mine closest to us. I followed, grateful they'd shortened their long strides to match mine. The two talked about the mines' condition, especially the one lost to the blast, how it would affect output, and whether it could be reopened. They went over administrative matters, too. They spoke Devian out of courtesy to me, but their conversation was boring. I tuned them out.

We were about thirty šīzu from the center mine's entrance when someone shouted, "Där är hon!"

A sea of miners surged forward. In seconds, we were engulfed. I took a discreet look around. I might be short, but I am by no means small. Standing in the midst of these big, burly men and women made me feel tiny and a little bit scared. Being frightened by the hakoi was a new feeling for me.

Laughing and jabbering in Syrenese, the miners clapped me on the back, touched my uniform, my hair, and my face. I plastered on a grin, hoping I was fooling everyone about enjoying this. Then I was hoisted onto someone's broad shoulders and paraded through the throng. More hands clapped my thighs and knees. I flinched by reflex, but willed my body to keep still so I wouldn't fall off the miner carrying me. In my peripheral vision, I saw Piri and the Laerd at the edge of the crowd, laughing. I didn't think it was funny.

For a good twenty minutes, I was carried through the throng until it seemed every miner had at least a chance to see me. "Okej, sätt ner henne!" Piri's stentorian voice rang out. I heard her clearly even over the crowd's excited babbling.

The miner lowered me to the ground, and the horde broke apart. Finally, I had space to breathe. I peered ahead. Someone was pushing their way through. A moment later, a young hakoi man with strong, rugged features stood before me. With a shy smile, he held out a large piece of clear, unadorned rock, and gently placed it into my upturned hands. My breath caught. It was white thalin, rough-cut and highly polished. The refracted light produced a rainbow of colors. It was exquisite.

The young miner appeared nervous, as if expecting me to reject his homespun gift. I gave a deep bow. "Kea leboha. Mwen pral trezó li toujou. I shall treasure it always." A murmur swept through the crowd. Someone obviously spoke Devian because a deafening cheer went up. After it had died down, I heard Piri's booming voice again.

"Det räcker! Åter till arbetet!"

The miners erupted into good-natured grumbling and headed for the mine entrances. I assumed they were going back to work. After the crowd had thinned, I walked over to Piri and the Laerd and looked from one to the other. "That was...quite a welcome."

Piri smiled. "To me and my people, you're a hero." She turned to the Laerd. "I'd better get back to work, too. Devi Amash's buyers are coming tomorrow, and I have to be ready." She paused. "Are you going to take the Moreva into the mine?"

"If it's all right with you, yes."

"That's fine. You know where you can and can't go. " She looked at me. "Why don't you let me take that? I'll put it in my office, and you can pick it up before you leave."

I handed her the rock and smiled. "Thank you. That's very kind of you."

"Well, thalin *is* a bit heavy to carry around. And you can't exactly put this piece in your pocket." Piri gave us a nod. "Have a good tour." She strode toward a steep-roofed, single story building. Next to the mines, it looked like a toy.

I turned. "So...where to?"

"We're going to Mine Number One. It's active, so you can see how it works. And there's something in there I want to show you."

"Lead the way."

Our pace was leisurely as we chatted about village affairs and my work in the lab. "How are your plants coming along?"

"Nicely. Much bigger than they were two days ago. I might be able to start harvesting next marun." I paused. "I'm itching to get back to work on my project. I can't rush it, but if Kherah gets hit with the fever this summer, having the cure would save so many lives." My lips tightened. "Not to mention the suffering."

We arrived at the mine entrance. Bending over a large box, the Laerd picked out two yellow hats with what looked like a small light on the front. He handed me one. I rapped it a few times. The hat, whatever it was made of, was solid.

"Put it on. It'll protect your head from falling rocks."

My eyes went wide. "Falling rocks?"

He laughed. I realized it was one of the few times I'd heard him do that. I liked the way it sounded, a rumbling from deep inside his chest.

"Well, this *is* a mine. Sometimes blasting loosens the rock in the ceiling and pieces fall. Don't worry—we're not going anywhere near the blasting area. It's just a precaution, and a required one."

"All right." I put on the hat. It promptly slid sideways.

"Hm. Let's see if I can find a smaller one." The Laerd dug around in the box. "This one should be better."

I set it on my head. It was still too big, but at least it stayed put. "This works."

He nodded. "Ready?"

"Ready."

I climbed into a little cart and studied the mine's hewn walls. Something heavy *thunked* on the cart's cargo bed. Climbing in, the Laerd started it up. To my surprise, its motor was silent. *Battery-powered. Huh.*

Rolling deeper into the mine, the Laerd explained the mining process, from the initial blasting to the thalin's final preparation for market. He showed me where the pieces were separated from the rock and then according to color. "The different colors have different chemical compositions. Red is the most common, and that's the kind we use for fuel—heating, machinery, cars, and so on. It's also the most dangerous because flammable gas sometimes collects in pockets where the thalin is concentrated. They were working with red thalin when the mine blew up. The other colors—green, yellow, and blue—are used for industrial purposes, like hardening metals. White thalin—the piece the miners gave you—is the rarest of all. Like the rest, it's got industrial uses and is used for jewelry, too." He gave me a sideways look. "A piece the size of the one you were given is very valuable."

I cocked my head. "How come you know so much about mining?"

"I used to work here."

"Really? Who sentenced you?"

He smiled. "No one. I only sentence people to the mines when they raise hell, like that young man who—"

"Jarl."

"Oh, so you found out his name? Anyway, mining is hard, dangerous work. Juvenile antics have no place here, and the miners won't put up with it. I knew they'd straighten him out."

"Hyme told me as much. So why did you work here?"

"Because I liked it. There's something about hard work that gives you real satisfaction at the end of the day, like you've accomplished something meaningful."

"Why'd you quit?"

"Urla—my heartsbound—thought it was too risky. So I went to the farms." He snorted. "As if farming isn't as dangerous as mining."

I gave him a grim smile. "I know. I've done my share of reattaching body parts."

We were on our way back when he took a hard right into a tunnel that had it not been for the cart's headlights, I wouldn't have known was there. He drove about sixty šīzu, then stopped the cart and shut off the power. The lights went out, too. I had never seen such absolute darkness.

He switched on his hat's light. "Turn your light on."

"How?"

Instead of answering, he leaned over and did it for me. The bright beam lit up the immediate area. I could see the tunnel's rough walls, and a little ahead. As far as I could tell, the tunnel ran straight. Beyond the light's range, its inky blackness seemed to go on forever.

The Laerd hopped out of the cart, then helped me onto the smooth floor. I watched him lift a huge lantern from the cart's rear. *So that's what I heard.* He checked it over, then let out a soft grunt.

I eyed the lantern. "Where are we going?"

"One of the places we're not supposed to go."

"So it's not just me. You break rules, too."

He grinned. "Only when the chances of getting caught are low."

Taking my hand, we walked deeper into the tunnel. Electricity crackled through me, but the feeling was almost smothered by my curiosity. The tunnel reminded of some of the darker, forbidden reaches of the É where Eresh and I used to play as children. I peered at the wall. What looked like large doorways had been cut into it. If that's what they were, I didn't want to know where they led. We bypassed two, stopping at the third.

"Here we are." Giving my hand a little squeeze, he led me through. Tiny sparkles of red, blue, green, yellow, and white flashed in my hat's light. "Where are we?"

"You'll see." He turned on the lamp.

My jaw dropped. We were in an enormous room, with glittering pieces of thalin projecting from the walls and ceiling. Swiveling my head, I took in the sight. It was beautiful and dazzling, as if I'd entered into the heart of a multicolored jewel. "Astoreth. This is...incredible." I couldn't stop staring. "Do all the rooms look like this?"

"This is the only one."

"How'd you know it was here?"

"I was one of the crew who cut this part of the mine. Sometimes on my days off, I'd sneak in just to look at it."

"Will they mine it?"

"Eventually."

"What a shame. Can't they preserve this one room?"

"It doesn't work that way."

"Oh."

Leaving the big light behind, we walked deeper inside. I turned. The thalin colored the Laerd's bronze skin, making him look as if he was made of stained glass. He stepped forward. Staring through glinting, hooded eyes, his look was feral. I tried to step back, but my body wouldn't move. Then he swept me into his strong arms and kissed me hard, knocking my hat to the floor.

My brain short-circuited. Time stopped. I knew nothing but the feel of his soft lips locked on mine, his dancing, probing tongue, and his musky scent. His body heat scorched me, even through my uniform. Throwing my arms around his neck, I wrapped my legs around his waist and pulled him closer, drinking in his kiss like a thirst-crazed woman parched from the desert suns.

He pulled away, then set me down. I stood mute and blinking until my brain jump-started itself. We stared at each other, wide-eyed, for a good minute. Then he cleared his throat. "Come on. We'd better go before someone comes looking for us."

He picked up my hat and set it on my head. Miraculously, the lamp hadn't broken. The Laerd switched off the big lantern. Except for our head lamps, the room was plunged into darkness again.

He took my hand as we left the room. My brain threatened to short out again, but I held it together. We walked to the cart in silence. I climbed into the passenger seat while he stowed the lamp in the back. Then he got in and fired up the cart, its headlights illuminating the black rock surrounding us. Leaning over, he switched off my hat's lamp, then did the same to his. He turned the cart, and we were on our way.

We'd almost reached the main track when he killed the motor. "Someone's coming," he whispered. I listened and heard a low-pitched whine. I realized I'd heard it for some time but hadn't understood what it was. In the darkness, we watched a larger cart trundle past. Its whine grew fainter. When it had completely died away, he started the cart again and pulled off. In a moment, we turned right onto the well-lit main track. Minutes later, were back where we'd started. Easing the cart into a slot with the others, I got out while he returned the lantern to the storage room.We walked to the administration building to pick up my thalin piece from Piri's office. Thankfully, she wasn't in. The Laerd scribbled a note while I cradled my rock. Outside, he seemed to be in a hurry to get to the car. He didn't take those long strides that forced me to trot to keep up, but I had to walk fast. He opened the passenger side door, and I slid onto the seat. Then he climbed in on driver's side. He turned with an apologetic look. "Moreva—"

"Don't. But it can never happen again."

His expression settled into that neutral mask I'd grown to know so well. Without another word, he started the engine and we drove away.

We didn't speak. The wind blowing past my face, I thought about our kiss. *What happened back there?* It wasn't the first time I'd been kissed, but not even my first kiss had felt like that. This had felt like a lightning bolt. I thought about that morning on the ridge, the way his stare had mesmerized me. *And why do I feel those sparks whenever he touches me?*

Entering the village through the rear gates, the Laerd circled the plaza and stopped in front of my tower. Clutching my rock, I climbed out the car. Before he could drive away, I rested my hand on the door's sill. "Laerd."

He turned.

"Thank you for taking me to the mines today. I...enjoyed it."

His expression didn't change. "So did I, Moreva."

He pulled off. I watched the car circle back around the plaza and kept watching until it disappeared around the corner. *What's he thinking? I don't...* I shook my head. Confused by my feelings, I pushed open the door and stepped inside.

The Moreva of Astoreth

After tossing and turning for hours, I finally sat up and turned on the light. *Why can't I sleep?* I knew part of it was because of what had happened at the mine yesterday with the Laerd. But it wasn't just that. It was as if there was something important I'd left undone. Pondering for a few minutes, it dawned on me. *My dance and meditation ritual.* Aside from my mission, I'd long since learned it helped me to sleep, too.

I rolled out of bed, splashed my face, then hurried to the É. Dimming the lights, I chose my music. It was a long piece, so I didn't put it on loop. I touched the panel, and the sound of strings, woodwinds, and brass filled the air.

I started dancing and as always, it wasn't long before I lost myself. But this time was different. Instead of becoming the dance, I became the music, the spiraling notes from the woodwinds and brass, now soaring on the back of the strings...

And then I really am soaring. I look down. I'm flying over the familiar landscape, with its green rolling hills, stands of trees, and the river. It's just as beautiful as it was before, but I'm not here to admire the scenery. I look around. A black dot on the horizon is growing larger and larger by the second. Narrowing my eyes, I gird myself for the fight. *This time, I will rip its red heart out.*

I wheel, and with a mighty flap of my wings, speed toward my nemesis. Just when it looks like we'll collide, I fly up, flip, and land on its back. I start ripping out beakfuls of feathers from its neck. The black bird rolls over and over, but I'm able to hang on. Then it goes into a fast, tight roll. I'm thrown off.

Fluttering, I try to regain my balance. The black bird dives at me. I recover, fly up, and then veer to the left. The black bird flies past, nearly clipping me with a wing. It wheels to face me. Now it was exactly where I'd wanted it to be. Not realizing I was so close, the black bird startles when I dart forward and grab hold of its red jewel with my feet. It screams.

I give a fierce tug. The jewel doesn't budge. I haul on it.

Still nothing. The black bird stabs at me with its great beak. I bob my head this way and that, managing to avoid it. But I can't avoid its beak forever. I'm about to give up when I hear another scream, familiar, but different from the black bird's. My hearts leap. My friend, the big brown bird with the white spots, has arrived. In moments, the black bird's beak is no longer poking at my head. From its jerking and rolling this way and that, I know it's fighting the other bird.

I strain at the jewel. Finally, I feel movement. With a cry of triumph, I yank again.

A searing pain explodes at the back of my skull. I let go and tumble downward. I try to flap my wings but can't. I pick up speed. The ground comes closer and closer, faster and faster. Just when I think I'll crash, a brown and white-speckled blur crosses my sight. I settle onto a feathered back.

Hold on, little one. I am going to land.

I dig my feet into the brown bird's feathers. After a few hops, it comes to rest on the riverbank. Stretching one wing, I slide off its back and roll onto the grass. I lay still, my head throbbing.

A valiant try, little one.

But not good enough.

It is frightened. That is good enough for now. But it also means it will be even more dangerous when you face it again.

So what do I do next?

What you are doing.

I—

You will know when you are ready. My friend spreads its wings and shoots skyward.

Wait! Wai—

Waking, I lay on my side, just as in my vision. The seero had turned itself off. Head pounding, I tried to sit up but could barely move. I waited. A few minutes later, I managed to drag myself to my feet. Dizzy and swaying, I shuffled to the entrance but when I bent to pick up my slippers, I almost fell over. I slapped my hand against the wall for support.

Pawing at my shoes, I managed to get hold of them. I climbed the stairs, holding onto the wall. It seemed to take forever to get to the top.

Inside my apartment, I shuffled to my uniform draped over the chair and touched the bar. "Time," I croaked.

"Sixth hour, thirty minutes Ekban."

Good. Five hours until the morning service. I should be all right by then. I set the alarm for three-thirty Gor and dropped my shoes. I frowned. There was something on the back of my neck. I probed under my hair, and my fingers came away wet. Peering, my eyes widened.

It was blood.

I shambled to my healer's kit and pulled out a bottle of bactericide and a soft cloth. Folding it, I soaked and then pressed the saturated cloth to my neck, wincing at its sting. A minute later, I dropped the cloth into the trash. Reaching into my bag, I took out my roll of nuskin, tore off a small piece, and bandaged my wound. By the time I had to get up, it should be just a scab, if that. If not, I'd slap on another piece of nuskin, and my hair would cover every trace of it.

Stumbling to the bed, I crawled under the furs, then turned out the light. I thought I'd fall asleep right away but didn't. My bird friend's advice echoed through my mind. *Keep doing what I'm doing.* I blinked at the ceiling. *I don't know...it just feels like I should be doing more. But what?*

Sighing, I let it go. My head hurt too much. *I should get a headache pill. Except I don't want to move.* I tried a sleep trick, and it worked.

But my dreams were anything but pain-free.

Chapter Sixteen

Head still pounding, I dragged myself out of bed. The last thing I wanted was to give the service but I hadn't a choice. Digging in my healer's kit, I found my headache pills and swallowed two of them dry. After showering, I felt my neck for the bandage, peeled it off, and ran my fingers over the spot where the black bird had stabbed me. Not even a scab. My headache was gone, too.

Dressing in my garb—black today, with gold body glitter—I threw on my cloak and left the apartment. If nothing else, I needed to robo-mop the É's floor. I didn't think I'd gotten blood on it, but then I didn't know how long I'd been unconscious. There could be a spot or two.

I set up the altar and purified the air while the robo-mop did its work. Kneeling before the altar, it wasn't long before I heard the twenty on the stairs and the sound of several quiet voices. When they had settled into place, I began the service. I spoke like a somnambulist, intoning the words I knew by hearts. A tiny sigh of relief escaped me when it was over. If anyone had noticed my lackluster performance, they were kind enough not to say so. After the penitents had left, I cleaned and purified the É again, then trudged back to my apartment.

I started shucking my garb before I'd taken a second step. Slippers, shoes, thigh stockings, corset—a trail of clothes leading to the bed. I fell onto the furs, my face in the pillows. But I couldn't stay like that, not if I wanted breakfast. I thought about skipping it to sleep. *If I do, I'll feel even worse by lunchtime.*

Resolving to nap after nourishment, I got up, noticing I'd decorated the fur with specks of glitter. *Oh, well. I'll just brush it out later.* After showering a second time, I peered into the mirror. My skin was clear, smooth, and supple. *A little cream won't hurt.* Scooping a glob from the jar, I rubbed it in. *Better*. Plastering on my makeup, I dressed, and then tapped the bar. "Time."

"Fifth hour, fifty minutes Gor."

I stepped outside my tower. The tension in the air hit me like a wall. *What in Astoreth's name?* I frowned and started walking. Nothing seemed amiss. There were villagers who, like me, were headed to the hall. Others plied the sidewalks. The hairs on the back of my neck were standing straight up. They were watching me. Whenever I made eye contact with someone, they quickly looked away. It was odd, but I wasn't going to let it bother me. I strode along as if everything was normal.

There was tension in the dining room, too. I noticed the Laerd deep in conversation with Rausch, a council member. I took my seat. "Good morning, Hyme. What's going on?"

He gave me a confused look. "Good morning. I believe we're about to eat breakfast."

"That's not what I meant. Don't you feel it?"

"Feel what?"

"The tension. It's like the whole village is waiting for something to happen."

He smiled. "I don't feel anything like that. Your imagination, maybe?" He squinted. "You didn't sleep well last night."

"You're right."

"I hope you're planning to nap this morning."

I shook my head. "I was going to, but I need to check my corolis patient. See if my cure is working. I'll take a nap after lunch." I sighed. "I hope I'm not so tired I can't sleep."

"I have a little something for that."

I chuckled. Hyme had "a little something" for everything.

Outside, the sense of nervous excitement seemed to have escalated. "Hyme, are you sure there's nothing going on?"

"I'm sure."

That told me the matter was closed. I gave a little shrug. *All right.*

We entered the lab. I headed for the skratz cage and peered inside. *Hm. Color's better, but it's still too slow.* Plopping into my chair, I picked up my tablet and started calculating a new formula.

As it turned out, I didn't take a nap after midday. Between my own work and helping Hyme with his, I was busy until dinnertime. Walking out of the dining hall, he gave me a little vial. "Drink this before going to bed. It'll help you relax."

"Thanks, Hyme."

"Don't mention it."

The service seemed to take forever. After it was over, I felt so tired I thought I'd pass out. "Might not need Hyme's concoction after all," I muttered while trudging to my apartment. I started stripping my garb as soon as I walked in the door.

Ready for bed, I set Hyme's sleep aid on the nightstand. *I'll drink it later if I have to.* Then I decided to open the shutters. It would stay warmer if left closed, but it was cloudy out, so I didn't have to worry about the moons' light keeping me awake. And the furs would keep me plenty warm enough. I opened all of them.

Yawning, I crawled into bed and in moments, fell into blissful oblivion.

⊙⊒⊒⊒⊒⊙

The sound of drumbeats woke me. I struggled to open my eyes, but my lids were like weights. I gave up. *I'm dreaming, anyway.* I rolled onto my side and pulled the furs over my head. But the drumming didn't stop. Managing to pry my eyes open, I sat up and listened. *That rhythm...I've never heard anything like it. What's going on?*

Turning on the light to its lowest setting, I scooted out of bed and opened the window overlooking the plaza. The drums were much louder now. Leaning out, the glow of what had to be a terrific bonfire silhouetted the village's rear wall.

This bore investigation. I dressed, closed up my room, and left.

I opened the tower door a crack and peeked outside. No one was around, so I ventured out. *Some kind of party and they didn't invite me?* If so, I wasn't surprised. I'd done a good deed, but that didn't mean they'd taken me into their hearts. I tugged on one of the rear gate's huge stone doors, pulling it just wide enough for me to slip through.

My jaw dropped. *What in Astoreth's name?* Only three or so nindan from the road, it seemed the entire village was out here, ringed around a good-sized shallow pit. The Laerd, shirtless with eyes closed and arms outstretched, stood on a raised platform. The bonfire raging behind him made the scene surreal.

I moved forward, careful not to make any noise. My steps shortened as I came closer. By now I could make out individual faces. A few I recognized. From what I could see, all seemed to be lost in some sort of rapture. The bonfire's heat, the beating drums, made me dizzy. I reached the edge of the pit and looked down.

What I saw made me sick. My dizziness disappeared, replaced by a deep, burning rage.

At the bottom of a pit, an unconscious woman lay stretched on her stomach. Large pillows supported her hips and neck. Naked from the waist down, at least thirty men were in the pit with her. They were taking turns.

"Stop," I screamed. I jumped into the pit and started dragging the men away. "Stop it! Leave her alone! Voi bastardi, leave her alone!"

"Få Morevan härifrån!" the Laerd thundered, heard even over the bonfire's roar.

Someone grabbed my arms, then pinned them behind my back. Someone else clapped a hand over my eyes. A third yanked my feet from under me. They hauled me out of the pit. I fought, my screaming competing with the bonfire's roar. I zapped the one whose hand covered my eyes. A yelp, and the hand was gone. I twisted my neck to zap the next one. A gag stuffed into my mouth, a bag thrown over my head, and then a net thrown over me. I was hauled away, still trying to fight.

Without warning, the one holding my feet dropped me. Something clicked. I went airborne, landing hard on the floor. The door slammed. Another click. I frowned. In a second, I understood. That old lock below the bioscan—the one Eresh told me didn't have a key—did in fact have a key, and I'd just been locked inside my tower.

I untangled myself from the net, snatched the bag off my head, and then the gag from my mouth. Jumping to my feet, I banged on the door. "Oi! Let me out of here!" I ran to the barrack's door and pounded it, though I knew no one would hear through the thick rock. Then I had an idea. I took the steps two at a time to my apartment, yanked open the battlement door, and ran to the Laerd's apartment. I grabbed the door handle and threw myself against the door.

Locked. But then, why wouldn't it be?

I plodded back to my room and started pacing. What had been going on? The sex was obvious, but for what? Did it have some sort of higher meaning, or was it just a night out with the boys?

I was about to go back to bed when the battlement door slammed against the wall. I whirled. The Laerd, face contorted with rage, stood behind the threshold. "How dare you interfere with our ritual? You had no right," he roared. He stormed inside and banged the door shut.

"Ritual?" I shouted. "You call that a ritual? What in Astoreth's name kind of ritual was *that?*"

"She asked—"

"Don't tell me she asked for it. There isn't a woman in the world who'd *ask* to be gang-raped by thirty men!"

"You don't understand—"

"Oh, I understand. You people are barbarians!"

His eyes narrowed. "You have a lot of nerve, Moreva," he said through his teeth. "Eresh told me about this Ohra-Sin ceremony of yours. Twenty at a time, eh? I'll bet you've fucked the entire garrison by now." He looked me up and down. "Religious rites my *ass*," he said, his voice rising. "Astoreth is nothing but a whore, and so are you!"

I stared, slack-jawed. Then I jumped straight up and gave him a brutal slap. His head whipped to the side. "Blasphemy!"

Before my feet hit the floor, a stinging pain across my cheek came sailing out of nowhere and the next thing I knew, I was tumbling head over heels on the bed.

"How—who the hell do you think you are?" he shouted.

My mind clouded with red rage. Call me a whore? Hit me? For that, I'd teach this hakoi a lesson he'd never forget.

I launched myself from the bed, zapping him at the same time.

"Skit," he yelled, face twisted in agony. Recovering, he clenched his jaw and plucked me out of the air in mid-flight. Slamming me against his chest, my arms were pinned. But I wasn't helpless. I stiffened the fingers on each hand, twisted my wrists, and gave him two hard jabs.

He gasped, then dropped me. I executed a back flip, giving his knees a savage kick in the process. Landing feet-first on the bed, I watched him go down, his mouth a rictus and eyes squeezed shut.

They popped open. His stare was colder than I'd ever seen it. He leapt. I shifted to move out of the way, but my foot caught in the blanket. I glanced down. I shouldn't have.

The Laerd plowed into me. For a moment I went airborne, and then fell hard with him on top.

My breath whooshed out. In a lightning move, he jerked my arms over my head. I twisted this way and that, trying to find leverage, but couldn't.

"Stop, Moreva. You can't fight me anymore," he growled. "You're caught, and you know it. You'll stay caught until I decide to let you go, and don't you *dare* do what you did to me again!"

I stopped fighting because he was right. I was about to zap him when his star-colored glare turned from ice-cold fury to confusion, to wonder, and then to raw, blazing desire. "Tehi," he whispered.

My eyes widened. For the first time, I understood what it meant to want someone, someone to quench a burning, terrible thirst I didn't know I had. I wanted this hakoi man and no other. My lips parted.

"Tehi," he whispered again.

"Yes," I whispered back. He stared for another second and then struck, delivering a bruising kiss.

My body responded, and my juices flowed. He let me go and in an instant our clothes were gone. We rolled on my bed, clawing at each other. I raked my nails across his back and felt wetness. Holding tight enough to bruise me, he chewed at my breast. Giving a hard shove, I threw him off and bit into his shoulder, tasting blood. We were fighting again, the bed our battleground.

He bulled his way into me, stretching me wider than ever before. It hurt, but I found pleasure in my pain, and was soon swept away. He dug into me, shoveling, and then pounding me like a belye mouton. Tears poured down my face. I didn't want him to stop. Ever.

After what seemed like hours of frenzied lovemaking, we rolled off each other, gasping and utterly spent. I lay on my back, blissfully unaware of anything but the electric shocks radiating through me.

Then I came to my senses.

I bolted upright. *My vow...Astoreth, what have I done?*

I panicked. "Laerd," I said, panting, "you have to leave. Leave me, please. Now."

He looked confused. "Wh-what?"

"Please. Just leave me."

I squeezed my eyes shut. When I opened them, the deep hurt etched on his face was heartbreaking.

He shook his head. "If you say so."

"I say so. Please."

He gathered his clothes. I closed my eyes again. A minute later, the door opened, then shut. Rolling onto my side, I curled into a ball and cried until I had no more tears.

⦿⊐⊒⊒⊏⦿

Later that morning, I stood before the window in my apartment, hands clasped behind my back. Staring through the glass, I didn't see the brilliant spring sunsshine, or the birds flitting about. I didn't see the trees, now almost in full leaf. I didn't notice the smell of smoke from the long burnt-out bonfire. The only thing that registered was my soreness, a constant reminder of what I had done.

The battlement door's bell chimed. "Tehi," a familiar, rumbling voice said over the loudspeaker.

I said nothing, nor did I move. A few minutes passed. The door opened. I didn't turn around. Then it shut, its soft thump sounding loud in the apartment's quiet.

Footsteps on the rug, and then I felt the Laerd's gaze boring into my back. My lips tightened, then relaxed. "Have you come to gloat because I broke my sacred vow to Astoreth?"

He didn't answer at first. "No. I came to apologize. For what I said."

I nodded.

The silence lengthened. "I'm not sorry for what happened last night."

"Neither am I," I whispered. Then, louder, "Astoreth help me, neither am I."

Two more steps behind my back. "Tehi, I love you. I've always loved you. And you've broken a second vow. You love me, too."

"What makes you say that?"

"Your body told me everything I needed to know."

I bowed my head. He was right. Even now, I yearned for him to hold me, kiss me, and make love to me. I turned, my eyes filled with tears. "I...I know it's what you want—what I want—but it can't be, Laerd. I told you that day on the ridge. I was born into the É's service. Everything about me—my body, my soul—is pledged to Astoreth. She and the É own me. What I gave you last night was not mine to give."

Crossing the rug until he stood only inches away, he rested his hands on my shoulders. "I don't care about your É, Tehi. Out there," he jerked his head at the window, "you'll be whatever you have to be. But inside these rooms, you are mine. And I am yours. You said you were lonely. With me, you'll never be lonely again."

I squeezed my eyes shut, and then opened them. Two tears, one from each eye, tracked down my cheeks. "Laerd, no."

"I won't take no for an answer."

Now my tears came in full. "Please. Don't make this any harder than it already is."

He rubbed my shoulders. "I'm not making it hard, Tehi. You are. Give in to me, Tehi. Just give in."

"I...I can't."

Giving my shoulders one last squeeze, he dropped his hands and nodded. "All right." He walked to the door.

I couldn't believe he was being so calm about this. "Laerd, wait—"

"Do you know anything about hunting?" he said without turning around.

I blinked, confused. "N-no."

Now he did turn. "Hunting is more than just learning how to aim and shoot. The most important lesson is patience. The more patience you have, the more likely it is you'll come home with dinner." His star-colored gaze was piercing. "I'm a patient man, Tehi. I'll wait for you. For however long it takes."

"You sound awfully sure of yourself."

He gave me a small smile. "I've never been so sure of anything in my life." Opening the door, he stepped through and was gone.

❧

"Tehi. Tehi. Tehi!" Hyme snapped.

I jumped in my chair where I'd been playing with a hairless skratz. "Oh! I'm sorry. Something I can get for you?"

He sighed, clearly exasperated. "I asked you for canus powder. You gave me praeslip. If I'd mixed that in, these pills could have killed someone or at least have made them very sick. This is an apothecary, Tehi. We can't afford to make mistakes."

I hung my head and then looked up. "I'm sorry. I won't do it again."

Setting the jar of powder on the counter, he walked over to me and rested a hand on my shoulder. "What's wrong? You've been moping for five days. You've hardly eaten, and you haven't worked on your project. All you've done is check your beacon, give your services, and play with your skratz."

I said nothing for a long while, just kept scratching my little skratz between its ears. "Hyme, what was that night about?" I said without looking up.

"What night?"

"The night of that...that..."

"Oh. That night." He took a breath. "It's an ancient funerary rite. Back when our people were truly communal, when someone died, it wasn't unusual for a favored woman or man to choose to die along with them. The sex is a way for the one who chose to die to take a piece of their friends with them, so both will have company in the afterlife. And Vors Leften had a lot of friends."

I looked up. "Why did she want to die?"

His lips tightened. "Said Vors meant everything to her, and she couldn't go on without him. The Laerd and I—and several others—tried our level best to talk her out of it, but Aeryn insisted."

"Did she—"

"No, she didn't feel a thing. I shot her with enough kerrian to knock down a pirsu."

"What happened next?"

"I gave her a lethal injection. Then we dropped the bodies into the bonfire." He tilted his bald head. "But that's not what's bothering you, is it?"

I shook my head.

"Out with it."

I put the skratz back in its cage and returned to my chair. I didn't say anything at first. Then, in a rush of words, I told him everything that had happened between the Laerd and me that night, sparing no details. Well, a few details, but nothing he couldn't figure out for himself. I told him about breaking my vows to Astoreth and what it meant. "There's no repenting over this."

I told him about the Laerd's and my conversation the following morning. Falling silent, I stared at the floor.

The lab was quiet.

"Do you love him?" Hyme finally said.

"Yes." My voice was bleak.

"Then go to him."

I raised my head. "But what about my vows?"

"What difference does it make now? They've been broken. You can't take back what happened, Tehi. So you might as well follow your hearts."

⬡⬡⬡⬡⬡

For hours after the evening service, I paced my apartment, trying to figure out what to wear when I went to the Laerd. *I have to stop thinking of him that way. Teger. Not Laerd. Not dicknut.*

My vestments were out. I thought about wearing a uniform, but those clothes didn't belong to me, and I didn't want any reminders of the É. Not tonight. "Guess I'll go naked," I muttered.

My head snapped up. That was what I'd do. Teger had said that when in our rooms, we belonged to each other. He would have to take me as I was. Wiping off my sacred makeup, I stepped into the shower and scrubbed hard, determined to rinse away every vestige of the É. I sniffed. *Bonbon stick.* Pouring more soap, I vigorously rubbed it into my scalp and hair, then rinsed. I took another sniff. Nothing.

I raked a comb through my hair and checked myself in the mirror, not that there was much to check. Staring at my face, it hit me. *I'm not wearing makeup.* It felt odd, knowing someone outside the É would see me without it. I shrugged. *I'll get used to it.*

Standing before the door, I blew a heavy breath. I was ready, but I was also a bundle of nerves. I breathed in a slow, deep breath through my nostrils and let it out through my mouth. And again. And again. Calmer now, I stepped outside.

My skin prickled in the chilly night air, and the stones' cold seeped through my feet. Shivering, I wrapped my arms around me. I'd never crossed the battlement at night, and between the walls and the roof, it was pitch black. My pace slow, I hoped I was walking in a straight line.

Sensing I'd reached his door, I felt for the bell and pushed the button.

It opened at once. Without a word, Teger took my hand and gently

186

pulled me into his room. Holding me tight, we stayed like that for a long while, not speaking. Then he swept me off my feet, carried me to his bed, and laid me on the soft furs. I watched him undress. Then he crawled into bed. He smiled.

I smiled back.

We made love, not mad and untamed, but slow and sensuous, with just as much passion. We brought each other to the brink of climax again and again, only to pull back at the last minute and start over. When we were both whimpering in frustration, we let go. Our lovemaking ended with both of us reaching screaming orgasms. The noise we made didn't matter. No one would hear us through the tower's thick, impenetrable walls. We made love until completely spent.

We drew up the furs and cuddled. He stroked my hair. "You look better without all that makeup."

"I feel naked."

"You *are* naked."

I giggled.

We fell silent. "What took you so long?" he whispered after a long while.

"I had a lot to sort out."

"Did you talk to Hyme?"

"Yes." Anxiety shot through me. I struggled to get up. "Oh, no. I didn't think—"

He pulled me down and gave me a kiss. "Relax. Everybody talks to Hyme. He knows how to keep his own counsel."

I snuggled closer. "Good," I said, my voice muffled by the furs and his chest. Then I poked my head out. "I had a pet name for you."

"What's that?"

"Dicknut."

He roared with laughter. When it had subsided to chuckling, he gave me a little squeeze. "I deserved it. I *was* a dicknut to you."

Silence fell again, then I shifted to look into his face. "I've been wondering. You said you've always loved me. What's that about?"

His star-colored gaze turned serious. "I fell in love with you the minute you stepped off that airship."

"Then why—"

"What could I do? I couldn't just sweep you into my arms and declare my love. And I thought I was being unfaithful to Urla's memory. So I denied it. I guess that's why I was such a dicknut. But when the ura tried to kill you, and you came down from that tree and fell into my arms, I couldn't deny it anymore. I knew I loved you. I will always love you." He smiled. "And you?"

"The first time we made love. Though there were hints before that." I told him about how the ground had seemed to shift when he'd held me under the tree. "And that staticky feeling I get whenever I touch your bare skin...I didn't know what it meant."

"Are you getting that staticky feeling now?"

I kissed his chest. "Oh, yes."

We snuggled under the furs, basking in each other's warmth. My body hummed.

He stirred. "One more thing."

"What?"

"Remind me never to tangle with you again. My sides where you jabbed me still hurt."

"Then don't pettula mi."

He snorted. "Believe me. I won't." A moment later, he said the last words I wanted to hear. "What time do you have to get up?"

I let out a small sigh. "Um, two Gor."

"You sure? It's six Ekban now. You won't get much sleep. And you'll be taking an awfully cold shower."

"Then make it three. The water should have heated up by then, and I can always nap after breakfast."

I could almost feel his smile. "Need some company?"

"That'd be nice."

"Wish I could. But after breakfast I have to go to the fields and inspect the spring planting, talk to the farmers about what's needed."

Without warning, he pulled me on top of him.

We made love one last time for the night, and for the first time, slept in each other's arms.

Chapter Seventeen

The third sun rose. Summer was upon us.

The battlement proved perfect for Teger's and my nocturnal comings and goings. The high wall prevented anyone inside the village from seeing us, and its steep, sloping roof did the same for those outside the gates. By tacit agreement, we almost always slept in his apartment. He'd come to my room one night, hours after the service, to find me still dressed in my garb. I'd stood before the mirror, tears running down my cheeks. After helping me undress, he'd picked up my bottle of makeup remover and smeared a dollop over my face. Then, pointing me toward the bath, he'd given me a little push. After showering, he'd d taken me by the hand, and we left my room.

Inside his apartment, he'd bolted the door and had then taken me into his arms. Trembling, tears had welled in my eyes. "Teger, I feel like such a fraud."

"Shh, shh, min älskling. No talk of the É in here."

I'd looked up and nodded. "What does min älskling mean?"

He'd smiled and stroked my still-damp hair. "My beloved." Then he'd kissed me, sweet and tender.

After that, we only slept in my apartment when I had to work late composing sermons. We never made love while there, and my dreams were troubled. I often woke to find him stroking and kissing my hair, murmuring soothing sounds to help me go back to sleep. Sometimes I couldn't, so he'd tell me stories about his people, full of drama, intrigue, and betrayal. Though they took place thousands upon thousands of years ago, he insisted they were true, handed down from generation to generation, word for word. I smiled but kept quiet. Everybody knew the Devi, ageless and immortal, created Peris, its flora and fauna, the morevs, and the hakoi twenty-five hundred years ago.

One night, in the middle of one of his stories, I started shaking. He stopped. "What's wrong, älskling?"

My teeth chattered. "It's just an anxiety attack. It'll be over soon."

"Do you get them often?"

"This is my first, but I know the signs."

He didn't say anything for a moment. "What are you anxious about?"

"Us. I'm worried about what will happen if we're found out. I mean, we both know— "

"Pretend I don't."

"Huh? Why?"

"Sometimes it's better to talk these things out. What will happen to you?"

"Astoreth will execute me for breaking my vows."

"Even though you're her granddaughter?"

"It doesn't matter. Serving and loving only Her are two most important vows a morev takes, and the punishment for breaking them is death."

We fell silent. "What will happen to you?"

"I'd be branded a traitor. Which means I'd either swing from the battlement or be dropped into the mine."

I untangled myself from him and rose onto one elbow. "A traitor? Why?"

"Our hatred for the Devi runs deep. It might have happened long ago, but the atrocities committed against my people have never been forgotten." He paused. "Or forgiven." I said nothing. *That spawning and breeding experiment...what in Astoreth's name* happened?

Neither of us spoke for a long while. "Feel better, now?"

I let out a little snort. "Not really. But I should try to sleep." I lay down and snuggled against him. He was asleep in minutes. I listened to his soft snoring. Eventually, I slept, too.

⊙⧥⧥⧥⧥⊙

The following morning, I stood over a flask half-full of jinyan solution and cooli leaves, watching the liquid come to a boil. Jinyan was a powder that, when mixed with water, broke down all organic and inorganic contaminants, resulting in ultra-pure water that wasn't exactly fit to drink, but its use would have no effect on experimentation of whatever kind. It didn't take much jinyan to purify a bottle of water but having to use it for every experiment meant supplies dwindled fast. I'd ordered enough to last for at least four or five arhu to be delivered on the next garrison supply run. I'd ordered more hairless skratzes, too.

I'd begun harvesting my plants a couple of days ago and was now preparing reductions for a new red fever serum. I'd already made reductions from reddic root, calmyra, gilti, and kaklin. Cooli was the last.

I picked up the flask with a pair of tongs and set it on the heat-proof pad next to the burner. Back home, not only could I have made the five reductions at once, I wouldn't have had to touch anything until the serum had been formulated and tubed. We'd been taught how to make what we needed the primitive way in the event—however unlikely—there was a power failure in the É, or we didn't have access to the needed equipment. Like now. The Devi didn't make all-in-ones small enough to fit into a trunk.

Never mind. Astoreth, I'm just glad to be working *on this again. Between the vandalism and having to wait for my plants, it's been over an arhu. And summer won't wait.*

After the cooli reduction cooled, I strained it with finer and finer meshes until it ran clear blue. The liquid still held tiny particles, but this was the best I could do. I'd never worked without an all-in-one before. I hoped it wouldn't matter.

I poured a measure of the five reductions into a small tube, gave it a vigorous shake, then held it to the light and inspected it. Orange and blue globules floated in the mixture. I shook the tube and again held it to the light. This time the liquid was a uniform brown.

Dropping my new serum into a metal rack, I stepped over to the supply chest at the far end of my table, pulled out a pair of abra gloves, and drew them on. The abra would keep impurities on my hands from contaminating the experiment. I snatched three disinfectant towels from the holder, then retrieved a small, clear rectangular box from the chest. I wiped the inside down with one of the cloths and threw it in the trash. Opening a different drawer, I took out two disposable syringes, and with the box, stepped back to the rack. Wiping down the syringes and the serum tube, I lay one syringe in the box, and filled the other with serum. The empty one was for the virus.

I turned to the cage and coaxed a hairless skratz into my palm. Setting the little beast on my head, I winced as its claws dug into my scalp. Box in hand, I went to the deep freeze and picked out a virus-filled tube.

Now I had to get my experiment up and running before the virus came out of dormancy. It was unlikely, considering the vial would be in the open air for only a few minutes if that, but I couldn't take any chances. Inside the closet, I opened the environment's airtight chute, then shoved the skratz and the two syringes inside. I fit the vial into its slot. Slipping my hands into the six-fingered manipulators, I extracted a minute amount of the virus with a syringe and injected the skratz. When finished, I threw the syringe into an acid vat, watching it dissolve until there was nothing left. I re-capped the vial, scurried to the freezer, and replaced it in its box.

Now I had to wait two hours for the virus to manifest. I filled some of the time by cleaning up from my experiment, writing up lab notes, and re-reading earlier lab notes. Finishing, I swiveled in my chair, thinking about which plants to try next if this serum didn't work.

Then it dawned on me that Hyme hadn't come back to the lab. While I'd been making my reductions, he'd said he was going to his apartment to do some research. That had been almost three hours ago.

I'd started to get up when he walked through the apartment door, yawning. I laughed. "Some research."

He chuckled, looking sheepish. "I started, anyway. The next thing I knew I was waking up."

"Must have been some really interesting stuff."

He chuckled again. "How's your experiment coming along?"

"Still waiting for the virus to show up. Shouldn't be too much longer, though."

The bar on my uniform beeped. "There it goes. I'll be right back." In the closet, I peered through the clear, lysite chamber. The skratz had turned bright red and round, whitish pustules peppered its body. I slipped my hands in the manipulators and gave the little beast a shot of serum. Pursing my lips, I stared at it for a few seconds. *Astoreth, let this one live.* I let out a light snort. I could pray all I wanted, but this was science.

I walked out of the closet. "All done."

"Good. It's almost lunchtime. We should go."

Walking across the plaza, I lifted my face to the sky and took a deep breath. The rays from the three suns caressed my skin. I was working on my project again, and I was in love. Contentment wrapped me in its warm embrace. "Isn't a beautiful day? I can smell the forest and the loam from the fields."

Hyme gave me a sideways look. "And the livestock too, I imagine."

I laughed. "That, too."

Mjorans on the plaza greeted us with nods and smiles. "Hyme, is it my imagination, or do people seem happier?"

"I've noticed it too, over the years. It's the weather, I think. Winter can get wearing in the mountains. It's cold, usually cloudy, and the days are short. I don't have proof, but I think it has to do with the hours of light we get. Now that the days are longer and there are fewer cloudy days, we get the light we need to lift our spirits."

Inside the dining hall, his thoughts seemed to bear him out. It was noisy, full of chatter and laughter. The atmosphere had been much more subdued this past spring. Lunch was served and I dug in with gusto. I finished my plate before Hyme had eaten half of his.

"You have an appetite today, Tehi."

"Guess it's all that lecturing you gave me about these northern plants after breakfast. I'm especially interested in terbone grass. That sercin sounds promising."

"My, I haven't had terbone grass in years. Too high up the mountain for these old bones."

"Oh, you're not that old."

He smiled. "Tell you what. Why don't we get the Laerd to take you up the mountain? I'll say it's for us, but then I'll have a last-minute emergency and won't be able to go. That way you two can spend some time together."

"You're devious. Thank you." In my peripheral vision, I noticed a man standing nearby, smirking and staring at me with hate-filled eyes. I dismissed him. I got the same looks from other Mjorans. By now I was used to it.

After lunch, we cornered Teger as he was leaving. "Laerd, the Moreva and I would like to harvest terbone grass tomorrow or the next day, at your convenience."

He never glanced my way. "Day after tomorrow's good. What time?"

Switching to Syrenese, the two men hammered out the details of our trip as if I wasn't there. I gave Teger sharp looks, but I didn't mind being left out. It was an act to keep our illicit romance secret. In public, instead of snapping at or ignoring one another, we treated each other with cool, polite indifference, which we thought appropriate after the mine disaster.

"All right," Teger said, switching back to Devian. "We'll leave after breakfast. I'll have a car waiting."

At the appointed hour, I dug out two large and deep collection bags and a trowel from a closet while Hyme watched. "Try to get both the red and blue terbone grasses. We can explore the properties of each. And try to get the roots too, if you can. That's where the sercin is concentrated."

I stepped out of the lab and saw Teger waiting in the car. It was a different type than the one we'd taken to the mine. Instead of long and low, this one was boxy with large wheels and sat high off the ground. The only similarity was that it had no roof. I noticed his gun securely fastened in a rack on the back of the vehicle.

"Hyme not going?" His tone was chilly.

"Said he had an emergency," I said, my tone just as chilly. Stowing my bags in the back, I walked around to the passenger side and climbed inside.

He fired the engine and was about to put the car in gear when someone called out.

"Laerd, vänta!"

We turned to see Rausch running toward us. He caught up to us, panting. "Laerd, vart ska du? Vi skulle prata om —"

"Imorgon vid två Tryn, Rausch. Kommer du inte ihåg?"

Rausch furrowed his brow. "Åh. Ja." He peered at me. "Vart tar du henne?"

"Ingen med dig att göra."

"Men vad händer om —"

"Vi säger så här. Om något händer, du hanterar det. Om någon ger dig problem, berätta för dem att jag sa så."

Rausch stepped back from the car and stood a little taller. "Ska göras, Laerd."

Teger pulled off. In seconds, we were out of the village and on the road. I turned. "What was that about?"

He rolled his eyes. "Oh, we're supposed to talk about some crisis going on in his section, but he got his dates mixed up. We're supposed to talk tomorrow at two Tryn. Then he wanted to know where I was taking you, and I told him none of his business. I told him if anything happens while I'm gone, he should handle it and if anyone gives him a problem, to tell them I said so." He sighed. "Rausch means well. He wants to be Laerd but knows he can't beat anyone in a fight. Besides, he's a terrible administrator. His section is always in some sort of trouble. For some reason, the people keep electing him." His lips tightened. "If something does happen, I just hope there'll be a village when we get back."

"So that's how you get to be Laerd? You fight for it?"

He sighed again. "Old, old custom. Take on all comers, the one left standing wins. But these days, a Laerd has to be a good administrator and fighting for the job sure as hell doesn't guarantee that. I've tried to convince people we should elect the Laerd just like we do the Council. So far, no one's listened. I think they just like to see a good old-fashioned, bare-knuckled fight."

"How long have you been Laerd?"

"A little over a year. People were unhappy with the old Laerd, so they called for a new one. My heartsbound was dead, so I thought why not? I had nothing to lose."

"Who was Laerd before you?"

"A man named Lars Geren."

"Is he still in Mjor?"

He shook his head. "There's no shame in losing, but he took it pretty hard. He packed up his family and moved to Gurm."

"What's Gurm?"

"A city to the west of here."

My eyes widened. "You have cities?"

He smiled. "Of course. Did you think we all lived in villages like Mjor?"

"Well...yes."

"Gurm is one of our largest, over two million."

"Astoreth, that's bigger than Uruk."

He smiled again. "Why are you surprised? You *do* have demographers back home, don't you?"

I gave him an ascerbic look. "My sociology classes were ages ago. And demographics isn't part of the curriculum in life sciences."

He laughed.

We rode in silence for a while. "Do you think you're a good administrator?"

"Haven't been any calls for a new one...yet."

We passed the turnoff to the mines, and about six da-na later reached an intersection. An airborne globe shone with a bright orange light that turned blue in the next instant. Teger stopped the car, and I watched the traffic passing before us. Our light turned orange again, and that traffic stopped. He made a right turn, and then we were off.

The suns's heat and the wind blowing my hair felt wonderful. Oncoming traffic zipped by. We came to another, globe-less intersection. Barely slowing down, Teger navigated a raised curve and then merged into heavy, speeding traffic. Cars zoomed by us left and right, some carrying children who stared and pointed at me.

After three hours or so, we left the busy road and got onto another one. The traffic here was much lighter. We'd traveled about four da-na when he turned left onto an even smaller road.

Now, traffic was almost nonexistent. I looked over my shoulder. There was one lone car far behind us that disappeared as we drove around a bend but reappeared on the straightaway. I faced front again. Every so often I'd see an oncoming car. In the distance, I could see the road twisting its way into the mountains. "Where are we going, if I might ask?"

"To a pond I know on Bret Mountain. These mountain ponds are the only places terbone grass grows."

I cocked my head. "How do you know where all the best places are to find what Hyme and I want?"

"Remember all those stories I told you about when I was a boy? Well, to keep me out of trouble, Hyme took hold of me and tried to teach me the healing arts. Too bad I had no talent for it. But the lessons stuck, and so did the places to get the best plants."

About thirty minutes later, we turned off that road and onto another one, not much more than a paved track. After twenty minutes, we turned right onto a dirt trail. Teger was an expert driver, roaring up the rutted mountain road as if it was something he did every day. The road ended, and he shut down the engine. Getting out, he freed his gun from the rack, then reached in the cargo area and pulled out a medium-sized, insulated box with handles. "We walk from here."

I picked up my bags. "What's that?"

"Lunch. We're missing it, so I had the kitchen staff fix us something to eat." He winked. "One of the perks of being Laerd."

We started walking along an overgrown, winding path through the woods. Higher and higher we climbed. I was getting hot. I was about to ask how much further we had to go when we broke out of the woods into a small meadow carpeted with brilliantly colored wildflowers.

"There you go," he said, sounding cheerful. "Have at it."

I took a few steps and stopped. The terbone grew in the pond's center. Hyme had told me they grew in water. I'd been prepared to go wading, but I didn't think I'd have to go swimming to get them.

Teger peered. "Something wrong?"

"Uh...no. I mean, how deep is the pond?"

"Not deep. About this high." He put a hand on his waist.

"Oh." Given his height, water would be almost over my head.

Realization spread over his face. "Ah. I can get them for you if you want."

"No, I'll get them." We walked to the pond's edge. He laid his gun and the lunch box on the grass and stripped. I frowned. "Why—"

"I'm going swimming while you get the terbone. I'm hot."

"What about—"

"Like when we went for the skagwort. No predators this high up. But I didn't want to leave the gun in the car in case one decides to wander by." Stark naked, he ran for the pond.

While I undressed, he splashed into the water. "Come on. The water's fine."

I folded my clothes. Trowel in hand, I ran for the pond. I splashed in and almost dropped the trowel. Scurrying to the bank, I stood on the grass, shivering.

"What's wrong?" he called.

"I thought you said the water's fine. It's freezing!"

"It's fine to me."

"That's because you have hide for skin."

He laughed. "You'll get used to it. Besides, you want your terbone, right?" He lay back, floating.

I sighed. *Well, I can take this a little at a time.* I stepped to the pond's edge and put a foot in the water. It came up to my ankle. Then I put in the other foot. Step by step, I waded into the pond until I was immersed. I swam to the stand of terbone.

"Now for the hard part," I muttered. I took a deep breath and dived. The plants were a lot bigger than I'd thought. I started digging around the nearest one. When I thought I'd dug enough, I pulled at it. Nothing happened. I dug deeper. Still nothing. I tried a third, and then a fourth time, but no matter how deep I dug, the plant refused to come out.

I surfaced. *There's got to be another way.*

"Having trouble?" Teger said from behind.

Treading water, I looked over my shoulder. "No, I'm...well, I guess so. The roots go pretty deep."

"You don't have to get the whole root. Just cut the taproot with the trowel and you'll have enough. Or didn't you notice its serrated edges?"

I rolled my eyes. "Now he tells me."

He chuckled and floated off.

Taking a lungful of air, I dived again. I cut the plant's taproot and came up with a red terbone in hand. Turning my head, I contemplated the pond's edge. Swimming back and forth for each plant would be a pain. *Wait.* I let go of the terbone. It floated. *Perfect.* All I had to do was cut and let the plants float until I was ready to go.

Some time later, a hand rubbing my bottom caught my attention. I surfaced. Teger stood behind me, smiling. "Don't you think you've harvested enough?"

I looked. Terbone—a lot of them—floated on the water. I looked at the grass stand. I'd made a big dent in it. *Hope Hyme and I can use them all.*

"I'll help you get these out, and then we can lie in the suns and dry off." He gathered an armload and waded off. I gathered the rest and followed, half-swimming until my feet touched bottom. We spread our loads, then settled on the grass. I noticed his gun lay between us but didn't think anything of it. I closed my eyes, enjoying the heat. After the pond's chill, it was welcome.

"Let's eat."

I opened my eyes. Rolling my head, I saw he'd sat up and was opening the lunch box. "You're hungry? Already?"

"Aren't you?"

I raised my brows. All that harvesting had been hard work. "I guess I am."

He pulled out two wrapped parcels and two bottles. Unwrapping the first, he took a quick look, then handed it to me. "Yours. Vegetarian."

Sitting up, I peeked inside. Between the bread slices were sprouts, maizur, and red, juicy sherbots. It looked delicious. I took a bite. It *was* delicious.

He handed me an open bottle. "Here. It's ale. Not the kind I usually drink but just as good."

I sipped. Strong, tart, and spicy, it went well with my meal. I took another sip, then bit deeper into my bread and filling. It and the ale were gone in no time.

Stowing the trash and the bottles in the box, we lay back in the sunslight. I felt drowsy and at peace. I didn't want to go to sleep, so I rolled onto my elbow. Teger lay with his hands behind his head, eyes closed. I watched him for a minute. "What are you thinking about?"

"My heartsbound."

"Oh." A few moments passed. "Do you miss her?"

He shrugged. "Sometimes. Not as much anymore." He rolled onto his elbow. "Urla was a good woman, a good heartsbound. We had a good heartsbonding. But I always thought there was something missing, something I couldn't place. Since I've known you, I know what it was."

"What?"

He looked deep into my eyes. "Passion. I loved her, but not like I love you. Sometimes I feel like I could just burst. I have to have you, älskling. Oh, pfft," he rolled onto his back again, "there just aren't any words to tell you how I feel. I didn't have that with Urla. Eventually, I would have been unhappy in our heartsbonding, not knowing why." He closed one eye and peered at me. "Does any of this make sense?"

I smiled, giving his jaw a light caress. "Yes, it does."

The hairs on the back of my neck stood up. We were being watched. "Teger—"

"I know. Be still." In one swift move, he rolled over, grabbed his gun, and fired into the trees. He then leapt to his feet and ran into the woods.

CRACK!

I jumped to my feet, too. I had opened my mouth to call him when he stepped out from the foliage. "Missed. But he won't be back."

I sighed in relief but choked when I realized what he'd said. "He?"

"Or she. That was no animal. That was a hakoi."

"Are you sure?"

He shrugged. "I don't know of any other animal around here that runs on two legs."

"Why was he here?"

"Spying on us."

"Why?"

"I don't know."

"How long do you think he'd been there?"

"I don't know that, either."

"Do you think he heard us?"

He shrugged again. "We weren't exactly shouting." Walking to the pond's edge, he sat, laid his gun down, then patted the grass. "Come sit."

"Shouldn't we be going?"

"Why?"

"Well, in case we're—"

"Our watcher is long gone, älskling. What's the point of spying on someone who knows you're there?"

"Well, all right." I walked over and sat close. He smiled and pulled me closer still. The next thing I knew, we were rolling about in the bright purple grass, making sweet, glorious love amidst the wildflowers. When we'd finished, I collapsed on top of him, panting. "Min älskling," he whispered, stroking my hair.

The suns warmed my back, and I felt drowsy again. Teger poked me in the ribs. I raised my head. "Now we should go," he said with a mischievous grin. I climbed off him and stood on wobbly legs. Taking my hand, he led me to the pond. We waded in, and splashing each other, rinsed away the evidence of our lovemaking. We lay in the suns again, and after we'd dried off, dressed.

He helped me gather the terbone and stuff them into the collection bags. Taking one, he picked up his gun. "Here. You carry the lunch box."

We started walking. My thoughts churned. *Who was spying on us? Someone from the village, or just someone walking by?* I gave my head a little shake. *That's stupid. We're out in the middle of nowhere.*

What are the chances it was someone out for a stroll? A knot of anxiety formed in the pit of my stomach. Teger didn't seem worried about it, but whoever had been spying on us now knew our secret. What were they planning to do with their new-found knowledge?

Without warning, Teger stopped, and I bumped into him. "Mm. Must have hit him." He pulled a leaf off a tree and showed it to me. There were spots of dried blood on it. "When we get back, ask Hyme if anyone came in with a gunshot wound."

Reaching the car, we threw our bags and the lunchbox into the back. I rested my hand on the edge of the cargo bed, watching him secure his gun to the rack. "Teger, who knew we were coming here?"

"Everybody. Hyme was talking loud enough to wake the gods."

"No. Who knew we were coming...here?"

He looked up and gave me a small smile. "We were followed."

I remembered the car far behind us on the mountain road and told him about it.

"It's possible. Maybe even probable. But without more, it's pretty meaningless." He looked at the ground. "Come here." He pointed to a set of wheel tracks. "Those belong to our spy."

"We didn't make them?"

"No. Our tracks are over here." He pointed to a set that ended at our wheels. "I'll ask the pool clerk whether anyone signed out a car like ours when we get back."

We climbed into the car. He touched a lighted blue panel and it started with a roar. I eyed the narrow track. "There's no place to turn around."

He frowned. "We don't need to turn around."

Teger proved as adept at driving backward as he was at driving forward. In no time at all we were on the mountain road, heading back to Mjor. The trip in didn't seem to take as long as the trip out. Too soon, I saw the village walls and sighed.

He looked at me sideways. "What's wrong?"

"I just don't want today to be over, spies or no spies."

"There'll be other days."

"I know, but..."

He patted my hand. The familiar thrill washed through me.

We rolled through the village gates, and he pulled up beside the lab. He helped me take the bags of terbone out the back. "Thank you for taking me out today, Laerd," I said, making my voice as expressionless as possible.

He bobbed his head in a short nod. Getting back into the car, he drove off, leaving me standing with two big and heavy bags of terbone. I carried them inside. "I'm back!"

Hyme entered the lab from the apothecary. "Excellent, excellent," he crowed, rubbing his hands together. He raised his brows. "You didn't have to get *that* much."

"I know. I lost track and kept digging until Teger suggested I stop."

"I'm sure it'll be fine. What we don't use, I can trade for knowledge. Terbone isn't as precious as helly, but it's still worth a lot." He looked at the wall timepiece. "Dinner isn't for a few hours yet, so why don't we start sorting these?"

"Let me check the beacon first."

"Fine."

Ten minutes later, I was on my way back to the lab. Walking, it occurred to me that since becoming Teger's lover, I'd been neglecting my dancing and meditations. *I'll start again tomorrow.* What I was trying to do was too important to let lapse.

For the next hour or so, Hyme and I sorted the bounty I'd brought back. We separated the red terbone from the blue, then hung them up to dry. He had to string extra rope to hold all the plants. While we worked, he lectured me on terbone's properties. Some of it I'd heard before, but the review was well worth it since it helped me to understand the new data.

After all the plants had been hung, I noticed a faint, terrible odor that seemed to grow stronger by the second. I wrinkled my nose. "What's that awful smell?"

He chuckled. "Guess I should've warned you. Terbone stinks while it's drying."

"How come I didn't smell it at the pond? They were drying in the suns."

"It takes a while. Besides, you were outside. Even if it smelled then, the breeze would have taken it away. Don't worry, it doesn't get much stronger than this. And it disappears after a day or so."

"I hope so. I can't imagine trying to work in this stink."

"Come upstairs. It won't smell up there, and we can have some iced tea."

"Sounds like a good idea."

Inside, I took a deep sniff and was grateful to smell only the musty odor of old nupaper. While he bustled about getting our drinks, I made myself comfortable in one of the fireplace chairs.

He emerged from the kitchen and handed me a tall, condensation covered glass. "Here you are." He sat in the chair across from me.

I sipped. "It's delicious."

"It's a blend of mynt and ruse. Very refreshing on a hot summer's day."

I smiled. "You haven't felt hot until you've spent a summer in Uruk. Most people stay inside in the air conditioning all day and only come out at night after it cools down." I sipped again and set the glass on the table. "Hyme...did anyone come in today with a gunshot wound?"

"Oh, my. No. What happened?"

I told him about the hakoi who'd spied on us and how Teger must have shot him because he'd found blood on the tree leaf. "So, I was wondering..."

He shook his head. "They could have gone to any healer in any village. Healers aren't exclusive. People travel all the time and get sick, break bones, and so on. It's a healer's duty to attend to all who come for treatment, wherever they're from."

I closed my eyes and let out a tiny sigh. Learning our spy's identity was going to be harder than I'd hoped it would be. Maybe Teger learned something useful, but I'd have to wait until tonight to find out. Meanwhile, there was one thing I could do. I opened my eyes and gave Hyme a big smile. "So tell me about mytle."

"Tell me about cooli."

"Deal. You first."

He began lecturing, and we traded knowledge until dinnertime.

◦ ⌐ ⌐ ⌐ ⌐ ◦

I stepped into Teger's apartment to find him closing the shutters at the window overlooking the plaza. The other two were closed. He'd dimmed the lights until they emitted a warm, soft glow. I walked over and took him into my arms. He slipped one arm over my shoulder and stroked my hair. "Älskling," he whispered. "You always smell so good."

"Mm. So do you."

Letting go, he led me to a fireplace chair and sat. Curling on his lap, I lay my head against his chest. "Were you able to find out anything from the car pool?"

"No one hired a vehicle like ours today. But then, I was pretty sure there wouldn't be a record."

I told him what Hyme had said about getting treatment for a gunshot wound. "He could have gone anywhere for healing. Is that true for hiring a car, too?"

"Some villages, like Mjor, have an ordinance that only residents can hire cars. Other villages—the larger ones, usually—don't. Some have the ordinance but don't enforce it. And then there are the cities. Anybody can hire a car there."

"So he could've hired a car almost anywhere."

"I think we can rule out the cities. They're too far away. No, it has to be from one of the closer villages."

"What's the closest?"

"Niren. About fifteen da-na. It's bigger than Mjor, too." He chuckled. "You were right. We *are* a backwater village. If it wasn't for the beacon, we wouldn't even be on the map." He fell silent. "I wish we could find out if anyone in Niren hired a car like ours within the last day or so. I would love to get some names."

"Why can't we?"

"Because we're not the police. Only they could get information like that."

"So let Muts do it."

"Can't. It's not a crime to follow someone. And if no crime's been committed, there's nothing Muts can do."

I thought about the distance between Mjor and Niren. "How often are cars hired in Mjor? And when someone hires a car for longer than a day, are they allowed to park on the street? Or do they have to return it to the pool for pick up the next day?"

"Not too often. Besides, there aren't that many cars for hire. If someone hires for longer than a day, there's no need to return it to the pool. They're allowed to park on the street. Why?"

"Well, let's assume someone picked up a car in Niren. Fifteen da-na isn't that far, but it's far enough. Seems it would take a lot of effort to pick up a car in Niren and drive it to Mjor. I think this was an overnight trip."

"Maybe. But how would they get to Niren in the first place? No, there were two people involved in this. Someone hired a car in Niren or wherever and drove it to Mjor."

"So we ask if anyone noticed a car parked on the street overnight."

He shook his head. "Assuming it was an overnight trip, they probably parked in an alley. They aren't lit, and it'd be unlikely anyone would notice a car out there."

I bit my lip. "Tell me something. There's only the one road leading out of Mjor to that highway. Shouldn't we have seen anyone following us?"

"Not necessarily. Whoever was following probably had a good idea where we were going. There are a couple of ways to get Bret Mountain, but they gambled we'd take the most direct route. If they were driving over the speed limit—which I'm sure they were—catching up to us wouldn't have been hard. They'd know. That white hair of yours is like... well, a beacon."

"How did they know Hyme wasn't coming with us?"

"Älskling, Hyme is old, a lot older than he looks. He's delivered so many people here, I'm sure he's lost count. He delivered not only me but my parents, too. You know his saying, 'too far up the mountain for these old bones'? Well, it's true, and everybody knows it, including our follower."

The apartment was quiet. I shifted on his lap. "All right. We've figured out a possible how. Now, who?"

"I have my suspicions. The two men who tried to beat you up, Hert and Prag Harst. You remember them, right?"

"How could I forget?"

"Well, I think it's Prag."

"Why?"

"Remember I said you'd made a couple of enemies? Those two spent an arhu in jail for assaulting you. Both lost their jobs at the tannery. Hert's working at the mine, but Prag refused. So now he's jobless with no money and back living with his parents. I'm sure he blames you for everything—he's that type—so now he's going to get back at you by trying to prove you're having an affair with me. And if he does..."

"I get recalled to Uruk, and you…you…" Tears welled in my eyes.

Teger gave me a squeeze. "To Prag, I'm just collateral damage, älskling. It's you he wants."

I gazed into his eyes. "So what do we do now?"

"We have to be hyper-vigilant. Every time we leave Mjor, whether by car or on foot, we have to assume we're being followed."

"Even if Hyme's with us?"

"Even then." He looked at my feet. "And it's good you've been wearing those slippers. Everybody knows your apartment is across from mine. Hard shoes would echo on the battlement and someone might hear, especially if they're listening for it." His lips tightened. "And finally, I have to figure out a way to get that disc."

I frowned. "What disc?"

"The one he used to record us. You didn't think he was just watching, did you?"

"I didn't think anything at all."

"Well, I can guarantee you he's got us on vid. I just pray he hasn't made copies."

The apartment was quiet again. Teger prodded my back. "Come on. Let's go to bed."

My eyes widened. "How can you sleep at a time like this?"

He grinned. "I didn't say anything about sleeping."

"You're incorrigible."

"That's me."

I kicked off my slippers. He slipped an arm under my legs and carried me to bed. I watched him undress. For a good long while, I forgot about our problems.

Drowsy after our lovemaking, I was falling asleep when something occurred to me. "Teger?"

"Mm?"

"How much money did Prag make at the tannery?"

He lifted his head from my breast. "Couldn't have been much. Tanning doesn't pay all that well."

"Hm."

"What?"

"If Prag has no job and no money, where'd he get the money to buy a recorder?"

Teger grinned. "Min älskling, you're brilliant. He could have bought it ages ago but maybe not. I'll check it out later." He laid his head down, and in seconds, was snoring softly.

For about ten minutes, I lay wide awake, my thoughts and worries chasing each other. Then my drowsiness returned, slipping over me like the night slips over the mountains. Just before I fell asleep, an image appeared in my mind's eye.

Kepten Yose.

Chapter Eighteen

In the two marun after we'd been spied upon, we went out three times to gather herbs and plants. Not that Hyme needed them—Teger just wanted to test his spy theory. Hyme went with us twice. The first time he came with us, we were followed. The second time we weren't. The third time, Teger and I went out alone, and our spy came along.

"It's Prag," he said while I lay in his arms that night. "I spotted him hiding behind a tree."

"So now we know who it is and why. The only question now is who's behind it."

"Right. Oh, that reminds me. I want to show you something." He got out of bed and retrieved a small box from his closet. "Look." Pulling out a soft green bag, he upended it, and a small, slim silver rectangle fell into his palm. "This is a recorder. I bought it at Wyn's shop today. I told him I'd be recording Council meetings and wanted something really good. He showed me this—it's the best this company makes. And it's expensive. See that slot? That's where the disc goes. It comes with software, so you can play back your vid on a computer or hook it up to a projector and play it on a big screen. And the microphone is really sensitive. I tested it by setting the recorder on the tripod I'd bought on one side of the room and from the other, whispered a childhood rhyme. The mic picked it up loud and clear."

I held out my hand. "May I?" He gave it to me. Inspecting it, I peered into the disc's slot and examined the button controls. "I've never seen anything like this."

A sly smile appeared on his lips. "Well, we *are* pretty backward up here."

My eyes widened. "Wait, I didn't mean—"

He laughed. "I know. Just teasing."

I gave him a look. "Anyway, you're saying something like this would have picked up every word we said."

"Most likely. But what's important is Wyn told me Prag bought the same model just over two marun ago."

"How'd he pay for it?"

"Cash. He's been telling everyone an elderly aunt died and left him an inheritance. Nobody believes him, but his parents aren't denying it."

My brows shot up. "So you think his parents are in on it, too?"

"No. The Harsts don't have a lot of money, and I think Prag is paying them to keep quiet." He put the recorder away and returned it to the closet. Then he climbed into bed and cuddled me.

"Do you think the Council will want your sessions recorded?"

"Don't think so. I just said that so Wyn wouldn't think I was prying."

The apartment was quiet. I blew out a heavy sigh.

"What's wrong?"

"I'm scared, Teger. Aren't you?"

"Of course. But we can't let fear paralyze us. This is a game, älskling. The hunter and the hunted. And Prag's the hunter."

"Some game. The stakes aren't win or lose. They're life or death."

"Yes, but in this game, the roles can switch. The hunter becomes the hunted."

I rose onto my elbow and frowned. "What do you mean?"

"Think about it. Prag got us on vid when we were at Bret Mountain, and the evidence is damning. But he recorded us two marun ago. So why hasn't he aired it yet? Why does he keep following us around?"

I didn't have an answer, so I said nothing.

"It's because he wants more ammunition. He doesn't want there to be any questions about our involvement. Catching us once on a mountaintop is one thing. If he can record us making love or whatever at different times and in different places, it would be solid proof."

I thought about it. "Well, that makes sense. So what do we do now?"

"We go out flower hunting as often as we can. Keep Prag busy. We'll stay on our best behavior, though. He doesn't need any more ammunition than he already has." He paused. "I just pray he doesn't make a move before I'm ready to make mine."

"You have a plan?"

"It's getting there. But I can't do anything until after Cirkus."

"Cirkus?"

"Ancient custom. It's a fair held once every five years, a way for young people from other villages to meet and maybe find mates. The idea is to bring new blood into a village, especially the smaller ones. Cuts down on inbreeding. This year it's Mjor's turn to host." He fell silent for a moment. "Don't know how much longer the tradition will last. Seems young people these days head to the cities to find work and mates."

"How come you didn't go to the city?"

"I thought about it, especially given my—ahem—history in Mjor, but decided not to. I went to work in the mines, and then I met Urla. Besides, from what I've heard I really don't think I'd like the city. I'm a village boy at hearts."

I snuggled against him. "Well, I'm glad you didn't go."

"Me, too."

I closed my eyes. "Tell me. You said you're working on a plan. Does that mean we're the hunters, now?"

"Not yet. But if all goes well, we will be." He gave me a little squeeze.

We fell asleep, and the next thing I knew the alarm was ringing. I pulled the furs over my head. "Nooo."

Teger laughed. "Up. Up, and face the day."

"You're mean."

"You don't know how mean I can be."

"Show me."

He rolled over, and we made love. I giggled afterward. "You can be mean to me anytime."

"I love being mean to you." He prodded me. "But you have to get up. You've a service to run."

I wagged my finger. "No É talk in here."

"Guilty as charged. Now, go."

I looked at the intercom timepiece—he'd taught me how to read it—and with a small cry, scooted out of bed. I had about thirty minutes. Kissing him a hasty goodbye, I stuffed my feet into shoes and ran for the door. Since the night he'd led me naked out of my apartment, I never wore clothes when I went to him. I didn't want any reminders of the É while there. Slippers whispering on stone, I barreled toward my apartment and burst inside. Ten minutes later, I was running downstairs.

I hadn't set up the É last night. Rushing like a madwoman, I got everything ready. No sooner had I settled before the altar, I heard boots on stone. While they undressed, I found my center and calmed.

I set a stately pace for the service. It lasted forty minutes, probably a record for me. After the penitents had gone, I sensed I was being watched. I let out a minute sigh. I was tired of it and wanted some peace. "What can I do for you, Kepten?"

"How is the Laerd treating you these days, Moreva?" he called from the landing.

Fear flashed through me, but I squelched it. I looked over my shoulder. "What do you mean?"

"I saw how he disrespected you the day you arrived and wanted to know if he still disrespects you."

Getting to my feet, I turned and gave him a level stare. "We've reached an accord."

Yose smiled. "Ah. That's good to hear. Very good, indeed." He made no move to leave.

I let out a theatrical, impatient sigh. "Is there anything else I can do for you, Kepten? I really don't want to miss my breakfast."

"Oh, of course. My apologies. I will see you after midday, Moreva." He saluted and disappeared from the entrance.

Troubled, I set up the É for the evening service. Taking one last look around, I threw my cloak over my shoulders and returned to my room.

❧

Sitting in Teger's apartment later that day, I told him what had happened that morning. "He was trying to throw me off guard. He knows. Or at least suspects."

"How did he behave during your meeting?"

"He was his usual, cold self. All very correct before his superior officer."

He tapped a finger on the desk. "At least we know now where Prag is getting his money from."

A hazy memory surfaced, and I blinked a few times. "Yose," I said, my voice soft. I sat up. "Yes, that has to be it. Which means Prag's in touch with him." Then I frowned. "But Yose doesn't have that kind of money."

"How do you know? Do you know how much he's paid?"

"No." I sat back and bit my lip. "But surely the soldiers' pay is banked for them. I mean, what would they spend money on up here?"

"Maybe they get a stipend or something. That's something you can ask the next time you see him."

"Well, how about this? I'm sure they're paid in Devian money. I can't imagine them being paid in Syrenese coin."

Teger's look turned thoughtful. "True. Which means he's is paying Prag in Devian. So the question is where Prag is getting the money exchanged. The bank here doesn't have a relationship with the Devi. So where's he going?"

I didn't have an answer for that one, so I said nothing.

He smacked his forehead. "Of course. Why didn't I think of that sooner?"

"What?"

"The mines. We're not the only mine that sells to the Devi. Piri told me they pay them in Devian money, so the villages got together and set up a central bank that sets the exchange rates. Every mining operation has its own bank. Prag used to work at the mine, in administration. He's got to know somebody who works for the bank and is paying him—or her—a cut to exchange the money and keep quiet about it."

Neither of us spoke. I pursed my lips. "Let's say we're right. How do we prove it? Yose's being in contact with Prag breaks the Protocol. I don't know if what Prag's doing with the money is illegal but—"

"It is. We're not allowed to have Devian money. One of the laws the Council at the time passed when the beacon was built."

"Fine. But it still doesn't answer the question of how we're going to prove all of this."

Teger gave me a big smile. "I haven't the slightest idea." He sobered. "Maybe something will come up." He looked at the intercom's timepiece. "You've been here long enough. I'll see you tonight."

He walked me to the door. I gave him a short kiss and left.

The thumps of my boot heels as I walked across the battlement sounded thunderous. I wondered if they could be heard below. *Doesn't matter. I was there on official business. Well, mostly official.*

Opening my apartment door, I headed for the control room. During the long ride up, I thought about Yose and Prag, and how we would prove they'd broken the Protocol. I didn't come up with any answers.

I reached the top and stopped. Silence. The computers were dark. So was communications module. The only light came from the triple suns outside.

Running to the converter's cabinet, I flung open the door and leapt inside. Fumbling, my fingers found the wires. They were snug in their sockets. I felt for the main cable. Jiggling it, the power flashed on, then off. The cable had come loose. "Astoreth." I jammed it into its socket and the control room came to life. Beeps and buzzes greeted my ears, the sounds of the computers resetting themselves. I stepped out of the closet and looked at the communications module. Its green message light was blinking. Sweeping my gaze over the terminals, the fat, colorful cylinder slowly rotated at the proper speed, and the signal output panel shone bright blue. Everything was in order. I hurried to the module and covered the panel with my hand. "Astoreth-69."

A Devi's white-maned, blue-violet head floated before me, face angry. "Astoreth-69, where have you been? You've been offline for over two hours."

"Greetings, High One. The main converter cable disconnected itself."

"Disconnected itself? What do you mean?"

"It slipped from its socket. This converter is so old it was probably around before the Great Pantheon created Peris. I request a new one."

"Your impertinence is noted. And you have to go through the proper channels. Fill out a requisition form and message it to Supplies. It's up to them to decide whether you get a new converter. Give your report."

"Rotation speed seven-point-five, signal output normal at eighty-two."

"Report acknowledged and submitted. And Moreva? Don't let this happen again." The Devi's head disappeared.

"Don't let this happen again," I muttered. "Like it's my fault the cable slipped."

I looked around. Where was the requisition form? *Eresh hadn't said anything about that.* I searched everywhere, even opening the computer cabinets. Nothing. I sat before the module, staring while I tried to think of someplace I hadn't looked. Then I had an idea. In the manual, there was a section I hadn't looked at because it didn't seem relevant. Could that be where the form was located?

I hurried over to the electronic reader. Grabbing it, I scrolled through its contents, found the section, and tapped the screen. The table of contents appeared. I scanned it. *Oh. It's just an appendix.* I looked through it, anyway.

No form. Disappointed, I returned the reader to the shelf. Then I saw something else. A razor-thin tablet lay on the shelf underneath. I picked it up and switched it on. I scrolled through the table of contents, watching carefully. *There it is.* I tapped the title, and the requisition form appeared.

I studied it. "Doesn't look too complicated." Returning to my chair, I pulled up the keyboard and started typing. When finished and satisfied, I plugged the tablet into the module and sent the form to Central. Then I tapped my timepiece. "Time."

"Fifth hour, ten minutes Tryn."

Good. Got time for a quick session before dinner. On my way down, I wondered if Supplies would send me a new converter. Eresh said I'd be ignored. I snorted. *Sure he's right.* Inside my apartment, I stripped to my underwear and frowned. I hadn't had any visions lately. I wanted to kill the black bird and be done with it.

You will know when you are ready.

"I'm ready now," I muttered.

Inside the É, I chose my music on the seero. The sound of strings and drums filled air. I began to dance. But it didn't clear my mind. Overwhelmed by a rush of anxiety, I tripped over my feet and fell.

Sitting up, I hugged my knees and buried my face. I started shaking. Would Prag air his recording before Teger was ready? Would Yose report to Astoreth his suspicion I was having an affair? Or would he wait until Prag gave him a copy of the disc to prove it? And Astoreth...what would She do? Would She really execute me? Her own granddaughter? She'd executed my mother, but then She didn't have a choice. Now She did. She made the law, and She could break it. Would She choose my life over Her law?

I've taken Her and everything else for granted. Being Her granddaughter was like a shield, protecting me from the punishments others would have suffered if they'd done all the things I had, especially missing

Ohra-Namtar. As Jaleta and Eresh had said, She would have executed anybody else. Me, I was sent to the Syren Perritory for a year. But with Teger, I was sure I'd gone too far.

After my shaking finally stopped, I got up and switched off the seero. Turning, I nearly jumped out of my skin. Yose stood in the doorway, staring at me. How long had he been standing there? Why didn't I sense him? Did he see my anxiety attack? *Doesn't matter. I'll just say I had a vision or something.*

I took a small breath. "May I help you, Kepten?"

"Yes, Moreva. One of my troops has fallen ill. Would you come take a look at him, please?"

"Of course. Let me get my things."

He saluted and disappeared from the doorway. After his footsteps faded, I hurried over to it and peeked around the corner. The barracks door was open. I ran to my apartment, threw on my uniform and grabbed my healer's kit, then left.

Yose met me at the door. After my usual "as you were," he led me to a bed where a pale and sweating young man lay. His body twitched. "What's his name?"

"Pavet Kila."

Setting my kit on the bed stand, I dug around for my diagnostic wand. I slid off the dust sleeve, then pulled back the sheet. Starting from his head, I passed the wand over Kila's body, paying close attention to the letters and numbers flashing on the screen. When finished, I put the wand away and turned to Yose. "He's got a viral infection, but it's not contagious. How long has this man been here?"

"Two arhu."

"Have you been on field maneuvers lately?"

"We completed one the other day."

I reached into my kit for the jar of antiviral pills I'd brought from Uruk but stopped. My lips pursed. Instead of the pills, I pulled out a pair of nuskin gloves and snapped them on. Kila moaned as I lifted his arm. "I know it hurts, Kila. But I have to do this." Manipulating his arms and legs, I found nothing. Then I turned his head and saw a tiny, swollen bite mark. I motioned to Yose. "That's it. Look."

He peered at the mark. "What is it?"

"Looks like he was bitten by a weral, a type of fly common here in the summer months. Most people show no symptoms, but Kila wasn't so lucky." I reached into my kit a third time and pulled out a jar of dark green pills Hyme and I had developed while I'd waited for results in my fever experiments. Doling out fifteen, I poured them into a smaller jar, then shook out two more from the larger jar. "We'll give him two pills now, and then one every two hours. Make sure he's got plenty of water by his bed. He's in the morning group for services, isn't he?"

"Yes."

"Give me a call at three Gor, and I'll decide then whether he can go. Get him a pitcher of water with ice."

Yose barked an order, and a female soldier ran into the kitchen. Emerging with pitcher of ice water and a glass, she handed them to me. I filled the glass, then set it and the pitcher on the stand. Turning, I helped Kila sit up, dropped the pills on his tongue, and held his head while he drank. After helping him to lie back, I peeled off my gloves and threw them into a nearby wastebasket.

I picked up my kit. "That's all I can do for now." Then I remembered. "Kepten, could I speak with you in your office?"

He gave me a puzzled look. "Of course."

We walked inside. "Kepten, what do your troops do for entertainment? I'm curious."

His lips tightened. "They gamble, mostly."

"With what? Chips?"

"Money. Most of their pay is banked, but they get a small stipend every arhu to spend at our commissary on things like megsticks."

"And you allow gambling?"

"Many of my troops aren't vid players. They have to have something to do, so yes."

I resisted the urge to smile. "Thank you. I'll be going, now. Remember, call me at three Gor."

"I'll certainly do so, Moreva." He saluted and walked me to the barracks' door.

Once in the stairwell, I did smile. Unwittingly, Yose had just told me where Prag was getting his money.

I told Teger about the call I was expecting, so we spent the night in my apartment. Besides, I needed to dictate a couple of sermons. I also told him what I'd learned that after midday.

He smiled. "Wonderful. We still can't prove anything, but the pieces are falling into place."

Later, he asked if I wanted to go flower hunting, as he called it, tomorrow after lunch. "We haven't been in a while, I've got a hole in my schedule, and Prag needs something to do."

"Yes. Hyme needs charry." I kissed his nose. "I suppose you know where to get some?"

"Do you doubt?"

We fell asleep, and at precisely third hour Gor, the intercom rang. Half-asleep, Teger reached for it, but I slapped his hand away. "Yes, Kepten."

"It's three Gor, Moreva. You said I should call you."

"I'll be right down." I filled Teger in on the sick trooper while I dressed. "He should be much better by now. Those pills are powerful." I picked up my healer's kit and walked down to the barracks. Most of the garrison was asleep, but those that weren't started to stand. I shook my head.

Even from here, I could see Kila was much better. Yose joined me at his bedside. Although the pavet's skin was still pale, some of his color had returned. He was no longer shaking or sweating, either. I opened my kit, doled out more pills, and set them on the bedstand. "Keep him in bed today. He should be all right by tomorrow."

Kila looked disappointed. I smiled. "I'll give you an extra dose of our Most Holy One's love and forgiveness the next time you come to service." He brightened at that. "You should try to sleep, now. I'll be by later to see how you're doing." I gave Yose a short nod and left the barracks.

I let myself into the apartment. Teger was still in bed. "Don't think we're going flower hunting today, älskling." He tipped his head toward the battlement. "Look outside."

I opened the door to see sheets of water sliding off the roof. Rain pounded against it like a drummer gone mad. I clucked in disappointment. "No, I guess not." Sighing, I closed the door and sat on the bed.

"Time to get ready for the service?"

I sighed again and nodded.

"What's wrong?"

"I'd rather stay here with you."

"Well, you can't."

"I know." I stripped off my uniform while he watched with an appreciative look. Then he rolled out of bed and started to dress. "I should get going, too. Get some work done before breakfast. It'll be that much less to do later."

I walked over and gave him a hug. "I'll see you tonight."

"You'll see me at breakfast."

I slapped his bottom. "You know what I mean."

He gazed into my eyes. "Yes, I do." Without warning, he lifted and gave me a kiss that quickly turned passionate. He set me down a minute later, and then headed for the battlement. Opening the door, he flashed a smile over his shoulder, and was gone.

My lips tightened. I'd been looking forward to our flower hunt. Prag would follow us, but at least I'd have a break from Yose and his spying. "Nothing to be done about it now," I muttered. *Maybe the rain won't last too long. If it ends before lunch, we still might be able to go.*

I pulled out my garb for today, the one I hated because it fit me so badly. That and the rain only fueled my annoyance. "Nothing to be done about that, either." I struggled into it, tugged at it here and there, trying to make it as comfortable as possible. It was a lost cause. Gritting my teeth, I rolled my eyes and gave up.

While my makeup dried, I gathered the rest of my things and laid them on the bed, then peeled off the mask. Wrapping in my cloak, I picked up my crop and shoes and left to ready the É for the morning service.

Chapter Nineteen

We didn't go charry hunting that after midday, the next day, or the next. It rained torrents. Outside, it was impossible to stay dry. Like the rest of the villagers, I mostly stayed indoors, usually at the lab. The times I did have to venture out, the plaza was almost always deserted. The fountain had been turned off, too.

Five days into our never-ending rainstorm, I stood before the sterile enviroment's chamber, staring at the results of my latest experiment. The hairless skratz, now a brilliant shade of red, lay on its side with eyes open. The pustules covering its body looked a little larger than they had when I'd given it my latest serum. Like its predecessors, I'd watched the little beast die, convulsing until the end.

I let out a tiny hiss. *Another one. That makes twenty-eight. I'm missing something...but what?*

Slipping my hands into the manipulators, I picked up the dead skratz and dumped it into the acid vat. The acid bubbled, and then seemed to boil. The skratz's body was tossed about, buffeted by the roiling liquid. I watched it dissolve until there was nothing left.

Stepping to the chamber's far side, I pressed a black square on top of a squat canister with a hose connected to the cylinder. The square blazed orange. Acid gas filled the chamber. When the chamber looked as cloudy as it did outside, I lifted my finger, and the square went dark. After a minute or two, the cloud dissipated. I studied the chamber. *I've enough hairless skratz for now, but I'll definitely need to have more brought on the next supply run.*

My lips tightened. *The rate I'm going through them, it's a wonder no one's said anything about it.* I'd been ordering hairless skratzes two boxes at a time, each box holding forty skratz. I'd kept the number of boxes low so as not to arouse suspicion. But it also meant I'd been putting in lot of orders. *I wonder if anyone would raise brows if I asked for three boxes. Or four.* Then I sighed and shook my head. *I'll think about that when the time comes.*

I stepped out of the closet. Hyme stood at one of the long counters, pouring viscous liquids in varying bright colors into molds. I walked over. "What are you making?"

He looked up. "Gel candy. Laced with a very mild sedative, I might add. It's children's day the day after tomorrow, and I need these for the little ones." He paused. "And their parents."

"Why?"

He chuckled. "I didn't make any for the last children's day, and it was absolute bedlam. Children screaming at the sight of a needle, refusing to take medications, parents pulling their hair out...it's a wonder they didn't have me swinging from the battlement. So, this time, I'm not taking any chances." He gave me an inquiring look. "How was your experiment?"

I let out a long sigh. "More of the same. Not exactly encouraging." I paused a beat. "I'm going to my tower. Have to look after the beacon and then get my exercise."

"All right. Coming back afterward?"

"Yes. I want to write up my lab notes before dinner."

"Very good. See you then."

I donned my rain cloak, then stepped outside. It was raining just as hard as ever. I reached the corner and scanned the sky. From what I could see through the downpour, the lowering clouds were dark gray shot through with bands of lighter gray, all shifting with the wind. It was depressing to look at. *Just how I feel.* It also reminded me of that awful vision I had during Ktana.

I lifted my head and let the rain pummel my face. Then I threw back my cloak's hood. In seconds, my hair was dripping. I started across the plaza and stopped. Unfastening the clasp at my neck, I slipped off my cloak and let the rain soak me. Cloak over my shoulder, I started walking again, deliberately splashing into deep puddles and feeling the wetness seep through my boots. By the time I reached my tower, I was a bedraggled mess. *Exactly how I feel.*

The bioscan lock clicked, and I stepped inside.

The next marun, first day, the clouds disappeared, and the suns returned like long-lost friends. Mjorans reappeared on the plaza. The fountain was turned back on. Village life returned to normal.

"Do you want to go flower hunting the day after tomorrow?" Teger said that morning after breakfast. His tone was cold. "You said the marun before last Hyme needed charry. I've time for it if we leave right after breakfast."

In my peripheral vision, I saw Prag hanging about, obviously listening to our conversation. "Yes. I'm not working on anything that needs my immediate attention."

"All right. I'll have a car waiting."

"Thank you."

He brushed past me. Turning, I caught Prag glaring with undisguised hatred. A second later, he looked away, hailed someone I couldn't see, and hurried off.

Watching him, I recalled a conversation I'd had with Teger about how Prag could have possibly known about our affair. We'd been so careful. Hashing out various possibilities, I'd finally remembered. He'd been the man smirking and staring when Hyme had suggested Teger take me to gather terbone. And he'd understood every word.

I gave Prag's retreating back one last look. Then I too left the dining hall and headed for the lab.

On the appointed day, Teger and I set off from Mjor. We were going to a different mountain this time. Hof Mountain was closer to the village, about an hour or so away. Instead of taking the main roads, he took the back ones that twisted and turned into the foothills, and then into the peaks. Every so often I looked back. Once, I thought I caught a glimpse of Prag's car, but I couldn't be sure.

We came to a turnoff. He stopped the car, and we stared at the unpaved track. The rains had turned it into mud. Even the ruts, now filled with water, had almost disappeared. "You sure you want to do this, älskling? You'll get your uniform and boots dirty."

"I've got other uniforms and boots. Besides, Hyme really needs the charry."

"All right," he said, sounding doubtful. Making the turn, he drove along the narrow, precipitous track, weaving around the water-filled ruts as best he could. We inched our way up the mountain. He grimaced. "Pray we don't get stuck."

"I'm praying Prag does."

The incline leveled out somewhat at the track's end where we got out of the car. I grabbed my collection bag from the back while Teger freed his gun from the rack. Then he reached into the back seat and pulled out a small satchel.

"What's that?"

He grinned. "Provisions."

"But you just had breakfast."

"But I might get hungry again."

I shook my head. "You eat enough for three hakoi."

"Have to keep my strength up."

He led the way into the woods. We walked for about a half hour up a steep slope and then we came to the stand of charry. While I clipped leaves and stripped bark from the middling-sized bushes, Teger walked a perimeter, keeping an eye out for predators. "We're not going that high up," he'd said.

I finished about an hour later, my bag bulging. "Ready when you are." I paused. "Did you see Prag?"

"He left about five minutes ago."

"If we hurry, maybe we can catch him."

He shook his head. "Let him go. We're not the hunters, yet."

We walked in silence. Standing by the car, my keen hearing caught the sound of Prag's vehicle. He wasn't far away. "You know, I still—"

I looked around, feeling uneasy. Something was different, but I couldn't say what. There was just...a *wrongness* about it. I frowned.

Teger peered. "What?"

"I-I don't know. Something doesn't—*look!*" I pointed at the mountain. The ground was quivering, almost rippling. Then a rumbling sound.

Still holding his gun, Teger leapt over the car's hood and grabbed my hand. "Run!"

I didn't ask questions. Clutching my bag, I ran with him. We crashed through the woods, dodging trees, and leaping over fallen logs. The rumbling grew louder. Despite his long legs, between my fear and my Devi speed, I had no trouble keeping up with him. Every so often, he'd look up. He did so one final time and jerked me around so that we now ran up the mountain, instead of across its face.

Just as we made it to the top, the rumbling turned into a roar. Wide-eyed and panting, I watched the mountainside rupture a scant hundred šīzu below us. A huge section slid away. The rushing, deep brown tide spread outward, faster and faster. Mature trees and boulders were carried in its wake, tossed about like toys.

Minutes later, all was quiet. Not even birds sang. I squeezed his hand. "Wh-what happened?"

"Mudslide. It's rained so much the ground basically liquefied." He blew a heavy breath. "That was close." Lips tight, he pointed to the carnage. "And the car's down there, somewhere." He shook his head. "Looks like we'll have to walk home. Good thing we're not that far away."

Hand in hand, we started walking. There was no trail, so we had to blaze through the forest, pushing tree branches out of our way or ducking under them. The smell of last year's decaying leaves permeated the air, overlaid by the acrid smell of mud. On and on we walked. We stopped several times while he consulted a round, flat object he'd pull from his pocket. Sometimes we changed direction, sometimes we didn't.

"What's that thing you keep looking at?"

Teger stopped. "A kompass. It's a way of finding your bearings. Come here. I'll show you." He pulled me closer. "See this arrow? It tells you which direction you're going. Mjor is northeast of here, so as long as the arrow points to the northeast, we're generally going the right way."

"I see." I bit my lip. "Are we going to have to spend the night out here?"

"Yes, why?"

"Oh...nothing."

"Don't 'oh, nothing' me. What's wrong? Haven't you ever spent a night in the open before?"

"No."

Dropping the kompass into his pocket, he wrapped me in his arms. "My poor, sheltered älskling." He looked down and smiled. "Don't worry. Animals will leave you alone...most times."

My eyes widened. "Most times?"

"Unless you're sick or injured. Besides, I still have my gun. Loud, sudden noises will almost always scare off a large animal."

"All...all right."

He let go and took my hand. "Come on."

We started walking again. "Do you always carry your kompass with you?"

"Only when I'm out flower hunting with you and Hyme. I carry it just in case...well, you saw what happened."

After about an hour, he called a halt. "Are you hungry? It's got to be after lunchtime."

Pleased I could be of use, I tapped the bar. "Time." Nothing happened. I looked down. It was dark. "Oh."

"You're out of range. Your timepiece works on rayun waves but at a different frequency than your beacon. It's the same wavelength my flat-comm uses." He pulled the slim rectangle from his belt and pressed its rim. A white light blinked. "See? No signal." He cocked his head. "Hadn't you ever noticed your timepiece was off on our flower hunts?"

"No...I mean, I don't look at it. I just tap it." I squinted. "Don't you carry a timepiece?"

"Yes, but it broke last marun, and I haven't had it fixed." He chuckled. "That'll teach me to procrastinate." Stepping closer, he stroked my hair. "Now...back to my question. Are you hungry?"

"Yes."

"Then let's eat." Leaning his gun against a nearby tree, he opened his shoulder bag's flap and took out two bars wrapped in shiny white paper. "Here you go."

I turned it over. "What is it?"

"Food bars. Each one of these is equal to a complete meal. Tastes good, too."

Unwrapping it, I took a bite. It *was* good, sweet, salty, and spicy all at the same time. Not wanting to eat too fast, I took little bites, savoring the flavors. "I like it," I said between bites. Finishing it, I looked up to see he'd already finished his. He took the wrapper and stuffed it into his bag.

"Ready to move?"

I nodded.

"Let's go." He grabbed my hand. By now, we'd left Hof Mountain behind and were walking along relatively flat, if rocky, perrain. The going was easier, but my boots weren't made for walking any real distance, and my feet hurt. I was tired, too. My last endurance event had been well over a year ago, and I was out of shape. We hadn't really stopped to rest since we'd started our long walk.

Teger didn't seem tired at all. He strode along as if he could walk all day and night.

So I gave a prayer of thanks when he stopped and said we should find a place sleep for the night. He squeezed my hand. "Let's try over he—aargh!"

His fall jerked me forward. I almost fell on top of him. Letting go at the last minute, I threw myself to the side, landing on my hip. It hurt, but I barely noticed. "What happened?" I shouted.

"Fell into a hole." His voice sounded strained. Bent double, he worked his foot out. "There." He put his foot on the ground, then cried out again. Face contorted with pain, he balanced on one foot, the other dangling behind him.

"Oh, no," I breathed, trying to stem my rising panic. Teger, injured? How were we to get back to Mjor now? Then the healer in me kicked in. Forgetting my panic, my priority was to see to my patient. First, I had to get him comfortable. "Where was it you thought might be a good place to spend the night?"

"Over there." He pointed to a cluster of rocks about forty šīzu away. I dropped my bag and ran toward it. Navigating the low rise, I turned. The rock cluster made a rough U-shape, providing protection from the back and on the sides. It was large enough for two people if they didn't mind being close. The top was exposed, though. I shook my head. Teger couldn't go any further so this would have to do. I prayed it wouldn't rain again.

I ran back to where he waited. "I think it'll work. Give me your pack." He handed it to me, and I slung it over my shoulder. Picking up my bag of charry, I wrapped my arm around his waist. "Put your arm around my shoulders. Use your gun and me as crutches."

"But älskling, I might ruin my gun."

"You can get a new one."

"That's not the—"

"Do you want to stay out here?" I said, glaring.

"No, but—"

"Then do it."

Twisting his lips, he draped an arm about my shoulders. I took a small step forward. Teger hopped at the same time. I was too short to make the ideal crutch, but I was all we had. It took us a few tries to find our rhythm. Once we did, our progress was steady. We reached the rock cluster, gingerly navigated the low rise, and faced our shelter for the night.

He eyed it. "No top."

"I've already prayed to Astoreth it won't rain."

He gave me a sideways look and a small smile appeared on his lips. I got the feeling that he wasn't talking about the possibility of rain.

I helped him sit, then stretched out his long legs. Unlacing his boot, I tugged at the uppers until the gap was wide enough for my fingers to slip inside. His ankle was swelling. If I didn't hurry, I wouldn't be able to get my fingers in there at all. "All right. When you fell into the hole, did you hear a popping or tearing sound, or did you feel something like that?"

"Yes. Something tearing."

I probed his ankle, putting light pressure on the bones. "Does any of that hurt?"

"No."

I pressed the tendon holding the ankle joint together. "Does this—"

"Aaugh!"

I laced up his boot, making sure it was firm but not tight. "You have a moderate to bad ankle sprain. That's all I can tell you right now."

"Shouldn't I take off my boot?"

"No. Your boots are heavy enough to provide support and compression for your ankle, and that's what you need." I looked around. *We could use some ice. Maybe there's a stream nearby...the water should be cold enough.*

My lips tightened. It didn't matter. Even if there was a stream, we didn't have anything with us to carry water. Then I remembered what Hyme had told me about ebera, a common vine with painkilling properties. I wondered if there was any nearby. I dug into my bag for the cutters. "I'll be right back."

"Where are you going?"

"Going to find something for your pain. I won't get out of sight from where we are." I began walking, looking over my shoulder every now and then, making sure I could still see the rock pile. I'd gone about thirty šīzu when I saw the vines hanging from a tree up ahead. I looked back and could see only a sliver of rock. I bit my lip. I didn't want to get out of sight of the shelter, but Teger needed all the help he could get. Walking the last fifteen šīzu, I reached the tree and started chopping at the closest vine. I cut a long specimen. Carefully retracing my steps, I returned to the rock pile.

By the slant of the suns's rays through the trees, it would be dark soon. *Better hurry it up.* Setting the ebera next to him, I moved his leg out of the way, then gathered piles of wet leaves. After making a large mound, I lay my bulging bag on top. Then I gently positioned his leg on top, elevating it. I stepped back to assess what I'd done and was pleased I'd gauged correctly. The elevation angle was as high as his hearts.

He peered at my handiwork. "What'd you do that for?"

"Keeps down the swelling and bruising." Picking up the ebera, I sat next to him. "Here. Take this and chew on it. Swallow the juice. It'll help kill the pain."

He took the vine and inspected it. "Ebera, huh?"

I smiled. "Hyme taught you well."

"This stuff also gets you high."

"Good. You won't notice your pain."

He started chewing. After about five minutes, he sighed and lay the vine in his lap. "I feel wonderful." He draped his arm around my shoulders. "I'll take the first watch."

I frowned. "Watch?"

"Yes. One of us has to stay awake while the other sleeps. Just in case some nosy cheret decides to take a look at us."

"What's a cheret?"

"A very large katt. You remember the ura? They're not nearly that big, but they're big enough. A lone man—or woman—wouldn't stand a chance."

"Are...are there any more animals out here that might want to take a look at us?"

"Of course. Most will leave you alone, but cherets are curious creatures."

"You're not doing this just to scare me, are you? Because it's working."

"No, älskling, I'm not."

"How will we see them if we have no light?"

"We can hear and smell them, can't we?"

"So what do I do if one comes by?"

"Fire the rifle. They're skittish and will run from a sudden, loud noise." He kissed my hair. "Don't worry. All you have to do is press your finger on the trigger and squeeze. Don't try to aim at anything. Here, I'll show you."

He picked up the gun and showed me how to hold and fire it. It looked easy enough. "Now press gently."

I did so.

CRACK!

The recoil threw me back into the rock wall, stunning me. A few seconds later, I sat forward and gave my head a small shake. "Astoreth. You didn't say anything about that."

"I'm sorry. I'm so used to it, it didn't occur to me."

"I suppose I'll live."

He looked around. "We should eat before it gets full dark. Where's my pack?"

I felt beside me. "Right here." I pulled out the food bars. "These are the only two left."

"Well, I didn't expect to be stranded in the mountains."

I unwrapped one for him and then the other. We ate in silence. I didn't realize I was hungry until my first bite. Shoving the rest of the bar into my mouth, I barely tasted its spicy goodness. After we'd finished, I stuffed the wrappers into the bag and laid it beside me.

We watched night fall, growing darker and darker until it was pitch. I heard small creatures scuttling about. Something to my left rustled the leaves, making little grunting noises. I heard another rustling further away. I could tell it was larger than the creature I'd just heard. Was it a cheret? How would I know? I huddled closer.

"Afraid?"

"Yes."

"These mountains are huge, älskling. The chances of any of the big predators finding us are pretty small." He gave me a squeeze. "We'll be all right. I promise."

We said nothing for a long while. He nudged me. "Look up."

I did. The moons hadn't yet risen. Through a break in the canopy, I could see the sky with its pinpoints of sparkling light. Some of the sparkles were blue, others were pink, and still others had a yellowish cast. And there were so many of them, crowded in this small patch of sky. They were beautiful.

"I love you like the stars, min älskling," he whispered.

I smiled. "Like the stars."

Neither of us spoke for a while. "I think I'll teach you Syrenese," Teger said.

"Why?"

"Because I want to. Besides, wouldn't you like to know what other people are saying about you?"

"They talk about me?"

"Sure. It's not all bad, though." He chuckled and gave me a little squeeze. "Just joking."

"No, you're not."

He said nothing for a moment. "But really...would you like to learn?"

I thought about it. I could've easily learned Syrenese long before—I'd been immersed in it since coming to Mjor—but I'd shut my ears and mind. *Now, though...* I smiled. "Yes. Yes, I would."

"Good. We'll start tomorrow. Don't let anyone know you speak our language, though."

"Why?"

"Just a precaution. But you need to sleep, now."

"All right." I nestled under his arm and in moments had dropped into oblivion. In the next instant, it seemed, he nudged me. "Wake up, älskling. It's your watch now."

I yawned. "Mhmm. Where's the gun?"

"Right here." He passed it to me. "Be careful."

I felt around and my fingers found the long barrel. I took it in both hands and laid it by my side. "I'm all set. You can go to sleep."

Ten minutes later, he stirred. "I can't sleep. I keep thinking about what's going on in Mjor. Who's in charge? Great gods, don't let it be Rausch." He sighed. "This is no good. I have to—"

"I'll sing you a song. It's one we use for babies."

"I'm not a baby."

"Hush." I started singing, a slow, simple tune that altered brain waves to induce deep slumber. Within minutes, I heard his soft snoring. "Works every time," I whispered.

I basked in my success, but it didn't last long. Shivering, my hearts beat faster. I felt more alone and afraid than ever. It was one thing to be out here and have Teger to talk to, but I didn't have that now. The trees hid most of the moonslight. My senses were on hyper-alert. Every sound seemed magnified by the darkness, and I heard every one. The night birds' stuttering cries. The rush of wings as they flew past. The rustling of leaves, signaling some creature going about its business. Shadows moved everywhere. Was that a cheret? An ura? Or some other beast I knew nothing about? I lay my hand on the gun, resassured by its presence. My hearts slowed a bit. *Astoreth deliver us.* That made me feel even better.

An ululating cry split the night. I jumped. *What was that?* More important, where was it? Close by? Far away? I couldn't tell. I peered into the moving shadows. *Is it real or my imagination?* I thought about what Teger had said. *Most predators will leave you alone, except if you're sick or injured. He's injured.* Did this mean the beasts would come sniffing for him?

I pulled the gun into my lap and felt around until my finger lay on the trigger. No matter what happened, I would be ready.

Time passed. The shadows seemed to grow closer. Then one of the shadows detached itself from the others. *Wh-what...* It was coming toward us. I waited. Soft footfalls. Then the rank odor of an animal. My hearts pounded. I raised the gun, aimed at the moving shadow, and pressed the trigger.

CRACK!

"Awwrr-rrr!" something screamed. I felt Teger start at the same time the recoil slammed me against the rock. The beast's crashing through the forest sounded unnaturally loud. My chest heaving, I gripped the gun hard, too frightened to let it go.

"Älskling," his soft, gravelly voice sounded beside me. "You can give me the gun, now. I'm awake."

"B-but what if it comes back? Or if th-there's another one?"

"I'll take care of it."

I loosened my grip on the rifle and passed it to him. Blood rushed back into my hands. The gun rustled the leaves when he set it beside him. His arm tightened around my shoulders. "You did well, älskling."

"Oh, Teger, I was so—"

"I know." He kissed my hair.

We sat in silence, watching and listening for more dangers that might be lurking. We didn't see any. Well, I saw plenty, but I knew they were just shadows from the trees.

He nudged me. "Look up."

I raised my head. The sky was lightening fast. Moments later, the forest filled with birdsong. Small striped mice and other creatures skittered about in search of breakfast.

We'd survived the night.

⚬▨▨▨▨⚬

About an hour later, we decided it was time to go. Over his protests, I made Teger chew more ebera. "There'll be less pain when you get up."

I moved his injured leg and gathered the pile of leaves. After I'd scattered them, I picked up our bags, threw them over my shoulder, and then squatted. "Just like yesterday. Use the gun and me as crutches."

"Wait." He cracked open his rifle and emptied the bullets into his palm. There were precious few of them. "Put these in the bag."

"Why?"

He smiled. "So I don't accidentally shoot you or myself while we're walking."

I dropped them into the bag, and he draped his arm over my shoulders. I looked at him. "Ready?"

"About as ready as I'm going to get."

"All right. On the count of three. One, two, *three*." His face twisted as we strained and wobbled getting to our feet. We almost fell a couple of times, but we managed to stand. His face relaxed, and we started to move.

We'd gone about five šīzu when he stopped. "Hold on. I want to see something." We hobbled to the left and soon came upon a large splotch of dried blood. "You hurt it bad, älskling. That's a lot of blood."

"Do you think it'll die?"

"Maybe. Depends on where you hit it."

"Do you think it was a cheret?"

"Don't know. Can't see any footprints."

233

I thought about maybe having killed whatever it was I'd shot. It had been necessary, but it still saddened me.

Holding the rifle in the crook of his arm, he pulled out his compass, studied it, and then pointed almost straight ahead. "That way."

We started moving. It was slow going, mainly because we had to watch for rocks lurking beneath the leaves. But our progress was steady. Limping through the forest, he began my Syrenese lessons. First came the standard greetings. Then he named things—tree, stone, leaf—which I repeated. He gave me little quizzes by pointing to a leaf, his bag, or to himself, and I named them. Like when he'd taught me the Syrenese numbers, I was a stellar student.

Every so often, we'd stop so he could check his kompass. This time, he stared at it with raised brows, then looked around. "We should be coming across a road soon."

He was right. Less than an hour later, we came to one of the back roads. I'd never been so glad to see a sign of civilization. "Is this one of the roads we took to get to Hof Mountain?"

"As a matter of fact, it is. We came out much closer to Mjor than I'd thought. If all goes well, we should be there by nightfall."

I nearly cried in relief.

We started hobbling again, stopping only so he could chew more ebera. I knew he was in great pain, but he never complained. I admired him all the more for it.

"We should rest, Teger."

He shook his head. "I'm fine. I'll let you know when I'm tired."

My lips tightened. He would do no such thing. But if he thought he could go on, then we would.

Hours later, an engine rumbled behind us. We looked back. A boxy car like the one Teger had hired sped along the roadway. Slowing, it came to a stop upon reaching us. The driver was no one we knew. He looked us over. "Du ser ut som du behöver lite hjälp."

Teger smiled. "Snälla. Kan du ta oss till Mjor?"

"Säker. Stig på."

He looked down. "He's going to take us to Mjor."

I helped him into the car. Then I climbed into the back with our bags and the gun. The man put the car in gear, and we were on our way. I listened to their conversation, straining to catch a few words I'd been taught today. I recognized "Laerd," "stone," and "rifle." There were a few other words I recognized and figured he was telling the man about the mudslide.

In no time, we were rolling through the village gates. A cry went up from the crowd standing in front of the sessions hall, where Muts had apparently been relating the latest news about us. Mjorans surged forward. They surrounded the car, clapping Teger and our rescuer on the back, slapping the fenders, and creating a general ruckus.

Someone pushed their way through the crowd. "Låt mig genom. Låt mig genom!" It was Hyme. He reached the car and peered at the pain lines on Teger's face. "Vad har du gjort med dig själv?"

"Skådad min fotled."

I knew "fotled" meant "ankle," so I guessed Hyme had asked if he was hurt. When the crowd saw Teger had been injured, some came forward. "Nej, nej," Hyme said, trying to wave them off. But they would not be deterred. Two men and a woman picked him up and carried him to the hospital. The crowd followed.

That left me and the man who'd given us a ride alone. We watched the mob's retreat. He turned to me. "Populär Laerd eller hur?"

I hadn't a clue what he'd said so I nodded, hoping it was the right thing to do. The man smiled, so I assumed it was. I smiled back. Climbing out, I grabbed our bags and the rifle from the back, then slung the bags over my shoulder. I bowed as best I could, considering I was trying to hold on to two bags and a gun at the same time. "Kea leboha."

His smile disappeared. He stared for a few seconds, then pointed. "Deh-vi."

"Ja. Yes." I braced, waiting for him to spit at me. He didn't. A thoughtful look crossed his face. He smiled again. "Adjö."

I returned his smile. "Adjö. Goodbye."

The man grasped the steering horns and roared toward the gates. He waved. I waved back. He shot through the opening and was soon lost to sight.

I was so tired the only thing I could think about was passing out. But I had to get this bag of charry to Hyme, return Teger's bag and gun to his apartment, check the beacon, and then go see Yose. Somewhere in between all that, I had to shower. I wondered if I'd be in any shape to conduct a service tonight.

Lab first. I willed one foot to move. Instead, I sank to my knees and slumped in the street.

"Tehi," someone called. "Tehi!"

My head felt heavy as a slab of thalin, but I managed to look up. Hyme and a small crowd of Mjorans ran toward me. The next thing I knew, I was picked up by several pairs of arms. I tried to protest. No words came out.

They took me to the hospital. By now, I was so dizzy, people were just a blur. Someone stripped off my filthy uniform, dressed me in a gown, and laid me on a bed. I hardly felt the needle penetrate my arm or the sheet tucked under my chin.

Closing my eyes, I fell into oblivion.

◑ᴿᴿᴿᴿ◐

I awoke with a start. *Where...am I?*

Hearing a chuckle, I rolled my head to see Teger lying on the bed next to me, grinning. "About time you woke up."

"When did I go to sleep?"

"Yesterday."

"What time is it now?"

"Time for dinner."

I struggled to get up. "Oh, no! I have to—"

"Stop that!" a voice snapped. Hyme strode into the room. "You don't have to do a thing. I've already notified Kepten Yose that I'm treating you for exhaustion and severe dehydration. I'll let you out of this hospital when I'm good and ready. The garrison and the beacon will just have to get along without you."

I fell back on the pillow. "All right. Whatever you say."

He sat at the foot of the bed. "How do you feel?"

"Groggy."

"Are you hungry?"

"A little."

"Good. Dinner will be here soon. I've ordered vegetable soup for you."

"Sounds delicious."

The room was quiet for a moment. I looked at Hyme. "So how did you find out about the mudslide?"

"Guess who," Teger said.

I turned my head. "Prag."

Hyme nodded. "He claimed he was on his way to visit a friend in Strind—that's another village—when he was almost caught in it and was forced to turn back. Said he thought he should warn people if they wanted to take that route."

"But he said nothing about us."

"If he did, he'd have to admit he was following us," Teger said. "And he wasn't about to do that."

"I raised the alarm as soon as I heard about it," Hyme said. "That was just after lunch. When we found the car pinned under a boulder at the mudflow's edge, we feared the worst."

A chime sounded. "Be right back." He got to his feet and left.

I looked at Teger. "There's got to be something we can do about Prag. I mean, leaving us maybe to die is a crime, isn't it?"

"No. It's despicable, but not a crime." He smiled. "Don't worry. I've got a plan. If it works, we'll never have to be bothered by Prag again."

"What is it?"

"Not telling. If it doesn't work, it's best you don't know."

I said nothing for a few moments. "Are we the hunters, now?"

He grinned. "Oh, yes."

I smiled a little. "How's your ankle?"

"Better. Hyme says he may let me out of here tomorrow. I'll have to wear a brace for a while, though."

"Did you rip any tendons?"

"No, thank the gods."

Hyme and a woman walked into the room with food trays. He set my soup on a portable shelf and rolled it in front of me. It smelled heavenly. The woman set Teger's dinner before him, a platter laden with meat and vegetables. We started to eat. Soup had never tasted so good.

After dinner, Hyme talked to us for a while, then declared it was time for us to sleep. We protested, but it was no use. He turned down the lights and after warning us not to stay up, left the room.

"I'm not sleepy," Teger grumbled.

"I'll sing you a song."

"Do that. I liked that song."

I sang my lullaby, and in minutes, he was asleep. Now it was my turn. I pushed my consciousness down until I felt as if I floated. I pushed some more, spiraling further downward into sleep.

My last thoughts were of Prag and what Teger had in mind.

Chapter Twenty

After Teger's and my ordeal on Hof Mountain, our bond deepened. In public, our formality was tinged with a new respect, as befitting former enemies who'd shared a harrowing experience, and came out the stronger and wiser for it. The Mjorans treated me differently, too. They showed a warmth that had been absent before, even after the mine disaster. On the street, they'd greet me with friendly smiles and sparkling eyes. I wondered if it meant they'd begun to accept me.

"Don't read too much into it, älskling," Teger said. "You saved those miners' lives and saved mine as far as they're concerned, but you're still Devi to them. It doesn't mean they think enough of you to invite you into their homes, much less heartsbond into the family."

It was discouraging because I'd come to like the Mjorans. They were a strong, intelligent, and independent people, the complete opposite of the hakoi back home. A pang of sadness lanced through me. *The hakoi back home aren't like the Mjorans because the Devi bred those traits out of them. It was necessary, but...still.*

Even though I was now fluent in Syrenese, we mainly spoke Devian. "Don't want to slip up," Teger had said. Hyme and Teger were teaching me to read and write in Syrenese, I was teaching both to read Devian, and the three of us were learning to write in my native tongue. Writing wasn't difficult, but it was frustrating. I was used to typing, my fingers flying over the keyboard to get my thoughts down. Writing by hand was too slow. I often got impatient forming the letters and numbers, and sometimes forgot what I was writing about even as I was writing it.

Another Ohra-Sin came and went. Maybe it was because I knew Teger was waiting for me in my bed, but this time, I didn't mind so much. Or tried not to.

Meanwhile, the Mjorans had been preparing for the Cirkus celebration, which was now at a fever pitch. Mjor's colors—a blue field crossed by yellow diagonal stripes—were seen everywhere. Other colors, bright and gay, were in evidence, too. Pennants affixed to the streetlights lining the plaza waved in the breeze, and bunting decorated the canopies of the shops and windows. A soundstage had been erected at the plaza's far end, near the rear gates. Cooking aromas permeated the air day and night. The villagers, including children, scurried about fetching and carrying. And Teger was in the middle of it all, directing the activity like an orchestra conductor.

I was busy too, not on my project, but helping Hyme to get ready for the inevitable illnesses and mishaps, from simple headaches to lacerations from falls. "I hope it won't be more than that, but we must be prepared," he'd said. We sorted the extra supplies he'd ordered, the nuskin, woolly balls, splints, and other assorted paraphernalia. Most important were the healing herbs and other plants he needed for his ointments and cures. He sent me to the woods and fields, usually twice a week, to get what he needed. Teger came with me. For him, our flower hunts were a welcome break from the hubbub in the village.

Prag always shadowed us. One day, a marun before Cirkus was to begin, Hyme sent us out for yet more skagwort. We decided to hike to the ridge since I'd pretty much denuded the vines in the nearby woods. Walking, he draped an arm about my shoulders. I looked up. He nodded, and I slipped my arm around him. On the ridge, we gathered all the skagwort flowers, pods, and vine bark we could, then lounged in the purple grass. Leaning over, he gave me a deep, passionate kiss. When it was time to leave, we took our time, holding hands almost all the way back to the village.

That night I asked why he'd done this. He smiled. "Two reasons. One, I've been thinking about it, and I don't want Prag to lose interest and show what he has before I'm ready. And two," he looked into my eyes, "I couldn't stop myself."

I kissed his cheek. "So when do you think Prag plans to tell the world about us?"

"Since he hasn't said anything yet, not until after Cirkus. And by then, I'll be all set."

Then it was Cirkus time. Half a marun before it began, caravans of revelers arrived in these great, elongated boxes on wheels and were directed to park outside the gates in a designated area. Others arrived by car. They too were directed to park outside the gates.

I watched with increasing interest. "Where will all these people stay?"

"Well, the ones who came in husbils—they're like small houses on wheels—will stay there. People who came by car will either stay in the village or they'll camp. Most will camp, though. Our hotel isn't big and even with so many of us opening our homes to guests—for a price, of course—there's not enough room for all of them."

On the first day, I stood at my window overlooking the plaza. People were greeted by three Mjorans wearing wide belts. On one side of the belts hung rolls of green nupaper. On the other hung a large, soft bag with a drawstring closure. Money was exchanged, and the hawkers pulled a length of nupaper from the roll and tore them into two strips. Buyers were given a piece from the strips or sometimes a length, depending how much money was spent. The other nupaper pieces were shoved into the bag.

More Mjorans walked about the plaza hawking the green nupaper. Even Teger took part. I noticed Prag spent a lot of money on these strips, buying them from every carrier he spotted. After buying a strip from Teger, I saw my lover's smile after Prag had turned away. He tore off one small green rectangle from the strip he'd kept and put it in his pocket. No one noticed. The rest he stuffed into the bag. It wasn't long after that he passed his roll of green paper, belt, and the money he'd collected on to someone else. He threaded his way through the crowd to his tower and disappeared inside. Emerging a few minutes later, he melted into the growing throng.

That night, sitting on his lap, he said I should stay in my apartment until Cirkus was over. "Laerds from other villages will be here, and I'll be expected to host them in a private setting."

"Every night?"

"No, but I don't know which nights. And I'll be so busy I might not get a chance to tell you."

"Not even at mealtimes?"

"Oh...should have said. Tonight was the last night for regular mealtimes. From now until the end of Cirkus, the dining hall will be open twenty-eight hours so people can eat whenever they get hungry."

"Then you should give the Laerds formal invitations. That way you'll know, and I can stay overnight."

He gave me a sly look. "Don't like sleeping in your own bed?"

I kissed his nose. "Of course...as long as you're in it."

Snuggling against his chest, when I heard his gentle snores, I knew it was time for bed. I hopped off his lap and gave him a shake. "Come on. Bedtime."

He jerked awake. "Wha—?" He blinked a few times, then gave me a sheepish smile. "I'm sorry. I must be more tired than I thought."

I helped him out of the chair, led him to the bed, and helped him undress. We slipped beneath the furs and in a moment, he was snoring again.

Lying in his arms, I thought about having to stay in my apartment until Cirkus ended. Alone, I rarely slept well. Guilt and anxiety dogged me, and my dreams were anything but pleasant. Sleeping with him helped keep them at bay. But if he said I should stay alone for the marun, then I would.

I wasn't looking forward to it one bit.

⊙═╤═╤═╤═⊙

People were still arriving on the third day of Cirkus. From my window, I gazed upon the sea of hakoi jostling each other as they tried to make their way around the plaza. Music blared from speakers set up around its perimeter. Shop owners shouted to the crowd their special Cirkus deals. The throng's excited jabbering added to the cacophony. Mjor was bursting at the seams.

I was supposed to meet Hyme at the dining hall in a few minutes. I left my apartment and, in the vestibule, opened the door a crack and peeked outside. Most of the mob had their backs to me, so it was unlikely they'd notice me join them. I took a deep breath and stepped out, making sure I heard the bioscan's click. Taking another breath, I began threading my way through the horde.

It was slow going. People stepped in and out of my way. Though I kept to the crowd's edge, there were some who noticed me. "Deh-vi. Deh-vi." It sounded like an epithet. Sometimes it was accompanied by a hiss. I kept my head down. At least no one spat at me.

A pair of long, trouser-clad legs blocked my way. My head snapped up. It was Piri Nyag. She bowed. "Moreva Tehi. May the Most Holy One turn Her face to you."

I bowed in return. "And to you, Piri Nyag."

She turned to a young, broad woman standing beside her, holding a child who couldn't have been more than two. "Moreva, this is Grylla Moren, one of the miners you saved in the mine collapse. She wanted to thank you in person."

Grylla stepped forward. "I'm honored to meet you. I'm a single mother with no living relatives, and I don't know what would have happened to my baby if you hadn't the courage to break your Protocol and free us. Thank you." She smiled.

I let Piri translate for me. Returning the young woman's smile, I bowed. "I'm honored you wished to meet me, Grylla Moren. I'm pleased I could help." Piri translated my short speech into Syrenese.

Grylla's baby started to fret. The girl, who'd been staring at me with wide eyes, strained against her mother's hold, her chubby arms stretched toward me. Grylla gave me an inquiring look, and I nodded. She held the baby out. Taking her, I held her close. The little girl fingered my face, pulled at my lip, and pinched me, no doubt intrigued by my blue-violet skin and makeup. She rubbed her palms against my cheeks, then looked down. They were clean. She looked up with eyes wide in amazement. Staring into my golden eyes, she poked one. I managed to close my lid just in time. Grylla gasped, but I glanced over and shook my head. The toddler grabbed one of my white curls and pulled. Then she let go, giggling when my tress sprung back into place. She did this several times, laughing with glee.

In my peripheral vision, I could see some in the crowd had turned to watch. Most looked horrified, but there were a few who smiled. Grylla let her toddler to play with my hair for a few more minutes, then took her. The little girl objected, but Grylla whispered something in her ear. She quieted.

"Have you had breakfast?" Piri said.

"No, I was on my way to the dining hall."

"Well, we've eaten so we won't keep you. I hope to see you again before Cirkus is over."

"As do I, Piri."

We bowed again. She and Grylla disappeared into the throng.

I finally arrived at the dining hall. Entering through the side door, I saw Hyme sitting on the dais. I took my usual chair. "Sorry I'm late," I said in Devian. "I ran into Piri Nyag from the mines and she had with her a young woman who wanted to meet me." I told him about the toddler playing with my face and hair.

He laughed. "Quite all right. I was a little late myself, trying to get through the crowd." He looked at the counter where the kitchen staff was serving up plates of food. "No service today, so you need to get in line."

"All right." Before I could rise, I noticed a middle-aged man wending his way toward us with plate in hand. He reached the dais and handed it to me. I dipped my head. The man smiled and walked away.

Hyme raised his brows. "Very thoughtful, our Laerd."

"What do you mean?" I said between bites.

"You were served. He must have told the staff to bring your food so you wouldn't have to stand in line. Makes of sense, considering how we feel about the Devi. Mjor's guests don't know you the way we do, and I can see how there might be trouble if you ended up standing in front or behind the wrong person."

That made me love Teger all the more.

I finished my meal. Hyme picked up our plates and walked them to a bin piled with used nupaper plates for recycling. We left the dining hall and headed to the lab, threading through the raucous mob. After a few detours, we made it to the building. Inside, Hyme disappeared into the apothecary to open the shop.

The lab was quiet, and I let out a tiny sigh. It was nice to be able to hear myself think. I walked to the skratz cage and peered through the lysite. The little beasts looked back at me with eyes bright. *I really need to work. But if it's as busy as Hyme thinks it will be, I wouldn't be able to get anything done, anyway. Too many interruptions. The two hours it takes for the virus to manifest is one thing, but there's no way I'd be able to make new serum, not with everything I have to do to make it.*

Hyme walked in and donned his lab coat as I slipped into mine. At the counter, he started making a batch of pills. The chime rang. He left to answer it. Through the open door, I heard the murmuring of voices. The chime rang again. Minutes later, he returned.

"Selling a lot of these headache pills." He smiled. "As I knew I would. And it's only the third day."

"So I guess your stock should be pretty much depleted by the time Cirkus is over, right?"

"Yes. I'll have to send you out for more supplies."

I laughed. "If there's any left. We pretty much emptied out the woods these past two marun or so."

We worked in companionable silence for most of the morning. Then it was time for lunch. Afterward, we had just stepped outside the dining hall when Hyme asked, "Coming back to the lab?"

I shook my head. "I need to check the beacon right now, then get my dance and meditation session in. I'll come after that."

"Very good. See you later."

We parted ways. Like this morning, I skirted the crowd, trying to make myself inconspicuous. I thought I was doing well until I was shoved from behind. I almost fell into the man in front of me. I turned. A huge hakoi woman with hands on hips glared. "What are you doing here?" she shouted, her words slurred. "Get out. Nobody wants your kind around!"

I didn't move.

"Did you hear me? I said get out!" She took a step forward.

I still didn't move. I lived in the village. She didn't. And I'd be damned if I was going to let her run me off.

She took another step. When I didn't step back, she balled her hands into fists and swung. I ducked. The power behind her swing spun her around. She stumbled.

A crowd had circled around us. "Get her," I heard someone shout. "Get the Deh-vi," someone else called. The rest took up the chant. "Get the Deh-vi. Get the Deh-vi!" The woman swung at me a second time, and I danced out of the way. People started laughing, which only infuriated the woman more. Eyes narrowed, she rushed me. Again, I stepped out of the way. Unable to stop herself, she fell into the crowd. They pushed her back inside the makeshift ring. I glanced around. Money was exchanging hands.

I kept my distance. Every move she made, I countered with one of my own. I had yet to lay a hand on her, but I knew this game was only going to last so long. I didn't want to get into a fight. Sooner or later though, one of her thrusts was going to come too close, and I'd have to defend myself.

Behind the woman, someone bulled their way through the mob. She swung. A meaty hand grabbed her arm and spun her around. It was Muts, and he did not look happy. He jerked the woman's arms behind her, pulled a plaztik restraint from his pocket, and then tied her arms behind her back. "Go on," he shouted to the crowd. "It's over. Go have fun!"

Muttering in obvious disappointment, the crowd left. Muts turned and cocked his head. I nodded. He gave a short nod, then hauled the woman away.

I reached my tower without further incident. Inside my apartment, I sat in a fireplace chair, thinking. *Astoreth. What happened back then? Why do they hate us so much? It's been twenty-five hundred years. Hyme talked about atrocities...but it was so long ago. Wouldn't they have gotten over it by now?*

"Guess not," I murmured. I gave my head a slow shake, then sighed. *Should check the beacon now.* Crossing my room, I wondered what kind of atrocities the Devi had committed. Maybe I'd ask Hyme about it later.

In the control room, the cylinder glowed white. I adjusted it and then inspected the converter's wiring. The main cable had started to slip again, and I jammed it into its socket. I jiggled it. The connection was firm. I called Central and made my report.

In my apartment, I undressed and headed for the É. Setting the lights on continuous burn, I chose my music, a strings only selection. The rich, full sounds swelled, and I began to dance.

When my legs were wobbly, I sat before the altar and closed my eyes. My body relaxed. The floating sensation stole over me, as did the swirling clouds. The familiar green landscape appeared.

...

I hover on the air currents, searching for the black bird. I don't see it. I fly toward the horizon. That's where it's always appeared before. My powerful wings carry me like a missile seeking its target. I'm spoiling for a fight, and I'm going to find one. The land below me is just a blur. I fly on and on, but I still don't see the black bird.

I grow tired and settle on the riverbank to rest. Curious, I walk to the bank's edge and look into the mirror-like water. Something's different. Then it dawns on me. I'm larger than I was before. My chest is much broader, and I sport the hooked beak of a raptor. I look down.

Wicked-looking talons grace my toes. The gold jewel on my breast is bigger and brighter. I stare at my reflection. *Why do I look this way?*

A shadow passes overhead. My head jerks up. It's nothing—just a passing cloud. I wonder where my friend might be. I have some questions I'd like to ask. I wait, but he doesn't show.

...

The vision faded. I opened my eyes and frowned. *I don't understand. Why was I larger? And alone? Where was black bird? Does this mean I won?* I shook my head. *Maybe it didn't mean anything at all.* Getting to my feet, I looked around. *I should get back to the lab. I'll clean later.* I turned off the lights and returned to my apartment.

Music and laughter came through the closed windows. Heading for the bath, I wondered about the time and stopped at the chair where I'd draped my uniform. I tapped the bar. "Time."

"Fifth hour, thirty-two minutes Tryn."

My brows rose. The trance had lasted for over an hour. I took a quick shower, threw on my clothes, and left. Outside, I hurried through the crowd as best I could. I got a lot dirty looks, but no one bothered me. I stepped into the lab.

Hyme burst inside from the apothecary. "Tehi—thank the gods. I'm running low on antiemetic syrup and I haven't had a chance to fill more bottles. Would you do that for me?"

The apothecary's chime rang. Without giving me a chance to answer, he whirled and raced away. I smiled. "Of course, Hyme." I walked over to his set-up for bottling the syrup and got started. The ninth bottle was almost full when he returned. "How many bottles do you need?"

"No limit. When you run out, I'll make some more."

"Why don't you give me the formula and let me do it? That way you won't have constantly run back and forth. In fact, if you'd give me the formulas for everything, I can make those, too."

He beamed. "That would be a huge help." Then he frowned. "But what about your own work?"

"You need me more."

"You're wonderful, Tehi."

"Teger tells me that, too." We laughed.

While I poured syrup into the bottles, he bustled about, collecting his formulas. He set them on the counter next to my bottling operation and headed to the apothecary. The chime rang as soon as he opened the door.

The street door opened, and Teger fairly leapt inside. For a moment, the sounds and smells of Cirkus invaded the lab's quiet. He slammed the door. Head swiveling left and right, his eyes held a wild look. "I need someplace to hide."

I frowned. "From what?"

"From the madness out there."

"But it's only the third day."

He clapped his hands over his face. "I know," he groaned. Dropping his hands, he walked over to me and slid his arms around my shoulders. "I'm sorry. I should have given you a proper greeting." He gave my hair a single stroke. "God eftermiddag, min älskling."

"Good after midday, yourself." Standing on tiptoe, I kissed his chest.

"What are you doing?"

"Helping Hyme. He's had so many customers since Cirkus began, he's running out of medications. So I'm making them up while he minds the store."

"You're wonderful."

"He told me that, too."

Chuckling, he lifted me until we were face to face, then gave me a soft and gentle kiss. Pulling away, he gazed into my eyes. "I have to go, älskling," he whispered, setting me on the floor.

"So soon?"

He sighed. "As Laerd, I have to be seen. That means walking around with a big, silly grin plastered on my face, talking to people, playing the games, posing for pictures...you know."

"I don't, but I'll take your word for it."

He smiled. "I'll try to come by again sometime. You'll be here?"

"Yes, except for services and checking the beacon."

"What about your dance and meditation sessions?"

"Hyme needs me. Those can wait."

"You're wonderful."

"You keep telling me that."

"It's true." He held me for a minute or two, and then grimaced.

"All right. Now I really have to go." Dropping his arms, he walked to the street door and looked over his shoulder. "Until later."

I blew him a kiss.

He caught it. Opening the door, he stepped through and was gone.

I returned to filling bottles. I'd just filled the last one—fifteen in all—when Hyme walked inside. "Finished with those, yet?"

"They're ready." I arranged the bottles on a nearby tray. He picked it up. "I'll need more headache pills next. Can you mix those up for me?"

"Of course."

He nodded, then disappeared into the apothecary. I mixed the headache formula and poured the powder into the pill press. The rest of the after midday flew by. I didn't stop working until Hyme came in to tell me it was time for dinner.

⬤▰▱▰▱⬤

I didn't see Teger again until the last day of Cirkus.

Hyme closed the shop early. "I want to see this." We left the apothecary and threaded our way through the crowd.

"See what?"

"The lotteri."

"What's that?"

"It's a way of gambling. You buy a ticket, and if your ticket wins, you get a prize."

"How do you get a ticket?"

He turned. "Didn't you see all those Mjorans walking around with the green rolls on belts when you were out?"

"Yes."

"Well, they were selling tickets."

"Oh." We started walking again. "What's the prize?"

"A one marun, all-expense paid trip for four to Gurm."

"Astoreth. That's some prize."

"Indeed. I just want to see who wins."

We staked out a spot near the crowd's edge. The blaring music died. Teger and a councilwoman walked on stage, the woman carrying a huge jar filled with green bits of paper. I smiled. *Ah...I see.*

"All right, everybody," his voice boomed over the sound system. "The moment we've been waiting for. The prize, for those who don't

249

know, is a one marun, all-expense paid trip for four to Gurm."

The crowd roared. Many waved their ticket strips above their heads.

He held up his hand for silence. "All right, let's go." The council-woman shook the jar. When she stopped, he plunged his hand inside, fished, and withdrew it with a single ticket clutched between his fingers. "And the winner is…" He peered and rattled off a string of numbers, then rattled them off again. He looked up. "Anybody got that ticket number?"

A shout rose up from the middle of the crowd. "Me. Me. I've got it!"

The mob groaned.

"Come on up and claim your prize."

When I saw who mounted the stage, my smile widened. Teger had pulled it off. The winner of the lotteri was none other than Prag Harst.

"Congratulations. You'll be leaving for Gurm in two days. Who are you going to take with you?"

Prag's face shone. "I'd like to take my parents and my brother Hert if he can get the time off. He's a miner."

Teger smiled. "I think I can arrange that if I ask Piri nicely." He faced the crowd. "Thank you all for coming. Enjoy this last day of Cirkus. There are great bargains in the shops, so support Mjor's economy by spending the rest of your money. We've enjoyed having you and we hope you had a wonderful time."

The crowd laughed and began to disperse.

"One more thing. Those who've found provisional mates, please go to the sessions hall to sign your contracts."

The music started again and Hyme and I headed back to the apoth-ecary. I tapped his arm. "What contracts is he talking about?"

"Didn't the Laerd tell you the reason for Cirkus?"

"Yes, but he didn't say anything about contracts."

"Well, those who find mates sign a one-year contract. If they decide they're not suited at the end of the year, they can part without conse-quences." He gave a little shrug. "It's a little more complicated if there's a child involved—visitation rights, and all—but couples are usually care-ful about that." His look turned thoughtful. "It's always amazed me how well the system works. From what I hear from healers in other villages, there are very few who part after the year is up."

"So where do they live?"

"Anywhere they want. If someone from Mjor found a mate from another village, they can either stay here, or go to the other's home village. Or they can apply to live in another village. Or they can go to the city."

"Is that how you met your wife? Through Cirkus?"

He chuckled. "No, I met her on one of my trading trips. Her father didn't approve of me. Nyla, headstrong as she was, convinced me to run away with her. So I did."

We reached the apothecary. Hyme unlocked the door and walked behind the counter. I stood on the threshold. "Is there anything else you'd like me to make up for you?"

"I think I've enough. People will be leaving tomorrow. This is the biggest party night of Cirkus, and I've plenty of headache and stomach pills as well as antiemetic syrup in stock."

"All right. I'm going to my apartment. I'm ahead of myself on sermons, and I'd like to keep it that way. See you at dinner."

"See you then."

I shut the door and grit my teeth against the music blaring from the loudspeakers. Walking, I kept to the mob's edge, as always. I heard hisses and threatening whispers, but no one tried to block me. Standing before my tower, I looked around to make sure no one was paying attention and stepped inside.

After all that din, the abrupt silence set my ears ringing. I started up the stairs, stopping when I reached the É. Staring into the darkness, I remembered I still had to clean it. *Later. I've plenty of time.*

Inside my apartment, the shutters were open. Music came through the windows. It was still loud, but not so much. I walked to the window and looked out. The crowd had thinned since yesterday. They milled about, some with seeming purpose and others without.

The music faded. I looked at the soundstage. A band, eight men and a woman, was setting up. They arranged several large black boxes around the stage, then took out their instruments, some stringed, some tubular. One sat before a rectangular orange box with spindly legs. They announced themselves, and the horde cheered and whistled. The ruckus eventually died down, and they began to play. To me, sounded more like noise than music.

I plopped into a fireplace chair. Spying my tablet, I leaned over and picked it up. I closed my eyes and tried to concentrate but couldn't. My attention wandered, from the music and the raucous crowd outside, to thoughts of what Eresh and Teger might be doing now, to my latest vision, and other places. I gave up. Setting the tablet on the table, I walked to the window. Several couples danced inside a ring formed by the crowd. Some were good, some were very good, and others were terrible. But everyone looked like they were having a fabulous time.

The battlement door opened. I jerked my head around. Teger crossed the threshold and grinned. "Oh, good. You're here."

I ran to him and leapt. Catching me by the waist, we peppered each other with kisses. After a minute or two, he set me on my feet. I looked up. "What are you doing here?"

"Hiding. I come here whenever I need a break. This is the last place anyone would look for me." He paused. "I hope you don't mind."

I snorted.

He took my hand, led me to the chair, and pulled me down onto his lap. "I thought you were helping Hyme."

I leaned against his chest. "He said he has enough medicines to last until Cirkus is over, so he didn't need me."

We fell silent, enjoying the nearness of one another. "Great gods, I've missed you," he whispered.

"Mm-hm."

Minutes passed. I closed my eyes, inhaling his scent and trying the block out the music outside.

"How do people find mates in this madness? Do they walk around with a sign or something?"

He laughed. "No. We hold dances and 'get-to-know-you' parties. Usually by eighth day, they've paired up. After that, it's just a matter of formalities."

"I bet all the pretty ones are taken first."

"Not necessarily. It may look like fun and games, but it's serious business. They're looking for mates, not passing fancies."

"So how many people signed up?"

"Twenty-six. All of them found mates, too."

"Is that usual? I mean, all of them pairing up like that?"

"I don't know. I've been to Cirkus, but I never put myself out there."

I leaned against his chest again. A few minutes later, he gave me a squeeze, pushed me off his lap, and took both my hands in his. "I have to go. Tonight's the big party night and I have to be everywhere. I don't even know if I'll make it back by morning."

I walked him to the door. He opened it and let out a small sigh. "I'll be so glad when this is over." Bending down, he planted a kiss on my hair. "I'll see you tomorrow sometime. Maybe." He left.

I closed the door. If I hadn't been so busy over the past marun, I probably would've gone insane. But our lives were about to go back to normal. "Me too," I whispered. "I can't wait until Cirkus is over, either."

I returned to the chair and plopped onto its cushion. Picking up my tablet, I steeled myself to focus. It wasn't long before I'd thought of several topics. *Hm. I'll do as many as I can before dinner.* I started dictating. After finishing the last sermon, I tapped the bar. "Time."

"Sixth hour, forty-seven minutes, Tryn."

I'd better go. Setting the tablet on the table, I left my apartment. At the bottom of the stairs, I took deep breath, then pulled open the door and stepped outside.

Keeping my head down, I started for the dining hall. No one hissed. No threatening whispers. No one spared me even a glance. I noticed the tall mugs, some frothing, that seemed to be in almost every fist. Several people swayed and stumbled as they tried to make their way through the crowd. I smiled. *Guess they're too drunk to care about a Devi wandering around.*

I entered the hall and saw Hyme was already seated. I pulled up my chair. "Hello."

He turned. "Tehi. Any problems getting over here?"

"Not this time. It was as if I was invisible."

"Excellent."

While we ate, he talked about the knowledge he'd traded with the other healers. "It's a good thing you cut all that terbone. I've traded most of what I didn't keep for myself. Among other things, I've got a new microscope, ideas for a couple of formulas I've been having trouble with, and a first edition of a textbook on herbs and plants I've coveted for years." He smiled. "You made me a rich man. I should send you out for the rarer medicinals more often."

I laughed. "Anytime."

After dinner, we lingered in the dining room, chatting about his newly acquired knowledge. Finally, I tapped the bar. "Time to service."

“One hour, four minutes.”

“I need to go. I’ll see you tomorrow.”

“Good night, Tehi.”

Walking to my tower, I was ignored again. While dressing, I thought about how the Syrenese healers shared knowledge. In Uruk, finding new cures was treated like a competition between and even within the És, with healers working on their projects in secret. *How many more cures could we find if we pooled what we knew? By now, we might have even found the red fever cure.* But I knew sharing knowledge would never catch on among É healers. The habit of secrecy was too deeply ingrained.

I checked myself in the mirror. Satisfied, I threw on my cloak and left to set up for the evening service.

Chapter Twenty-One

The night after the Harsts left for Gurm, I lay in Teger's bed, watching him dress for his first foray on his mission to find Prag's disc. When finished, he spread his arms and did a slow pirouette. "What do you think?"

Clad in black from head to toe, nothing he wore, not even his makeup, reflected any light. "You look like a shadow."

"Good." He picked up a small, slim cylinder from his desk and thumbed it. A spot of bright white light appeared. Nodding once, he put the cylinder into his pocket. Then he picked up a small, soft-sided case and checked the contents.

"What's that?"

He looked up. "Lockpicks."

I gaped.

He grinned, teeth glowing against the black paint. "Told you I'd been a bad boy." He walked to the door and looked over his shoulder. "Don't wait up."

Near dawn, he returned empty-handed.

This repeated for seven nights. I was a nervous wreck. Somehow, I managed to act as if nothing was wrong, but it was getting harder and harder. During services, I couldn't center myself and slipped more than once while delivering my sermons.

On the evening of the eighth day, Yose stayed after I'd dismissed the penitents. "Moreva. Permission to speak frankly?"

There was a quality to his voice, a kind of silky smoothness I didn't like. "Of course."

"Is anything wrong? You seem tense."

I gave him a steady stare. "No, Kepten. All is well. Why?"

"I noticed you stumbled during your sermon tonight. And you did it the night before, too."

"That's because I didn't memorize them well enough."

"Busy at the lab?"

"Yes, but what business is it of yours?"

He smiled. It wasn't pleasant. "It's important that our Moreva give her whole being during our services. That's when the Most Holy One speaks to us, and we need to absorb every word to feel Her comfort and love."

"I understand, Kepten. I will do better next time."

"I'm sure you will, Moreva." Saluting, he left the Temple.

After Teger returned to the apartment, I told him what had happened. He smiled and gave me a squeeze. "Patience, älskling. I'm on the hunt. Don't worry, I'll find the disc before they get back."

"You sound awfully optimistic."

"Let me put it this way. I know now where the disc is not."

I wasn't sure how that was supposed to make me feel better, but I said nothing.

On the ninth night, less than twenty-eight hours before the Harsts were due, he returned to the apartment with the disc in his gloved hand. "You see, älskling? I told you I'd find it."

"Where was it?"

"Prag's desk. In a hidden compartment."

"What do you think he'll do when he finds it gone?"

He grinned. "Nothing. I put a different disc in there. He has so many others piled on his desktop I doubt he'll notice one missing." He set the disc on his desk and stripped off his gloves. "Do you want to see it?"

"Have you looked at it?"

"Of course. I had to make sure I had the right one."

"All right."

I climbed out of bed while he booted up the computer. Slipping the disc into its slot, a picture immediately blossomed on the screen. I recognized it at once. It was the meadow where he'd taken me to harvest terbone.

"Passion," his deep voice filled the room. "I loved her, but not like I love you..."

He skipped to a different spot. The vid showed us making love. My eyes widened. "You mean he came back? Even after you shot him?"

"Mm-hm."

"Why didn't we sense him?"

He grinned again and winked. "We were busy. Seen enough?"

"Yes."

He popped the disc out of its slot and set it on the desk.

A stab of anxiety speared me. "Do you think he made a copy?"

"Don't think so. I went through his discs one by one. I searched every spot that looked like it could be a hiding place. This is the only one I found. If there's a copy, he's already given it to Yose. That obviously hasn't happened because if it had, you'd be in Uruk by now."

"True." I let out a tiny sigh of relief. "Now what?"

"Now we destroy it." He walked to his weight set and flipped over a section of the rug with his foot. Selecting the largest weight, he dropped the disc and let the weight fall. It hit the floor with a bang. Picking it up, he inspected the shattered disc and nodded. He set the weight on the rack. Stepping over to a small closet, he retrieved a broom, a dustpan, and a nupaper bag. He swept the shards and deposited them and the disc's sleeve inside. Crushing the sack in his large hands, he threw it into the fireplace and rearranged several bricks so it couldn't be seen. He looked over his shoulder. "We'll burn it come winter."

I frowned. "Why don't we burn it now?"

"Because no one lights a fire in the summer, silly."

"Oh."

Teger began stripping off his black clothes. "How come you have those?"

"They're for night hunting. Helps us blend in."

"How do you see?"

He rummaged in his closet for a minute, then returned to the bed holding what looked like a flexible black loop. "Here. Put this on. Make sure it covers your eyes."

I slipped the loop over my head.

"Now. Watch." He turned off the light.

The room went black for a split-second, and then I could see as if it was midday. I turned my head. He stood in the same spot, hand on the switch. "Wait...did you turn the light back on?"

"No. The room is pitch." He flipped on the light.

I took off the band and handed it to him. "How does it work?"

"There's a fluid inside that's ultra sensitive to light. It can pick up and amplify a single photon." He yawned, then looked down and winked. "I'm going to take a shower. Don't go anywhere."

"Never." I picked up the black band and inspected it. *Their technology...so much more advanced than I'd thought. That'll teach me not to make snap judgments. About anything.*

He returned about ten minutes later and crawled into bed. "Think you'll sleep better now?"

"Absolutely," I said, snuggling against him.

And I did.

⊙⊐⊒⊐⊒⊐⊙

Getting ready for the service the following morning, I slipped into my little pink dress. It was a bit loose. *Must've lost a few pounds.* Plastering on my makeup, I peered into the mirror. Satisfied, I threw on my cloak and left.

My performance was flawless. While cleaning the É, I noticed Yose standing in the doorway. His face was neutral, yet there was a sour look in his eyes.

I straightened. "Yes, Kepten?"

"I just wanted to remind you of our meeting today. It's time for my marunly report."

He listened to the service. I knew what day it was, and he knew I knew. He'd hoped to catch me in another slip-up. I smiled. "Thank you, Kepten. I will be there."

Yose saluted, then disappeared from the doorway.

After breakfast, Hyme and I were on our way to the lab when a young girl handed him a flyer. "Huh. Fourth time this morning I've gotten one of these."

"What is it?"

"There's an emergency Council meeting set for tomorrow, at five-thirty Tryn." He gave me a sideways look. "I'm pretty sure I know what it's about."

"I'm pretty sure, too."

258

"Are you ready?"

"Yes."

He nodded once. "Good."

At five-thirty Tryn the following day, Hyme and I took our seats on the dais in the sessions hall. Most of the councilmembers were already seated. Teger hadn't arrived yet.

Hyme had told me that at a meeting like this, he would normally sit with the audience, but Teger had thought it important to hide my fluency in Syrenese. To do that, he would act as the official translator.

I looked around. It seemed the entire village was here—standing room only. In the big room's center, a stand held a slim computer with a box beside it. A large white screen had been placed against the far wall. Prag stood next to the computer with a sleeved disc in hand. I leaned over. "How can Prag call an emergency meeting? I thought only councilmembers could do that."

"Anyone can call a meeting if it's important enough to affect the entire village."

Teger strode into the room. Ignoring me, he clapped a few of the councilmembers on the back before settling into his seat. If he was nervous about this meeting, he didn't show it.

He banged his gavel and the room quieted. "This meeting will now come to order." He fixed Prag with a bland gaze. "Mannen Harst, you have business before this Council?"

Hyme whispered in my ear.

Prag smiled. "Yes, Laerd. If I may give some background first?"

"Proceed."

He cleared his throat. "Thank you. As we all know, Hyme needs plants and herbs from the forest and fields to make his medicines. Before Moreva Tehi arrived you, Laerd, would assign someone to go with him while he searched for what he needed. After the Moreva's arrival, she went with him, but no one else. Then something changed. Suddenly it was you, Laerd, and always you, who went with Moreva Tehi while she searched for medicinals even at the expense of carrying out your duties as Laerd. Why was that?" He cocked his head and gave Teger a hard stare.

Teger stared back, unperturbed. "Because Hyme, you, and me are the only ones who speak Devian."

"Why did you never assign me to go with her?"

"You and your brother attacked her. Did you really think I'd give you a chance to do it again?"

Hostile muttering filled the room, and the temperature seemd to drop a few degrees. The villagers obviously hadn't heard about it. Their rancor was heartening; they were on my side. So far, anyway.

Teger rapped the gavel. The room went silent.

Prag seemed unnerved but plowed on. "Be that as it may, it seems that—"

"Will you get to the point, Mannen Harst?"

He straightened. "Very well. I charge you, Laerd Teger, with having a love affair with Moreva Tehi. You are a traitor. And I demand the Moreva be recalled immediately."

The hall erupted with cries of outrage, judging by the Mjoran's faces. It was impossible to tell whether it was directed at Teger and me or to Prag. Teger banged the gavel so hard I thought it would break. It had no effect. "Silence!" he roared. The lavmic amplified his deep voice. I would swear the walls shook.

It worked. The room quieted. I heard whispering as well as the rustle of clothing while those in the back jostled one another to get a better view.

Teger's stare had turned cold. "That is a serious allegation, Mannen Harst. I take it you have proof of this supposed affair?"

Prag smirked. "Oh, yes. I have the proof right here."

A hush fell over the room.

He flipped a switch on the black box. The screen glowed white. He slid the disc out of its sleeve, then inserted it into the computer's slot. The machine whirred. Turning, Prag stared at me with an evil grin.

A vid of a man and a woman having sex popped up on the screen. Animal-like grunting sounds came through the speakers. The man was Prag. The audience tittered, and soon erupted into raucous laughter. He spun around. "No," he shouted. "No!"

A scream tore through the air. The young woman pictured in the vid rushed down the aisle, hands balled into fists. Without breaking stride, she let fly with a punch that knocked Prag into the stand. He and the equipment crashed to the floor. The vid disappeared. She whirled and ran through the main door.

Teger banged his gavel, again to no effect. "Enough!" he shouted. The laughter quieted, though muffled giggling could be heard. "Is this your idea of a joke, Mannen Harst? Because I am not amused."

Jumping to his feet, Prag spun and stared at me, madness in his eyes. "You," he howled. In three bounds, he was up on the dais. He leapt, and hands closed around my neck. We went flying backward, chair and all. I hit the floor hard. Shouts and screams rang in my ears. Prag repeatedly banged my head against the floor. Stars danced behind my eyes. He squeezed my throat tighter and tighter.

My world went black.

I came to and opened my eyes to see Teger's frightened face hovering over me. "Moreva. Moreva! Can you hear me?"

His voice sounded far away. My hearing cleared, and I realized he was shouting. I opened my mouth, but no sounds came out. I nodded. Several hands helped me to my feet. I sagged against someone who helped me into a chair. My head and neck throbbed. Looking out over the room, I saw the villagers milling about, some wearing frightened looks like Teger. Others looked angry, and still others looked to be in shock. Their excited babbling made my head hurt even more.

Prag was nowhere to be seen.

"I think this meeting is over," Teger's voice rang out. I carefully turned my head. He'd returned to his seat.

"What about Prag Harst?" someone shouted. "He should swing from the battlement!"

"There will be no swinging today. Mannen Harst will be dealt with according to law. Thank you for coming." He banged the gavel once and stood.

The crowd began leaving amid much murmuring and the occasional bark of laughter. Teger walked over to me. "Moreva, I think you should go to the hospital and let Hyme look you over."

"I'm all right, Laerd." My voice was raspy.

"It would make me feel better." Though his tone was neutral, the look in his eyes told me he would brook no argument.

"I think the Laerd is right," Hyme chimed in.

Teger's and my gazes locked for a moment longer. Then I looked down and nodded. He helped me to stand. Hyme took a firm grip on my elbow and guided me out of the hall, then straight to the lab. Inside, I turned and held up my hands. "Hyme, I really don't think this is necess—"

"You heard the Laerd. And I do think it's necessary. You've had quite a shock."

In the patients' room, he pointed to a bed. "Up." Then he adjusted the panel's settings for positive energy flow. "I'll be right back. You need something for your throat. You're going to be very sore and no doubt you have a headache. I have something for those, too."

I smiled. I didn't have to tell him I had in my healer's kit whatever I needed to take care of myself. He knew. But he wanted to see to my needs. Teger wanted him to see to my needs. It was nice, being fussed over. I'd never had that before.

Teger stepped through the doorway. "How are you feeling?"

"You know, I'm really quite all right."

"You don't sound like it."

I patted the bed. He sat and looked into my eyes. "Älskling, why did you let Prag do that to you? I know your reflexes. You had plenty of time to move out of the way."

"Well, you'd mentioned that he'd already attacked me once. You saw them—they were upset. I wanted to show everyone Prag had it in for me, so he made up this story about us having an affair. Between the disc and his second attack, he can shout the truth from the rooftops, but nobody's going to believe him now." I smiled.

He didn't smile back. "I appreciate your reasoning, but I don't appreciate you putting yourself in harm's way. Prag meant to kill you. You should have heard him screaming when Muts dragged him away."

I covered his hand with mine. "I'm sorry. But it just seemed—"

"I know. Like a good idea at the time." He leaned over and kissed my forehead. "Hyme probably won't keep you overnight, so I'll see you later. Just don't get any more good ideas, eh?"

"I won't."

He stood just as Hyme came bustling into the room. "Don't leave yet." Teger sat. "Here," he said, handing me a few pills and a glass of water. "These will help with the soreness and your headache." I popped them into my mouth, followed by a swig of water. "And this will help your throat." He handed me a small bottle of what looked like syrup. I upended it.

He looked at Teger. "I'm going to keep her until dinner. After that,

I want you to walk her to her tower. If she shows any signs of flagging, bring her to me immediately."

I sat up. "Oh, now Hyme, that's—"

He swiveled his head and scowled. "Keep quiet."

I kept quiet.

Teger nodded. "I'll do that." He left the room.

Hyme turned. "Lie down. You need to get some rest. I'll be back later."

I fell back into the pillow. Already I felt drowsy. There must have been a sedative in the syrup he gave me. "Hyme…"

"Yes?"

I gave him a sleepy smile. "Thank you."

"No thanks needed, Tehi. Now sleep."

⊙ᗒᗒᗒᗒ⊙

Later that night, Teger picked up the pile of nupapers he'd been working on at his desk and straightened it. "Done." Standing, he stretched and turned. "I thought you'd be asleep by now."

"I slept until dinner, remember?"

"Mm." He stripped off his clothes. Leaving them in a pile where they dropped, he climbed into bed and pulled me close. "How's your throat?"

"Fine. I'm not sore anywhere, either. Hyme really is an incredible healer. You're lucky to have him."

"Don't I know it."

We said nothing for a long while. Then he gave me a squeeze. "You know, Prag might be out of the way, but we haven't seen the last of this. There's one more."

"Yose."

"Yes."

"But he doesn't know anything except for what Prag told him. He's gone. Yose can't hurt us now."

"That's not the point. He broke the Protocol. I won't let him get away with it."

"How in Astoreth's name are we going to prove it? Ask Prag? Aside from Yose's insinuations to me—if you could even call it that—there's nothing to go on."

263

“True. But aren’t you a little concerned about where Yose was getting the money to pay Prag?”

“It came out of his own pocket.”

“How do you know?”

I opened my mouth, then closed it. “Oh.”

“Oh.” He said nothing for a moment or two. “Tell you what. Even though you could say it involves the garrison, don’t tell Yose about the meeting. He’ll figure out soon enough something must have happened when Prag doesn’t come around for his money. Meanwhile, we’ll just wait. Maybe he’ll let something slip.”

“And if he doesn’t?”

“I’ll just have to figure out something else.” He kissed my hair. “Time for sleep.”

“I told you, I’m not sleepy.”

He grinned. “I can make you sleepy.”

“How?”

“Like this.” He pulled me on top.

It worked.

Chapter Twenty-Two

For almost an arhu, I watched the third sun rise later and later, lower and lower in the sky. The days were still warm but getting shorter, and the nights longer and cooler. One morning, the small sun didn't rise at all.

Summer was at an end. And I was halfway through my tour as beacon steward for Astoreth-69.

I turned from the window overlooking the rear of my tower. Teger was still asleep. I watched him for a while. With Prag out of the way and the evidence of our love affair destroyed, he was safe. But I wasn't. I still had to go home. Once I had, there was no way I could hide my love for him. I wouldn't even have to say anything. Astoreth knew me to my core. She would know what I'd done, and I'd be executed for breaking my most sacred vows.

"Hearts divided cannot serve," I whispered. I thought about my mother. Like hers, my hearts weren't divided.

My hearts belonged to Teger.

I shimmied out my garb and hung it in the closet. After a quick shower, I saw he'd awakened, and crawled under the furs with him.

"Good morning, älskling," he said, his voice heavy with sleep.

"And a good morning to you." I kissed his nose and then, worming my way under his arm, cuddled him.

"How did the service go?"

"Wasn't one of my best."

"I'm sure it was fine."

We lay in each other's arms, enjoying the morning quiet and our warmth. A long while later, he stirred. "I'd better get moving if I want to eat." Untangling himself, he climbed out of bed. I sat up and watched him dress in a long, collarless, loose-fitting white shirt with matching drawstring pants, then stuff his feet into a pair of brown soft-soled slippers.

He returned to the bed and sat on its edge. Smiling, he traced my jaw with his index finger. "I'll see you at breakfast." Then he left.

I lay back for a few minutes, feeling the familiar electric shocks fade. Then I too got up. Picking up my uniform, I went over it with a critical eye. The enzymes were failing, though I knew no one else would notice. Tomorrow or the next day, I'd have to pull a fresh one from my trunk. But it was fine for now.

At the vanity, I applied my makeup, and raked the comb through my long, tight white curls. My thoughts returned to the end of my tour and what would happen to me. *Will She be merciful and grant me a quick death? Or will She make an example and leave me to die in the desert like my mother?* I stopped combing. My lips tightened. I sincerely hoped She'd opt for a quick death.

I shook my head. There was no point dwelling on it. I was going to die for my sins, and there was nothing I could do about it. Meanwhile, I would make the best of what I had in the time I had left and be content with it. I started combing again, trying hard not to think about my death.

Then, in mid-stroke, an idea came to me. I stared into the mirror. The odds weren't good, but there might be a way I could survive a return to Uruk. I might even be able to return to Mjor. There were many factors to consider, and I had to think carefully through each one. But the crucial factor was that I had to be the first to find the cure for red fever.

And I had only eight arhu in which to do it.

⊙◲◲◲◲◲⊙

In the control room, I sat before the communications module, idly swiveling back and forth. *Come on, Eresh. Call me.* The panel stayed dark.

Sighing, I walked to the windows' control switch. *Could use a little ventilation in here.* I covered the panel with my hand, and four of the eight windows opened. A breeze wafted inside. I breathed in the freshness for a minute, then returned to the chair. I started swiveling again.

I'd been doing this for three marun. After my dancing and meditation session, I came here for my stewardship duty. Instead of leaving,

266

I stayed an extra half hour to forty-five minutes, hoping for a call from Uruk. So far, there'd been nothing. And I didn't dare make a call. It had been an emergency, but I knew how lucky I'd been last spring that Eresh had been at the board when I called. If Astoreth had found out I'd called, She'd also know I'd brought my research to Mjor. If She did, there was no telling what She would have done. But it was important that I talk to Eresh. He could give me the key piece of information I needed for my plan to succeed.

I tapped the bar. "Time."

"Fifth hour, fifty-six minutes Tryn."

I sighed again. *Better get back to the lab if I want to get some work done before dinner.* I got up and had taken a step when the green light started flashing and the alarm buzzed. My heartsbeat sped up. I fell back into the chair and smacked my hand against the panel. "Astoreth-69."

Eresh's head bloomed before me, a big grin on his face. "Greetings, Tehi. How are things going up there?"

"Eresh!" Barely containing my excitement, I smiled. "All right, considering."

"Is the Laerd still treating you badly?"

I hesitated. "We've come to...an understanding." I wondered what to say. Then I knew. I told him about the mudslide and how it had changed our relationship. "We're not exactly friends, but he doesn't scowl every time he sees me. A couple of times, he's even smiled."

"Good. That at least makes it easier for you. How's it going monitoring the beacon?"

"Not too bad, considering the problems I've had with the converter. I asked for a new one, but they haven't sent anything."

"And they won't. Trust me."

A moment of silence. "How about you? How are you doing?"

"Oh, I'm well enough, I guess. Believe it or not, sometimes I wish I was still beacon steward."

My jaw dropped. "Really? Why?"

"É life is so regimented. It seems like the bells are ringing every other minute, calling us to do this or that. I...I've had some difficulty readjusting."

"Nothing that's gotten you into trouble, I hope."

"No, no...it's just that I miss being able to do what I want when I want. You'll find out when you get back."

I said nothing. I'd be coming back to the É, all right. The question was whether I'd survive it.

"Is Yose up to his old tricks?"

"He spies on me often as he can. I'm in the lab a good part of the day, so there's nothing he can do about that. But when I'm in the É or going upstairs to my apartment, I sometimes catch him from the corner of my eye."

"Yes, he did that to me, too. How's the work on your red fever project coming along?"

"I'm making progress...I think. But how did you know?"

He frowned. "Know what?"

"That I was working on my project."

"Why wouldn't you be?"

I blinked, and then realized. *Oh...he was here.* I took a breath. "Astoreth said I couldn't bring it because it would be too dangerous."

He laughed. "That's my Tehi. You weren't about to let a little something like Astoreth's direct order stop you."

"Don't tell anyone, all right?"

"Oh, please. You know I wouldn't do that." He paused. "You got the habitat I sent?"

"Oh, yes. It's fabulous. You sent all the plants I've been working with most and then some. And thank you for my cooli. That alone is worth three talents." My hearts beat a little faster. "Do you know if anyone has found a cure?"

"No."

"Are you sure?"

He snorted. "Of course I'm sure. If somebody had, the whole world would know by now, including you."

I breathed a sigh of relief. "Good. I want to be the first."

"I'm sure you will. Just keep at it."

In the background on Eresh's end, I heard a bell. He sighed. "Time for tenth-hour prayers. I'll give you a call again when I have the chance."

"All right. And it'll get better. You'll see."

"Yes, I suppose so. Take care of yourself, Tehi. And tell Hyme I said hello. Signing off." He ended the transmission.

I stared at the green panel, now dark again. Tears welled in my eyes. "Goodbye, Eresh," I whispered, knowing this was the last time I'd talk to him.

Knuckling back my tears, I left the control room. Descending the tower steps, I thought about Eresh. He'd be fine, though I could see how readjusting to É life would be difficult. He was right about the constant interruptions. Until I came here, I'd never spent so much time in a lab. Now I couldn't imagine it any other way.

At the bottom of the steps, I looked to my left and saw the barracks door was shut. *Yose must have something better to do today than spy on me.* I pulled open the door. The day was beautiful, bright and sunny but definitely on the cool side. *Won't be long before I'm wearing my winter uniforms again.*

The next aftermidday, I sat a fireplace chair going over my lab notes when Teger walked in from the battlement. "I was pulling out my winter coats and thought about you."

"Why?"

"I want to see what you have."

I pointed to the closet. "In there."

He hauled out the red quiltsuit and a mound of furs. Holding them up, he looked over and studied me. "That's what I thought. Much too big. We'll have to get a quiltsuit and furs made for you."

He returned the winter wear to the closet. "We'll have to get you a pair of snowshoes made, too."

I frowned. "You have special shoes for snow?"

"They fit over your boots. The snow gets pretty deep, and the shoes keep you from sinking into it."

"Oh. Well, the É will pay."

"Of course it will. Put in the requisition after we see the furrier, the quilter, and the shoemaker."

I nodded. "So when do you want to do this?"

"How about now? If you're not too busy."

I thought for a moment. *I've already checked the beacon today, so...* "Sure." I picked up my tablet.

Teger eyed it. "Why're you bringing that?"

"I'm going to the lab after we're finished."

We went to the furrier, a kindly old man who took my measurements. Besides a coat, I needed a hat and gloves. "Give me about ten days, and I'll be ready for her final fitting," he said. At the quilter's, I was fitted for a suit that would also be ready in a marun. The shoemaker was our last stop. I explored the shop while he and Teger conferred. I picked up a boot and turned it over in my hands. Then I picked up a snowshoe. Flat on the bottom, it was far longer than my foot with upturned toes. The straps, I figured, were for holding it on the wearer's feet. *How can anyone walk in these things?*

"Moreva," Teger said in Devian. I turned. "You need to be fitted for your boots and snowshoes. Sit over here." He pointed to a chair in the shop's center.

I walked over to it. The shoemaker bustled about, picking up various objects. Sitting on a small stool, he bent down and measured my right foot in my boot, then set my foot on his lap. He took a stylus from behind his ear and made several notations on a piece of nupaper. Lowering my foot to the floor, he did the same with my left. He nodded and smiled. I smiled, too.

Teger looked at his wrist timepiece. "I've still got work to do, so I need to get back."

Giving the shoemaker a wave, we left the store. Walking across the plaza, I looked up. "What work?"

He chuckled. "Well, I couldn't say I was headed over to your place."

"I told you, I'm going to the lab."

"Oh, right. Damn."

"What?"

He looked down and grinned.

I rolled my eyes and then frowned. "Wait...he took my measurements in my boots. Wouldn't that make my feet bigger and the fur boots too small?"

"Yes, but he's making allowances for that. Pedar—that's his name— has been doing this for years and can figure out exactly how wide and how long your foot will be in your new boots and snowshoes."

Entering the lab, I walked to my table, switched on my tablet, and scrolled to where I'd left off. I'd just gotten an idea for a new formula when Hyme came in from the apothecary. I looked up.

He smiled. "Hello, Tehi. I thought you'd be here earlier."

"Teger and I went shopping for new winter wear. Nothing in my closet would fit."

"Ah." He stepped over to one of the long counters, pulled the pill press to him, and poured in a medium-sized bag of blue powder. Then he started the machine.

The press's whine and the racket made by the finished pills shooting into the hopper made my ears hurt. *Better type instead of dictate. The mic won't pick up my voice over all that noise.*

About five minutes later, I caught a faint whiff of smoke. Frowning, I checked the burners on my table. They were cold. I checked Hyme's burners. They were cold, too.

"Hyme, do you smell something burning?" I shouted.

He stopped the press and sniffed. "No, can't say I...wait. I do smell something. Wonder what it is?"

"Let's go see."

We headed for the apothecary. The smoke smell was much stronger in here and stank of chemicals. We frowned at each other. Hyme walked to the door and stepped outside, with me on his heels.

I froze. The control room was on fire.

Thick, oily-looking black smoke billowed from the tower's windows I'd left open. When I could move again, I sprinted across the plaza. A group of children were seated on the ground staring, but I didn't waste time by going around them. I leapt, hurdling over their heads. Reaching my tower door, I hopped from foot to foot, waiting for the bioscan lock to disengage. "Hurry, come on, hurry!" I muttered. Just when I was about to break the thing, it clicked. I threw the door open and hurtled up the stairs, shoved the door open to my room, and barreled over the threshold.

I yanked open the door to the beacon tower. Smoky tendrils wafted toward my apartment. I raced through the tunnel, jumped on a lift, and set the controls for full speed. It shot up, then stopped with a jerk. I was nearly thrown off.

The smoke was so thick, I couldn't see a thing. *Astoreth. Why aren't the auto foamers working?* No foamers meant I had to put out the fire the hard way. I prayed it hadn't grown so big I couldn't deal with it myself.

I dropped into a crouch. Coughing, I felt along the wall until my hand closed on the fire extinguisher. I hauled myself to my feet, clutching the heavy rectangle under one arm. Now I needed to find the switch plates for the exhaust fans and the siren. Moving forward, I dragged my fingers across the wall until I found them. I read the raised letters with my fingertips until I found the right one. I pressed my hand against the panel. Nothing happened. I pressed again. Still nothing. I took another step, my fingers sliding over to the next plate. I pressed the panel. The fire siren set up a piercing wail.

I didn't have time to wonder what had happened to the exhaust fans or what had happened to the garrison. The flames I could see through the smoke were growing by the second. Dropping into a crouch, I crab-walked toward the fire, spraying the green, viscous goo as I moved along. My lungs and throat burned, but I kept going. I was sure the old converter had caused the fire. *If they'd sent me a new one like I'd asked, this wouldn't be happening.*

My head spun from inhaling smoke. I rallied against it, knowing I would die if I lost my way. On and on I went, battling the fire and my own body as I crossed the floor. I looked up. The room was still ablaze, but the flames had lessened.

I stood to stretch my legs and turned my head in time to see flames leap over the non-flam barrier I'd laid down. Stepping forward, I slipped on a patch of the green muck and fell. My temple connected with a solid thump against something hard. I fought to stay conscious, but it was no use.

My world turned black.

⊙⊐⊐⊐⊐⊐⊙

"She's coming out of it," someone said.

I made a tiny frown. *Who's coming out of what?*

Then I remembered the fire and hitting my head on something. But where was I now?

I opened my eyes. The hospital. Hyme hovered by my bed, looking anxious. "Tehi, can you hear me?"

I tried to answer but couldn't. That was when I realized I'd been given an endotracheal intubation. With that hose going down my throat to ventilate my lungs, there was no way I could talk. I nodded.

"You've been in a coma from severe smoke inhalation. The tube's there to keep your throat from closing up completely. Your lungs have been—"

I nodded again.

He smiled. "Sorry. I got carried away. I know you know."

Teger entered the room. "She awake?"

"Yes."

"May I talk to her?"

Hyme hesitated. "You have three minutes." He left.

Teger leaned down and kissed my forehead, then sat on my bed. "I brought you something. I figured you might be able to use it." Handing me my tablet, he must have seen my elation because he chuckled. I turned it on. A keyboard appeared at the bottom of the screen.

How long?

"About two days."

Who?

"Me. I saw the smoke and knew you were in there. I'd no idea you needed rescuing, though."

How?

He grinned. "You left the doors open."

Did you put out the fire?

"No. It was still burning when I ran out of there."

Anything left?

"From what I hear, not much. The control room is going to have to be completely rebuilt."

"Time," Hyme called and bustled into the room. "Out, Laerd."

"Can I have fifteen more seconds?"

He sighed. "All right."

Teger picked up my hand and kissed it. "I love you," he said, giving it a gentle squeeze.

Love you more.

Hyme tapped his foot. "Laerd, you really must leave now. Tehi needs to rest. I'll let you know when she's up for having company again."

"All right, all right. But you call me the minute she is."

"Agreed. Now shoo!"

Teger laughed as he left the room. Hyme stepped up to the bed, syringe in hand. I picked up my tablet. *What's that?*

He looked at the screen and then at me. "Concentrated olarian. Do you want some or do you think you can sleep on your own?"

I hesitated. I knew what went into some of Hyme's sedatives—they would knock out an ura. But if this was just olarian, that was different. And this tube was uncomfortable. I nodded.

He gave me the shot.

The next time I woke, the tube was gone from my throat. I opened my eyes to see Hyme enter the room. He walked to the bed, perched on the high stool next to it, and smiled. "How do you feel?"

I opened my mouth.

"Don't. Use your tablet."

I picked it up and started typing. *That wasn't just olarian.*

"No."

I glared.

His smile died. "Tehi, when we're hurt, sleep is the best medicine. Your Devi blood…a simple olarian shot wouldn't have put you down long enough, nor would you have slept deeply enough. You know that."

I screwed my lips and nodded.

"I'm sorry I didn't tell you the truth, but I also didn't want you trying to balk me."

My lips loosened. *All right.* I set the tablet aside.

He patted my hand. "You have a visitor." I grinned, but he shook his head. "It's Kepten Yose. Do you feel up to seeing him?"

My grin melted into a frown, and I nodded once.

He walked to the door to the hospital's small waiting area and pushed it open. "Kepten, she'll see you now." He left the room as Yose entered.

Yose stood at the foot of the bed and saluted. His face was stern. "Moreva, I'm sorry to bother you at a time like this, but I need to ask you some questions about the fire."

Eyes narrowing, I grabbed my tablet. *You dare to question me, your superior officer and a Moreva?*

He smiled. It wasn't pleasant. "Yes, Moreva. On the order of our Most Holy One. She is most unhappy that Her beacon was destroyed."

Prove it.

"Of course." He pulled a tablet, much smaller than mine, from his pocket. He walked around the bed and handed it to me.

I switched it on. Astoreth's miniature head appeared, Her look severe. "Moreva Tehi. Concerning the fire, you will cooperate with Kepten Yose in any manner he sees fit until the investigators arrive." My lips tightened. A holo was easy to fake. I touched a small indentation on the tablet's side. A tiny numeric keyboard appeared. I pulled out the tablet's stylus and punched in a series of numbers. Astoreth's head vanished, replaced by an alphanumeric code floating above the tablet. I stared at it, wide-eyed. The message came from Her personal computer. Besides me, only three morevs at the É—all technicians—knew Her identification code. The message could still be a fake, but it was highly unlikely.

I turned off the tablet. Giving him my most ferocious glare, I nodded once.

Hyme came into the room from the reception area. Yose turned. "Healer, this is official business. You must leave."

Hyme's jaw set. "The Moreva is my patient. Her well-being comes before your official business. I am here to monitor her condition. If you upset her in any way, *you* will be the one to leave. Is that understood?" He brushed past Yose, perched on the stool, and glowered.

Yose stared back. His jaw tightened, then relaxed. "Understood."

He turned. "We've determined the cause of the fire. It was the converter. Did you check the beacon that day, Moreva?"

I picked up my tablet. *Yes.*

"Was all in order?"

Yes.

"No loose or frayed wires or cables?"

No.

"Would you swear to that?"

Yes.

"Well, if all was in order when you checked the converter, how do you think the fire started?"

I shrugged.

"I'll tell you. The converter's main cable, which you just swore was in fine working order when you checked it, shorted out and caused a power spike. That, in turn, caused the converter's meltdown which started the fire." He stared with hooded eyes. "Are you still willing to swear all was well when you checked the beacon?"

I knew what he was doing. He was trying to hold me responsible because I was lax in my stewardship duties. I gave him a stiff nod.

"Very well. I have just a few more questions, and then you can get your rest." He paused. "When my people entered the control room, they noticed a series of footprints much too big to have been yours. They followed these footprints to the lift and down to where they disappeared in the tunnel. Moreva, do you know to whom those footprints belonged?"

I was about to type "no" when a familiar, rumbling voice answered for me.

"They're mine," Teger said. He stepped into the room from the small reception area.

Yose turned. "Yours?"

I waved my hand behind Yose's back, trying to get Teger's attention. No one must know he'd been in the tower. He'd broken the Protocol and would go to prison. But now that he'd admitted it, what could be done?

Teger walked to my bed and smiled. "Yes. Mine."

Yose straightened. "Then I'm afraid, Laerd, you'll have to come with me."

His smile didn't waver. "Slow down, Kepten. I have a few questions, too."

"I don't answer to you."

"Maybe not, but I'm sure the Moreva has questions of her own. You do answer to Moreva Tehi, don't you?"

"She's in no condition to—"

"I'm sure the Moreva wouldn't mind if I spoke for her." He looked down. "Permit me?"

I nodded.

His smile died. "Where was the garrison while the tower was burning?"

"Out on maneuvers."

"The entire garrison? You left no one behind to see to the safety of the tower?"

"Of course not. There was a guard—"

"On duty, yes. One lone guard who told me he'd face a military tribunal if he left his post for any reason and who tried over and over to contact you. You never responded." He tilted his head. "I've talked to several of your senior personnel—"

Yose's face darkened. "You had no right!"

"I did. Under the Protocol, I'm empowered to do anything I think necessary to ensure the safety of Mjor. That fire could have endangered us."

I thought that a bit of a stretch but of course, I said nothing.

"Your personnel told me you left fifteen troops behind but ordered them to practice virtual maneuvers instead of being on alert for any danger to the tower. Hooked up to those machines, they could neither see the lights nor hear the siren. They may have well as gone with you."

Yose's eyes widened. "Are you blaming me for the fire?"

"No, I'm blaming you for not being there to help put it out." He paused. "How do you think the Most Holy One would react if She knew her granddaughter almost died because the garrison was unavailable? That it took a villager willing to risk prison to save her life?"

Yose stared at me.

I nodded.

He looked back at Teger, his eyes narrowed to slits. "Defending the Moreva, are you?" he sneered. "That's just the kind of thing I'd expect from her lover."

Teger smiled again. "I've heard that charge before. It was never proven." He frowned a little. "But Kepten, how did you hear about it? It was an internal affair. There are only two people in the village authorized to speak to you, and both of us are in this room. I know I didn't tell you." He looked at Hyme. "Did you?"

"No."

He turned to me. "Maybe it was the Moreva."

I shook my head.

He looked at Yose and raised his brow. "Well, Kepten?"

"I don't answer to you."

"I'm speaking for the Moreva."

Yose said nothing. A trickle of sweat slid down the side of his bald head.

Teger's eyes narrowed. "Then I'll tell you how you heard about it. From Prag Harst, one of my villagers. He somehow contacted you saying he could prove the Moreva and I were having an affair but needed money to do it. So you gave it to him. But he came back to you for more, always more, and you paid. That brings me to another question. How did you get the money to pay Harst?"

"I don't know what you're talking about."

Teger stepped forward until he was a scant two šīzu away from him, looming over the much shorter man.

Yose stood his ground.

They glared at each other. "Lying does not befit the proud tradition of Astoreth's military, Kepten. I'll ask again. How did you get the money?"

Yose didn't answer. He seemed to be weighing whether it was safer for him to say nothing, or to confess all. He blinked a few times, then took a breath. "At first I paid him out of my own wages," he said in a strong, clear voice. "But when he demanded more, I could no longer do that. So I put in a requisition for a small pay raise for my troops. I signed the Moreva's initials, and the requisition was approved. I used that money to pay Harst."

"And when he stopped coming around with his demands?"

Yose stood tall. "I distributed it to my troops according to rank and grade." He looked and sounded indignant.

"I think we've heard enough," a woman's voice floated into the room. A moreva stepped inside. She was an É investigator, identifiable by the insignia she wore on her right shoulder. Two morevi, also with insignia, accompanied her. A slim combination transmitter-receiver was clipped to her belt. Above the tablet floated a holo of Astoreth's scowling face. She couldn't see us—there was no cam here—but She'd been listening.

"Kepten Yose, I charge you with dereliction of duty, breaking the Protocol, and theft. You are relieved of your post immediately. You will return to Uruk to face My charges. You are to leave at once."

Yose seemed to sag inside his uniform. "Yes, Most Holy One," he said, sounding defeated. Then, as if remembering the military's proud tradition, he straightened. Chin held high, he marched toward the two morevi. The three men left the room.

"Tehi," my grandmother said. The last investigator turned the tablet to me. "I am glad you are all right, child. I owe a great debt to Laerd Teger for saving you. I will not be able to come see you, but I will be thinking of you daily. And Laerd Teger." The investigator rotated the tablet. "I absolve you of all responsibility for breaking the Protocol." Astoreth inclined Her head. "Kea leboha." The holo disappeared.

The investigator slipped her tablet into its sleeve. "I'll be going now, too. And I also give Laerd Teger my thanks. This is not the first time Kepten Yose has been investigated, but our results were always inconclusive." She turned to me. "I hope you're up and about soon. The garrison needs you." She gave each of us a nod and walked out.

Teger stepped over and sat on my bed. I started typing, then held up the tablet. *You were lucky.*

"You're right. For a minute there, I thought I was going to prison." He winked. "Would've been worth it. I've always wanted to see the inside of the tower, on fire or not."

We gazed at each other. His lips stretched into a sly smile. "Astoreth owes me, huh? Well, I know who I'm going to collect from." He kissed my forehead. "You get some rest. I'll see you tomorrow." Giving my shoulder a squeeze, he left the room.

I lay back in the pillows. Hyme slid off his stool. "The Laerd is right. You need to rest now. Miss you in the lab."

Miss you and the lab, too.

"Are you in much pain?"

No, not too much.

"I'll give you something for it. Be right back."

When he returned, he held a syringe. I raised my brows.

"Just a little bit of kerrian."

I nodded, and he gave me the injection. The effect was almost immediate. The pain in my chest was gone. But all the excitement had exhausted me. My eyelids drooped.

"All right, I'll leave you now."

I barely heard him and didn't see him leave. In a moment, I fell into a deep, peaceful sleep.

◎ ⊐⊏⊐⊏⊐ ◎

Fifteen days after Hyme had discharged me from the hospital, Teger and I stood in front of the beacon tower, watching an airship settle over the landing pad. It hovered about ten šīzu off the ground. When the glow beneath its belly had faded into nothingness, the pilot shut down the engines. The sudden quiet was disconcerting. The only sound was the breeze soughing through the trees.

In the near silence, we awaited the arrival of my new second in command. Behind us, the garrison stood at attention.

A hakoi in uniform exited the aircraft. From here, I could tell it was male and a Kepten. He walked toward me. Stopping about three šīzu away, he saluted, face impassive. He was taller than Yose, but not by much. It didn't matter. Short as I was, I'd look up to him, anyway.

"Kepten Stiren reporting for duty, Moreva."

"Very well, Kepten. Welcome to Beacon Astoreth-69."

"Thank you, Moreva."

"Kepten, this is Laerd Teger, Chief of Mjor."

"Laerd. A pleasure to meet you."

"Likewise, Kepten. Welcome to my village. I must get back to my work, now. A good day to you." He headed for Mjor's giant stone gate.

I'd no idea what to say next, so I said the first thing that came into my head. "The garrison is ready for your inspection, Kepten."

He nodded once and pivoted toward the garrison. We walked along the orderly rows of soldiers, not speaking. After our inspection, I pointed to four troopers and directed them to unload the airship. I turned to Stiren. "I'll show you the barracks now." We headed for the tower doors. A soldier broke formation to open and hold the door for us. I didn't know if that was protocol, but it wasn't until then that I remembered to dismiss the troops. The garrison followed us inside at a respectful distance.

I gave Stiren the tour. I took him through his quarters, the kitchen, and the room with the virtual combat trainers. We walked up the short flight of steps to the barracks door, and I rested my hand on the bioscan lock. "This door leads to the É. I hold morning and evening services, and you're in the evening group. Service starts at one-thirty Durm."

We walked to Stiren's new office. He sat behind the desk, and I took the visitor's chair. I smiled. "Do you have any further questions? Anything you'd like to know?"

He inclined his head. "Thank you for the briefing, Moreva. These are the kinds of things you can only learn on the ground. But I do have one question. Without a comm, how do I get in touch with you?"

"There's an intercom behind you. You can call one of three people on it—Hyme, the village healer, the Laerd, and me. If I'm not in my room, I'm usually at the village's laboratory. Call Hyme, and he'll let me know. If I'm not in my room or at the lab, there isn't any way to get in touch. Just leave a message."

"I see. Permission to speak frankly, Moreva."

"You may."

"I understand, and I'm sure you do too, that one of my duties is to report to our Most Holy One the morev's conduct, and I make my report marunly."

I frowned. "What are you getting at, Kepten?"

"I had the opportunity to speak with Kepten Yose before his execution. He told me about the rumored affair between you and the Laerd. He said he never reported it to our Most Holy One because he had no proof."

He stared as if expecting a reply.

He wasn't going to get one. I sat immobile, my hard gaze riveted on his, and said nothing.

Stiren seemed unperturbed. "After that villager came to him with his allegations, Yose claimed his suspicions were fueled by his frequent attempts to contact you by intercom in the middle of the night. Sometimes he even rang your doorbell. Either way, you did not answer, when by all rights you should have been in your quarters."

I stared for a moment longer, then took a deep breath. "Kepten Stiren, I do not have to answer to you, but I will if only to put this matter to rest. First, despite what Kepten Yose may have thought, I am under no curfew and am not required to be in my apartment at any given time. Second, I am a healer. I am often at the lab late, which may stretch into the middle of the night. During those times, the Kepten never once tried to contact me there. Third, I am a poor sleeper. At night, it is my habit to turn off the intercom's chime except when I am expecting a call. The same goes for the doorbell." I paused. "Have I responded to your concerns, Kepten?"

He gave me an unreadable look. "Yes, Moreva. And you should know that unlike Kepten Yose, I am not a suspicious man by nature. My only interest lies in your ministering to the spiritual needs of this garrison. As long as those needs are met, I will have nothing to report."

I stood. "Thank you for your candor, Kepten. It is much appreciated."

"As is yours, Moreva. Please, allow me to see you out."

The garrison came to attention as soon as they spotted me. "As you were." The soldiers went back to their various activities.

Stiren followed me to the barrack's door and pushed it open. I stepped over the threshold, then turned. "I will see you at the evening service."

"Yes, Moreva." He saluted and the door shut.

I climbed the stairs to my apartment. Though it was early after midday—lunch was only an hour ago—I thought I might as well check the beacon. Doing it now would save me a trip from the lab later. Besides, despite my strict orders, I'd learned the gods didn't care when the daily report was called in as long as the report was called in daily. I patted my pocket, feeling its slight bulge. And while in my apartment, I could refill my vial.

Rounding the staircase turn, my inner ear played back the conversation I'd just had with Stiren. Teger and I were safe enough from him. He'd made it clear he was only interested in the garrison's spiritual well-being, not me. I hadn't realized it until now, but a huge load had been lifted from my shoulders.

Feeling lighter than I had in arhu, I skipped up the remaining stairs and entered my apartment.

Chapter Twenty-Three

Long before the morning service, I tramped across the plaza, footsteps echoing on the paving stones. The suns wouldn't rise for hours, and the dark suited my mood. Three arhu had passed since summer's end. I was no closer to finding for the red fever cure now than I had been then.

I'd left Teger sleeping in his bed. He didn't understand my rush to discover the cure—I hadn't told him my plan—but he'd gotten used to me leaving so early. Every so often, I'd catch him watching me with a worried look. "You should rest, älskling," he'd say. "These early mornings and late nights are too hard on you. Maybe you haven't noticed under all your makeup, but you've got dark circles under your eyes."

I'd noticed. I'd chosen to ignore them.

A strong breeze kicked up. I shivered. *Be winter soon.*

My mind went blank until I reached the lab. Standing outside the door, I blew a heavy breath. Condensation wreathed around my head. Pushing it open, the lights flickered. I set them for continuous burn. I shrugged into my lab coat, blew out another breath, and opened the closet door.

I hesitated, staring into the darkness. Then I stepped inside. Walking to my habitat, I rolled back the cover and saw it was morning. *I should check my plants.* Strolling along the aisle, I looked for dead leaves and other signs of blight. There were none. I checked the water supply, dipping my hand into the bucket and examining the water cupped in my palm. It was clean. The bucket would need filling soon, but it could wait.

I straightened and dried off with a nearby towel. Lips tight, I stared at the sterile chamber. *I don't want to see. I know what's in there.* I approached the environment with slow steps, looked inside, and gasped. I fled the closet and ran to Hyme's apartment. "Hyme. Hyme. Wake up," I shouted, banging on the door. "Wake up!"

Hyme, in his nightwear and half-asleep, finally opened the door. He peered out. "What's wrong, Tehi? What's happened?"

I grinned, hopping from foot to foot. "It's not what's wrong—it's what's right. Come see, come see!" I ran to the closet and skipped inside.

He entered a moment later and walked over to me. "All right. What's this about?"

I pointed to the environment. "Look. What do you see?"

"I see a dead skr—wait. It's color—it's not so bright a red. And no pustules."

I beamed. "Right."

"What did you use?"

"Just cooli and linmen, can you believe it? I can't believe I didn't think of that before. But that's the key—a mixture of southern and northern antivirals. Now I just have to find the right ones. Oh Hyme, this is the furthest I've ever gotten." I threw my arms around him and hugged tight.

He loosened my grip. "My antivirals are at your disposal."

I let my arms fall. "Thank you. And believe me, I'll use them."

"Of course you will. Now if you'll excuse me, this old man needs his rest."

I ducked my head. "I'm sorry. It's just that—"

"I know. I would have done the same." He smiled and left me alone.

I listened to his footsteps, then heard his door open and shut. I waited. Not hearing anything more, I dipped into my pocket, drew out a vial of pills, and popped one into my mouth. It tasted awful, and I barely resisted the urge to spit it out. The pill was decil, a potent, extreme energy mixture Hyme had shown me how to make not long after I arrived. Right now, it was perfect for my needs, though I had to alter the formula because of my Devi blood. In minutes, new vigor rushed through my body. I'd been taking them whenever I started feeling worn but no more than two a day, just enough to get by. Decil was highly addictive, and I was sure I had enough hakoi blood to succumb if I wasn't careful.

Slipping my hands into the manipulators, I picked up the dead skratz, dumped it into the acid bath, and watched it dissolve. I pulled my hands free and rested a finger on the canister's dark panel. It blazed orange, and acid gas billowed into the chamber. When the clouds had dissipated, I left the closet.

I opened the cabinet where Hyme kept his antivirals and studied the glass tubs. "Baryn ought to be good." Spying a nearby stool, I lugged it to the cabinet and climbed on top. I took out the tub of dried seeds, setting it on the counter. I made six trips, retrieving a different stock of seeds each time. After lining up the tubs, I grabbed seven jars with lids from the cabinet beneath the counter.

I dragged the grinder toward me. Filling the hopper with baryn seeds, I closed the cover and tapped a lighted green square. The grinder sprang to life, its irritating, high-pitched whine setting my teeth on edge. Powdered baryn flowed from the chute into the jar. After the last dregs had trickled into the jar, I pulled it from under the spout, capped and labeled it, then set it aside. Taking out the grinder's blade, I washed it at the sink. I peered. *Looks clean enough.*

I put the blade in the blow dryer, setting it for three minutes. While it worked, I wiped down the grinder's chute and other parts where the powder had sifted. A chime sounded, signaling that the dryer's cycle had ended. I took out the blade and inserted it into the grinder.

After filling the jars, I carried them to my table and arranged them in a neat stack. Shrugging out of my lab coat, I draped it over the chair. I reset the lights, took one last look around, and then stepped outside.

Not even the barest hint of dawn played about the mountaintops. I skipped to my tower. Inside my apartment, I laid out my garb and made plans. After breakfast, I'd clip the most potent antivirals from the habitat and start working with those and the ones I'd taken from the cabinet.

A thought that had been hovering at the back of my mind burst to the fore. I hoped it wouldn't take too long to find the solution. I might be headed in the right direction, but I was running out of time.

Tightening my lips, I dressed and headed down to the É.

⊙⊐⊐⊐⊐⊙

Two marun later, I returned to my apartment from the lab, late as usual. My weariness made each step feel like I was slogging through mud. I was looking forward to sleeping, no matter how little. Walking inside, I was surprised to find Teger sitting in a fireplace chair. I grinned. "Why, hello there. What are you doing here?"

"Waiting for you." He sounded stern.

My grin died. "Why? I mean, I know why, but—"

"Sit. We need to talk." He pointed to the empty chair.

I stepped over and sat. "About what?"

"You."

My hand flew to my chest. "Me?"

"Yes." He leaned forward. "Tehi, you have got to stop working like this. I know how important finding the cure is to you, but you're burning yourself out. Have you looked in a mirror lately? Those circles under your eyes are bigger and darker than ever. You can see them even through your makeup. And you don't eat. You bolt half your food, and then you're off to the lab. You've lost so much weight your uniform hangs on you. You look sick, and people are starting to notice. They've been asking Hyme and me about you."

"What do you tell them?"

He spread his hands. "What can we tell them? At least I can say I don't know. But you're putting Hyme in a tough position. He just says you're working on a special project you won't tell him about."

I said nothing. It never occurred to me that my hard work might affect others, especially Hyme.

"And you've got an Ohra-Sin in about a marun or so. I've seen you come back from that rite—you're practically dead on your feet. If you keep on the way you're going, you'll be in no shape for it. You have to stop, Tehi. Otherwise, you'll end up in the hospital for exhaustion and miss the ritual. If you do, just think about what Astoreth will have to say about *that*."

We stared at each other.

His eyes narrowed. "Where are you getting the energy to run like this?"

"Meaning what?"

"Don't play coy with me. You sleep on the whole maybe three hours a night. This has been going on for, what, over two arhu? I told you how you look. You have to be using something to keep up."

I gazed at the rug. *Should I tell him? I don't want to lie.* I looked up and hesitated. "Decil," I said in a low voice.

He started, eyes looking as if they'd pop from his head. "Decil?" he shouted. "Are you crazy? Wait'll I get my hands on Hyme—"

"Hyme had nothing to do with this," I snapped. "I made them myself."

"He showed you how to do it, didn't he?"

"That was a long time ago. I didn't tell him what I was doing now, so there's no way he'd know." I paused. "And I'm not addicted if that's what you're thinking."

"How many do you take a day?"

"Two."

"That's all it takes."

"For you hakoi. Not for me."

Teger said nothing for a moment. He stepped over and held out his hand. "Give them to me."

By now I was exasperated. I wanted to go to bed, not stay up and argue. "I told you. I'm not addicted—"

"Give. Them. To. Me."

I glowered. With a heavy sigh, I reached into my pocket, pulled out an almost full vial of pills, and tossed it to him. He caught it and without a word, marched to the bath. I heard the commode lid open and then *plink, plink* as the pills hit the bowl. Then it flushed. He returned and made a show of throwing the empty vial into the fireplace. "Don't you ever do anything like this again," he growled.

"I can always make more."

His glare burned. "But you won't. Promise me."

I bit my lip. I didn't want to make that promise but knew if I didn't, he would watch me like a skyrin. I didn't want that, either. "I promise."

"Good. Now. This is what you're going to do. You're going to rest for a marun. No going to the lab. After that, no lab work until after breakfast. You can work after evening services, but no more than two hours. And don't try to stay longer because I'll come get you. I know you've stopped your dance and meditation sessions. You should get back to it. I—"

"Who are you to tell me how to live?" I snapped. "I'm perfectly capable of handling my own life, thank you."

He raised his brow. "Oh? And who's the one hooked on decil?"

"I told you, I'm not addicted!"

"We'll see when the withdrawal symptoms start."

"There won't be any." My eyes narrowed. "I'll admit I've been working too hard, but I'll be damned if I let you dictate what I can and can't do. Here are my terms. Five days of rest. After that, I'll do lab work before breakfast if it suits me and for up to four hours after evening services." Glaring, I folded my arms across my chest.

"What about your dance and meditation sessions?"

"I'll just have to see about that."

We scowled at each other. Then he threw up his hands. "Fine. We'll do it your way." He gave me a meaningful look. "Starting today. Are you ready for your morning service?"

"No."

"All right. It's six-thirty Ekban now. Set your timepiece to three-thirty Gor. That's only four hours sleep but it'll have to do. And you'll have enough time to dress and get everything ready."

Allowing him this chance to salvage his dignity, I set the timepiece and undressed. He was right about the uniform's poor fit. It was supposed to be on the snug side, especially the trousers. I gave a little push and watched them pool at my feet. My underclothes bagged at the knees and sagged at the waist. Astoreth would be apoplectic if she saw me.

I took off my blouse and draped it over the chair. My bra drooped at the shoulders. I crawled into bed. Teger crawled in after me. We lay side by side, not touching. "Still angry with me?" I said, my voice low.

"I was never angry with you. I'm afraid for you." Rolling over, he took me into his arms and kissed my hair. "Älskling, nothing is so important that you have to ruin yourself like this," he whispered. "Not even your red fever project."

How about my life? I wanted to say. *Should I tell him what I'm trying to do?* I bit my lip. *No. I'm not ready.* I hadn't yet thought out all the details, and I wasn't sure the second project I'd started, as crucial to my plan as finding the cure, would work. Anxiety raised its ugly head, but I held it in check. I needed to sleep, not fret. Closing my eyes, I used an old sleeping trick.

The next thing I knew, my uniform's timepiece was buzzing. I blinked, struggling to wake up. *Decil. I need a decil. They're in my pocket.* I started to stir when I remembered Teger had flushed them. Staring at the ceiling, my eyes threatened to close again. *Astoreth. Am I going to be able to make it through the service, never mind the rest of the day?*

I heaved a sigh. No time to think about it now. Dragging myself out of bed, I shuffled to the chair and turned off the alarm. I trudged to the bath. My shower helped wake me some, but not much. I shuffled to the closet. Taking out my red corset, I wrapped it around me and fastened the hook at the waist to keep it in place while I fastened the rest of them.

I'd started fastening the fifth hook from the bottom when my hands began shaking. Then my fingers went numb. My eyes widened. Hyme had said these were classic symptoms of decil withdrawal. But I'd been so careful. Could I have made a mistake in altering the formula? I fumbled with the hook, willing my trembling hands still and to make my deadened fingers do what I wanted.

"Need some help?"

I looked over my shoulder. Teger stared, his expression that unreadable mask I knew so well.

"Uh...no." I went back to fastening the hook but still couldn't do it.

"You sure?"

The shaking and numbness disappeared. The hook slid into its slot. I looked over my shoulder again and smiled. "I'm sure."

He didn't smile back.

Got to get out of here. If the symptoms started again, that was the last thing I wanted him to see. Fastening the remaining hooks, I plastered on a makeup mask and pulled on my stockings while the paint set. Peeling it off, I stuffed my feet into slippers, ran to the closet, and grabbed my cloak.

I turned. Teger's face was like stone. I smiled again. "See you at breakfast."

He nodded but said nothing.

His look made me nervous. I fled my apartment and nearly tumbled down the stairs. Inside the É, I set up the altar. My hands shook a little and the numbness crept into my fingers, but it didn't last. Ready, I knelt and waited for the morning penitents.

The service was going well. My hands didn't shake, my fingers didn't go numb. My voice was clear and strong. Then, in the middle of the sermon, I forgot what I'd written. Hyme had told me short term memory loss was also a withdrawal symptom. So I did the only thing I could do. I improvised, taking bits and pieces of sermons I remembered and weaving them into whole cloth. Finishing my homily, I cropped the backs of the penitents, then dismissed them.

Gathering the incense and candle holders, I dropped them into the glass, wood, and brass bowls, and headed for the closet. Three steps from the door, I started shaking. A distant roaring rang in my ears. My hands went numb. The bowls tumbled from my grip, and I faintly heard the glass one shatter. I collapsed. A searing pain drilled through my wrist. Helpless, I writhed on the stone floor.

Then I was booted into another reality.

I lie on the green grass, my wings flapping in spasms. The black bird looms, kicking me with its taloned feet. Every so often, it stabs me with its great beak. Yet its kicks and pokes don't draw blood. It caws again and again, laughing. I want to fight, but my spasms won't let me.

I could tear you apart right now, the black bird says in a rasping voice. *But I will not. I want the pleasure of fighting you to your death.* It laughs again and launches itself into the air.

The seizure ended, and my vision disappeared. I lay on the floor, gasping. My brain spun. It wasn't long before it registered pain, and that brought me to my senses.

I looked down. A spear-like glass shard had punctured my wrist. Teeth clenched, I pulled it out and watched my blood drip into a small pool of water from the shattered bowl.

Need my kit.

I struggled to my feet, crossed the É on wobbly legs, pulled off my shoes and stepped into my slippers. Holding on to the wall, I climbed the stairs to my apartment. I staggered to my kit, found the antiseptic, and washed my wrist. Then I took out a bottle of antibiotic and squeezed it into the hole. Last, I pulled out a roll of nuskin and scissors, cut off a strip of bandage, and wrapped it around my wound.

I stumbled to a fireplace chair and fell into it. Nausea set my stomach quivering. Bending forward, I dropped my head into my hands, wondering how long this would go on. One thing was certain, though. The way I felt now, I was in no shape to leave my apartment, let alone eat breakfast.

I finally lifted my head, without a clue as to how much time had passed. Pawing at my uniform draped behind me, I found the bar and tapped it. "Time," I croaked.

"Sixth hour, forty-seven minutes Gor."

Breakfast was almost over. My knees shook as I got up. Stepping out of my slippers, I unhooked my corset and tottered to the closet. Fumbling with the hangar, after several tries, I managed to hang it, then stuffed it inside. I rolled off my stockings, balled them into a wad, and threw them at the basket filled with more stockings. I missed. I looked for my shoes and remembered I'd left them in the É.

I felt sick again. Lurching to the bed, I crawled under the furs and pulled them up to my chin. My body trembled. Squeezing my eyes shut, I prayed I wouldn't have another seizure. The trembling stopped after about ten seconds. Thankful, I relaxed and was almost instantly asleep.

Teger's stroking my hair woke me. He smiled. "How are you feeling?"

My lips twisted. "I've been better. What time is it?"

"After lunch."

I startled. *What?* Then I lowered my eyes. "How did you know?"

"I could tell you were having trouble hooking your corset. That's never happened before. And you dressed so quickly. Usually you linger a bit, talk to me. Not this time. You wanted to get out of the room before your hands started shaking again, right?"

I nodded.

"What happened here?" he said, touching my bandaged wrist.

I told him everything, and he wrapped me in a warm hug. We lay like that for a long while, not speaking.

He kissed my hair. "Are you hungry?"

"No."

"You should eat something. Here, I brought food."

He helped me sit up. I turned my head and saw a little basket resting on the nightstand. Grabbing the handle, he set it on my lap and lifted the cover. "It's not much. Just a small smörgås."

I looked up. "Thank you."

His response was a gentle smile.

I picked up the sandwich and bit into it. It tasted like ashes. I finished it in three bites. One would have been enough, but with him watching, I knew I had to eat it all.

"See? You *were* hungry." He took the basket, setting it back on the nightstand. Saying nothing, he took me into his arms again, and began stroking my hair.

I grimaced. "I need to clean the É."

"Do you feel like doing that?"

"No, but it needs to be done, and I don't want to wait until the evening service."

He helped me out of bed, steadying me when I began to wobble. "You sure you want to do this?"

"I'll be all right. If the shaking starts again, I'll just come back to bed." I picked up my uniform.

"By the way, I told Hyme what happened," he said while I dressed.

I stopped pulling up my trousers. "I wish you hadn't done that."

"Well, I thought he had a right to know."

No, he didn't. But it was too late to argue about it now. "How did he react?"

"About what you'd expect. He was angry at first, then blamed himself. I told him it wasn't his fault."

I fastened my trousers. "I dread facing him."

"Don't. He understands."

He doesn't. Neither of you does.

I slid my feet into slippers, and went for the door, trying to walk steady. I looked over my shoulder. "Love you. See you at dinner."

He smiled and nodded. I felt his gaze as I stepped out. Holding on to the wall, I started down the staircase. The farther steps seemed to swirl, making me dizzy. By concentrating on my feet, it wasn't so bad.

It took almost five minutes to reach the É. I stepped over the threshold and headed for the closet. The closer I came, the more of the chaos I could see. Bowls, incense and candlestick holders and more lay strewed on the floor. I saw the shattered glass bowl that had cut me. My lips tightened. I hoped I was in good enough shape to clean up the mess.

It didn't take as long as I'd expected but it exhausted me. I turned out the lights and with shoes and crop in hand, carefully made my way upstairs. Inside my room, I walked to the open closet and shoved my shoes into the storage unit on the floor. My crop followed. I shucked my uniform and peered at it. *Starting to wrinkle. Need to pull out a clean one tomorrow.* I set the timepiece to wake me an hour and a half before dinner. That would give me time to make myself presentable and check the beacon, too.

I shuffled to bed and burrowed beneath the furs. Getting

comfortable, I remembered I hadn't showered after the morning service and still wore my sacred makeup. *Why didn't he mention it?* My brow quirked. *Doesn't matter.* I was too ill this morning to shower and knew Teger didn't care about my makeup. I pulled the furs over my head and fell asleep.

When the alarm woke me, I slowly opened my eyes and gazed at the ceiling. The alarm's blare, loud and irritating to begin with, seemed even louder and more irritating. I blinked. *All right. I feel better. I think.* I rolled out of bed, being careful not to jostle my brains, and stood. After making sure I was stable, I headed for the bath. Turning the shower knob all the way to the right, near-scalding water cascaded over me. I didn't flinch. I stayed in the shower for a good while, getting out only because I knew dinner would be served soon.

I felt cleaner than I had in arhu. The decil had given my skin an uncomfortable, oily feel, and no amount of bathing could get rid of it. I suppose that in itself was a good reason to get off the drug. The other was that over time, decil ate away at the body's internal organs, guaranteeing a long and agonizing death.

I donned my uniform and tapped the bar. "Time."

"Sixth hour, thirty-nine minutes Tryn."

Oh. I'd better hurry. I slipped on my boots and stepped over to the vanity. Makeup mask in hand, I stared at my reflection. The dark circles under my eyes looked as if someone had blacked them. I shook my head. Fitting the mask, I peeled it off and threw it in the trash.

Once my stewardship duty was complete, I headed for the dining hall. Walking down the curved staircase, again I had to hold on to the wall for support. At the bottom, I peeked inside the darkened É. Tendrils of anxiety wormed into my mind. Would the evening service be a repeat of this morning? I squashed them. *I'll worry about that later.*

Entering the dining room, I saw Hyme was already seated. He turned when I pulled out my chair.

"How are you feeling, Tehi?"

I gave him a small smile. "Better than I have any right to feel."

Dinner was served. I speared a molun, popped it into my mouth and chewed. Like the smörgås, it tasted like ashes, and I had to force it down my throat. I speared another and forced that down, too. I didn't have to look up to know that Teger and Hyme were watching me eat.

To satisfy them, I cleaned my plate, but my stomach felt awful, as if I'd swallowed a stone.

After dinner, Hyme and I stepped outside. "Will you be able to perform your service tonight?"

"I'll be fine. I'm much better than I was this morning."

"Good. If you like, come to the store tomorrow and keep me company."

"I just might." He was referring to Teger's and my bargain, but our bargain had said nothing about the apothecary.

Entering my tower, I had a fleeting thought to cancel tonight's service. *No.* If I did, Stiren would have to report it to Astoreth. I'd have to explain to Her why I'd canceled, and that meant I'd have to confess all. I took my time climbing the stairs. It seemed like forever before I got to my apartment.

I walked in to find Teger sitting in a fireplace chair. A sense of déjà vu and not a little annoyance washed over me, but I gave him a bright smile. "Checking up on me already?"

He snorted. "Of course not. You promised. I just came over to see how you were doing. Are you going to do your service tonight?"

"Hyme asked me the same thing. The answer is yes."

"You feel up to it?"

"Not really, but I have to do it." I cocked my head. "Don't you sometimes have to work even if you don't feel well?"

"Yes, but—"

"But what?"

"I worry about you."

"There's nothing to worry about." I didn't feel nearly as sanguine as I sounded, but I wasn't going to let him know that. "Now shoo. I have to get ready."

"If you don't mind, I'd rather stay here." His gaze was resolute. I knew that look. He wasn't going anywhere, whether I liked it or not.

"Then stay." I undressed and decided against taking another shower. I could always remove my secular makeup with a wet cloth. I picked my red corset from the closet, brushed off the bits of herizab and salt that still clung, then fitted it around my waist. His gaze bored into my back while I fastened the hooks, but my hands didn't shake nor did my fingers go numb. Reaching into the closet again, I pulled out a pair of stockings and slid them over my legs. Last, I dug out my shoes and crop.

After putting on my sacred makeup, I reached into my healer's kit and rooted for my scissors. I cut the bandage off and inspected my wound. Only a tiny scab remained. *It's fine. Nobody's going to notice.*

The only thing left to do was to re-read my sermon to make sure I'd committed it to memory. Settling into the chair, I picked up my tablet and read it. Then I closed my eyes and recited the sermon aloud. I opened them to see Teger nodding and smiling.

I lay my tablet on the table. "Time to go. I'll see you after the service." I left the apartment and let out a tiny sigh. *Please, Astoreth—no symptoms while I'm setting up and during the service.*

It turned out I had nothing to worry about. I set up the altar without trouble and had no memory gaps while giving my homily. No problems cleaing up, either. I returned to my apartment.

Teger looked like he hadn't moved. I smiled. "It went—"

"Very well, I thought."

My jaw dropped. "You were there?"

He grinned. "I was peeking around the corner. I've always wanted to see one of your services. I thought the cropping at the end was a nice touch."

"You shouldn't have." It came out rougher than I'd intended.

His grin died. "Are you mad at me?"

"Let's just say I'm annoyed. But I'd appreciate it if you didn't do it again."

He ducked his head. "All right. I won't." Then he gave me a sly smile. "Tired?"

"Not as tired as I thought I'd be."

He grinned again. "Good."

I undressed, and he helped me into another one of his jackets. This one was heavier than the other I'd used just a few marun ago. I wouldn't be toasty warm, but it was warm enough, and we were only going a short ways. He opened the door, and I stepped through. Arms about each other, we crossed the battlement.

Chapter Twenty-four

My five-day abstinence from the lab passed faster than I thought it would. I spent most of it in the apothecary with Hyme, talking about my project and learning about new herbs and plants that might be useful to my second project. Lucky for me, he even had most of them in stock.

"Why are you interested in those, Tehi? You don't need them for your red fever research."

I gave him a sweet smile. "All knowledge is useful knowledge. Right?"

We laughed, and he said no more about it.

By the end of the second day, my sense of taste returned. At meals, I savored every bite, reveling in the different flavors bursting over my tongue. Ravenous hunger was another withdrawal symptom, so Teger made sure I had a second helping at each meal. Which I ate with as much gusto as the first. It was a far cry from what I'd been taught, that moderation was the key to achieving balance between body, mind, and spirit.

The fourth day, I restarted my dance and meditation sessions. I didn't have any visions, but I'd forgotten how good it felt to lose myself in music and movement, the way it cleared my mind and led me to my center. *Cure or no cure, I'm not letting my work get in the way of this again.*

The night of the fifth day, I lay wrapped in Teger's arms, his soft snores barely registering as I stared at the ceiling. Without decil, my work would slow down by half, something I could ill-afford. True, I had been addicted, and that was my fault. But even if I hadn't been, would he and Hyme have objected so strongly to my using it if they knew why I was taking it? Why it was so important I be the first to find the cure? Should I have told them about my second project? That the two projects might well save my life?

I let out a little sigh. *Doesn't matter, now. I promised I wouldn't take decil anymore. I've cut my lab hours. And it's not like I can work faster. Rushing through an experiment would be inviting disaster. All I can do is pray I'm close enough so this slow-down won't affect me too much.*

The sixth day finally came. The circles under my eyes had disappeared, and though I was still thin, from my uniform's fit, it was obvious I'd gained back some weight. Hyme and I headed for the lab after breakfast. It was all I could do to keep from running. Walking inside felt like coming home.

At my table, I inspected the large plaztik tarp draped over it. "What's this?"

"I put it there to keep down the dust. I didn't touch anything else."

Pulling off the tarp, I inspected my equipment. Everything was just as I had left it. Well, almost. The base I had left to gel five days ago had turned into a useless sludge. Another base I'd left to cool had crystallized. It was useless, too. I grimaced. I'd lost everything, but at least I had my lab notes to tell me where I'd been and what I'd been trying to do.

I looked around and then at Hyme. He'd been watching me. "I'm sorry, Tehi."

I shrugged. "Nothing to be sorry about. I'm the one who went and got herself addicted. The formula I'd worked out was obviously wrong. Probably should have used less krato." I grabbed a plaztik spatula and started scraping the sludge from the beaker, pouring the viscous stuff into a metal bucket.

The lab was quiet. I scraped at the sludge from the beaker's bottom. It wasn't working. The sludge had hardened, and I needed something heavier and stiffer than plaztik. Scanning my worktable, I spied a metal one. I dropped the plaztik into the beaker with the gel and started scraping with the other. It worked much better.

"Would you do it again?" Hyme said.

"Do what again?"

"Make decil."

"I gave Teger my word I wouldn't. And I know how important that is to your people. I would never betray his trust."

"What if you hadn't promised?"

I stopped my scraping and looked up. "What are you getting at?"

"Just wondering. Let's say nobody knew you were an addict and you weaned yourself off without anyone noticing. Would you experiment again, making more decil? Maybe using less krato?"

I fixed him with a steady stare. "Yes."

"Why?"

"Because I have to be the one who discovers the cure. And the more hours I can squeeze out of the day, the better." Nervous now, I went back to my scraping. We were on dangerous perritory. I was not going to tell him my plan, and if he kept asking questions, I would be forced to lie. I didn't want that.

"I don't understand how the Gods can do this. You've told me how it works. If you're the first to find the cure, your É will sell it to others for an exorbitant price. And they'll have no choice but to pay." He shook his head. "It's unconscionable. Hakoi lives are at stake."

I breathed a tiny sigh of relief. "It's part of the game the Great Pantheon play with each other. To them, the hakoi are expendable." I paused, and added, "As are morevs."

"Your Gods are cruel."

Our Gods. But I wasn't going to get into that debate.

I shrugged. "It's the way things are." I picked up the beaker with the crystallized solution and began chipping at the residue. I could feel Hyme watching me. "Well, I'd better open up the shop."

"All right." In truth, I was glad to see him go. Cleaning up my ruined experiment, talking about decil, and thinking about my shortened lab hours had soured my mood.

My chipping was getting me nowhere. *Soaking should help.* I collected the soiled beakers and spatulas and set them in the sink. I opened the hot water tap. When it had warmed enough, I filled the beaker with the crystals and set it aside. Drawing on a pair of nuskin gloves, I poured soap into the sludge-soiled beaker and started scrubbing.

I'd just finished polishing it when the door opened. Teger strode over the threshold. I let out a tiny groan. I didn't want to see him.

He reached me with a wide smile. "Älskling. What are you doing?"

I didn't smile back. "Cleaning."

Draping an arm around my shoulders, he peered into the sink. "Cleaning what?"

I didn't answer.

He frowned. I watched him stare at the beaker with the crystals. Some of it had melted, clouding the water. Understanding spread across his face. "Oh." He looked at me. "It was for the best, älskling. And you can always do the same experiment again, right?"

I wanted to slap him. Instead, I simply glared.

His eyes narrowed. "All right. I'm sorry your experiment was ruined. I'm sorry I caught you using decil. I should have let you stay addicted to the stuff and kill yourself. Is that what you want to hear?"

I said nothing.

He dropped his arm. "Fine. I'll just come back when you're in a better mood."

"Good idea."

Eyes narrowing to slits, he spun around and marched out of the lab.

I breathed a sigh of relief. Picking up the beaker with the now-soft crystallized solution, I got to work. After I'd finished, I gathered and carried them to my worktable.

Pulling up my swivel chair, I switched on my tablet. My lab notes for the ruined experiment appeared. I started reading. Two pages in, I frowned. After another few pages, my frown deepened. I'd made several mistakes running the experiment that even a first-year apprentice wouldn't have made.

I turned off the power. Setting the tablet on the table, I leaned back and closed my eyes. That the experiment had been ruined no longer mattered. It had been doomed from the start. And I knew why. *My conversions for the decil were way off…it's a wonder I didn't kill myself.* I sighed. I'd have to go over all my notes since I'd begun taking it to see if I'd made other mistakes.

"Tehi."

I jumped, and my eyes flew open. Looking over my shoulder, I saw Hyme standing at the street door. "What's happening?"

"It's time for lunch."

"Oh." I walked over to him. "Let's go."

Hyme was uncharacteristically silent as we crossed the plaza. At the hall's side door, I'd curled my fingers around the handle when I felt his hand on my arm. I turned.

His face wore an earnest look. "Tehi, I'm sorry for what I said about your Gods, about Them being cruel. Just because Their ways are different from mine doesn't give me the right to judge Them. I hope you'll forgive me."

I smiled. *Our gods.* "You're forgiven. And no offense taken."

He smiled back. "Thank you. Now let's go in and eat."

As usual, I had two helpings. Hyme and Teger had told the curious that I'd been ill with myzgote and was now much better, though still a bit weak. It was as good a lie as any since no one in Mjor knew enough about morevs to know we don't suffer from the same illnesses as the hakoi.

On the walk back to the lab, Hyme was much more animated. We talked about my project without being specific, and I told him about my mistakes. "I hope I won't have to repeat my earlier experiments. We're talking over two arhu worth of work. That would really set me back."

Three people were standing in front of the apothecary when we arrived. He headed for the shop. The customers waved, and I did, too.

At my table, I shrugged into my lab coat and pulled up the chair. Picking up my tablet, I settled in and started reading. Some time later, a sliver of sunslight appeared in my peripheral vision that quickly brightened. I looked up as Teger poked his head through the open door, giving me a wary look. "May I come in?"

I stood and set the tablet on the chair. "Of course."

"You're not going to bite me, are you?"

"No, I just had lunch."

Relief washed over his face. Hurrying over, he wrapped his arms around my shoulders and drew me close. Laying my head on his midriff, I gave him a hard squeeze.

"You still love me," he said in a low voice.

I looked into his face and smiled. "Yes, silly." I let out a small sigh. "I'm sorry. I was in a really bad mood and took it out on you."

"What was wrong?"

"Coming back here, seeing everything ruined...I'm over it, now."

"Good."

The next thing I knew, I'd been swept off my feet. I wound my arms around his neck and gave him a peck on his lips. He responded with a deep, satisfying kiss. After pulling away, he gently lowered me to the floor. Still holding me, he stroked my hair. "I have to go now. Duty calls. I just wanted to see how you were doing."

"I'm fine."

"Then I'll see you at dinner." He walked to the door. Pulling it open, he looked over his shoulder. "By the way, you're filling out nicely. Your uniform is starting to look good on you again." He grinned, winked, and was gone.

I slowly wagged my head. "That man is incorrigible," I whispered.

Alone once more, I settled back into my chair and started reading again. Hyme bustled in and out, but I barely noticed. Reading the notes for the experiment I'd done before the one that had been ruined, I was glad to see I'd made no mistakes.

I checked my timepiece, and my lips twisted. I needed to check the beacon. Since the control room had been rebuilt, there was hardly a reason to keep an eye on anything, but I had to call in my status. As far as I was concerned, it was time wasted when I needed to be catching up.

Walking across the plaza, it occurred to me that instead of practicing my dance and meditation ritual after monitoring the beacon, I could do it tonight after my four hours at the lab were up. It would give me more time before dinner to set up the experiment and get it underway. I didn't worry about Teger objecting to my new schedule. He'd said he wanted to see me dance. Well, now was his chance.

Satisfied with my new plan, I stepped inside my tower.

❖

Four days passed. My new experiments had gone better than I expected. But tonight, I wouldn't return to the lab. Tonight was Ohra-Sin, and I hated it as much now as I ever did.

"Is it fun?" Teger had asked before the ritual last arhu. He'd been lying on the bed, watching me get ready.

I'd stopped plastering makeup on my leg and looked up. "Is what fun?"

"Ohra-Sin. I mean, it's an orgy, isn't it?"

I'd shrugged, trying to feign indifference. "Yes, but I wouldn't call it fun. It's just something I have to do, that's all."

Right now, I was alone. I thought about the ritual. *What makes the garrison and Teger so different? They're all hakoi. With the garrison, even the thought of them touching me makes me want to throw up. But Teger...no. I want his touch, I need it. Is it because I love him? Is that the difference?*

302

I ripped the last piece of makeup plaster from my arm and headed to the É. Purifying the air, I then set up the altar. I lit the braziers around the pool and turned out the lights. Last, I chose the ritual's music. I looked around. The candles burned bright, and the É was growing smoky from the incense. I knelt before the altar and prayed, imploring Astoreth to fill me with Her love. I raised my head and stared into a candle flame, wondering if She would answer this time. With a small sigh, I rose and walked to the pool. Sinking onto my pillow, I sat in sacred lutos and waited.

The penitients arrived a short time later. After the É quieted, I waited about ten minutes, recited the opening prayer, then dove into the pool. The troops followed. Eyes closed, I gritted my teeth at the seemingly myriad hands and lips on my body, but I didn't fight them. They swarmed over me. My jaws were clenched so hard I thought my teeth would break. A tongue probed my lips. The ritual compelled me to open my mouth. It shot inside, licking and probing. I wanted to bite it. I also wanted to vomit.

My heartsbeat sped up. I felt them balloon, growing larger with each pulse. Sharp, excruciating pain lanced through me. *Astoreth! The decil...am I having a delayed seizure?* Frightened, I started thrashing, fighting to shove the penitents away. They piled on me. I couldn't breathe, couldn't think. It never even occurred to me to zap them.

Then my body swelled. My skin was being stretched to its limit. The pain was unbearable. All I could do was ride out the seizure and hope it didn't get any worse.

It got worse. My skin stretched further and began cracking, splitting apart. Agony drove me out of my mind. I screamed. Bubbles shot from my mouth. I sucked in a breath to scream again. Water rushed into my lungs. I tried to claw my way to the surface, but I couldn't. There were too many bodies in the way.

A deafening thunderclap accompanied by an eye-searing lightning flash was the end. I burst. My skin ripped as if made from the thinnest nupaper. My brain shredded. I somehow managed to scream one last time, and then...nothing. No sound, no light, no feeling, no thoughts.

An explosion of bright, bright colors. The entirety of colors in the universe swirled in a never-ending dance of circles, spirals, diamonds, trapezoids, pentagrams, and every other geometric shape, in sizes from atomic to gargantuan. At the same time, a wall of *sound* crashed through the cosmos. Its reverberations pulsed, rocking the foundation of all that is, all there was, and all that will be.

Little by little, a feeling of substance materialized. It was a body, weightless and tumbling as if lost in the depths of space. An impression of myriad needles pricking. Consciousness slowly coalesced. A sense of being crept to the fore.

Wait...I-I'm not dea—

A shaft of white-hot light pierced my skull and then rushed through the rest of me. Its burning heat shot from every orifice. I was in too much agony to scream. A split-second later, the horrible pain stopped. My third eye opened.

What is THAT?

A glowing, amorphous...*something* throbbed inside a translucent casing. Its pulsing rhythm reminded me of a heartsbeat. It spoke to me in a language without words, without sound. Yet I understood, not with my mind, but with my hearts. When it finished speaking, a burst of tiny, twinkling lights showered over me. Then my mind understood. It had spoken the language of love, the kind of love that knows no bounds. And that love was now mine.

At that moment, I felt my love for everything there is—the rocks, the flora, the fauna, and Peris itself. I felt my love for everything that isn't, the vast, unknown regions of nothingness and imagination. For the first time, I embraced my hakoi-ness and loved myself for who and what I was. I loved the hakoi, no matter who they were or where they were. I simply *loved*.

Ecstatic, I plunged headlong into Ohra-Sin, an eager participant instead of a passive vessel. I touched them as they touched me, spreading the universal love that binds us all.

The gong sounded. We climbed out of the pool. I gave the benediction and bade them to go their way in peace, with joy in their hearts. In my peripheral vision, I noticed a few penitents look up. They'd never heard me say that before. Then I did something I didn't think I'd ever do after an Ohra-Sin, not for a moment.

I smiled.

Chapter Twenty-five

The next morning, I woke to find Teger in my bed, sitting up and reading from my tablet.

I sat up and stretched while letting out a mighty yawn. "God morgen." Fully awake now, my skin prickled from the room's chill. I scooted back under the blanket and looked up. "Aren't you cold?"

He lay the tablet on the nightstand and slid under the blanket. "God morgen älskling. Not really."

I wormed my way under his arm. "Astoreth, you *do* have hide for skin." I kissed his chest. "What are you reading?"

"A history of Peris. Astoreth wrote it."

"Not exactly light reading."

"But it's...interesting." He paused. "How did Ohra-Sin go?"

"It was wonderful. I have to tell you—"

"No, you don't. I've a very good imagination."

I shifted to look into his face. "Yes, I do. I have to tell you everything."

"You're not just talking about the ritual, are you?"

"No." I took a deep breath and told all. About what it was like for me as a child, the way the Devi children treated me in school and how I learned to hate the hakoi and the part of me that was hakoi. I told him about growing up, hating the other morevs because of their hakoi blood, and how I lorded my own mostly Devi blood over them. "And I was more than happy to use my power on them whenever I wanted, for any reason or no reason." I told him about how I didn't want to become a healer because it forced me to serve the É's hakoi. About how I treated my patients as if they were worse than dirt. And about how my bigotry had landed me in Mjor.

Teger didn't speak for a long time. "Yet you fell in love with me. Why?"

"I've asked myself that question Astoreth knows how many times. I honestly don't know. But I'm glad I did."

"So what happened last night?"

I smiled. "A revelation. I finally understand the meaning of love and what it means to love. I can't put it into words, but I know that it's all around us and inside us. All we have to do is allow ourselves to feel it."

"Like the way I love you?"

"That's part of it." I kissed his chest again. "And you know what else?"

"What?"

"I don't feel guilty anymore for loving you." I climbed on top and gave him a deep kiss. "Make love to me," I whispered.

"But—"

"It's just a room where I keep my things, Teger. It doesn't matter." I kissed him again.

Cuddling under the blanket afterward, a surge of happiness filled me. There'd be many things to learn and discover from my new perspective, and I couldn't wait.

Thank you, Grandmother. Thank you for helping me find my way to Love.

⊙⊒⊒⊒⊒⊙

My high from Ohra-Sin lasted two days, and then all my self-hatred, guilt, and anxieties came rushing back.

After the morning service on the third day, while climbing the stairs to my apartment, I started thinking about my grandmother. *I wonder what She's doing right now. Probably getting ready for Ktana. I'd love to see Her.* A tendril of worry crept into my mind. *But what would She do if She saw me? I've betrayed Her in the worst possible way. She'd know, and She won't forgive. She'll throw me into one of the É's underground cells, for who knows how long, and then...then...* In the next second, my foreboding exploded into a full-blown anxiety attack. Running up the stairs, I burst into my apartment, threw myself into a fireplace chair, and curled into a tight ball. I shook, and my hearts pounded. My teeth chattered so hard it hurt. A torrent of tears poured down my cheeks. *How could I have done this to Her? I-It's...why did I have to fall in love? Why?* Why?

During the attack, I had no sense of time passing. In the middle of a panicked thought, a small voice echoed in the back of my mind. *Being in love with him is nothing to be ashamed of, to feel guilty about—it's proof of Astoreth's divinity. Celebrate your love. As for what might be, it may come to pass, or it may not. You don't know the future. All you have is now.*

Hearing that, my shaking subsided, and after a final few tremors, I felt like myself again. I thought about what the little voice had said. *Celebrate my love... It goes against everything I've been taught, everything I promised to Astoreth...but it feels...so* right. *I have to make peace with it...with my love, and with myself.*

Dancing and meditation helped, but it wasn't enough. While meditating, I concentrated on the recapturing the love that had infused me during Ohra-Sin. It always manifested, and I bathed in the pure light that brought joy to my mind, body and spirit. But my self-loathing never failed to return. About a marun after Ohra-Sin, I didn't leave the É after my meditation session, just sat with my head in my hands. *Why can't I make the feeling last? I don't feel like that when I'm with him. It just... disappears, and I feel nothing but love. If only I could be with him all the time...but that's impossible. We can't give ourselves away.* I let out a heavy sigh. *Maybe I'm trying too hard? What else can I do?*

Three days later, I stood before my table in the lab mixing a cooli sap reduction. "Tehi," Hyme called from behind me.

I turned. His face wore a puzzled look. "Something I can do for you?"

He gave his head a little shake. "You've been different these past few days. You're just as driven as you've always been, but...you smile a lot more, and sometimes you hum while you work. Like now. You've never done that."

I shrugged. "Guess I'm happy, Hyme. Happy in my work, happy spending time with you and Teger, just...happy." Elation filled me. He sensed the love I had worked so hard to become. Yet I had no sense of pride, of having accomplished a goal. It just was.

He smiled. "Well, I'm glad to see it."

That evening, about two hours before the service, I donned my lab coat and sorted what I'd need for my next fever experiment. While my back was turned, Teger stepped into the lab. "God kväll, you two."

I looked over my shoulder. "And god kväll to you," Hyme and I said almost at the same time.

While the two men chatted, I gathered my equipment—two syringes, one filled with serum, and a red fever vial from the deep freeze—and hurried to the closet. After setting up the experiment, I gazed at the skratz for a few seconds, then popped the vial from its slot. I left the closet.

The lab was quiet. Hyme and Teger watched me with worried looks. I couldn't blame them. I held in my hands the deadliest virus on the planet. One misstep, and Mjor would be devastated. I returned the vial to its box and set it in the deepest part of the freezer. Then I gave the two men a reassuring smile. "All done," I said in my brightest voice.

Teger exhaled the breath he'd obviously been holding. "Good. So what now?"

"We wait for the virus to take hold. That'll be two hours."

"Won't you be running your service?"

"The skratz won't die before I get back. Anyway, I'm going to check my plants."

Reentering the closet, I rolled up the habitat's cover. All the light rods were shining bright. *I'll clip some leaves.* Picking up a pair of cutters and a small basket, I stepped inside. The rods gave off so much heat, it felt like a day back home. I strolled along the aisle, inspecting the plants and pulling off the dead leaves. I dumped them into the compost bin.

By now, I was sweating inside my uniform, but I kept pacing up and down the aisle, weighing possible candidates for my new serum if the last one didn't work. Though faint, I heard Teger and Hyme talking. I stopped at the bushy maram plant. *Hm. Maybe this one?* Maram wasn't as potent as other anti-virals, but it might make a good supplement to my linmen and cooli base. I clipped the leaves of other plants I hadn't tried, too. A few minutes later, I looked into my basket. *That's enough.*

I rolled down the habitat's cover, then tapped the bar. "Time."

"Forty-four minutes Durm."

I raised my brows. *Been in here longer than I thought. The service is in forty-five minutes. I'll check the skratz first, then go.* Standing before the environment, I set my basket on the floor and looked inside. The little beast was sick—it had turned pink—but it wasn't yet time to give it the serum.

Standing at the closet door, I heard Teger and Hyme still talking. I opened it a crack.

"—tell her the truth?"

"I don't think that's a wise idea," Hyme said.

"Why?"

I closed the door. I figured they were talking about one of the village women, and it was obviously a conversation I wasn't supposed to hear. *Well, I don't have time to wait until they've finished.* I threw the door wide and stepped out. "Time for me to go. I'll sort and press these leaves after I get back."

The two men startled. My eyes darted from one to the other. "What? Did I interrupt something?"

"No, no," Hyme said. "Not at all."

I set my my basket on the counter. "See you when I get back, Hyme."

"See you then."

Teger and I left. On the walk, I outlined my plans for the evening. "I'll go back to the lab after the service, give the skratz a dose, and finish working on those leaves. Then I'll do a dance and meditation session."

"All right. Your place or mine?"

"Mm...mine." Reaching the plaza's edge, I breathed in the crisp night air. "I didn't think I'd like cold weather, but I do. So invigorating. Air conditioners can't begin to match it."

He snorted. "Wait until winter. Then we'll see how much you like it."

We parted ways. Two hours later, I rushed to the lab. Hyme was nowhere to be seen, so I slipped into my lab coat and ran for the closet. Opening the door, even from here, I could see the skratz had turned the familiar bright red and was covered with pustules. Shoving my hands into the manipulators, I injected the serum, then stepped back into the lab.

I pulled out the press from cabinet below the counter and set it beside the basket of leaves. *I'll start with the maram.* I picked out the orange and red striped ones, dropped them into the hopper, and turned on the press. Its foot mashed the leaves, squeezing them until the sap rained into a small bottle I'd placed under the drain. When the drips slowed to nothing, I picked up the bottle and capped it. Then I chose the next batch of leaves.

When all the bottles had been filled, I put them into the basket and took it to my table. After recording my notes for this evening's work, I slid my tablet into its padded sleeve, then headed outside. I thought about the music I'd choose for my session. *Something without too much energy.*

Stepping inside my tower, I climbed to the landing and hesitated. *It'd be easier to do it now instead of going all the way upstairs and back.* I entered the É and undressed. I chose my music. The room filled with the sound of drums beating a complex, syncopated rhythm. I began my dance. When the seero shut itself off, I walked on shaky legs to the altar and sat, folding my legs into sacred lutos.

No sooner had I closed my eyes, a hard blow bowled me over. Struggling to right myself, I was knocked over again, tumbling head over tail—

Tail!

I open my eyes. I am the blue-violet bird, and the black one has barreled into me. Before I can get my bearings, it barrels into me a third time. I spin through the sky, desperately flapping my powerful wings. After regaining control, the black bird comes at me a fourth time. But I'm ready.

I fly up and roll over. As it passes me, I grab a beakful of neck feathers and tear them out.

The black bird screams with rage. I arrow toward it, my talons spread wide. I will rip the red jewel from its chest and destroy it. But the black bird has other ideas. It too spreads its talons. Our feet lock together. Whirling about each other, we plummet toward the ground. We crash. Our talons unlock, and we bounce away from one another.

I lay still, stunned by the impact. Recovering, I look for the black bird. It lay on its side. I flap my wings and leap, my raptor's beak wide. I will pluck its eye out. The black bird rights itself and hops sideways, out of my reach. I land and spin around. Only a šīzu away, it grabs one of my lead feathers and pulls. The feather breaks. I jump backward. Instead of squaring off, it leaps at me with talons spread. One of its feet closes around my chest jewel, and the black bird launches itself skyward.

My chest is burning agony. I scream and feel my jewel pop. I do the only thing I can—I clamp my razor-sharp beak around the black bird's leg. Bones crunch. I taste something bitter and foul.

With a deafening screech, the black bird lets go. Panting, I roll to the side and look down. Blood pours down my chest. It slows as I watch. I look up. The black bird, now limping, is coming for me again. I'm not ready for another round, but I have no choice.

Our battle rages on. I rake my talons over the black bird's shoulder. Green ichor flows. It tries to peck my eye out. I twist my head and suffer a deep hole in my neck. But my blood loss is taking its toll. I'm tired, my reflexes slowing. The black bird renews its attacks with vigor.

With a mighty flap, I launch myself into the sky. I'm not flying away. The battle is almost over for me, and I know it. If I'm going to die, I will die in the air where I belong, not on the ground.

I turn my head. The black bird is right on my tail. I fold my wings and drop several šīzu. It flies over me. I've gained a little breathing space, but it won't last long. The other bird wheels overhead and dives at me.

This is it, the last round. I'm too weak to fight. It's all I can do to stay airborne. Buoyed by the air currents, I hover, waiting. Then I have an idea. It's so farfetched it probably won't work, but it's the only chance I have. Right before it crashes into me, I fold my wings, dip, and then flip upside down. I'm exactly where I'd wanted to be, one foot resting on the black bird's breast. I clamp my talons around its jewel and pull with all my strength. Its beak tears at me, jostling my torn jewel. I'm in agony, but I don't let go. I pull harder and harder. Finally, I feel movement. The other bird's screams are now of pain.

Squeezing my eyes shut, I wrench as hard as I can. The jewel rips free. Bowled backward, I tumble through the air. I right myself and watch the black bird. It hovers, ichor pouring from its breast and dripping from its mouth. Eyes filled with rage and hate. Then it disintegrates. A mass of black feathers rain landward and disappear as they fall.

I want to cry out in victory, but I'm too weak. My pain is excruciating. It takes every bit of concentration just to fly. I soar along the wide river. I will drop the jewel into its deepest part, where it will be lost forever. Except I can't fly any farther. My wings fold, and I drop several šīzu. I try but can't stretch them to slow my fall. Helpless, I plummet faster. *Where's my friend? He's not even going to come say goodbye?*

Something crashes into me. I let out a squawk. Was the black bird alive again? I twist my neck left and right. I can't see anything. I struggle again to spread my wings but they don't move. I'm hit again and go tumbling. The river flashes below me. *Wait—I wasn't flying* this *close to the water, was I?* A third body blow, and then I'm over the water. I fall in with a great splash and go under.

This is perfect—instead of going splat, I'm going to drown.

But I don't drown. I'm buoyed to the surface and pushed toward the bank. I peer into the clear water. I can't see what's holding me up or pushing me. Moments later, I struggle onto its edge and stare into the river's depths, wondering. Then I realize I'm no longer exhausted, no longer in pain. I look down. My jewel, instead of hanging loose, is firmly wedged into my breast. The furrows where the black bird had raked me with its talons are gone. I stretch my wing. My broken feather is healed.

You won, a familiar voice sounds beside me.

I turn. It is the brown speckled bird.

You have conquered your hate.

And almost died trying.

A light breeze ruffles our feathers. *No one said it would be easy.*

We sit on the riverbank, silent. I cock my head. *Who are you?*

A friend. Though we are birds, I feel its smile.

Another few moments pass in silence. *I must go now,* the brown bird says. It points a wing at my foot. *Keep that.*

I look down. To my surprise, I still hold the black bird's jewel in my talons. *Why? I was going to drop it in the river.*

The river does not want it. And the jewel will forever remind you of what you were and what you could be again if you let it.

You mean the black bird isn't dead?

Oh, no. It waits and watches. And if you allow your hate to grow, you will be back here, fighting the same battle for your soul.

My eyes widen. *My soul?*

The brown bird gives me a look. *You did not know? That this was about reclaiming your soul?*

I...well, no. I thought it was just about me getting rid of my hate.

Your hate was a black blot, devouring your soul. You were very close to losing it. Did Ginzu not tell you that?

I startle. *How do you know about Ginzu?*

My friend said nothing. I feel its smile again.

I bob my head. *I will remember.*

Good. Farewell, Tehi. We will not meet again. The brown bird spreads its wings and lifts into the sky.

I watch until it isn't even a speck in the distance. I look at the river. Then I too launch myself skyward. I have no idea where I'm going, but I fly on and on, the jewel clutched in my foot.

Then all fades to black.

I woke, sprawled before the altar. Sitting up, I swiveled my head. *It...looks the same.* A feeling of weight draws my attention, and I see the jewel is still in my hand. Bringing it to my face, I peered into its depths. A dim light pulsed within, one I knew only I could see.

My brown friend had been right. The beast was not dead.

I walked into the closet and slid the jewel into my uniform pocket. *I'll clean the É now and set up. More time to stay in bed with Teger.* Task completed, I dressed and headed for the entrance. On the landing, I pulled the jewel from my pocket and smiled. Then I skipped up the steps to my apartment, where my lover waited for me.

Chapter Twenty-Six

Winter fell upon Mjor with a vengeance.

For three days, gale force winds whipped through the streets. On the plaza, awnings over the shops were ripped from their moorings and sailed away to crash into the village wall. Some sailed over the wall. People were bowled over, barely able to get to their feet. The elderly were advised to remain indoors whenever possible, and the school had been closed. Several merchants didn't open their stores. Inside my apartment, the wind whistling through the tiny crevasses in the stone shutters set the windows rattling. The only places where quiet reigned were in the É and the lab.

On the fourth day, while on my way to breakfast, a sudden wind gust knocked me flat. My chin smacked against the pavement. Stunned, I couldn't move. After my wits returned, I tried to get up and was promptly knocked down again. A pair of strong arms lifted me. "Kea leboha," I panted. On my feet, I turned to see who it was.

Teger. He circled an arm around my shoulders and held tight. "Put your arms around me," he shouted above the howling wind. I clutched his waist. Together, we made our way to the dining hall. The wind threatened to blow both of us over, but we reached it without being blown away.

He pulled open the door. The wind ripped it from his hand. It banged against the thick stone, and then the wind flung both of us inside. Teger fought to pull the door shut. "Hoo," he said, and blew a heavy breath. He gave me a sideways look. "How do you like the cold, now?" He peeled off his coat and hung it.

I shrugged out of my coat. "Is it always like this? The wind?"

"Sometimes. Not often."

"When will it stop? Or will it?"

"Give it another day or so. The wind will die down, and everything will go back to normal." He smiled a little. "You should fall down more. It's the only time I get to hold you in public."

I felt my chin. It was sore, but not swelling. I matched his smile. "How about you keep me from falling? You could always walk me to the lab after breakfast."

"But you'll have Hyme to hold on to."

"So? Then I'll have both of you. No way I'll fall, then."

His smile broadened. "Done."

We walked into the main room. Hyme looked up when I pulled out my chair. "Good morning, Tehi."

"Good morning."

"I'm glad you made it. I wondered if I should have come to get you. I hope you didn't fall in all this wind."

"Yes, I did. Twice. The Laerd rescued me." I sat. "He saw me fall and held me while on our way here. He's walking us to the lab after breakfast, too. Just in case." I smiled.

He looked puzzled. "But—" Then he smiled back. "Well, between the two of us we should keep you on your feet."

Breakfast was served. The gale shrieking through the closed shutters could be heard even above the chatter in the room. By now everyone was used to it and the whistling had become little more than background noise.

While eating, Hyme started a discussion on botany. "There are other plants, like the masich bush, that bloom only in winter. Later in the season we can harvest some." He took a bite of his kommelas. "Maybe."

"Maybe?"

He sighed. "It's going to be a tough winter. The snow might be too deep to go out, even in snowshoes."

"How do you know?"

"Whenever the winds come down from the mountains this early, we're always in for a bad winter. Record-breaking low temperatures, snowfall, things like that. We'll get a lot of use out of our quiltsuits this year. And..."

"And what?"

He put down his fork. "I've seen a lot over many, many a year, Tehi. And I've noticed a pattern. Remember I told you Mjorans are a sturdy lot? Well, they are. But when winter starts off like this, for some reason there's sickness. A lot of sickness. Sometimes, I'm not even sure what I'm treating. I fear we'll lose a number of small children and our elderly this season. Especially our elderly." He picked up his spoon. Staring into his cup, he stirred his kafe, seeming lost in its depths.

Watching him, I knew he was talking about himself.

I patted his shoulder. "Come on. Let's get to the lab. We have work to do."

He looked up and gazed at me for a long moment. "Yes. Yes, we do."

Finishing his kafe, we left the table. Teger was waiting for us in the hallway, and we helped one another into our furs. The three of us looked at each other, then stepped out into the brutal wind.

◎⇌⇌⇌⇌◎

The following night, I woke from a sound sleep. Something was different. Still in a fog, I tried to figure out what it was. Then I realized it was quiet. No whistling sounds coming through the windows. The terrible winds had stopped.

Yet there was something else. It was quiet, but somehow, it was the quality of the silence that piqued my curiosity. Carefully disentangling myself from Teger's arms, I climbed out of bed and tip-toed to the window overlooking the plaza. I unlatched the windows and shutters, then opened them. My breath caught. The roofs of the buildings lining the plaza, and the plaza itself, were covered in white, fluffy looking stuff that seemed to glow and sparkle in the streetlamps' light. Its beauty was stunning. "So this is snow," I murmured, transfixed.

An arm about my shoulders brought me out of my trance.

I looked at him. "It snowed, Teger," I said, my voice full of wonder.

"I can see that."

"Let's go outside."

"Not now, älskling. We'd make tracks and though it's unlikely, someone might get the idea Prag was telling the truth."

"Oh."

He squeezed my shoulders. "Tell you what. We'll go out early, before breakfast. We'll have every reason to be out and you can do your exploring then."

"All right."

He smiled and gave my jaw a gentle caress. "Now. Close up and come back to bed. You're letting all the heat out. And you have to be up in just a few hours."

For the first time, I felt the cold and shivered. After closing up, we climbed back into bed.

Minutes passed. I stared at the ceiling, unable to to sleep. Several tricks later, I still stared at the ceiling. I started to get up. "I can't sleep. I'm going to dictate a sermon."

He pulled me back down. "You'll do no such thing," he growled. "You're going back to sleep."

His tone irritated me even more. "And who's going to make me?"

"I am."

And he did.

❖❖❖❖❖

I didn't clean the É after the service, wanting as much time as possible to play in the snow before breakfast. Ten minutes after returning to my apartment, I was ready to go. Clumping down the steps—my boots were heavy—I reached the bottom, pulled open the door, and gasped. The snow was just as beautiful from this angle as it had been from the window. Excited now, I ran outside.

The snow came halfway to my knees. I lifted my foot and gave it a kick. It was soft, like powder. In the lamplight, I watched the tiny snowflakes hang in the air like glittering colored jewels before settling to the ground. I tried sliding my feet, thinking I'd kick up even more snow. I almost fell over. It was heavier than it looked. Lifting my knees high, I took a step. Then another. In a moment, I was marching through the white powder, looking back at my tracks and giggling.

After I'd tired of this, I picked up a small mound of snow and licked it. It tasted like ice-water. That wasn't surprising. We'd learned about snow in school, and I knew it was made of frozen water vapor. I just couldn't help trying it for myself.

Gazing at its whiteness, I wondered if the snow was as soft as it looked. I flung myself forward, landing face-first. I landed harder than I'd thought, but not so hard it hurt. I rolled onto my back and splayed my limbs. I closed my eyes. *Swimming!* I thrashed about, laughing.

"We call those snow birds," a familiar, gravelly voice said.

I opened them. Teger loomed over me, smiling. I squinted. "Snow birds?"

Instead of answering, he helped me up and helped brush the snow off my coat. He pointed to the ground. "Turn around. Look."

I studied the mark. It did look like a bird, the wings made by my arms, and the tail by my legs. "It's pretty."

"Come on. I'll show you something else."

"What?"

"You'll see."

I stared. He had a look in his eye, one I knew all too well. He was up to something.

We walked a ways onto the plaza and stopped. "Stand here." Then he walked about thirty šīzu away. He bent down, picked up a mound of snow, and shaped it into a ball. Then he looked up. "Ready?" he called.

"Ready."

He threw the snowball. It hit me in the chest. Surprised, I brushed the snow off the fur. "What did you do that—"

Before I could finish, another snowball hit my chest. Then another.

Now I was annoyed. He wanted a fight? I'd give him one. I picked up a mound of snow and shaped it. I looked up. He'd pulled his arm back to throw another snowball. I didn't give him the chance. I let fly my little ball and hit him square in his stomach. I bent down to gather more snow.

"Now you get it," he yelled.

"Oh yes," I muttered. "I'm about to show you how much I get it."

He threw his ball. I jumped out of the way. Before he could pick up more snow, I threw mine. It left my hand like a shot and caught him on the shoulder. He grinned, scooped up a handful of white powder, and flung it.

I ducked. The ball sailed over my head. I made another snowball and while stooped over, hurled it and hit his thigh.

"Oh, ho. You catch on quick. Let's see if you can hit a moving target." He started running.

I did a quick mental calculation and pitched my ball. It smacked his arm.

Turning, his jaw dropped. "Where'd you learn to do that?"

I gave him a sweet smile.

We tossed more snowballs. In my peripheral vision, I noticed a crowd of villagers standing nearby, watching. Someone let out a whoop. The crowd surged forward. Some veered left, and others to the right, toward me.

The next thing I knew, the battle had been joined. Snowballs went flying from both sides. I couldn't avoid all of them but managed to dodge a fair number. I'd become adept at scooping snow, making balls, and throwing them in a matter of seconds. I laughed, and the snowball war raged on.

A shout went up that we were late for breakfast. An immediate cease-fire was called, and the crowd made a mad dash for the dining hall. Teger and I ran with them. Even the Laerd wasn't exempt from the rule on tardiness. We had less than a minute to get to our seats. We reached the entrance. Speeding inside, we threw off our furs, and hurried into the dining room. The dais was being served. I took my chair, and Teger slid into his just as the server reached him. She gave him a stern look. He grinned. Shaking her head, she reached into her cart, set a breakfast platter before him, and moved on to the next council member.

Hyme turned. "I watched you two out there. You're quite an opponent. Hard to believe you've never been in a snowball fight."

I leaned closer. "We have similar games back home, but we use treated sand instead of snow. It isn't all that different." I smiled. "Don't tell Teger."

After breakfast, we shrugged into our furs and headed for the door. "You're coming to the lab, aren't you?" he said.

"Of course. Why wouldn't I?"

"Just wanted to know."

Walking across the plaza, I thought the snow still beautiful, even though it had been trampled. "What will happen to the snow now?"

"We'll clear it, melt it down, and then dump the water into our reservoirs. That's where we get our water, you know. Snowmelt."

I hadn't known. Then I frowned. "Why did you want to know if I was coming to the lab? You know I always do."

"Because there's something you need to see."

My brows went up. "Really? If that's the case, let's get moving."

Reaching the lab, we stepped inside and hurried to the closet.

"Here," Hyme said. "This is what I thought you should see."

I looked into the environment's clear chamber. My jaw dropped. The little skratz I'd injected with red fever a day and a half before was still alive.

⁂

The skratz died three hours later. It wasn't unexpected, but that it had lived for forty-five hours after being injected was another breakthrough.

While my specimen lay dying, I studied my notes, going over the ingredients of the last serum and how much I'd used of each. The question was whether to add another antiviral to the mix or to increase the amount of the antivirals I'd used. Different calculations yielded different results, but the answers to some were closer than others. By the time the skratz died, I'd made an educated guess to increase the the stronger antivirals.

I tapped the bar. "Time."

"Second hour, twenty-seven minutes Tryn."

It was too close to lunch to start a batch of new serum or to take up my second project. I leaned back in my chair and swiveled. Hyme was at the counter, pouring a dark powdered substance into a conical flask. He picked up another jar of light-colored powder, measured it out, and poured it into the conical flask, too.

I sauntered over to him. Leaning against the counter, I inspected the flask. "What are you making?"

He poured in a third powder. "A children's cough syrup." At the sink, he filled the flask about half-full of water and returned to the counter. He set the flask on a ring stand over a burner and lit it.

I stared at the heat waves. "Think it's time to let everybody know I speak Syrenese?"

"Why?"

Looking up, I saw his frown. "Well, you said there'd probably be a lot of sickness this winter. If there is, maybe I could help in the apothecary, especially if you're out on a house call."

His frown morphed into a smile. "Actually, I make very few house calls. Most of the sick are able to get here on their own." He paused. "But what about your own work?"

"In case you haven't noticed, I'm usually sitting around waiting for results." I shrugged. "Just thought maybe I could help, that's all."

"I don't think it'll be necessary to let people know, but I'm sure I'll be calling on you, Tehi. Thank you."

By then the syrup was boiling, and it was time for lunch. On the plaza, we saw the plows hard at work. Most of the snow was gone.

Back in the lab, I began mixing another serum. The formula was complex, and it wouldn't be ready until long after the evening service. And the deal I made with Teger meant I'd have to leave before then. My lips tightened. *Damn me for making that deal. And if I had some decil, I could stay through the night.* But I had, and I didn't, so there was nothing to be done about it.

After the service, I worked as fast as possible. By the time I had to go, the only thing left to do was to inject the skratz with the virus. But it would have to wait. *Just a few more hours...* Sighing, I put my new serum in the refrigerator, then bundled into my furs. I tucked the tablet under my arm.

I stopped at Hyme's open apartment door. "Good night Hyme," I called. "I'll see you before breakfast."

"Good night, Tehi," his voice floated down. "I'll see you then."

I started the trek to my tower. It was snowing again, light, tiny flakes that looked almost like rain. Rounding the corner, I noticed a sheen of snow covering the plaza. *Wonder if it'll snow enough so the plows will have work in the morning.* My boots' thick, deep-tread soles made little noise against the pavement. A few people were about, even at this late hour. They waved as I passed. I waved back.

I thought about my experiment. I'd made a breakthrough, but it wasn't enough. The skratz had still died. My sense of urgency returned, and my steps quickened. I had less than four arhu to find the cure. At this rate, my tour would be over before I did, and my life would be forfeit. "Maybe I can experiment on two skratz," I muttered. But that wouldn't work. The enviroment's chamber was too small for more than one skratz and the manipulators. If the environment was full-sized, I could experiment on several skratz at once. I shook my head. *I'll just have to make do with what I have.*

Entering my tower, I decided against a dance and meditation session, but it did it occur to me to set up for the morning. I pulled off my boots and frowned after the É's lights came up. All was ready. *Must've done it after I checked the beacon. Great. One less thing I have to do tonight.* I stepped out and not bothering to put on my boots, headed for my apartment.

Inside, I felt the cold even through my furs. *Astoreth. Forgot to turn on the heat, too.* Then I shrugged. *Doesn't matter. I'm not sleeping here.*

I opened the heating grate, and a puff of freezing air brushed my face. The heat wouldn't be turned on until second hour Gor, but the room would be warm enough by the time I returned. I stepped onto the battlement. As always, Teger had left his door open a crack, giving me just enough light for me to see by. Pushing it open, he sat before a roaring fire, reading from a tablet I'd requisitioned from Uruk. I had told Supplies that my screen had broken. I'd only seen him use nupaper, so was surprised he'd known how to work it. "I've watched you," he'd said with a smile.

I shut the door. "What are you reading?"

"Oh, just another history of Peris."

"By now you must know more than I do." I stopped taking off my coat and peered. "This is what, the third book you've read about Peris's history? What's so interesting about it?"

"I find the Gods' interpretations...intriguing." He set the tablet on the floor, took my coat, hat, and gloves. Taking my hand, he led me to his seat. He sat and patted his thighs. I curled in his lap and lay my head on his chest.

"Did you finish your experiment?"

"No, I ran out of time."

"Mm."

We fell silent. I snuggled deeper into his arms, comforted by his and the fire's warmth. After a long while, he tapped my hip. "Let's go to bed." I slipped off his lap and started undressing while he watched, a small smile playing on his lips. Then he too shucked his clothes.

I crawled beneath the heavy furs, and he scooted in after me. After petting for a few minutes, he fell asleep. But I couldn't. *I should be in the lab, not in bed.* I tossed and turned, trying not to wake him. He woke, anyway.

"What's the matter älskling? Another anxiety attack?"

"No. Go back to sleep."

"How can I with you thrashing like that?"

Instead of answering, I jumped out of bed and plopped into a fireplace chair. "Is this better?"

His lips twisted. "No. Come back to bed."

"No. I need to think."

"You can think in bed."

I shook my head.

Looking exasperated, he got up and strode to the chair where I sat. "Come on. Get your clothes on." Before I could rise, he yanked his undershirt from behind me and slipped it over his head.

I pulled on my leggings and bra. By the time I'd dressed, so had he. "Where are we going?"

"To the lab."

I bundled up, slipped on my gloves, and started for the battlement door. "All right, I'll meet you outside."

"We go from here."

"But there might be people outside. There were when I came over."

"Knulla dem."

I didn't know what "knulla" meant but I could hazard a pretty good guess.

I grabbed my tablet. At the bottom of the stairs, he yanked open the door and marched over the threshold. I stepped out behind him and took a quick look around. Lucky for us, there was no one about.

It was still snowing. He strode across the plaza while I trotted behind. It was just like the old days, except this time he stopped and waited for me to catch up. Then he scooped me in one arm, and carrying me like a child, continued on his way. We reached the lab. Walking inside, I had to duck to keep my forehead from smacking against the lintel. He set me on my feet and almost slammed the door.

He jerked his head toward the closet. "Now. Go ahead with your experiment."

I didn't need to be told twice. In moments, I had my furs off and my lab coat on. With Devi speed, I hurried to the refrigerator, snatched my newest serum, and filled a disposable syringe. Then I rushed to the freezer and grabbed a vial. I zipped over to the cage, captured a hairless skratz, and dashed to the closet. It took me about a minute to set up.

Then I ran back into the lab and put the vial back into the freezer.

Relaxed now, I walked to Hyme's chair and sat. Teger eyed me. "I was getting dizzy just watching you. Do all morevs move that fast?"

I smiled. "I was in a hurry."

We said nothing for a few minutes. He gave me a look. "Two hours, right?"

"You have a good memory."

He grunted. "Wake me—"

Hyme's apartment door opened and he stuck his head out. "I thought I heard voices. What are you two doing here?"

I opened my mouth but Teger beat me to it. "She's finishing up the experiment she started before she left," he said, sounding grumpy. "We're here because otherwise I won't get any sleep."

Hyme chuckled. "Come on upstairs. We'll have some tea."

"You got anything stronger than that?"

"Of course. Come on up." His head disappeared.

We climbed the steep steps. At the top, Teger looked around. "This place hasn't changed since I was a boy."

Hyme laughed. "Yes, it has. It just looks the same. Go ahead, sit." He headed for the kitchen.

We sat on the couch. Teger snaked his arm around my shoulders and pulled me closer. I lay my head on his chest. Minutes later, Hyme reappeared with three big mugs, two of them steaming, balanced on a large wooden tray. He set it on the table, handed me my tea, then Teger his mug of ale. He took the last mug and settled into a fireplace chair. "So, what did you do this time?"

I sipped. "I hope by upping the concentration of linmen and cooli, I might get a better result."

"Better result than what?" Teger said.

Hyme's eyes widened. "She didn't tell you?"

"Tell me what?"

"The last skratz lived over a day and a half before it died."

Teger jerked his head around. "I want daily reports from now on."

"No. Every marun. That was our agreement."

"But—"

"But nothing. I've stuck to my bargain that I spend no more than four hours here after services, and I'm sticking to this one, too."

He let out a sigh.

Sipping our tea, Hyme and I discussed the properties of some of my other antiviral plants. Even Teger took part, making astute comments comparing my plants and some of the northern stock. "It warms these old hearts that you remember so much," Hyme said.

Teger raised his brow. "Are you joking? You drilled this stuff into my head deeper than a thalin corer."

Hyme and I laughed.

During a lull in the conversation, Teger glanced at his timepiece. "Your skratz should be showing fever signs by now. Let's go look." Setting his empty mug on the table, he headed for the stairs.

I entered the closet first. Sure enough, the skratz had fallen ill. Its skin had turned bright red, and if I looked closely, I could see the pustules forming. Shoving my hands into the manipulators, I picked up the serum, injected it, and then pulled my hands free. "Well, that's it for now. Let's pray to Astoreth this little beast lives."

Teger and Hyme glanced at each other. I wondered about that for a moment, but now that my experiment was underway, I was too tired to think about it. "Guess we'll be going now. Ready, Teger?"

"Oh, yes."

Hyme helped me into my coat while Teger shrugged into his. I picked up my tablet. "I'll see you before breakfast, Hyme."

"Of course, of course. Have a good night, you two."

We stepped out into the cold and started walking, both of us quiet. "Why is it so important that you be the first to discover the cure?"

My hearts sped up. *I'm not ready to tell yet.* Then an answer came to me. "It's a race. One I intend to win."

"What happens if you win?"

"You hakoi don't have to worry about the fever anymore."

"You know what I mean."

"No, really. The É will get all the glory. I'm just a scientist. I won't even get a mention in a footnote." I shrugged. "It doesn't matter to me. I just want to find the cure."

Astoreth's image appeared in my mind's eye. *And we can forget about Her making me head of research.*

Teger said nothing.

We continued our walk in silence, me getting more nervous with each step. "This is dangerous, Teger. Someone might see us."

"At this hour? Unlikely."

He pushed open his tower's door. I breathed a sigh of relief. The lights flickered. I realized this was only the second time I'd been in here. I hadn't noticed on our way down, but it was odd not seeing the É to my left. Instead, there were two great doors, now closed, that went from the floor almost to the ceiling. Together, they were as wide as the É entrance. I pointed. "What's that?"

He turned his head. "Storage."

We entered his apartment, and I didn't waste any time. The fire had long since died, and I could feel the chill on my face. Undressing, I slung my furs and clothes over the back of the fireplace chair, hurried to the bed, and crawled beneath the heavy furs.

Teger wasn't far behind. Slipping in beside me, he pulled me close. "Think you can sleep now?"

"Yes." I snuggled against him.

"Good, because you have to get up in a few hours."

"I'll be fine," I said, my voice muffled by his chest. Already I was falling asleep. The last thing I felt before it claimed me was Teger stroking my hair.

Chapter Twenty-Seven

The second skratz lived for two days before it died. The third lived two-and-a-half. The fourth lived three days, as did the fifth, and the three more after that.

I was on the verge of tearing my hair out. I was so close. No matter what I did, the skratz lived no more than three days. I was careful not to take out my frustration on Hyme, but Teger wasn't so lucky. The first time it happened, he wasted no time putting me in my place.

"I said I would, didn't I?"

A moment of silence, then his brow rose. "Älskling, I understand how you feel, but you will not take it out on me. Apologize."

I ducked my head. "I'm sorry."

After that, I was more careful, but it still seemed I was always apologizing. To his credit, he took my outbursts in stride. Whenever I did, he only smiled and gave me a tight hug.

Right now, I was alone in the lab while Hyme tended to a customer. Or rather, a patient. As he'd predicted, Mjorans had trickled in at first, but the trickle had become a tide this past marun or so. It seemed everyone had some ailment or another. In between my own work, he kept me busy making cures for the villagers' various conditions.

I'd been checking on my skratz every hour, and it was time to check again. I lay the dowel I'd been using to stir cough syrup on the counter. Inside the closet, I peered inside the chamber. The skratz looked no better than it had yesterday. The pustules were gone, but it was still bright red and its breathing labored. "Heal, damn you," I muttered. "Heal."

"What was that?" Hyme's voice sounded behind me.

"Nothing. Just talking to myself."

"Well, why don't you talk yourself into lunch? It's almost time."

After eating, Hyme had to speak with one of the diners, so I returned to the lab alone. Standing over the counter, dowel in hand and about to continue stirring the cough syrup he'd asked me to finish, I bit my lip. It hadn't been that long, but... *I should look in on my skratz.* I stepped into the closet and stopped.

It was dead.

I quick-stepped to the environment and stared in disbelief. It hadn't even lived as long as the others. Tightening my lips, I was about to slide my hands into the manipulators when a bolt of fury exploded through me. I sank to my knees and sobbed. *Why? What did I do wrong?*

A pair of hands under my armpits pulled me to my feet. It was Teger. He cupped my face, star-colored eyes full of concern. "What's wrong, älskling? Why are you crying?"

"Th-the skratz died," I hiccupped, and started sobbing again.

He lifted me, and my legs automatically locked around his waist. I threw my arms around his neck and buried my face in his broad shoulder. Holding me tight, he gently twisted from side to side, making those cooing, rumbling noises that always soothed me.

After I'd cried myself out, he tapped my bottom, our signal that I should get down. I slid to the floor. He smiled, though I didn't smile back. Stepping out of the closet, he led me to my chair and pulled me onto his lap. I lay my head on his chest while he stroked my hair. We sat that way for a long while, silent.

Eventually, he pushed me upright, his face serious. "Älskling, what if there isn't a cure for red fever?"

Anger zipped through me. "Don't say that." My voice rang through the lab. "Don't even *think* it."

"All right, all right." He pulled me back against his chest. "Calm down."

"There has to be a cure," I said in a low voice. "There just has to be."

After a minute or two, I got up. "I have to go dispose of my latest failure."

"Don't think of it as a failure."

"What would you call it?"

"Now you know what doesn't work. That's progress."

"I still—"

"Älskling. Remember what I told you about hunting? You're on a hunt. Be patient, or you'll never find your cure."

I nodded. He was right, but I didn't have the luxury of time. Every day, I was acutely aware of my deadline moving closer and closer. Entering the closet, I dropped the skratz and the syringes into the acid vat, then fumigated the chamber. Stepping out, I saw him standing at my table, holding an open-topped box made of thick, corrugated nupaper. He turned it this way and that, then upended and gave it a couple of hard shakes. Nothing fell out. He shook it once more, then set the box down.

He'd found the second part of my plan to cheat death. I'd been working on it while I waited for results and Hyme had nothing for me to do.

He turned. "What's this?"

I gave him a small smile. "It's a maze."

"A what?"

"A maze. Haven't you seen one before?"

He shook his head.

I walked over to him. "Let me show you. Skratz are fairly intelligent, and I'm doing a memory experiment. So, I built this out of scrap nupaper board." I reached into the cage and picked up a little beast snuffling in a corner. "I've been working with this one."

I gently set it into the box. The skratz looked around as if uncertain. Then it moved forward. At the first divider, it peeked around the corner, but didn't go inside. Then it crept along the corridor until it came to the second divide. It bypassed this one, too. At the third, it hesitated, then turned the corner. It squeaked and ran in circles, having walked into a dead end. After a moment or two, the skratz ventured out. It made a right turn and headed for the maze's beginning. Then it turned around started creeping again.

"Hello, you two," a voice called from behind us.

As one, we jumped and turned to the street door.

"What are you doing?" Hyme said, taking off his furs.

"Min älskling is showing me her latest experiment," Teger said.

He joined us. "Experiment, eh? I thought it was a game."

The three of us watched the skratz navigate the maze. By now, it had made it halfway through. It made several more wrong turns but managed to reach the end. I picked it up and scratched behind its ears.

The little beast shivered in delight. I tickled it for a moment longer, then returned it to the cage.

"So what are you trying to prove?" Teger said.

I shrugged. "Nothing. Just something to do." I hated lying, but I wasn't ready to tell anyone the truth. Not until I'd found the cure at the very least. But my experiment had gone well. Yesterday, the skratz had run the maze without error. This morning, just before breakfast, I'd injected it with a solution made from the juices of five plants I'd studied in Hyme's botany and herbology tomes. As I'd hoped, the skratz's memory had been erased. The solution needed fine tuning, but I'd definitely hit upon the right combination.

I touched the bar. "Time."

"Fourth hour, twenty minutes, Tryn."

"I have to check the beacon. And then I have to see Stiren for his report." I looked at Hyme. "I'll finish the cough syrup when I get back."

"Don't worry. I can finish it."

"All right." I bundled into my furs. "I'll see you later," I said, my voice muffled.

"I should be back by the time you've finished," Teger said. "If I'm not, just go on in."

I stepped out. Snow was falling, and it seemed colder than it had been before lunch. Walking across the plaza, I thought about the skratz that had died. *Too much pygo in the serum maybe? Or I shouldn't have added more maram? Hm...I'm pretty sure it wasn't the maram.* I sighed. *I'll have to go back to the serums I used for the first skratz that lived and start again.*

Inside my tower, I glanced into the darkened É. *Oh, right. I have to set up for the service. I'll do that after I see Stiren. By then, Teger should be there.*

Entering my apartment, I shed my furs and laid them on the bare wooden table. The chill seeped through my heavy uniform. I turned the heating grate's handle, and a small puff of warm air blew in my face.

I headed for the control room. On the long ride up, I pondered my serum. I'd used just about every combination of Hyme's and my antivirals. None had worked. There was something I was missing, but what?

All the equipment was in fine shape, as usual. I called Central, and as usual, had to endure a minor god's rudeness. I'd long since stopped letting it bother me. That's just the way they were.

Now, I had to see Stiren. Rounding the tower's bend, I noticed the door to the barracks was already open and walked faster. I called out "as you were" and headed for Stiren's office. The report was short. No disciplinary actions, a requisition for food, and which troops were due for rotation. I initialed it, then he popped the disc and handed it to me. Dropping it into my pocket, I gave my routine assurance I'd get it to the Laerd today.

I left the barracks and stepped into the É. Setting up took all of ten minutes. Surveying my handiwork, I nodded in satisfaction. I returned to my apartment, bundled up, then stepped onto the battlement. Pushing open Teger's door, I saw him seated at his desk, working on a pile of nupapers.

He grinned, leapt from his chair, and grabbed me by the waist. "Älskling." Lifting me high, he spun us in a circle. I hadn't even taken off my coat.

After hanging my furs in his closet, he carried me to the chair closest to the roaring fire.

I lay my head on his chest. "That was some greeting. You only saw me about an hour ago."

"I missed you." He kissed my hair.

We sat in silence for a long while before I raised my head. "Teger, why did you say there might not be a cure for red fever?"

He shrugged. "Just pointing out the possibility. Why?"

"Because I believe there's a cure for every illness. We just have to find it."

"Mm-hm."

"What's that supposed to mean?"

"What's what supposed to mean?"

I punched his shoulder. "Come on. Talk to me."

He took a breath. "Älskling, maybe the fever didn't come from Peris."

"Then where did it come from? Outer space?"

"Yes. Maybe a passing comet, a meteor strike, maybe even...aliens."

I snorted. "An alien landing? That's silly. The Gods would never allow it. They—"

"If they're Gods, why don't they fix it?"

"Because they're Gods, Teger. They know what's good for us, better than we do."

He gave me a dubious look. "Red fever is good for us?"

"Of course not. But we have to find the cure ourselves. It's one thing to talk about discipline and perseverance, but it has to be put into practice to do any good. Finding the cure is a teaching tool."

"A hard lesson to learn."

"The hardest lessons are usually the best lessons."

He grinned. "Speaking of hard—"

"Stop that. I have to get back to the lab. Discipline and perseverance, remember?"

His grin turned into a pout. "You wound me."

I kissed his neck. "I'll give you an extra dose of healing tonight."

"Deal."

I slid off his lap and straightened my uniform. Gathering me into his arms, he gazed down. "I love you, älskling."

I stared back with a tiny frown. His star-colored eyes held a strange look. There was love, but there was something else, too. Something akin to pity. "I love you, too. But I really have to go now."

"Of course. Let me get your things." He strode to the closet and brought out my furs. I was about to fasten my coat when I remembered. "Oh, yes. Here's the garrison's requisition for this marun." I pulled out the disc and gave to him.

"All right. I'll see to it they get what they need by tomorrow."

I drew on my gloves and opened the door. "Älskling." I turned my head. He looked serious.

"See you at dinner."

Wondering at his expression, I nodded. "See you at dinner."

Crossing the battlement, I thought about what he'd said. *Could it be true? The virus came from space and there's no cure?* I shook my head. I didn't believe that. I couldn't believe that. There had to be a cure. Besides, hadn't I come close already? Left untreated, the virus killed within a day. I'd kept several skratz alive for three times that long. That meant I was doing something right.

I pushed open my tower's door and saw it was still snowing, though harder than before. Forgetting my problems, I unfastened my collar, opened my mouth, and caught a few of the cold flakes on my tongue. I giggled. Re-fastening it, I started walking again.

I entered the lab. Hyme was stirring something in a pot over a burner. He looked up. "There you are. I was wondering where you'd gotten to."

I shrugged out of my coat. "Why? Did something happen?"

"No, it's just usually you don't take so long."

"Well, I had to see Stiren for his report. Then I set up the É for the service. After that, I went to see Teger."

He nodded. "Ah."

I laughed. "What's that supposed to mean?"

"Just 'ah.'"

Slipping into my lab coat, I plopped in my seat, and dictated a new entry for the dead skratz. I scrolled back through my notes until I'd found the ones for the first skratz to live three days and took careful stock of the ingredients I'd used. From there, I read the notes for each skratz until I came to the one that had died today.

I set the tablet on the table, leaned back, and rubbed my eyes. Looking over my shoulder, I saw Hyme pouring whatever he'd been stirring into molds. I joined him at the counter. "More candy?"

He looked up and smiled. "Not this time. I'm making medicinal soap."

"For what?"

"There's a rash people get, usually in winter, called 'scales.' If you saw it, you'd understand why it's called that. Anyway, it's a fungal infection, more annoying than painful, especially under layers of clothing. Bathing with this anti-fungal soap kills the infection. Then you smear on a moisturizer with most of the same ingredients as the soap. Clears it up in a few days." He tilted his head toward my table. "How are you coming along?" he said and started pouring again.

"Getting there, I guess. I'm trying to come up with a new formula based on the ones I've used before. Maybe the answer's there." I paused. "Hyme, Teger and I were talking and he suggested red fever didn't originate on Peris. He said the virus could have come from space. A passing comet, a meteor, or," I licked my lips, "aliens. That might be why it's been so hard to find a cure, or maybe there is no cure."

"What did you tell him?"

"I told him not to be silly. But what do you think? Could the fever have some kind of alien origin?"

He didn't answer at first. "Anything's possible, Tehi," he said, as if weighing his words.

"So you think—"

"No, I just said anything's possible."

"I think it unlikely, myself." I watched him for a while. "Well, better get back to work."

Some time later, a rumbling in my belly said it was time for dinner. I tapped the bar "Time."

"Sixth hour, forty-nine minutes, Tryn."

I lay my tablet aside and turned. Hyme was nowhere to be seen, but I noticed the door to his apartment was open. I walked over. "Hyme," I called. "Time for dinner. We'd better go now if we don't want to be late."

"I'm coming," his voice floated down the stairs. "Give me a minute."

I was fastening my coat when I heard his feet on the steps. When he appeared, he carried a thick book and gave it to me. "Take this. Go to your apartment and read it instead of coming here tonight."

Tracing the binding with my fingers, it felt leathery and slick—from some kind of animal, maybe. I opened it. The pages were slick, too. They definitely weren't made of nupaper, though I couldn't imagine what they might be. I turned the book over. "What's it about?"

"It's an encyclopedia of little-known properties of some of our most common—and uncommon—plants and herbs. Something in there might help you."

"Did you get it on one of your trading trips?"

"No. When I was a young man, a healer in one of the more remote villages died and left it to me. Why, I'll never know. I barely knew him."

"All right." *I really need to come back here tonight, but if he thinks it might be useful, it won't hurt to take a look.* I flipped the book open, turned to the last page, and saw a list of names. "What's this?"

"Those are the people who've owned the book. My name's at the bottom." He shrugged into his coat.

I did a quick mental calculation. My eyes widened. The encyclopedia was at least five hundred years old. "I can't take this. It's so old...it's probably priceless."

"Nonsense. It's a copy of a copy of a copy. If anything happens to it, I can get another."

"Well, I'll be extra careful with it."

"Good. Come on. We'd better go."

It was still snowing as we walked to the dining hall, just as heavy as before. I held the ancient book under my armpit to keep the moisture from it. At the table, I set the book to the side. Hyme didn't talk much during dinner, which was unusual.

After our meal, the council members trooped into the hallway. While putting on my furs, Hyme lay a hand on my arm. "I have to talk to the Laerd. I'll see you tomorrow." He stepped over to where Teger stood fastening his coat. "Laerd, I must speak with you," he said in Devian.

I frowned. That was odd. In public, he always spoke Syrenese, unless he was speaking to me. He obviously didn't want anyone to know he wanted to talk with Teger, but why? Curious, I dawdled a bit, pretending to have trouble fitting my hat. By now the last of the council members were walking through the door. I had to leave too, lest the two men figure out I was planning to eavesdrop. Then I remembered the encyclopedia. "Excuse me—I forgot my book."

They made room for me to pass. I strode into the dining room and grabbed the encyclopedia from the table. Returning to the hallway, I smiled. "I'll see you tomorrow, Hyme."

He nodded once but said nothing.

Outside, I started for my tower, my pace slower than usual. Behind me, I heard Teger and Hyme leave the hall. In my peripheral vision, I saw them heading toward the lab. Straining my ears, I could just make out their conversation.

"I'm going to tell her everything," Teger said. "I'm just waiting for the right moment."

"I told you once, it's a very bad idea. We're talking about her whole life, everything she stands for, her sole reason for being. Have you really thought about what the truth would do to her? If it doesn't drive her mad, she might turn on you."

"She deserves to know. And that's a chance I'll have to take."

"You're a fool, Laerd."

By now they were out of earshot. Keeping my slow pace, I thought about what I'd just heard. *This is the second time Teger's mentioned telling someone the truth. Who is she? And why would Hyme be so against it?* Sometimes the truth hurt, but it was nothing to be afraid of. I'd faced an ugly truth about myself and was a better person for it.

Reaching my tower, I set aside the mystery of Teger and Hyme's conversation. *Hm. Think I'll read for a bit before the service.* Opening the door, I stepped inside.

◎ᓕᓕᓕᓕ◎

Early the next morning, I sat in a fireplace chair, book on my lap. It was long after five Durm, and the embers from the dying fire gave off little heat. Setting the encyclopedia spine-down on the floor, I went to the pile of fuel bricks. Grabbing two of them, I eyed the pile. *Need more, soon.* Throwing the bricks into the fireplace, I watched the flames shoot up. They'd burn for at least an hour, and by then, I'd be ready for bed.

I turned. Teger was asleep, the tablet I'd given him on the nightstand. My lips stretched into a small smile. I envied his ability to sleep anywhere, and seemingly under any circumstance. Right now, the lights were at their brightest setting and the fire crackled and popped. Me, I could only sleep in darkness and quiet. Even his snoring, gentle as it was, awakened me. And it was a common occurrence.

I stepped over to the nightstand and glanced at the tablet. *What's he reading now?* I picked it up and read a few paragraphs. It was another history of Peris, this one written by the God of Waters, Ea-ki. He'd already read the histories by Astoreth, Amash, Hor-u, and Marduc. Apparently, he intended to read all twelve histories written by the Great Pantheon. My smile broadened. *The Gods would be pleased.*

I set the tablet on the stand. Giving him one last look, I returned to my chair. I looked down and noticed the encyclopedia was open at a different place. The pages must have flipped while my back was turned. I sighed. Though the pages were numbered, the book didn't list the entries in alphabetical order. And I hadn't made note of the page number where I'd stopped. I grimaced. *Should've used the marker Hyme gave me.*

I shrugged. *I'll just read what's here.*

I lifted the heavy book and set it on my lap. *Hm. Helly.* Settling back, I started to read. It was slow going. Written in an archaic form of Syrenese, I often had to stop to figure out the words. Teger had helped me while awake, but now I was on my own.

After forty-five minutes or so, I looked up and stared at the dying

338

fire, wondering why Hyme had insisted I read his book. It was interesting, but I didn't see how any of it could help me. My time would have been better spent in the lab.

I yawned. I'd been reading non-stop since the service had ended, and now my eyes felt as if someone had poured sand into them. I wondered what time it was. Twisting in my seat, I reached for my uniform slung over the chair's back and tapped the bar. "Time."

"Fourth hour, twenty-two minutes Ekban."

I should stop now if I'm going to be in any shape for the morning service. Well, I'll just read the rest of the helly article and then go to bed. I'll give the book back to Hyme at breakfast.

Blinking a couple of times to lubricate my eyes, I started reading again. I was almost at its end when the first line of the next-to-final paragraph grabbed my attention. I gawped and read it a second time. And a third. My hearts beat faster. My mouth went dry. In a second, I wasn't tired anymore. Excitement flooded through me, tinged with fear and hope. Fear that I was mistaken and hope that I wasn't.

Bolting from the chair, I ran to the bed and fell on my knees. I shook Teger's shoulder, hard. "Wake up. Please, wake up. I need your help."

His eyes popped open. "What is it, älskling? What's wrong?"

I lay the book on the bed and pointed to the paragraph. "Would you read the first line for me?"

An annoyed look passed over his face. Then, likely noticing the look on mine, it changed to curiosity. "Where, now?"

"This one."

He began reading aloud. "Though helly is normally used as a sedative, its sap, twice-reduced, has been proven to greatly enhance the body's immune response, raising the effectiveness of antiviral and antibacterial compounds tenfold."

He looked up with wide eyes. "Do you think—"

"I don't know. There's only one way to find out. I have to go to the lab." I grabbed the book and started to get up.

Teger caught my arm, then glanced at the intercom's timepiece. "It's only five Ekban. Let Hyme sleep. It can wait until after breakfast. Or even after your morning service. Besides, if you go now, you're breaking our deal, remember?"

I sat back. "But this is important. It could be the answer to everything."

"Even if it is, it can still wait. Your research isn't going anywhere, Hyme's store of helly isn't going anywhere, the book's not going anywhere, and—"

"Neither am I, right?" I said, grimacing.

He gave me a half-smile and nodded. "Come to bed. You need sleep."

"Who can sleep at a time like this?"

"I'll sing you a lullaby."

"You can't sing."

His half-smile turned into a wicked grin. "Oh, yes I can."

My lips twisted. I wasn't in the mood, and he knew it. Still, he was right about our agreement. I gritted my teeth. *I should never have made that deal.* Getting to my feet, I tucked the book under my arm. Marking the entry, I set the book on the chair's cushions, then returned to bed. He made room for me, and I turned out the lights. The embers in the fireplace glowed, but not bright enough to keep me from sleeping. Rolling over, I closed my eyes and yawned.

I could almost feel his smile. "I won't have to sing to you after all. Pity."

"Sorry to disappoint you."

"There'll be other times."

"Mm." I yawned again. But I still couldn't sleep. My tired body was at war with my brain's excitement. *I'd give anything for a decil right now. I could wait until he falls asleep, sneak out of here and go to the lab—*

I cut off the thought. That kind of thinking would only frustrate me, and then I'd grow resentful. I lay in the darkness, my mind racing. Maybe my approach had been the problem. Red fever brought the body's immune system to near collapse. Cooli supported the system, but its effectiveness was limited. I'd used it more for its virus-killing properties. And it had worked, up to a point. Now, armed with my new-found information on helly, it was time to change tactics.

My mind raced as I plotted my next move. Unbidden, memories of my battle with the black bird surfaced. I bared my teeth. *My enemy, I conquered my hate. And now I'm going to conquer you.*

Chapter Twenty-Eight

After breakfast, Hyme and I sat in his apartment, discussing my helly discovery and what it could mean for my work. I sipped my tea. "What made you think to give me your encyclopedia?"

He shrugged. "No reason. I mean, you were at a dead end. You'd tried just about every combination of plants from your and my supplies and kept coming up on that three-day limit. I just thought it might be useful."

"Have you read it?"

"Not all the way through."

I drained my mug. "I'd better see how my helly reduction is coming along. See you downstairs."

At my worktable, I peered into the conical flask over the burner. The second reduction was ready, so I took it off and set it aside. Dropping a clean beaker into my pocket, I carried the flask to the sink, grabbing an ultra-fine strainer on my way. The strainer caught small bits of helly leaves and roots as I poured the reduction into the beaker.

I set the flask and strainer in the sink, then returned to my table. Pulling out the top drawer of my supply chest, I drew on my gloves and picked out three disposable syringes—one for the virus, the second for the serum, and the third for the toxin I'd administer if the skratz lived. It might be wishful thinking on my part, but I wanted to be ready.

Dropping the first syringe in my pocket, I picked up the test tube and poured in the still-warm helly reduction, gave it a few vigorous shakes, and set it aside to cool a bit longer. When it had cooled enough, I filled the second syringe with serum, the third with poison, and dropped these into my pocket, too. Coaxing the skratz I'd used in my memory experiment into my hand, I went to the closet and shoved the syringes and the skratz down the environment's chute. I lingered for a minute, watching the little beast explore the chamber.

Reaching inside the freezer, I retrieved the box with the vials and opened it. My lips tightened. I'd used up the virus in the first vial and the second was about three-quarters empty. I was still confident, but that didn't mean my new serum would be the one. I had to find the cure soon, or I wouldn't have any virus left. And it wasn't as if I could order more.

I set up my experiment, injected the skratz, and returned the vial to the freezer. Now I had to wait. I wrote up my lab notes and set the tablet on the table. *Might as well start training another skratz.* I pulled out the maze.

Two hours later, it was time to check on my patient. I stowed the maze and put my trainee into its cage. Inspecting the skratz in the closet, its breathing was labored, and its skin had turned the familiar bright red with pustules. I slipped my hands into the manipulators and picked up the serum-filled syringe. Taking a deep breath, I injected it, then dropped the syringe into the acid. I stared at the little beast a moment, pulled my hands from the manipulators' sleeves, and left.

I returned to my worktable and pulled out the maze again. *Maybe another training session will keep my mind occupied.* I stuck my hand into the cage, lured the little beast onto my palm, and dropped it into the maze. It sniffed at the dividers. *Wonder how long it'll take this one to figure it out.*

"All done?" Hyme said from behind me.

I looked over my shoulder. "Yes. I'm trying not to hold my breath, but it's hard."

"Well, at least you have something to keep you busy. And if that doesn't work, you can always help me."

"True. Do you need anything?"

"Not right now."

I made a snap decision. "All right. I'm going back to my apartment and work on a sermon." I put the skratz and maze away, then bundled up. "See you at lunch."

"See you."

I barely noticing the falling snow, my thoughts whirling like the flakes around me. *Did I use enough helly? Maybe I should've concentrated the cooli and linmen blend a bit more? What about the maram?*

And the mytle? Like the helly, I'd used a double concentration of both antivirals. Should I have used them at all?

A knot formed in the pit of my stomach. The question I'd been trying not to think about burst to the fore.

Would the skratz live this time?

oꙮꙮꙮ

After that morning, I spent every moment I could in the lab. The skratz's condition didn't change much in the first two days, not that I expected it. The third day was critical. During the early hours of Ekban, I paced my apartment, biting my lip. I didn't feel the cold. The only thing on my mind was whether the skratz still lived.

"Come to bed, älskling," Teger said, his gravelly voice soft but not pushing or commanding. He knew the importance of this particular day. He'd been more than forbearing over the past several marun on this score, and I loved him all the more for it.

"I can't. I wouldn't sleep anyway."

"Maybe, but you've been pacing all night. You need to rest. Tonight is Ohra-Sin, remember?"

"I know that," I snapped. Then I sighed. "I'm sorry."

He said nothing for a long while. "Do you want to go to the lab?"

"No."

"Why?"

"I'm afraid of what I might find."

"That the skratz is dead?"

"Yes."

"But what if it isn't?"

I let out a long breath. "I'll wait. The longer I do, the more time the serum has to work."

"Then come to bed."

"Yes, I suppose." I slid under the furs and turned off the light.

He wrapped me in his arms. "You're cold."

"Am I?" I lay my head on his chest and stared into the darkness. Soon, his heavy, regular breathing told me he'd fallen asleep. I closed my eyes and tried to still my racing thoughts, using several different mental tricks. None of them worked.

Giving up, I opened my eyes. Staring at the ceiling, I was pondering

343

the formula I'd calculated for my latest serum when an idea for a different approach surfaced out of the blue. *Hm. What about adjusting...* While I thought about it, a weighty feeling settled in my gut. Then I gave my head a little shake and dismissed it. *Sounds good, but no. There's no solid basis for changing the ratios like that.*

The weighty feeling vanished.

The hours ticked by. I wanted to get up but Teger was right—if I couldn't sleep, the least I could do was rest my body for the ritual.

At long last, my alarm rang. I turned it off. Teger stirred and mumbled but didn't wake. I stretched, and then dressed for the service. Shoving my feet into slippers, I threw on my cloak and left.

The service seemed interminable. Once the penitents had gone, I bolted from the É without cleaning it, barreled up the stairs, and burst into my apartment. Teger wasn't there, so I quickly changed and raced downstairs.

Throwing open my tower's door, I sprinted across the plaza as fast as I could in my heavy furs. The plows were just starting their work and new-fallen snow hindered me that much more. After what seemed like a monumental struggle, I reached the lab and walked inside. I glanced to my right. The door to Hyme's apartment was shut, which meant he was either asleep or enjoying a morning cup of tea. *I won't disturb him.* Standing at the closet, I slipped on my lab coat, then entered. Holding my breath, I peeked into the chamber.

The skratz was alive. But the third day had not yet ended. Still, though its breathing was labored, its color was not so deep a pink as others had been at this stage. That meant something was working. What was working and how long it would work were different questions. For now, the skratz was alive, and that was the important part.

I stepped out and started for my worktable. Halfway across the lab, a flash of intuition stopped me in my tracks. *Give the skratz another injection,* a small voice echoed in my brain. *Double up on the helly. Cut back on the maram by one-half and substitute equal parts cooli and linmen.*

Jerking my head around, I stared hard at the closet door. My bones and gut felt heavy. As apprentice healers, we were told to always trust our intuition. I was never a believer in it, preferring to base my conclusions on cold, hard facts.

I thought about the heavy feeling in my gut while thinking about the serum formula last night. *Maybe I...*

I nodded once. *I'll do it.* There wasn't time to mix up a batch of serum before breakfast, so I'd start afterward. I hurried to my table and dictated the new formula into my notes. I heard a door open behind me.

Hyme smiled. "Ah. Good morning, Tehi."

"And good morning to you, Hyme."

"Ready for breakfast?"

"Almost." I dictated a few more observations about the skratz and set my tablet on the table. "Now I'm ready." We helped each other into our furs and left.

"Is the skratz still alive?" he said as we crunched through the snow.

"Yes. It's doing better than the others, but I've had an idea."

"Care to share it?"

I shook my head. "Let's see if it works, first."

"Fair enough."

During breakfast, Hyme did most of the talking. He told me he'd been reading the encyclopedia and all the new information he'd found. "Should have read it years ago. There's so much in there that could have helped me, especially with some of my more difficult cases."

I returned to the lab alone. After hanging my furs, I stepped into the closet. The skratz had taken a turn for the worse. Its skin had turned almost red again, and its breathing was more labored than it had been before breakfast. By evening—or maybe even after midday—it would be dead.

I set about mixing a batch of the new serum. When ready, I filled a syringe and hurried to the closet. I had my hand on the chute when I realized I'd be letting some of the virus into the air, even if a miniscule amount. I wouldn't catch the fever, but Hyme and Teger might. I stepped back to think, then had an idea. I could unhook the hose coupling on the gas tank and spray the inside of the closet afterward. The habitat shouldn't be affected much. The closet was huge, and the gas would be concentrated at its front end.

But there was the problem of the acid gas and me. I couldn't breathe it or get any on my skin. I blinked. *Well, the first one's easy. I'll just hold my breath.* I'd had breath training and could hold my breath for up to a half-hour. I'd be in the closet with the gas for under four minutes. *As for my skin...* I had another idea. A surgical suit and helmet should provide enough protection. And I'd wash the suit immediately to keep the acid from eating into the slick fabric. The downside was that the gas smelled terrible. *Hyme's not here...maybe the odor will have gone by the time he gets back.*

Running into the hospital, I threw open a locker door, pulled out a suit, and stepped into it. I carefully rolled up the sleeves, making sure the cuffs were tight around my wrists. I didn't roll up the legs. Leaving them as they were would provide protection for my boots. I just had to be careful about tripping. I worked a pair of tight gloves over my hands, then grabbed a helmet and fitted it over my head. Snatching the syringe, I ran back to the lab.

Making sure I'd shut the closet door tight, I hurried to the environment, then pushed the syringe into the chamber. I gave the skratz the new shot, ran to the environment's far side, and unhooked the coupling from the gas canister. Taking a deep breath, I held my finger on the release valve. Pressurized gas whooshed from the canister's hose. After about fifteen seconds, I replaced the hose connection and waited a few minutes for the gas to clear. When it had, I ran for the door, opening it just wide enough for me to slip through.

I rushed back to the hospital and stripped off the suit. On quick inspection, it didn't seem the worse for wear. I hung everything in the washer and started the cycle.

Again, there was nothing to do but wait. Pulling up my chair, I dictated the time I'd given the injection. Then I pushed the tablet aside and began drumming my fingers. What to do now? *I'll set up the maze. I don't feel like working on a sermon.* I grabbed the skratz I'd started training, then dropped it at the maze's start. I had to do this several times after it had boxed itself in dead-ends and couldn't seem to find its way out. The skratz I'd worked with before, now sick with red fever, had been quicker to learn.

By now a couple of hours had passed since breakfast, and exhaustion was creeping up on me. I returned the skratz to the cage, then put the maze away. Resting my hands on the tabletop, I let my head drop to my chest. I badly needed sleep if I was going to be in any shape for Ohra-Sin, but there was no way I was leaving the lab.

"Why don't you take a nap? I'll wake you in plenty of time before lunch so you can check on your skratz."

I jumped and turned. Hyme stood by the door to his apartment, watching me with a small smile.

"My eyes, right?"

"Right."

"Thanks. I'll do that." I slung my lab coat over the chair and glanced at the closet. I was tempted, but I knew there'd be no change, not this early. I headed to the hospital, switched on the positive energy flow to the nearest bed, and climbed up. I stared at the ceiling for a moment, then closed my eyes.

The next thing I knew, Hyme was shaking me. "Wake up, Tehi. It's about fifteen minutes before lunch."

I sat up and yawned. "Mm. Excuse me." I smiled. "Thanks, Hyme."

"You're welcome." He left the room.

I straightened my uniform, marched into the lab, and stepped inside the closet. It had been just under four hours since I'd given the skratz its shot. I peered into the chamber. The little beast's color was not as red as it had been before, but not by much. Still, it was an improvement.

We bundled up and left. "So how's your patient?" Hyme said as we walked across the plaza.

"A little better. I'm hoping it'll make it through the after midday."

I checked on the skratz again after lunch. Its condition was unchanged. I dictated my observations and leaned back in my chair. *Guess I could set up the maze...but that's too much effort.* I really didn't have anything to do to justify my being here but sitting and doing nothing made me feel useless. I swiveled my chair. Hyme stood behind the counter, watching something boil in a conical flask. "Need help with anything?"

"No. Why don't you get some more rest? That nap did you some good, but your eyes are still a little dull."

I shook my head. "I don't want to leave."

"Who said anything about leaving? Go back to the hospital. I'll wake you."

"Hyme, you're too good to me."

"I know. Now go."

In the patients' room, I lay on the bed and was asleep in seconds. Waking on my own, I tapped the bar. "Time."

"Sixth hour, thirty-four minutes Tryn."

What? I went down for my nap just after lunch and dinner would be served in less than a half-hour. I slipped on my boots and walked into the lab. Hyme was boiling more herbs. "You really shouldn't have let me sleep for so long."

"You needed it." He peered. "Your eyes look a lot better."

I watched the herbs dance in the flask's roiling waters. "Well, I'd better see about my skratz."

"Let me know how it's doing."

"Of course." Entering the closet, my lips tightened. What would I find this time?

I looked into the chamber. The skratz's breathing was still labored, but its color had much improved—a deep pink instead of red. Hope surged through me.

I allowed myself a smile. My nap had rested me, and I was confident Ohra-Sin wouldn't be a problem. Staring at the little beast, my bones and gut felt heavy. I closed my eyes, listening to my intuition. My smile broadened. I'd become confident about something else, too.

The skratz would live through the night.

⊙═╝═╝═╝═⊙

The fourth day found me in the lab before breakfast. I wasn't going to fool myself into thinking that just because the skratz had survived the night, it was out of danger.

I stood before the chamber, watching it. I had a syringe full of serum in my lab coat's pocket, debating whether to use it. The skratz's color had improved since last night—it was a medium instead of a deep shade of pink—and its breathing less labored. But it was obviously still very sick.

I decided to wait. After all, it was only early morning, and the skratz might improve as the day progressed. I'd check on it every hour or two. Walking to my worktable, I plopped into my chair and dictated the morning's findings. After that, I swiveled back and forth, thinking of nothing in particular.

Behind me, the door to Hyme's apartment opened. "Good morning, Tehi."

I swiveled around. "Morning, Hyme."

"Any change in your patient?"

"Yes. Its color is better, and it's breathing easier. I'll be watching it throughout the day."

He nodded. "Very good. Let's go get some breakfast."

Outside, it had snowed through the night and was still snowing. The street and sidewalks had been plowed, but the plaza had not. I persuaded Hyme to brave the plaza because it was the shortest and fastest route. Or so I thought. Hyme, being so tall, didn't have much of a problem walking through the snow. I did. It was past my knees. Between that and my bulky coat, it was a real struggle just to take a single step.

"Why don't we use the sidewalk? It'll be easier for you."

"I'm fine. Let's keep going."

We were almost late for breakfast. Slogging through the snow had taken a lot of my energy, and I was hungry. I dove into my meal. While the plates were being cleared, Hyme turned. "This time, we take the sidewalks."

I gave him a sheepish smile. "Yes, I suppose you're right."

We left the hall and I looked around. It was snowing even harder now, and the plows were out in full force. I counted six. They were having trouble keeping up in the heavy snowfall. As soon as they'd plowed a section of the street, it started filling up with snow.

"Pretty soon they're going to stop plowing because there won't be any point," Hyme said. Condensation wreathed around his head. "Means we'll be wearing our snowshoes. That'll make it easier for you to get around."

"I'll have to learn how to use them."

"It's not hard. The Laerd will teach you."

We walked on. The canopies over the shops—replaced after the windstorms—caught most of the falling snow, and the going was much easier. In the lab, I shrugged off my furs, and hurried to the closet. I stared into the chamber. The skratz's condition hadn't changed much since we left for breakfast, but the change was definitely for the better. Given the setback it had suffered yesterday, I kept the serum-filled syringe in my lab coat pocket.

At my table, I set up the maze. Luring the skratz I'd been training from the cage, I dropped it inside. The little beast sniffed the dividers, then started making its way through.

During the few hours I spent with the skratz, the apothecary's bell rang almost constantly. I had picked up the little beast and was about to drop it into the maze for the tenth time when Hyme burst into the lab. "Tehi, can you make more decongestant and anti-diarrheal pills for me?"

"Of course." I put away my experiment and got to work. Between monitoring my fever patient and making medicines, the rest of the day passed quickly. By dinnertime, I'd made enough of the medicines to last at least a couple of marun, or so I hoped. *I'll work with the skratz tonight, unless Hyme needs me.*

After the service, I returned to the lab and evaluated the skratz. There had been no change since lunch. Slipping my hands into the manipulators, I picked it up and turned it over. It didn't stir. I scratched it behind the ears. It still didn't stir. I set the skratz on the chamber's floor, and its legs twitched. It was the first movement I'd seen in four days. That might be a good sign, but I wasn't counting on it since it was still unconscious.

I walked over to my table and set up the maze. Coaxing the skratz into my hand, I dropped it inside. It ran through several times before it could do so without making a mistake. *Hm. I can't give it my drug tomorrow. Was hoping I could, but it's not ready. I'll have to keep working with it.*

All too soon, my four hours were up. I bade Hyme goodnight and headed for my tower.

The next morning, I was back in the lab after the service and checked on the skratz before I'd even taken off my furs. Its condition was the same. That worried me. It was as if the double-dose of helly I'd given it yesterday had run its course. *I'll give it another injection.* This time, I had to tell Hyme since he was in the lab. I left the closet and exchanged my furs for my lab coat.

I took a breath. "Hyme, when you're finished with that, I need to talk to you."

He looked up from his microscope. "We can talk now. What about?"

"I want to give the skratz another injection. Its condition hasn't changed since lunchtime yesterday. It's not getting worse but it's not getting better, either. I think the first shot I gave it has done all it can do, and I'd like to try a second." I paused. "So I'm asking your opinion. What do you think?"

"Well, let's have a look." Staring into the chamber, he rubbed his chin. "How long as it been like this?"

"Since three Tryn yesterday."

"And it's just after five Gor, now. Almost twenty-three hours." He gazed at the skratz with a thoughtful look. "I think you should give it another dose."

I stared. "That means opening the chute."

"Like you did yesterday?" He gave me a small smile.

My eyes widened. "How did you know?"

"I smelled the gas." He paused. "Tehi, why didn't you tell me?"

"The skratz was dying. I had to do something, and I didn't want you trying to talk me out of it." I ducked my head, and then looked up. "Are you angry with me?"

"I was. But I would've done the same thing if it'd been me." He smiled again. "So let's get to it. You used a surgical suit for protection?"

"Yes."

"Off to the hospital."

In the locker room, I pulled the syringe from my pocket and laid it on the counter. Hyme helped me into a suit and fit the helmet over my head while I worked on the tight-fitting gloves.

Back in the lab, I opened the closet door. He laid a hand on my arm. "I don't have to tell you to be careful, right?"

"Yes," I said, my voice muffled by the helmet.

"In you go."

I closed the door tight and gave the skratz the injection. Taking a deep breath, I disconnected the hose from its coupling, picked up the gas canister, and sprayed. I waited until the gas had dissipated, then slipped out of the closet. "All done."

"Good. Let's get that suit off you and into the wash."

We ran to the locker room. I stripped off the suit, hung everything in the washer, and started the cycle.

"So what was the formula this time?"

I told him. "I just had a hunch. I don't believe in hunches, but this time I thought it was worth trying."

"Always trust your hunches, Tehi. Sometimes it's all we have."

Back in the lab, I turned and sighed. "Nothing to do now but wait."

"It's almost time for breakfast, anyway."

Outside, it was snowing hard, and the temperature seemed to have dropped again. For me, each step was a struggle. The snow came almost to mid-thigh, and not a plow was in sight. "Guess we'll be wearing our snowshoes, now."

Hyme blew a heavy breath. "Earlier than usual, too."

After breakfast, my skratz looked like it had improved a little, but I couldn't be sure. I checked it hourly, and upon returning after evening services, its improvement was obvious, though it wasn't yet out of danger. Leaving the closet after checking the little beast for the umpteenth time, I headed for my worktable.

Now that the apothecary was closed, I had time for my memory experiment. To my surprise, the skratz ran the maze fifteen times without a mistake. Tomorrow morning after the service, I'd give it the memory-erasing shot. Hyme probably wouldn't be here, and I could do it without him asking questions.

I put the skratz into its cage and shoved the maze beneath the table. Straightening, I turned and spotted Hyme standing at the far counter with his back to me. "I suppose I should go. There's not much more I can do tonight."

He looked over his shoulder. "You've still some time before you have to leave. Why don't we go upstairs and have some tea?"

"That sounds wonderful."

Inside his apartment, I plopped onto the sofa while he went into the kitchen. We sipped and talked about the various herbs, plants, and their properties we'd learned from the encyclopedia. He'd read entries that I hadn't, so some of it was new. Two hours later, Teger came for me, wearing his electric blue quiltsuit and carrying the red one over his shoulder. "Temperature's dropped again. It's too cold for furs and the snow's too deep for walking without snowshoes. I left those downstairs."

Hyme shivered. "I guess I was waiting for that," he said, almost to himself. He looked up. "Would you like some tea, Laerd?"

"That'd be great."

Hyme disappeared into the kitchen. Teger sat beside me, worked off his skullcap, and pecked my cheek. "Any progress tonight?"

"Some."

Hyme returned with a hot, steaming mug and handed it to Teger. Hyme and I continued talking about the encyclopedia, then three of us spoke of village affairs. After a long while, Teger picked up the red quilt-suit and held it up. "I'll help you with this."

I eyed it. "I think I can do it myself."

"No, they're tricky to put on until you get used to it."

"I can—"

He raised his brow. "Don't get stubborn with me, älskling."

I gave him a small smile. He helped me slide my right foot into the suit and then the left, keeping up a running commentary while showing me how to handle the stiff material. "You have to make sure the seams are straight, so the suit will properly seal. If you don't, the heating filaments won't work, and you'll freeze to death. Or worse."

I watched him align a seam. "What could be worse than that?"

He looked up. "The suit could catch fire."

I swallowed hard. "Oh."

He fitted the skullcap over my head and straightened it. After closing the seal at my neck, he stepped back.

I turned in a circle. "So how do I look?" My voice sounded muffled.

Teger looked me up and down. "You look ready for the cold. I'll help you with the suit tomorrow morning, but you're going to put it on."

"All right."

"Let's go downstairs and get you into those snowshoes."

In the lab, he strapped the snowshoes to my feet while I watched. Then he had me practice walking, using two poles he'd brought with him for balance. It felt strange, walking with my legs further apart than usual. "You'll get used to it," Hyme said. I wasn't so sure, but I hadn't a choice.

After Teger decided I was ready, he grabbed my furs and we stepped outside. I gasped. The weather wasn't just freezing—it was mind-numbingly bitter. But the suit did its work, and seconds later, I was comfortably warm.

We started for my tower. He patted my arm. "How do you like our cold weather now, älskling?"

Planting my pole into the snow, I took a careful step. "As long as I'm warm, I could get used to it."

He let out a muffled chuckle. "You'll have plenty of time to get used to it, trust me."

We shoed in silence, mainly because I had to concentrate on

walking. By the time we arrived at my tower, my groin and inner thigh muscles were burning, and I knew I'd be sore tomorrow. *I'll skip dancing and meditation tonight. Give give them a chance to rest.*

I leaned my poles in the corner. Teger helped me unstrap my snowshoes. After unstrapping his shoes, we headed for my apartment. He supervised as I carefully removed my quiltsuit. "It's like I showed you, but you do everything exactly backward." Then he took off his own suit, with considerably more expertise.

The heat had long since been turned off, and it was cold. Teger rubbed his hands. "Why don't we light a fire?"

"Why don't we sleep instead?" I said with a small smile.

He grinned. "I know that look. You have no intention of sleeping."

My smile widened. I'd never tell him, but I didn't really want to make love. I just needed something to take my mind off the skratz. And our lovemaking had a way of taking my mind off everything. Stripping off our clothes, we left them where they'd fallen, ran for the bed, and dove under the furs. I turned out the light. Afterward, sated and drowsy, I curled against him and was almost asleep when he nudged me.

"Hm?"

"Do you think the skratz is still alive?"

"I hope so."

Silence. I was falling asleep again when he spoke.

"I lost my parents to red fever when I was seven."

Shock and dismay woke me up. "Oh, Teger, I'm so—"

"I guess that's why I was such a delinquent as a boy. I was grieving, but no one knew how to comfort me." My hearts broke for him, and I scooted up until his head lay on my breast. I kissed his hair.

"I love you, älskling," he said, his voice soft. A minute later, his deep, rhythmic breathing told me he'd fallen asleep.

"I love you too, Teger," I whispered. Staring into the darkness, I begged Astoreth that my latest serum was the cure, for his sake and the sakes for all the hakoi on Peris. It had to be the cure.

It just had to be.

❊❊❊❊❊

I didn't get to the lab the next day until after breakfast. Teger was called out right before the morning service. Thinking he'd be gone for only a few minutes, I was surprised he hadn't returned by the time I did. I took an extra long shower and was surprised even more when I stepped into my room and he still wasn't here.

After dressing, I sat in a fireplace chair and waited. And waited. And waited. I checked the time. Breakfast would be served soon. By now, I was irritated enough to put on the quiltsuit myself. I was on my feet when he appeared in the battlement doorway. He pulled off his skullcap and stepped inside. "Sorry. Had a bit of an emergency."

"What kind of emergency?" I snapped.

He stopped short and his eyes narrowed. "Are you angry with me?"

"Let's just say I'm a little annoyed. I wanted to go to the lab before breakfast."

"Älskling—"

I waved my hand. "Doesn't matter. I'll get over it." I picked up my quiltsuit. "Now help me into this thing."

He sat in the chair and supervised while I carefully worked my way into the suit. He had to help me only once, to straighten a seam I had trouble reaching. I put on my skullcap and sealed it. Tugging at the suit here and there, he then patted my shoulder. "All right. You're ready. Do you need help with your snowshoes?"

"I can do it. I'll meet you at the dining hall."

He nodded, and with a quick peck on my quilted cheek, stepped onto the battlement.

At the bottom of the stairs, I strapped on my snowshoes, grabbed my poles, and went out. Entering the dining hall, I saw Hyme had already arrived. Taking pains to peel off my suit, I hung it on the peg, hurried into the dining room, and pulled out my chair. "Did you check on the skratz this morning?"

"Good morning, Tehi. No, I thought you'd want to do that." He cocked his head. "You are coming over after breakfast, aren't you?"

I smiled. "Not even a herd of stampeding pirsu could keep me away." The words had no sooner left my mouth when breakfast was served. I ate in haste and got up to leave.

Hyme looked up. "Do you want help with your quiltsuit?"

"No, I can do it."

He nodded. I had a little more trouble getting into my suit than I thought I would, but I managed it. Once inside the lab, I ran to the closet.

Banging into the door with my shoulder, it flew open, and I rushed to the environment. I stared into the chamber. The skratz looked a lot better than it had last night. Its skin was mottled, light pink, and its normal pale, silver gray. Right now, it was more pink than gray, but the gray was gaining over the pink, even as I watched. Its heavy, labored breathing had eased, too.

"Looks like there's been serious improvement," Hyme said from behind me.

I spun around.

He gave me a little smile. "Sorry to scare you."

"No, no...it's all right." I turned back to the chamber. "You think so?"

"Don't you?"

"Y-yes...I think I was expecting something else."

"You've never gotten this far before. Really, you should expect anything."

I nodded and we left the closet.

"What will you do today, Tehi? Besides monitor your skratz every fifteen minutes."

I pulled off my skullcap. "Guess I'll work on my memory experiment." I thought of Eresh. "You know, when I came to Mjor, I thought I'd brought enough work to last me a lifetime. And I suppose it would have been a lifetime's worth in Uruk. But without all the interruptions, they're just a part of É life, I've been able to get so much done." I bit my lip. "I don't—" I caught myself. "Amazing."

"Eresh told me pretty much the same thing."

"He did?"

"Yes. Told me the freedom he had as beacon steward...he wasn't sure how he'd readjust." He cocked his head. "I've thought the same thing about you."

I didn't say anything. I hadn't told him what would happen to me when I returned to Uruk and didn't want to tell him because then I'd have to tell him my plans. I wasn't ready to do that. "Oh, I'm sure I'll get along." I started peeling off my suit.

He gave me an odd look through narrowed eyes. "I'm sure you will." Then he smiled. "Let's get to work."

I hung up my suit and went to my worktable while Hyme headed for the counter. I pulled out my maze and set up. Turning to the cage, I saw him take a jar of dried leaves off the top shelf. That reminded me. "Hyme, I've got a lot of your herbs, plants, and seeds over here. Do you want them back now?"

"Not at the moment. I'll just get them as I need them."

"Do you need any help?"

"No, I'm fine. I'm just making more decongestant, and then I'll open up the shop."

"All right." I picked up the skratz and then set it down. It had only been three or four minutes, but my curiosity got the better of me. I stepped into the closet and hurried to the environment. I let out a tiny gasp. The skratz's skin was silvery gray. I shoved my hands into the manipulators, picked it up and rotated it. Not a trace of pink anywhere. Laying it on the floor, I pulled my hands from the manipulators and stepped back. It looked as if it were sleeping.

I was almost too excited to work on my memory experiment. But it was just as important to my plan as the cure, so I steeled myself to do what was needed. I picked up the training skratz and plunked it at the maze's start. I couldn't give it the injection—not with Hyme in the lab—so I could only test its memory. It remembered. To make sure, I ran it through the maze again and again. Perfect, every time.

By now it was almost time for lunch, and I put the skratz and the maze away. It had been three hours since I'd checked my patient. I went to the closet. Hyme was right behind me. We said nothing as we hurried to the environment. I let out a little cry. The skratz was awake and moving about. I stared, my hearts pounding. The little beast, so plump when I shoved it into the chamber, now looked wasted and weak. Trying to explore, it stumbled and fell several times. If I allowed it to live, from past experience with the hakoi, I knew its recovery would be slow. Still, its eyes were bright and alert as it went about its investigations.

Hyme wrapped his arm around my shoulder and squeezed.

Tears sprang to my eyes, and my throat tightened. After years of research, hard work, frustration, and outright despair, I'd finally done it.

I had found the cure for red fever.

Chapter Twenty-Nine

That night, I paced my apartment, waiting for Teger. It was late. He was late. He was usually here by three-thirty Durm. Right now, it was long past that.

Pulling my heavy robe closer, I stopped my pacing and stared into the fireplace without seeing the flames' wild dancing. "Where are you?" I muttered.

A whoosh of frigid air announced that Teger had finally arrived.

I strode over to him. "Where have you been?"

He stood stock-still for almost a minute. "And a good evening to you, älskling." His voice was muffled by the skullcap, but his tone let me know I'd crossed a line.

"I'm sorry," I mumbled and took several paces backward.

Saying nothing, he began shedding his suit. His movements were slow, unnecessarily so, I thought, given his expertise. First, he unsealed the skullcap. Lifting it over his head, he shook out his long hair, then meticulously folded the cap in half and tucked it under his left arm. Then he unsealed the suit's torso, opening it to his crotch. After he'd done that, he carefully pulled out his right arm from the sleeve. Transferring the skullcap to his right armpit, he drew out his left arm. Now the garment hung loosely about his hips. Using both hands, he pushed the suit past his thighs to his knees. He undid the closures from the knee to the ankle on both legs. Then he began extracting his left leg from the suit.

I couldn't wait anymore and hurried over to him. "I found the cure," I blurted.

His head snapped up. He'd just pulled his right leg out of the quilt-suit, and for about five seconds, he stood balanced on his left foot, staring at me with wide eyes. A huge grin split his face. Dropping his skullcap, he kicked the suit to the floor and closed the distance between us in one long stride. Scooping me into his arms, he clutched me to his chest and danced about the room, twirling and singing in an off-key baritone.

A few minutes later, he fell into the nearest fireplace chair. I blinked, dizzy. He gave me a tight squeeze and stroked my hair. "So. Tell me about your cure."

I told him. "But I still have some work to do. I mean, I have to replicate my findings to make sure this one wasn't a fluke." I thought of the first injection I'd given the skratz and how that may—though however unlikely—have had an effect on the later two shots. "Anyway, the way I work is that if I do an experiment five times with the same results, then I know I've found the solution to whatever problem I'd been trying to solve."

"I take it you'll go to the lab after your morning service?"

"Yes. I need to make more serum, and I can get started on that before breakfast."

We said nothing for a long while. I closed my eyes, basking in the heat from the fire, the warmth of his body seeping through my robe, and the high from my success. Oh, I still needed confirmation, but I was confident my next five trials would turn out the same.

"Come, let's go to bed." His voice roused me from my reverie. I scooted off his lap. Towering over me, he stared into my eyes. As always whenever he did this, his star-colored gaze sucked me in until I was lost in their depths.

He took my hand and led me to bed. With a flick of his fingers, he undid the sash on my robe. Sliding his hands over my breasts, he pushed the robe off my shoulders. The heavy fabric fell to the floor. Without breaking eye contact, he leaned over and pulled back the thick fur blanket, and gently shoved me onto the bed.

I watched him undress, slow and deliberate, then join me. Since leaving the fireplace, his gaze had never left mine. He drew me close and laid on a deep kiss that sent shock waves through me. After a delicious forever, he pulled away and stared into my eyes again. "Thank you," he whispered.

"F-for what?" I whispered back.

"For helping us. For saving us."

"But—"

He kissed me again, then turned out the light. In the darkness, his arms slipped around me and squeezed tight. It was hard to breathe. A few minutes later, he loosened his grip and lay back on the bed, pulling me with him.

We didn't make love. Instead, his breathing turned slow and deep, a sure sign he had fallen asleep. I could have woken him up and insisted, but judging from the time he'd arrived, he'd had a long day. I sighed. *Well, guess I did, too.*

I breathed in deep, and slowly let it out. And another. And a third. My mind and body relaxed, and my desire drained away.

But I didn't sleep. Instead, I worried about the situation back home. *Has the fever hit Kherah? If it has, I'm sure Eresh would've left a message. I haven't gotten one...but that might not mean anything. If Kherah's in the middle of an epidemic, communications to beacons with live stewards have probably been cut. Astoreth will have drafted every morev in Her cities and towns to cope.* Another thought occurred to me. *The supply runs to Mjor haven't stopped. But they might be coming from one or two of Astoreth's other cities that haven't been hit. At least not yet.*

Then the question I'd tried hard to avoid shouldered its way to the fore. *If red fever has struck, and I have the cure...will I send it to them? Not sending it could save my life, but thousands of hakoi will die.* Thinking on it, my heartsbeat sped up.

Which would I choose—my life or theirs?

❄❄❄❄❄

The blizzard hit us about two hours after lunch.

I, being in the windowless lab cleaning up after my third—and successful—trial, had no idea what was happening. Hyme had gone out on a house call to deliver a baby because the mother was too far into labor to make it to the hospital in time. I didn't expect him back for quite a while.

So it was with some surprise that I opened the door to see snow coming down in a thick blanket. The weather bureau had predicted snow, but not like this. *Should I stay? If I do, I'll probably miss the service.* I shook my head. Heavy snows were the norm in Syren, and it'd be poor form to miss the service because of it.

I looked up. The gray sky gave off enough light that I could see, sort of. I stepped out and started for the corner. It was slow going. The snow was coming down so fast, it buried my feet every other minute. I had to stop so I could knock it off my shoes before continuing. At the corner, the visibility was even poorer. But I didn't let that stop me. I struck out across the street. This was a game between the snow and me, and as far as I was concerned, the snow would not win.

The wind picked up. The snow swirled faster. I looked down and realized snow that had already fallen was being hurled into the air. I swiveled my head. It was hard to tell if the snow was falling from the sky or being blown upward from the ground. Still, I could see a little ahead. I started shoeing again. My progress was slower than ever.

The bitter wind blew harder, and the temperature dropped. I shivered, even in my suit. Then I stopped short and blinked. All I could see was an unbroken expanse of white. I held up my hand, about a šīzu from my face. I saw a faint, red blob. Panic threatened to set in. I shook it off. *Just keep going in a straight line. I'll get to my tower.* I started shoeing, refusing to think I might not be walking in a straight line.

Hours seemed to pass. Lifting a hand to my brow, I peered about and then snorted. It wasn't as if I could see anything, but surely I should have reached the edge of the plaza by now. Had I? It was impossible to tell. *Maybe I'm closer to my tower than I think.* I stretched my arms and shoed about eight šīzu. Nothing. My lips pursed. *Well, I really hadn't gone far.* I stretched my arms again, and this time shoed a good four nindan. Still nothing. I let out a sigh. *Guess I'll just have to keep going.*

I bent to the wind and took a step. And another. After the fifth step, my legs gave way, and I fell in the snow. I was lost, and I knew it. Worse, the quiltsuit was not made for severely low temperatures like this. The filaments were working at capacity, yet I was freezing. And exhausted.

I could almost feel my body heat leaching out of my suit. Hot tears rolled down my cheeks, then froze. I was going to die out here. And for what? Surely Astoreth would have forgiven me for missing a service or two. My grandmother was demanding, but even She wouldn't want me to risk my life to pay homage to Her Holiness. Would She?

And Teger... My tears came faster. All my plans for a life together had been destroyed because of a blizzard and my own damned foolishness. Why didn't I stay where I was when I saw how thick the snow was coming down? I didn't treat sandstorms back home like this. Sandstorms were deadly. The only thing to do in a sandstorm was to seek shelter of any kind and stay there until it was over. I was learning in the hardest way possible that it was also true of blizzards.

I don't know how long I sat in the snow, crying and praying for Astoreth to save me. All I knew was that I was so, so cold, down to my very core. I couldn't stop shivering and was having trouble breathing. A hand squeezed my shoulder. My head snapped up. Hope surged through me. "Hello? Who's there?" I shouted. Straining my eyes and ears, I saw nothing but blowing snow and heard nothing but rushing air. Minutes passed. I didn't feel the squeeze again.

I started crying again. What had happened was obviously a hallucination. The reality was that I was dying. With no other choice, I began preparing myself for death. Then someone squeezed my hand. A gentle tug pulled me to my feet. A few more tugs, and I understood I was to follow. The unknown person leading the way, I shoed through the blizzard. I peered into the whiteness, trying to get a glimpse of my savior but the snow was too thick. Even my arm was just a blur.

We stopped about ten minutes later, and whoever had been leading me let go. A bolt of panic shot through me. *Calm down,* a little voice echoed. *You haven't been brought this far for nothing.* A couple of hard shoves at the small of my back, and I stumbled forward. I tried to regain my balance, but the snowshoes made it impossible. I fell against something hard.

Stone!

I pushed myself up, knowing I stood at my tower door. My hands roamed over it, searching for the bioscan lock. I stretched my arm to the right and felt the hard oblong box under my fingers. Holding it, I side-stepped until I stood before it, hearing its *click* even above the howling wind. I stumbled inside. Drifted snow blew in with me. I turned to thank my savior but saw only swirling snow.

Fighting the wind, I managed to shut the door. I shivered, hard. My body temperature was dangerously low, and I needed a hot shower this minute. Then I'd crawl under the heavy furs and sleep, maybe in my robe. I'd no idea what time it was, but it could still be late after midday. If so, and if I woke up in time for the evening service, I'd do it. If not, Stiren and Astoreth would just have to understand.

I started up the stairs. The tiniest bit of warmth caressed my face, the quiltsuit trying to do its work. But right now, it could never be enough.

The climb to my apartment took every bit of energy I had left. I swayed for a moment, then fell against the door. It flew open. The last thing I saw before hitting the floor was Teger rushing toward me.

⊙⊒⊒⊒⊒⊙

I awoke to find Teger fussing with the blankets, pulling up a corner here, tucking in a side there, and rearranging the cowl he'd obviously fashioned from one of the furs on the chair over my head.

He looked up. "You're alive." His star-colored glare was hard, and his voice low and tight. I'd seen him like this before. He wasn't just angry. He was livid.

"How long have I been out?" I croaked.

"A day."

I started to get up. "I have to explain to Stiren—"

He pushed me down. "You don't have to explain anything to anyone."

"But—"

"Stiren knows you're not here. At least he thinks you're not here. The intercom rang constantly when the blizzard started. That soon stopped. He even came up here a couple of times and rang the bell, but of course, you weren't in. I imagine he called the lab too and got no answer. So as far as he knows, you're dead."

"How do you know this?"

"I was here. Waiting for you after you didn't answer my ring at the lab."

Neither of us spoke for a minute or so.

"Of all the stupid things...Tehi, what in the gods' names were you doing out there? Why didn't you stay in the lab?"

"It didn't look that bad then."

"Where was Hyme?"

"Out delivering a baby. Besides, I had to run the service. I couldn't just let that go."

He leaned forward. "Yes, you could. Tehi, when you fell through that door, you were half frozen. I mean that. Your quiltsuit wasn't made for what you put it through. You've ended up with köldskador."

364

"What's that?"

He pulled the blanket back. "Look at your toes."

My toes were pallid, almost white. I frowned. "What happened?"

"That's köldskador. It happens when your skin freezes. It affects the toes and fingers first. If it's severe enough, you may have to have one or more amputated."

I thought my eyes would pop from my head. "Amputated?"

He gave me a slow nod.

I panicked. Amputate my toes? I tried to wriggle them. They didn't move. Then I realized I couldn't feel them, either. My head snapped up, my hearts pounding. "Teger, I can't feel my toes! Will I have—"

"I don't know. It looks like the freezing didn't go deep, but I won't know for another day or two. If we're lucky, the blizzard will be over by tomorrow. It'll take another day for us to be dug out, and when that happens, maybe Hyme can come here and take a look." He pulled up the blanket and tucked it under my chin. "You need to sleep."

"How can I sleep when I know my toes are going to be amputated?"

The look in his eyes softened. "I said I didn't know. That's a far cry from yes." His voice was gentle.

I wasn't convinced. It must have shown because he slipped off his boots and climbed into bed. "Whatever happens, it'll be all right, älskling."

"But—"

"Shh, shh. Sleep, now."

I nodded and closed my eyes. I was still scared, but I was also still exhausted. His scent, heartsbeat, and the smoothness of his shirt against my skin soothed me. My hearts slowed.

I yawned. Then I knew nothing.

◎ ⊐ ⊏⊐ ⊏⊐ ⊏ ◎

The tingling pain in my toes woke me.

I sat up and looked around. Teger wasn't here. I wondered how long I'd been asleep this time. Kicking off the blankets, I pulled my knee to my chest and lightly massaged my foot, hoping that would relieve some of the sting. It didn't. I massaged harder. That didn't work, either.

An icy whoosh of air hit me. "Stop that!"

I jumped and turned my head. Teger stepped through the

battlement door in his quiltsuit. "Why?"

"The tissue has already been damaged by the cold. Flexing will only make it worse. As a healer, I thought you'd have that figured out."

My eyes narrowed. "Well, I just thought—"

"Don't think. You've never dealt with cold-weather injuries before. Let Hyme teach you."

"How dare you tell me my—"

"Hello, Tehi," Hyme's voice came through the doorway. He crossed the threshold, healer's bag in hand. "I understand you've got a case of köldskador. Let's see it." He took off his skullcap and walked to the bed.

I lifted my right foot. Hyme set his bag on the floor and took it in one hand. Gently manipulating my toes with the other, he peered at them one by one. He did the same with my other foot, then lay it on the bed. "Doesn't look too bad. I'd say first degree. You might lose hot or cold sensations in your toes for a while, maybe permanently. It's hard to tell. Either way, you'll be all right."

"So you don't have to amputate?"

He laughed. "Oh my, no. You'd to have a much, much worse case of köldskador before I'd do something like that."

I glared at Teger. He looked at the ceiling.

"Bet it hurts now, yes?"

I turned back to Hyme. "Yes."

"Do you want something for the pain?"

"No, that's all right. It's more annoying than anything else."

He rummaged through his bag and pulled out a small vial. "Even so, here's some aleron—a mild painkiller." Unscrewing the cap, he looked up and eyed me. "Hmm...your Devi blood might mean you need a higher dose. So let's say you take two now, and two more when you get up in the morning." He shook out four pills and handed them to me.

"Has the snow stopped?"

"Yes. Late last night. When you come to the lab, I'll give you some burn cream. It'll soften the skin and help your pain."

"Burn cream? But I—"

"Köldskador is like a burn, caused by cold instead of heat."

"Oh." Teger handed me a glass of water. I took a swallow's worth and gulped down two pills, then took a second swallow. I frowned. "Hyme, how'd you get here?"

"The healer and Laerd are always the first to be dug out," Teger said. "Hyme wasn't at the lab, so he told the crews where he was, and they dug from there."

"What about me?"

"They're digging you out now. They'll be finished soon."

"I should tell Stiren I'm alive."

"After you're dug out. It's been this long, so he can wait a little longer."

I frowned. "Did you have to dig out the battlement to get here?"

Teger shook his head. "That awning is steep enough to keep it mostly clear. There's no problem."

"Oh." Then I remembered something. I looked Hyme. "How's the baby?"

He smiled. "*She* is just fine. So is the mother. Everyone else is recovering."

"Huh?"

"My, you should have seen that household when I arrived. The family was a wreck, thinking they'd have to deliver the baby themselves. It was a good thing I got there when I did. She crowned not long afterward." His smile broadened. "And of course, they were happy to be one of the first in the village to get dug out. It'll take at least three days before everyone is clear."

Teger's flatcomm whistled. He pulled it out of its holster, studied it, and then held it to his ear. "Laerd." There were several moments of silence. "God. Jag ska berätta det för dem. Adjö." He slid the comm into its pouch. "You're all clear, älskling. The crew has dug a path to the apothecary. You can call Stiren now."

I scooted across the bed and punched in the code for the barracks. "Moreva," Stiren said, sounding relieved. "Praise be to the Most Holy One."

"Yes, Kepten. I made it through, none the worse for wear." I looked at my toes. "Well, mostly. I take it the garrison is all right?"

"We're fine, though we're running a bit low on provisions. Have you heard from the Laerd?"

I glanced at Teger. "No."

"When you do, please ask him when the village will be able to start provisioning us again."

"I'll do that. Oh—and there will be a service tonight. Tell the evening penitents."

"You sure you want to hold a service, Moreva? It's long past the evening hour."

"Oh. Of course. I lost track of time. I'll hold the next service in the morning."

"Very good, Moreva. I'll tell them." He signed off.

I looked at Teger. "How long was I out this time?"

"Another day. And it's four-twelve Durm now. If you want a hot shower, you haven't much time."

"No, I'll wait."

Hyme fitted his skullcap. "Speaking of morning, I need to get back. Want to sleep in my own bed tonight." He picked up his bag and snowshoes. "I'll see you tomorrow, Tehi."

"Yes, definitely."

He walked to the door. "Until then," he said over his shoulder and left.

I stared at the door. "Stiren says the garrison's running low on food," I said without turning around.

"They are, eh? Well, I'm sure they're not the only ones, especially those with families."

I turned. Teger was peeling off his quiltsuit. "How long do you think it'll take to get them more?"

"A couple more days, maybe. We've got seven crews working day and night to get the village cleared." He paused, and his look turned thoughtful. "Go to the window. Look outside."

I threw on my robe and stepped to the window. My toes hurt. Opening it, I let out a gasp. All I could see was a blanket of white. "Astoreth."

"We probably wouldn't have found your body until spring."

A vision of my red, quiltsuit-clad frozen body flashed in my mind's eye. I shivered. "But I thought you said the crews were clearing the snow."

"They are. They're digging tunnels."

I turned. "Tunnels?"

"Yes. We could clear it like we do for the landing pad but that takes a lot of energy. So, we dig under it and then string lights along the ceiling." He shrugged. "Not that much different from opening a mountain for a thalin mine."

"And in the spring?"

"When the tunnels become unsafe, we collapse them."

"What do you do with the water?"

He gave me a questioning look.

I swept my arm at the snow. "That's a lot of water out there. What do you do when it melts?"

He smiled. "It's really not that much. Three šīzu of snow in a large bucket might make only a couple of inches of water. Anyway, there's a reservoir beneath us. As it melts, it sluices into grates and into the reservoir."

"Oh, yes. Hyme said something about that." I looked out again. "How much more snow do you think we'll get before winter's over?"

"It's still early. At this rate, it could reach the roofs."

Neither of us said anything for a few minutes.

"So you're going to the lab tomorrow?"

"After the morning service. I need to set up my fourth trial. I'd just cleaned up the last one when the blizzard started."

"All right. By the time you leave, the crews should have a good part of the rest of the plaza routes cleared, too."

I frowned. "How will I get to the lab? I mean, how will I know which tunnel to take?"

"It's simple. At each intersection, the crews paint the walls with small flags in the colors of whatever building you're trying to get to. The tunnel to the lab will have a picture of the lab's colors, so you'll know you're going the right way."

"I don't understand."

"I'll show you tomorrow." He yawned. "I'm going to bed. How about you?"

"No, I need to memorize a sermon."

"Well, don't stay up too late. You still need your rest."

"I've been resting for two days now."

He gave me a serious look. "You may feel fine, but after what you put your body through, you need to give yourself enough time to heal. Your toes are going to take several marun to heal as it is."

"All right." I walked to the fireplace, pulled out a fuel brick, and threw it into the flaming cavity. Settling in the chair, I picked up my tablet. Meanwhile, Teger had started to undress. I watched him from the corner of my eye while pretending to look for my place.

He did a few stretches. Except for his coloring and height—he was over seven šīzu tall instead of nine—he could easily be one of the gods. He looked over his shoulder and grinned. "Like what you see?"

My cheeks feeling about as hot as the coals in the fire, I fumbled at the tablet's controls. "Uh...um...well, yes."

"Good." He climbed into bed and settled in. His look turned serious again. "Remember, not too long."

"I won't. Promise."

He nodded once and rolled over. A few minutes later, I heard his gentle snores. Clicking through the files, it wasn't long before I found the sermon I'd given the morning of the blizzard. I liked to give the same sermon for the morning and evening services, so I wouldn't deliver that one. I flipped the page to the next sermon and scanned it. *This one.*

I tucked my legs under me, adjusted my robe, and began to read.

❧

After the morning service and a quick breakfast, Teger and I clumped down the steps. In the vestibule, I picked up my snowshoes.

He lay a hand on my arm. "You won't need those."

I looked up. He didn't have his shoes, either. "Why not?"

"Because the snow on the tunnel floors has been packed and smoothed flat." He pulled open the door.

My eyes widened. A perfectly formed tunnel, large enough for two people walking abreast, lay before me. Bright, bluish-white lights had been strung in an orderly row near the ceiling, and the walls appeared to glow. Even the floor seemed to give off its own light. There were tunnels beneath Astoreth's É in Uruk, but every inch of them had been painted with scenes from Astoreth's and É life. The beauty of this tunnel lay in that it was completely bare. I looked around. Well, not completely. A bright red square with even brighter green stripes had been painted on the wall to my right.

"Look familiar?" Teger's voice rumbled.

"My tower."

"Right. And you'll find flags like this throughout the tunnels. If you miss your turn, just go back to where you saw your colors last and go from there."

"You mean if I get lost."

He shrugged. "If you want to put it that way. But I doubt you will. We've got this system down to a science. As long as you know the colors of the building you're trying to get to, it's almost impossible to get lost. Even young children can find their way around without help."

Young Mjoran children, I wanted to say, but didn't.

He tugged my sleeve. "Come on."

We walked in silence. My head swiveled back and forth, looking out for the colorful painted squares. It wasn't long before I understood. At each intersection, flags had been painted in a vertical line. My tower's flag was in all of them. As for the rest, some of the patterns I recognized. Most not. I should have paid more attention to the buildings earlier, but I hadn't known what the colors meant. Eresh hadn't told me.

I saw a pattern that looked familiar and smiled. It was Hyme's apothecary and lab. We kept walking, following the signs. We made a final right turn and walked about forty šīzu until we reached the apothecary's door. The snow completely covered the shop's windows so we couldn't see if the light inside was on or not. A little sign hung on the handle. The store was open.

We stepped inside. The apothecary was empty, so we headed for the lab.

Hyme looked up as we came in and set a small jar on the counter. "I was wondering when you'd get here."

I smiled. "You're too impatient." We laughed, but Teger didn't. I turned. "He says that to me all the time. It's our little joke."

He nodded. "It's true."

I pulled off my skullcap and stuck out my tongue, then started peeling off my quiltsuit. When I had it halfway off, I noticed he wasn't taking off his suit. "Aren't you staying?"

"No. The Laerd has to see about his village. Inspect the tunnels, rap on doors to houses that have been cleared, check on people, things like that. By now the kitchen staff's houses should be cleared. Got to get the dining hall up and running as soon as possible." He sighed. "Going to be a long, busy day."

I felt for him. "I'll give you a nice massage tonight."

"I'll hold you to that. All right, I have to go." I heard the apothecary's chime, then the door open and shut. I looked at Hyme. "What's that you're making?"

"The burn cream I promised you. Sit down. Take off your boots and stockings."

I obeyed and laid one bare foot on my thigh. He picked it up, giving it a thorough inspection. "Good, good." He handed me the jar. "Here you go. Rub it in well so it soaks in nice and deep."

I scooped out a glob of cream, then rubbed it into my toes. The tingling pain stopped. I kept massaging until my hand was almost dry.

"Put a little more on it."

I scooped another glob and started massaging again.

"All right, that's good."

I repeated the process with my other foot, then put on my stockings and boots.

He cocked his head. "How do your feet feel?"

"I could have used this for the service. I thought I was going to die in those shoes."

"Well, by all means take it with you, though the pain should stop in another day or so. But you'll definitely need it today." He paused. "Even after the pain stops, keep using the cream. Your toes will heal that much faster."

"All right." I smiled. "And now, I need to get to work. I've lost two days behind this blizzard, and I'm anxious to finish up."

He gave me an intent look. "What will you do when your trials show you've really found the cure? You've worked on your project against Astoreth's order, and I imagine your punishment will be...harsh. The Laerd told me Kherah might have an outbreak this summer. And it's summer."

I looked at him for a long moment. "I've thought about that too," I said in a low voice. "I haven't gotten a message from anyone saying we've been hit. And I can't call to find out. I'm not allowed to call home in the first place—Astoreth's rules—and if there's been an outbreak, I might not get one. The only thing I can do is wait for news on the next supply run." I paused. "If there is one."

"And if there's a supply run, and you find out there's trouble?"

I turned my back, not wanting him to see the tears in my eyes. "I...I don't know."

His hand settled on my shoulder. "I understand, Tehi," he said, his voice quiet. "I'm not sure what I'd do, either." He turned me around and gave me a hug. Dropping his arms, he looked down and smiled. "But right now, we don't know for sure you've found the cure. So you'd better get to work."

I smiled back. "I guess I'd better."

Hyme returned to the counter, and I went to my table to gather what I'd need. I set up and injected the skratz. Waiting for the virus to manifest, I filled the time by going over my lab notes from three days ago and writing my notes from this morning. My uniform's alarm went off. Inside the closet, I slipped my hands into the manipulators, and gave the skratz a dose of serum. I stepped out of the closet. Thinking about what I'd do next, I stopped short. My eyes widened. *The beacon!* I hadn't called in for two days. I was in big trouble.

I ran to the rack, snatched my quiltsuit off its peg, and struggled into it.

"Tehi," Hyme called. "What's wrong?"

"Got to check the beacon."

Footsteps behind me. "Here, let me help you." He tugged at the suit, fitting it over my feet and legs while I worked on my arms. Then he patted me on the shoulder. "I hope all's well."

"With the beacon? I'm sure it's fine."

He gave me a serious look. "I meant with you."

"I'll think of something." I ran out of the building and raced through the tunnels, barely stopping at the intersections to make sure I was going the right way. It wasn't long before I spotted the first bright red and green flag. I ran faster. In minutes, I arrived at my tower and barreled up the stairs.

What would I say? Yose had told Astoreth I'd missed nine services between the mudslide and my hospitalization last summer. I'd given Central the reason when I'd returned to duty. They'd accepted it with grudging ill-grace and had warned me not to miss a report again or I'd be recalled. I had missed several reports since then, but that was because of the fire. Central hadn't been happy about that either. I knew in my hearts they weren't going to accept illness as a reason for missing my reports a third time. I had to figure out what to tell them, and it had to be good. Whatever might be going on in Kherah, I couldn't afford to go back. Not yet.

I tore off my skullcap and threw it to the floor. On the ride up, I thought and thought about what I'd say but couldn't think of a thing. In the control room, the first thing I noticed was the steady green light on the communications module. Central had called me, a bad sign. Taking my time, I checked all the machinery, trying to think. Nothing came to mind.

I finished my inspection and stared at the green light. I couldn't put this off any longer. With slow steps, I walked to the module and sat. My hearts beat faster. I covered the panel with my palm.

A goddess's head appeared, face twisted into a scowl. "Astoreth-69, where have you been? You haven't made a report in two days. You are recalled, effective immediately."

I opened my mouth, and then I knew. "Greetings, High One. Please wait. You haven't had a report because we've just been through a blizzard. It knocked out power to Mjor. The lifts weren't working, so I couldn't get up here. And the control room would have been dark. So would the bea—"

"The beacon was transmitting."

Astoreth! "Yes, but doesn't the beacon have its own power source?" I'd no idea if this was true.

"It does."

"But it's not connected to the control room." I'd no idea if this was true, either.

"That's so."

I breathed a tiny sigh of relief. "So, you see, though the beacon was on-line, the control room wasn't. Even if I could have somehow gotten up here, there was no way for me to get a message to you."

She stared for a long moment. I stared back, hoping I looked innocent. Her eyes narrowed. "All right, Astoreth-69. I accept your explanation. We'll send a tech to install a sep—"

"That won't be necessary," I said, trying not to sound anxious. "Mjor has agreed to put in a separate source for the lifts and control room. Their plan is to start work as soon as they clean up from the blizzard."

"Does Her Most Holy One know about this?"

I didn't hesitate. "Not yet. It will be in the next report sent by the garrison Kepten."

"Mm." She said nothing else for almost a minute. "Very well. Make your report."

"Rotation speed seven-point-five, signal output normal at eighty-two."

"Report acknowledged and submitted, Astoreth-69. Sign—"

"High One, wait!" I blurted.

Her face twisted into another scowl. "What is it?" she snapped.

I swallowed. "Do...do you have news of Uruk? They're due for a red fever outbreak, and we don't get the fever but I-I..."

Her look softened. "We've had no reports, Moreva. Not from Uruk or anywhere else in Kherah." Her tone had softened, too. "If we do, we'll make sure you're notified. Signing off." The goddess's head disappeared.

Relieved, I slumped in the chair and blew a heavy breath. My gaze riveted on the console, yet I didn't see it. Was my relief for Uruk or for me? I closed my eyes. "For me," I whispered.

And then a deep truth I'd been trying hard not to see since summer's end muscled its way to the fore. *What I'm doing...I'm severing every connection I have to Uruk and to Kherah. I am morev, but I don't want to be a moreva. I don't want to be an acolyte of Astoreth's Love. I'm willing to abandon everything I've ever known to be with him, to be here for him.* A tear trickled down my cheek. *And...it means I'm willing to abandon my grandmother.*

I bowed my head and sobbed. *I-I'm sorry, Grandmother. I don't have to leave...because I've already left.*

My tears eventually stopped. I stared at the console a moment. Wiping my face, I left the control room and headed for the tunnels.

Chapter Thirty

The fifth and final trial of my red fever cure had been a spectacular success. Though I'd used the same formula, the skratz had shaken off the virus faster than the others.

That had been three marun ago. Now, I stood over my worktable studying a second hairless skratz nestled in my palm. I scratched its ears. My memory experiment had been successful, too. The little beast had run the maze yesterday without flaw. Today, after giving it a dose of my drug, it didn't remember the route at all. It had sniffed its way around, taking almost all the wrong turns, before finally making it to the finish an hour later.

Mine wasn't the first memory experiments on skratzes. Conducted on a whim, researchers had made two remarkable discoveries. If allowed to spend a day together after hydration, skratzes recognized each other even after being separated for a marun. The second experiment showed they could be taught to press a particular lever to gain a reward—and remember the lesson for as long as they lived. And now, I'd proven they could be taught to run a maze.

I returned the skratz to the cage. Seeing its two hydration mates, it immediately scuttled into a corner. When the two came forward, the little beast began shaking and then rolled into a ball. Clearly frightened, the poor thing hid its head as if hoping the others would go away. I bit my lip. The only problem with the drug was that it wasn't selective. I hadn't time to refine it to that point. Instead, it acted as a bludgeon, erasing all memory.

But there might be a solution to that problem.

I turned. For once, Hyme wasn't puttering about the lab. He slouched in his chair before his worktable, his long legs stretched out and his hands behind his head. His eyes were closed. I watched him for a moment. "Hyme, do you know anything about hypnosis?"

He opened his eyes. "I was trained in it but haven't had much occasion to use it. My skills are probably rusty."

"Why don't we fix that?"

"Who'll be the subject?"

"Me."

He peered. "Why are you so interested in hypnosis all of a sudden?"

I shrugged. "Well, you're not doing anything, and I'm not doing anything, so I thought we could fill the time before lunch. Besides, we healers should keep all our skills up to date, right?"

"You've got a point there." He pursed his lips. "All right. Let me get my pendulum." His lips twisted. "Assuming I can find it." He disappeared into his apartment, and was back a few minutes later, grinning. "I actually remembered where it was. Amazing."

"May I see it?"

"Of course." He dropped the pendulum into my palm. I held it to the light and let it swing on its chain. It was beautiful. Shaped like a teardrop, it was made of white thalin, like the miners had given me last spring. Its faceted surface seemed to shoot beams of colored light in every direction. "This is gorgeous. Where did you get it?"

"It was a first-year present from my heartsbound."

"A woman of exquisite taste."

"Not really. She heartsbonded me, didn't she?"

We laughed. After our laughter had subsided, he pointed to his chair. "Sit. Let's get started."

Wheeling the other chair over, he sat and wheeled it closer until our knees almost touched. "All right, let's get you settled. Sit up straight. Put your arms on the armrests and keep your feet flat on the floor."

I squirmed in my seat.

"Ready?"

"Ready."

He held the pendulum at my eye level. Twisting slowly at the end of the chain, the pendulum's colored light beams spun. Starting his patter, his calm, soothing voice encouraged me to relax.

I'd been hypnotized before, so knew what to expect. Beginning in my toes, a heavy feeling crept over my feet and ankles. It slowly traveled through my calves, over my knees and into my thighs. The feeling sped up. It washed over my hips and trunk, then into my chest. Like a rushing tide, it spread through my shoulders and arms. Last, it shot into my neck and head. My body felt like the stones outside, weighty and immobile.

After relaxing me, he went to work on my mind. He suggested my consciousness rested in a dark box. This didn't work so well. The edges of my sight grew dim, but no more. He continued his patter. It still didn't work. He kept trying for another fifteen minutes or so, then gave up. Reversing my deeply relaxed state, I soon felt like myself again.

It was disappointing. For my scheme to work, I had to be way under, my conscious mind unaware of what was going on around me, my subconscious in full control. The only bright spot was we still time for him to practice his technique before my tour ended. Or so I hoped.

"You weren't completely under, were you?" he said as he dropped the pendulum into his breast pocket.

"No." I told him what had happened.

"Well, at least I can still relax my patient." He shook his head.

I smiled. "Don't look so glum. That's why we're going to practice."

He eyed me. "You're really serious about this, aren't you?"

"Of course. We can practice on each other."

"And we can practice whenever we both have some down time."

"Right." I smiled again. Now that I'd found the cure and knew my memory drug worked, I was going to have a lot of down time.

He looked at the wall timepiece. "Speaking of time, it's time for lunch."

"Good. I'm hungry."

We trooped to the rack and wrestled into our coats. Winter was slowly ebbing away. The tunnels had been collapsed and filled in. The buildings lining the plaza, at least those that caught the direct sunslight for most of the day, could be seen almost in their entirety. The days had warmed enough so we could wear furs instead of quiltsuits. We still had to wear snowshoes, though.

We headed for the dining hall. Shoeing across the plaza, he gave me a sideways look. "Bet you're ready for winter to end."

"No, I like it. Getting around can be a pain, but it's so beautiful. I love the way snow sparkles in the sunslight, like tiny pieces of thalin. And without their leaves, the trees look like sculptures."

"You see things differently than I do."

"That's because you're used to it."

Back at the lab, I helped him mix up medications, and after couple of hours or so, left to check the beacon. Shoeing across the plaza, I thought about our hypnosis experiment and bit my lip. *Will we have enough time for this to work?*

We'd better...or I was dead.

⊙⊐⊏⊐⊏⊙

That night, I sat before the fireplace putting the finishing touches on a sermon. The fire had died to embers. *Toss in another brick? No, we'll be going to bed, soon.*

In my peripheral vision, I saw Teger set the tablet on the low table. Leaning back, he rested his elbows on the armrests and tented his fingers before his chest.

I looked up. "Finished?"

"Mm-hm."

"So how many does that make?"

"Twelve."

"You know more than I do. I've read only three of the Great Pantheon's histories." I smiled. "So what did you think?"

He gazed at me without expression. "They're mostly lies, älskling."

My jaw dropped, and I bolted upright. "What?"

"You heard me."

"You blaspheme!"

"Yes."

My jaw worked but no words came out. Then my throat loosened. "How dare you," I shouted. "Astoreth would have your head for that!"

"Stop yelling. I'm sure She would. But it doesn't change the fact your Gods lied."

"I suppose you know the truth?" My voice had barely quieted.

"I do."

I sat back and waved my hand. "Then let's hear it."

"Are you sure?"

"You've gone this far. Might as well go all the way."

He nodded once. "First, your Gods didn't create Peris twenty-five hundred years ago. The planet's age is more like seven billion. Second,

your Gods didn't create the hakoi. We were already here. And third...
your Gods aren't immortal. They can die."

"And you can prove this?"

He stared. "I can."

I glared back. "All right. Do it."

"Meet me here tomorrow after breakfast."

"Done. Now get out."

He looked dumbfounded. "What?"

"You heard me."

His star-colored eyes turned cold. "Fine."

Without another word, he shrugged into his coat, then drew on his gloves. Clapping on his hat, he strode to the door and yanked it open, stormed outside, then slammed it shut.

○═╦╦╦═○

The following morning, I stood in front of my tower, waiting for Teger. The plaza was oddly deserted for this time of day.

A few minutes later, he came roaring around the square in the strangest contraption I'd ever seen. It had the high, boxy body of a car, but that was where the resemblance ended. Where the rear wheels should have been were metallic-looking treads that looked to be half the length of the car. Instead of front wheels, the vehicle was supported by two long poles, like snow poles, that were connected at the bottom to what looked like a pair of oversized snowshoes.

He pulled to a stop. "Get in."

When I heard his tone, I knew he was still angry about last night. *Well, so am I.* I unstrapped my snowshoes and swung my legs into the car.

"Put those in the back." He took my snowshoes and tossed them over his shoulder. They thunked on the cargo area's floor. Putting the car in gear, we sped off, picking up speed once outside the village gates. The ride was unexpectedly smooth. I looked out the window, then glanced at the speed-meter. There were no vehicles out, and he was taking full advantage of it. We came to the now-familiar intersection with the suspended globe, its light shining bright blue. Instead of stopping, he gunned the engine. We shot across the road.

In my peripheral vision, I noticed his clenched jaw and thought it best not to say anything about him running the light. "Where are we going?"

"You'll see."

Astoreth. The tension was thick, and this trip was going to be a nightmare if I didn't do something. *All right. I'll apologize first.* "Listen, I'm sorry I threw you out last night. It's just that…"

"Just what?"

"You told me my very being is worthless."

"How? I didn't say—"

"Think about it, Teger."

Silence reigned. "I see what you mean," he finally said, his voice quiet. "I guess I didn't have to be so blunt. I'm sorry. I didn't mean to insult you."

"You did more than insult me. But I forgive you."

The heavy mood lifted. I stared out the windshield, my thoughts wandering. Then I turned. "No matter what you think of the Gods, Astoreth saved me, you know."

"When was that?"

"When I was trapped in that blizzard. I thought I was going to die when something squeezed my shoulder. Then it took me by the hand and led me to my tower. I turned around, but there was nothing there."

"What makes you think it was Astoreth?"

"Who else could it have been? She heard my prayers and sent an avatar to rescue me."

He fell silent again. "You probably think we Syrenese don't have a religion, don't you?"

"Yes, you do. That funerary rite. Hyme told me about it. You believe in an afterlife, and that's religious concept."

"He also told you it was ancient, didn't he?"

"What's that got to do with it?"

"Everything. For us, it's just a relic from our past. No one believes in it anymore." He shook his head. "Aeryn wanted to die, and she wanted to die by the old ritual. That was her right, and we couldn't deny her."

I frowned. "What are you saying? That you don't believe in anything?"

"Yes, we do. We believe in Peris."

My eyes widened. "What? You worship the *planet?*"

"Not quite like that." He sighed, then took a deep breath. "A long time ago, we had gods. A god of wind, water, storms—everything. Gradually, we realized we had it wrong. So, we thought there must be one god instead of many, and we worshipped that. Over time, it finally dawned on us. There were no gods, there was no god. There is only Peris." He paused. "Älskling, Peris is more than a planet. The stones, the water, the air, and everything about Peris inside and out has created a sentient being. Like a spirit."

"So how come you don't worship it?"

"We do. Every time we open a mine, we thank Peris for its resources. The same goes for our crops, the animals we hunt, and everything else."

"And Peris takes care of you in return, just like the Gods take care of us."

"No, it's an acknowledgment. We are responsible for what happens to us. It has nothing to do with Peris. Like that mudslide. Do you think Peris was responsible for that?"

"Wasn't it?"

"Do you think Peris saved us?"

"Didn't it?"

"No and no. There was a mudslide because it rained torrents for a marun straight. We saved our own lives by keeping our wits about us."

Now it was my turn to fall silent. "So what does all this have to do with the blizzard?"

He didn't answer right away. "Peris saved you. Not Astoreth."

"Why would Peris do that?"

"I don't know. Peris has been known to intervene in individual lives but it's very, very rare."

"Well, I still think it was Astoreth who saved me."

He nodded but said nothing.

I stared through the windshield again, thinking about what he'd told me last night. Between that and what he'd just said, nothing made sense. A sentient planet? My lips tightened. *The Gods made Peris and everything in and on it. Their problem is they don't accept the Gods for what They are.*

We drove for hours. Then we left the highway and turned onto a side road. At least I thought it was a road. It was so covered with snow, I couldn't tell. He made several turns, and I realized we were headed into the peaks. We drove for another hour. He turned one last time and roared up the side of a mountain. The incline leveled out. After a half-hour or so, we stopped in front of a colossal door. "Where are we?"

"Skarsgard. It's a played-out mine. This is where we keep our records."

"Records?"

He fixed me with a steady gaze. "Everything about us has been recorded and stored away. Our history—our recorded history, anyway—from the earliest until now goes back over twenty thousand years."

I gave him a dubious look.

He peered through the windshield. "I think we can get in. The suns have melted most of the snow." He reached into the back and handed me my snowshoes. "You'll need these."

I opened the door and strapped on my shoes. The suns's blazing on the white, glittering snow was nearly blinding. Shoeing to entrance, I spotted a smaller door. It looked miniscule compared to the other.

Teger reached the door first. He tapped a small panel a few times. The door clanked once and began to rise. "How come you know how to get in?"

"It isn't a secret. Anybody can come here for whatever reason, whenever they want. All the Laerds have the code and will give it to whoever asks."

We entered the mine. Lights flickered. The door clanked, then descended. We unstrapped our snowshoes, leaning them against the wall. Teger set the lights on continuous burn, and we walked toward a bank of carts identical to the ones we'd used at the mine with the sparkling, thalin-covered room, except these were much cleaner. We shed our furs and stored them in the rear of the nearest cart.

He slid into the drivers' seat. "Hop in."

"No hats?"

"Not needed. This mine is played out, remember? No blasting in here."

I climbed into the cart. We pulled off and drove along a hallway that seemed to stretch almost as far as I could see. I marveled at the series of rooms lining the hallway on either side. There were so many of them. This place dwarfed the hall of records in Astoreth's É.

Then I frowned. If this was their hall of records, was it possible he was telling the truth? *No. Not that I think he's lying. Misguided, maybe. Anyway, I don't know what all this is, but Peris is twenty-five hundred years old and the Gods created it.*

Teger stopped the cart. "We're here." We walked across the hall to one of the darkened rooms. A sign over the doorway read "Krig."

"What does 'Krig' mean?"

"Wars."

The room was pitch. He stepped inside and reset the lights. I looked around. Rows and rows of shelves held slim volumes that looked to be a little wider than my tablet. *If their history is as long as he says it is, no wonder this place is so huge. Why didn't they make bigger books?*

We stopped at a shelf near the end of one row. Teger peered at the titles, selected one and held it out to me.

My brows shot up. These *were* tablets. *If they have tablets, why didn't I see any in Mjor?* I took it and looked up.

"Press the button on the bottom." A pinpoint of red light on the tablet's upper edge flashed once. Words appeared on the screen.

"Read. Aloud."

I started reading. My jaw dropped before I finished the first paragraph. I stared, wide-eyed. "The Gods are aliens?"

"Keep reading." His star-colored gaze was steady, his face set in that expressionless mask I knew so well.

The chronicle listed the Great Pantheon by name, including Astoreth. It told, in minute detail, the story of how the Devi had come to Peris in peace and friendship. They'd traded with the Syrenese, swapping their technology for thalin. But that hadn't lasted long. The Devi began rounding up the hakoi and had used them for breeding and spawning experiments to create a race of docile slaves.

I didn't finish the rest of it. Boggled, I looked up and stared. "This... this..."

He didn't give me a chance. "And then the war started."

I said nothing.

"The Devi gave us no quarter. Their favorite trick was to take prisoners into deep space—men, women, and even children—and shove them through the airlock." He paused. "They're still up there, you know. The floating dead."

"I—"

"Of course, we did our share. We couldn't fly into space, so we did the next best thing. We dropped them from our airships into the tallest, most rugged of Peris's mountains. Assuming they survived the fall—very unlikely—there's no way they could have survived the mountain weather. You think our winters in the valleys are bad? Up there, it's winter all the time. And ten times worse." He smiled. It wasn't pleasant.

I flipped my hand. "Oh, I'm sure they survived. The Gods are immortal, remember?" Then, realizing what he'd said, I squinted. "You had—have—airships?"

"Of course. We've always had them. We used the technology the Devi gave us to improve them."

"How come I've never seen one?"

He shrugged. "Like you said, we're a backwater village. The cities—like Gurm—are far to the west. There aren't any air routes over this way."

Teger fell silent. "And then your Gods..." He shook his head. "It's unforgivable."

"What?"

"They brought the red fever."

My jaw dropped again. "They...they did not!"

"They did. Red fever was unheard of until the Devi came."

My face grew hot. I still didn't think he was lying, but his re-education was going to be difficult. "Teger, I can't...I won't believe this. How do I know you just didn't make it up a week ago?"

He pointed to the tablet. "I taught you how to read our calendar. Look at the date."

I looked. The date showed the chronicle had been written twenty-five hundred years ago, at the same time the Gods had created Peris. I shook my head. "This doesn't mean anything. It could have been added yesterday."

His expressionless mask returned. "Come on."

"Where are we going?"

"Just come."

He took the tablet, shut it off, and put it back on the shelf. Then he strode out of the library, with me trotting behind. We climbed into the cart and drove off. Neither of us spoke. At the end of the huge hall, we stopped at another door. He placed his hand over a small, black panel embedded into the wall on his left. The door rose. We stepped into the pitch-black room. The lights flickered and then erupted with blazing intensity. When I could see, my eyes widened. My jaw dropped a third time.

Before me was a perfect replica of a Devi airship I'd seen only once. Long and sleek, it had the graceful, curving wings of an omara, the elegant, decorative wading birds kept as pets in the É gardens. I took a few steps, then started jogging across the gigantic room.

As I came closer, I saw the airship was not perfect. And it wasn't a replica. Some parts, especially the nose cone, looked charred, and the cone's tip was missing. It was covered with gouges, scratches, dents, and dings. It looked like there'd been some sort of accident. Then later, someone had tried to hammer out the worst of the damage and repair it.

I stretched my arm and stroked the cold metal. "Where did you get this?"

Teger still wore his stone-faced look. "The pilot crashed in the mountains. We brought it down piece by piece. We used the parts as a guide and built airships that were a match for anything the Devi could throw at us." He paused. "Once we owned the skies, the war was all but over and the Devi knew it. Besides, there were a lot more of us than there were of them, and they knew we'd keep fighting until the last man, woman, and child. So they withdrew."

"You're saying you beat the Gods in your war? I find that hard to believe."

"Well, if it isn't true, why aren't they here? Why aren't we slaves like the hakoi in the south?"

"All right...let's say I believe you. What happened to the southern hakoi? How come they're workers?"

He didn't answer at first. "They lost their war," he said in a low voice. "They begged us for help, and we tried. We sent troops and materiel, but by then we were exhausted. There was only so much we could do."

Neither of us said anything for a long while.

He shook himself as if shaking off bad memories. "Come. There's one more thing I want to show you."

"What?"

Instead of answering, he strode toward the other side of the vast room, stopping before a tall, black cylinder built into the wall. "The Gods are immortal, right?"

"Right."

"Then explain this." He flipped a lever and the cylinder slid open.

My mind boggled a second time. Behind a convex shield of lysite stood a minor god. Slack-jawed, I took in his white hair and blue-violet skin. And he was very dead, judging by the hole where his single heart should have been.

"Tell me again how the Devi are immortal."

"I...I..." Then I knew.

What he'd said was true, about the Devi being aliens, the war, their bringing red fever to Peris—all of it. I let out a wail and fell to my knees, sobbing. My entire life had been a lie. Everything I'd ever known was a lie. I wasn't three-quarters god, I was three-quarters alien.

Teger's hands on my shoulders brought me to my senses. "Leave me alone," I screamed. I glared, tears streaming. "Why did you show me this? Why?"

"Because I thought you should know." His voice was soft.

Stunned, I couldn't say anything at first. "You thought? You thought it would be all right to ruin my life? How dare...get out of my sight!"

He said nothing. Straightening, he towered over me. "Let me know when you're ready to go back."

"I'm not going anywhere with you ever again!"

He gazed at me for a moment. His lips tightened. Then he left.

I turned to the dead alien and dropped my head into my hands. My tears would not stop. I cried until I couldn't cry anymore. Raising my head, I stared at the body. Whoever he'd been, he was remarkably well preserved. Except for the hole in his mid-section, he looked as if he could be alive.

I don't know how long I sat on my knees, staring at the corpse. It might have been minutes or hours. Finally, I bowed my head. *Get up,* a small voice echoed. *It's time to leave. There's nothing for you here.* I nodded.

I didn't want to go anywhere with Teger, but he was the only way I could get back to Mjor. I wobbled to my feet and trudged to the door. He sat next to the entrance with his back against the wall. Knees drawn into his chest, his crossed his arms made a cradle in which he'd buried his head.

I stood over him. "I'm ready." My voice came out as a croak.

He looked up, his star-colored eyes filled with pain. "I'm sorry, älskling."

"You should be."

He hung his head, then struggled to his feet. Covering the panel with his hand, the door began its slow descent, settling on the floor with a soft thud. In my hearts, I felt something close, too.

We didn't speak during the long ride back to the old mine's entrance. After bundling into my furs, I stepped through the doorway and looked up. The suns had moved considerably since we'd arrived. We shoed to the car and climbed in.

A heavy silence hung in the air on the ride back to Mjor. I felt numb. My brain felt numb. Before I knew it, we were on the road leading to the village. We drove through the gates, stopping at my tower.

I made no move to get out, just stared through the windshield. I heard rustling, and then felt a light pressure on my arm. I turned. Teger gazed at me, an earnest look in his eyes. "Älskling—"

"I hate you." I shoved his hand off my arm. Grabbing my snowshoes, I got out of the car and stalked inside my tower.

❧

From then on, I avoided Teger as much as I could. It wasn't hard. Even in happier times, I really only saw him at mealtimes and at night. But relaying Stiren's requests was a different matter. That couldn't be avoided.

I rang the bell to his apartment. The door opened immediately. I handed him the disc without a word. We stared at each other. Then he took a breath. "Älskling, I—"

I walked away. Inside my apartment, the intercom rang. I pressed the "talk" button. "Yes?"

"Älskling, please—"

I released it. The intercom rang again. I ignored it. I locked the door to the battlement—as always, these days—wrapped in my furs, and headed for the lab. At my tower's door, I opened it and stuck my head outside. Teger was nowhere to be seen. I hurried across the plaza. I heard the desperation in his voice whenever he tried to talk to me. If he started dogging me, I wouldn't be surprised.

I slipped inside the lab. Hyme was crushing something with a mortar and pestle. I shed my furs, joined him at the counter, and peered inside the small cup. "What are you doing?"

"Crushing erleby resin. I use it in a syrup I make for late winter colds."

"Why don't you use the grinder?"

"The blades need sharpening, and I haven't gotten around to it." He handed me the mortar and pestle. "Here, why don't you do this for me while I see about the batch I'm making now? You have to grind it hard, though. Erleby is like rock."

"All right." I went to work. He hadn't been joking. It *was* like trying to crush rocks. But I didn't have any trouble. It gave me pleasure to envision Teger's face every time one of the resin pieces broke.

I was so engrossed in crushing Teger, I didn't hear Hyme come up and stand beside me. "How are you coming with that?"

I jumped. "Oh! Oh, fine." I held up the mortar. "Is this good enough?"

He chuckled. "Oh, my. I usually grind it into granules. You've made a powder."

"Will it be all right?"

"It'll be fine. Pour what you've got in here." He held out a beaker, and I dumped the powder inside. I poured a few more rocks in the mortar and started grinding again.

"He loves you, you know."

I shrugged.

"He didn't mean to hurt you."

"Then he should've kept his mouth shut."

"Tehi, please talk to him. Don't punish him like this."

"I'm not punishing him."

"Yes, you are."

I blew an explosive breath. "What do you expect me to do? I don't even know who I am anymore. My services...I just go through the motions. It used to mean something to me. Now it means nothing. He took my *life* from me, Hyme. How would you feel if someone did that to you?"

"I'd feel the same way. But instead of a loss, why don't you look at it as an opportunity?"

"To do what?"

"Reinvent yourself. Now that you're no longer Astoreth's, you can be anyone you want to be."

"But how? All that I was is all I know."

"That's the grand adventure, Tehi. Think about what you'd like to be and create your own future."

I said nothing. I thought about what might happen on my return to Uruk. If my plan didn't work, I wouldn't have a future. My eyes welled with tears. Maybe that was for the best. After all, where would I go?

"Will you talk to him?" Hyme's voice was soft.

Blinking my tears away, my lips tightened and then relaxed. I sighed. "Yes."

He smiled. "Good. Now, why don't you stop pretending you're grinding the Laerd to dust and break some more erleby for me? Once the batch I'm cooking is done, we can practice our hypnosis."

I smiled for the first time in days. "All right." I picked up the pestle and started grinding. By the time I'd finished, the syrup was ready. After it had cooled, I helped him bottle it.

"Let's practice now." We worked until dinnertime. Bundling up, we headed for the dining hall. Taking my seat, I noticed Teger looking my way. His face was bland, but his eyes spoke volumes.

After our meal, Hyme and I walked out the hall's door. He laid a hand on my arm. "Don't come to the lab tonight, Tehi."

"But we need to practice."

"Yes, but there's something more important you have to do."

I looked at my snowshoes and sighed. "I suppose I do. I'll see you tomorrow, then."

"All right. Good night, Tehi."

"Good night."

I shoed along the street, thinking about what I would say to Teger. What difference would it make? I no longer had a life. I felt stark naked. *Reinvent yourself,* Hyme had said. "And just how am I supposed to do *that?*" I muttered.

I stepped into my tower and trudged up the steps. Throwing my furs over a fireplace chair, I plopped into it, wondering if there was any-thing *to* say.

An hour or so later, it was time to get ready for the service. I felt no joy, no anticipation while I dressed. It was a chore, something I had to do because it was my duty. Flinging my cloak over my shoulders, I descended the stairs. *Why do I even bother? I'm not qualified.*

You stopped being qualified when you became his lover, a small voice echoed.

"True," I whispered.

So why is it any different now?

"Because then I believed."

I didn't whisper my usual litany as I lit the candles and incense. I was lighting them for Astoreth, but She was no longer my Most Holy One. I knelt at the altar and waited.

My voice sounded flat throughout the service. Even my cropping the penitents was lackluster. I wondered if they could tell I no longer cared. After cleaning the É, I picked up my slippers and headed for my apartment, still wearing my sacred shoes. To me, they weren't sacred anymore. They were just shoes.

I shucked my garb, leaving it in a pile on the floor. Smearing on makeup remover, I took a hot shower, almost hotter than I could stand. After my bath, I leaned back in a fireplace chair and stared at the ceiling.

How about this? You dicknut, you've totally ruined my life, and now you expect me to— I jumped to my feet. "Forget it. It doesn't matter."

At the vanity, I raked a comb through my curls. It was time to go. I reached for my uniform, then dropped my arm. I turned my head and stared at the furs slung over the chair. I would wear neither. The clothes belonged to the É, and for me had acquired a new symbolic meaning—not of faith, but of the Devi's lies. And tonight was not a night for lies.

I opened the battlement door and stepped out, hardly feeling the cold. My bare feet leaving tracks in the snow, I reached his door and rang the bell.

It opened immediately. We stared at each other for a moment, then he stepped back. I walked to the roaring fireplace and turned. "By showing me your chronicle, by showing me that dead alien, you stripped me bare, Teger. I am nothing. But I have one truth. No matter what She did to your people, no matter what you think of Her, Astoreth is still my grandmother."

He slowly shook his head. "No, Tehi. I left you with another truth."

The next thing I knew, I'd been swept off my feet. His face was inches away, his star-colored glare boring into my brain. "You're mine," he growled, and laid on a brutal kiss. Lightning crackled through me, and I knew it was true.

I was his. I would always be his.

After pulling away, he carried me to a fireplace chair. Curled in his lap, I looked up and gazed into his eyes. There were tears in them. "I thought I'd lost you," he said, his voice husky.

"I thought you'd lost me, too," I whispered. "But you have to help me."

"Anything."

"I don't know who I am anymore. Help me find myself."

He nodded and kissed my forehead. "I will."

I lay my head on his chest. We sat that way until the fire, burning so bright when I arrived, had dwindled to embers. He carried me to the bed and gently laid me on the furs. Then he slipped in beside me and turned out the light.

We made love for the rest of the night. By morning, I was exhausted. And I still had a service to run.

He stroked my hair. "You sure you're up to this?"

"I have to. Besides, it's not hard."

I started to get up, but he pulled me down and gave me a deep kiss. Ending it, I ruffled his hair and stood, then took a step toward the door. I hesitated. After being so warm, crossing the battlement naked was not going to be pleasant. "Here. Wear this." I turned to see him holding out his coat.

"But—"

"I'll get it during your service."

"All right." Bunching the coat around my waist so I wouldn't trip, I walked to the door and stepped out. Trying to ignore the snow's cold under my feet, I realized the despair and numbness I'd felt for the past marun had lifted. I grinned. I had two pieces to a new life. My future was still precarious, but even that looked brighter now.

Chapter Thirty-One

My tour as beacon steward was up in two marun.

Since our reconciliation, Teger had been acting strangely. I decided it was time to tell him my plan, but couldn't. Every time I tried to bring up the end of my tour, he shushed me.

"Teger, we really—"

"Shh, shh. It'll be fine."

If I persisted, he only smiled and held a finger to my lips or kissed me into silence. I lost my temper a few times, but even then he wouldn't talk to me, wouldn't say a word. Just smiled.

There were other changes, too. Teger was never a chatterbox, but now he was much quieter than was usual. Sometimes I'd catch him staring intently, seemingly at nothing. Other times, I'd feel his gaze on my back, and I'd turn to see him fixing me with a steady, unblinking stare. Then a slow smile would spread across his face.

It was unnerving. Many times, I thought to send a tendril of power to find out what was going on with him, but didn't. I'd done it once, but I vowed long ago that I would never invade his privacy like that again.

One after midday, Hyme and I were in the lab, discussing our latest hypnosis practice session when the door flew open and Teger strode inside. "Thought you'd be in here. We need to talk."

I swiveled my chair. "About what?"

"Us. We leave next marun, second day."

"Where are we going?"

"Away from here. From Mjor. Maybe to Gurm or one of the other big cities. I've got tickets as far as Uppala—that's a travel hub—and we can decide where to go from there."

My eyes widened. "Wait. You...you've been planning this all along."

Teger raised his brow. "Of course. You thought I was just going to let you go? Anyway—"

"But I can't just leave. I'll be arrested."

"Not if you're not here."

I shook my head. "Astoreth will come looking for me."

He grinned. "If She does, She'll break the Protocol, and that means She'll have another war on Her hands. I'm sure She doesn't want that."

"Teger, you're not getting it. All She has to do is spin a story about some rogue Devi on the loose, and *everyone* will be looking for me." I gave him a meaningful look. "And I won't be hard to find."

"Then we'll go into the mountains. I'll build a cabin, we'll grow our own food, I'll hunt—"

"What about the things we can't grow or hunt?"

"I'll make sure we're close enough to a village to buy what we need."

"And we'll do what for money?"

He let out an exasperated sigh. "Älskling, I'm trying to figure this out, and you're not helping."

"Listen to yourself. You would keep me cooped up in a cabin year after year until the day I die. Besides, weren't you the one who told me life in the mountains tends to be hard and short?"

"You're a healer."

"What if I can't get the herbs and plants I need? You could die from a simple cut. And what if it's something worse than that? Teger, without a clinic at the very least, one or both of us might end up dead sooner than you think."

"So what do *you* suggest?"

I licked my lips. "I go to Uruk."

His jaw dropped, and his eyes looked like they'd pop from his head. "Are you crazy? Astoreth will kill you!"

Hyme raised his hand. "Wait. What's this about Astoreth killing you?"

I explained the penalty for breaking my vows. "Being her granddaughter might save me, but I doubt it."

He clapped his hands once. "The Laerd is right. You can't go back. I have friends—"

"Who will have me, Hyme? Your friends might be willing to take me in, but what about the rest of the villagers? Look how hard it was to get the Mjorans to accept me, and a lot of them still don't." I looked at Teger. "And do you really think it'll be any easier in the cities?" I blew a heavy sigh. "Don't you see? The only place I can live in this perritory is Mjor."

Teger snorted. "You go back to Uruk, you won't be living anywhere."

Hyme frowned. "What do you have in mind, Tehi?"

I looked from one man to the other. "I have a plan."

"What is it?" the two men said as one.

I told them everything. "That's why I had to be the first to find the cure and the reason for my memory experiments. I developed a drug that erases memories from the conscious mind, and only the conscious mind...at least I hope. As for the hypnosis that's where you come in, Hyme. While I'm under, you'll shoot me with my drug and tell me what and what not to remember. You'll also tell me I'm still Astoreth's acolyte. With her psi power, the last thing I need is for Her to learn I know what She really is."

Hyme's frown deepened. "How will you get your memories back? Do you have an antidote for your drug?"

"I didn't have time to develop one. I'm counting on hypnosis, especially since we're only talking about erasing the conscious mind and not the subconscious."

He rubbed his chin. "I don't know, Tehi—"

Teger waved his hand. "It's too risky."

I stared at him. "Do you really want us to live our lives constantly on the run from Astoreth?"

"No, but—"

"Then it's settled. Hyme, we'll do it the day before I leave. That should give the drug time to spread through my system."

He looked uncertain. "I don't like the idea of you experimenting on yourself but...all right."

"It's a gamble, and a big one. But it's the only chance I have."

Teger eyed me. "Even if Astoreth doesn't execute you, what makes you think She'll allow you to come back here?"

I looked at him. "That's the second part of my plan," I said, and outlined it for them. "It's even riskier than the first part, but I know my grandmother. And I also know the kind of power games the Gods in the Great Pantheon play with each other."

The lab went quiet. "How will we know if it all worked?" Teger said.

I gazed at him. "Look for me on the garrison's next supply run. If I'm on it, you'll know. If I'm not..." My lips tightened.

He reached me in two long strides and crushed me against him. "Älskling, I don't want... I can't live without you. What am I to do?"

I gazed into his star-colored eyes. "Pray."

⊙⊐⊐⊐⊐⊙

Outside the village gates, I watched the airship settle on its landing pad. The pilot shut down the engines, and the glow beneath its belly faded. The door opened. A morevi in uniform, identical to mine, exited the ship. This would be Morevi Nareet from Irdu, another of Astoreth's cities.

He walked toward me, stopping about five šīzu away. We pressed palms and gave each other deep bows. "May the Most Holy One turn Her face to you, Morevi Nareet."

"And to you, Moreva Tehi."

"Welcome to the Syren Perritory." I turned to the blue uniformed hakoi standing behind me. "Morevi Nareet, this is Kepten Stiren, your second in command."

Stiren inclined his head and clicked his heels. "Morevi."

"The garrison is ready for your inspection, Morevi," I said.

We walked along the uniformed rows. After the inspection, Nareet dismissed the troops at my prompting. Then we walked over to Teger. His star-colored eyes were just as cold as they'd been when we first met. "Morevi Nareet, this is Laerd Teger, Chief of Mjor."

Nareet bowed. "May the Most Holy One turn Her face to you."

I bit my lip. How would he answer? Knowing him, he'd say something rude.

"And to you, Morevi Nareet."

I almost let out a sigh of relief.

He stared at Nareet. "I have village affairs to attend to. I will see you in the dining hall for lunch." He strode away.

Nareet frowned. "Is he always like that?"

"Like what?"

"So cold."

"Don't worry. He doesn't like us, but he'll be civil enough to you."

398

We slowly approached the village gates. It was so much like what Eresh and I had done a year ago, it almost seemed like a dream. I explained the village's bright colors and what they meant. We headed for the tower. I changed the bioscan to match his readings. I showed him the É, and then we ascended to the apartment. Already, I thought of it as his, not mine.

I gave him the nupaper with the village rules. "They're there for very good reasons. Don't break them."

Next, I showed him the bath and then the larder. "Last winter, Mjor had a blizzard. If it happens again, the larder will keep you fed until the village is cleared." I pointed out the door to the battlement. "Laerd Teger's apartment is on the other side. If you must see him—like when Kepten Stiren gives you his marunly requests for provisions—it's easier to get to him this way."

A pang went through my hearts. *Yes, it's very easy this way.*

Last, we toured the beacon control room. Unlike me, Nareet had been thoroughly briefed on what he was expected to do and thoroughly briefed on the Protocol. I pointed out the manuals, and then we were finished. We returned to the apartment.

I tapped the bar. "Time."

"Second hour, fifty-three minutes Tryn."

"You'd better get to the dining hall. They won't tolerate you being late."

Nareet raised his brows. "And if I am?"

I smiled. "You won't get fed."

Outside, I headed to the garrison's quarters. I didn't eat much. Afterward, I walked through the garrison's door for the last time. Gazing at the airship, I watched two troops load my trunks into the cargo hold. Teger walked through the gates and stood in his usual spot when greeting visitors. I met him and looked up. His face looked impassive, but his eyes showed his fear and misery.

"I love you," he whispered.

"Love you more." I hesitated. "Wait." I walked to the airship and returned with a large, heavy box. It was the thalin rock the miners had given me and my red jewel. I held it out to him. "Keep this for me."

His face melted into a mask of pain. He knew why I'd done this. If I survived, I'd be back for it. If I didn't, it was something to remember me by.

"Time to go, Moreva," the pilot called. I looked over my shoulder and saw him seated at the ship's controls.

I climbed inside and took my seat behind the pilot. The door closed. I looked out the window. Teger hadn't moved.

The pilot revved the engines, and the drives beneath the airship roared, their backwash blowing Teger's long, golden hair about his head. We lifted off. I watched him until I couldn't see him anymore.

I turned and let out a small sigh, wondering if I'd survive this last trip to Uruk.

⊙⊐⊐⊐⊐⊙

"So it was true, then." Astoreth spoke in that calm, quiet manner that meant she was enraged.

Head bowed, I knelt before Her golden throne in the É's Great Hall. I was sweating inside my uniform, even with the air conditioning running full blast. "Yes, Most Holy One."

"Are you pregnant?"

"No, Most Holy One. I took...precautions."

"At least there is that." She said nothing for a few minutes. "Give me one reason why I should not execute you."

"There is no reason, Most Holy One. I broke my most sacred vows to You. And I know not even being Your granddaughter will save me. But before you pronounce sentence, I would bargain with You."

"Bargain? With me?"

"Yes, Most Holy One. My life in exchange for the red fever cure."

"You defied me and took your research to Mjor? I demand you give me the formula. Now. Then we will see about sparing your life."

"I don't remember it, Most Holy One."

I could almost see my grandmother's jaw drop. "Surely you wrote it down."

"Yes, Most Holy One. But I hid it somewhere in Mjor. I don't remember where."

A wave of psi power hit me so hard it knocked me off my knees. Pain ripped through my head and hearts. I cried out, writhing on the black and gold tiled floor. As quickly as the pain had come, it was gone. I struggled to get up, my body on fire.

"Very clever, Moreva. You made a drug that erased your memory. But you also made an antidote."

"Yes, Most Holy One." I tried not to pant.

"Then here is my bargain. You will go to Mjor, take your drug, and get the formula for me. In return, I assure you a quick and painless death."

I didn't answer at first. My hearts beat faster. I took a deep breath. "No, Most Holy One. I do not accept Your bargain."

"You refuse me? You blaspheme! I will make you change your mind."

"You would torture me then, Most Holy One. You may execute me, but can You really find it in Your heart to torture me?"

The Great Hall was silent. An eternity seemed to pass. "No," Astoreth finally said. She said nothing after that, and another eternity seemed to pass. "What is to stop me from executing you now and then going to Mjor to look for the formula? It is mine. I am perfectly within my rights."

"The Laerd would never give his permission for You or Your troops to enter the village. If you did, the Protocol would be broken."

"And if I do break it?"

"You would start a war, Most Holy One. And I doubt the other Gods in the Great Pantheon would help you."

"Not if I told Them about the formula."

"Do You really want war with the Syrenese, Most Holy One? They provide most of Your thalin. You'd have to depend on the southern mines, and their output isn't nearly enough to sustain all the Gods and Their cities, towns, and farms. You wouldn't be able to fight a war."

"We have stockpiles."

"Yes, Most Holy One. But the war will be long and bitter. How long do You think Your stockpiles will last?" I paused. "And I would think You would want to keep the formula for Yourself. Imagine how many talents You could make selling it to the other É's."

"That is true."

More silence. And then, to my surprise, Astoreth laughed. "You are a cunning one, are you not, Tehi?" She chuckled. "Very well. I accept your bargain. Come here, child."

I looked up. She was smiling. I climbed the three golden steps and stood. She patted Her thighs. I leapt toward the throne and curled in Her lap, feeling like a little girl again. I gazed into Her golden eyes. "I-I'm sorry, Grandmother," my voice hitched. "I didn't mean to—"

"We never mean to fall in love. It just happens sometimes." Astoreth gave me a little squeeze. "It pains me you chose the Laerd over Me. But that too happens sometimes."

She fell silent. I knew she was thinking about my mother.

She stroked my hair. "Now. There is the question of your punishment."

I nodded.

She smiled. "Violating the Protocol is a very serious offense. So is disobeying me, not to mention breaking your vows. What should I do with you?"

"You could always exile me to Mjor."

Her smile broadened. "Why would I want to do that?"

"Because the Laerd saved my life from the fire in the beacon tower. You said You owed him a great debt." I paused. "I think he'll accept my exile as adequate repayment."

"I think he would, too." Her face grew serious. "But you know what this means, do you not? You can never return to Uruk or to Kherah."

"I know, Grandmother." I said nothing for a moment. "Will you come visit me?"

Astoreth smiled and caressed my cheek. "Of course, child." Her face turned serious again. "But from now on, you are no longer a moreva. You will stay in the worker's quarters until the next supply ship for leaves for Mjor. Until that time, you will wear the clothing I give you. You will have no contact with the morevs in my É, nor will you have contact with the Laerd. When it is time for you to leave, I will allow you to take one gown and one item you treasure. Choose wisely."

"Thank you, Grandmother."

"Now. I have many things to do. Go to the workers' quarters. You will be assigned a room. Stay there and wait for someone to bring you clothing." She peered through narrowed eyes. "Did I mention you will be eating with the hakoi?"

"No, but I don't mind. I...I learned a lot about love in Mjor."

"And so you did." She gave me a final squeeze. "Off you go."

I climbed off her lap. "But you do know that I love you, right, Grandmother? I mean—"

"I know, child. I know. Go."

I felt my way down the steps, bowed and backed out of the Great Hall. In the corridor, I headed for the worker's quarters. A small sigh escaped me. *I'm lucky to be alive.*

Arriving at a bank of elevators, I pressed the call button and a set of doors whispered open. Stepping inside the cab, I thought about my punishment. To my surprise, I didn't feel sadness over it. *I'll miss Kherah, and I'll miss the É, but there really isn't anything here for me anymore...if there ever was, except for Grandmother.* I thought about Eresh. *I'll miss him terribly. I wish I could say good-bye, to explain. It'd be easy to contact him...but I dare not disobey Grandmother. Not this time.*

I stepped out of the elevator and walked along the drab hallway leading to the workers' quarters. Stopping before the doors guarding the dormitory, I let out another small sigh. *I'll do what I have to do...but it's going to be a long six marun.*

The doors whisked open, and I walked inside.

⊙╤╤╤╤⊙

The airship lifted off, and we were on our way to Mjor. No longer a moreva, my passenger status was about equal to baggage. Instead of sitting up front behind the pilot, I was sitting in a jump seat with boxes piled around me. I was lucky she hadn't put me in the cargo hold.

The ship banked, then shot northward. A knot of anxiety formed in the pit of my stomach. The past six marun had given me plenty of time to think about my future, something I tried my best not to do. I got what I wanted from my grandmother; I escaped execution and was headed to Mjor. But what would happen once I got there? If the Mjorans didn't know about Teger and me before, they would know as soon as I showed up. And I knew what would happen. Teger would be branded a traitor, and either swing from the battlement, or be dropped into the mine. *And I'll be right there with him.*

My jaw tightened. *I don't care. They can execute us any way they want, as long as they execute us together.*

A few hours later, the airship's motion pushed me against the bulkhead, and I felt my stomach drop. *We're landing.* My hearts beat faster.

I heard the pilot give the "all clear," and the sound of many booted feet heading for the door. About five minutes later, two of the garrison began unloading the baggage area. They finally saw me sitting in the corner. As one, they startled. They'd only seen me in uniform or in my morevic garb. Right now, I wore my favorite dress, a floor length, off the shoulder gown with a plunging neckline, a tight bodice, and slits on each side almost reaching to my hips. The gown nicely set off my curves. Most startling to them, I knew, was that I wore no makeup.

The two men shoved several boxes aside. One trooper helped me out of my seat, and the other carried a delicate wooden frame, pointed at both ends, and strung with wire made from pirsu gut. I followed the troopers to the airship's exit.

Wild cheers and whistling greeted me when I appeared in the hatchway. I would have looked up to see what the fuss was about, but I had to concentrate on navigating the airship's steep stairs. Between my dress and slippers, tripping was a real danger. The troopers escorted me, one in front and the other, carrying my instrument, behind. On the landing pad, the trooper handed my piece to me.

I turned and my anxiety evaporated. Teger stood in his usual place when greeting the new morev. The cheering and whistling came from the mob of Mjorans spilling outside of the gates behind him.

But I had eyes only for Teger.

I started walking, my steps quickening until I was flat out running. In one fluid move, I set my instrument on the ground and leapt into his arms. Holding his face in my hands, I kissed him long and deep, and that familiar electric feeling exploded through me. He twirled me around. The villagers' cheering sounded far away.

After a not-long-enough eternity, he set me on the ground, his hands gripping my shoulders. Tears threatening to spill, his face shone with joy. "I thought…I thought I'd never—"

I rested my hands on his chest. "I know. Astoreth wouldn't allow me to contact you. Part of the deal I had to make."

His expression turned sour. "Tik."

I laughed. "Now, now. Don't speak of my grandmother that way."

He sniffed. "You smell funny."

"Astoreth made me live with the workers. They eat makira, a cabbage with a pungent odor. And taste. Pretty nasty, too. But don't worry—it'll fade."

He smiled, and then looked at the ground. "What's this?"

"My mother's harp."

"Will you play it for me?"

"Of course."

"Maybe you could play it for us, too."

"Us?"

"The village. I'm sure they'd love to hear you play and sing."

I laughed again. "I haven't been here five minutes, and you've already got me giving concerts."

"You don't have to—"

"Of course I will."

He gazed into my eyes, then looked me up and down. He peeked down my cleavage. "I love that dress."

"Thought you would. Astoreth allowed me to take one gown and one thing I treasured. So I took my favorite gown and my harp."

"You must be cold, though."

"I am."

He slipped out of his furred vest. "Here. Wear this. I'll have one made for you." He helped me put it on. "Come. Let's go inside." He picked up my harp in one hand and held mine in the other.

The Mjorans, who hadn't stopped cheering, clapped me on the back as we made our way through the crowd, some blows hard enough to make me stumble. "Where's Hyme?" I shouted.

"In the hospital," Teger shouted back. "We're going there now. Wait'll he sees you." He gave me a small smile. "We didn't change the locks. I guess it was our way of praying for you to come back."

I smiled and squeezed his hand.

We reached the lab. The villagers had followed us, their cheers subsiding to an excited babble. Teger turned to them. "Don't worry. You'll be seeing lots of her. But right now, we're going to visit with Hyme."

Hyme wasn't in the lab. I looked at Teger. "He'll be here in a minute," Teger said.

I looked up at him. "Well, I certainly wasn't expecting *that* kind of reception. What—"

He held a finger to my lips and smiled.

A second later, Hyme walked through the hospital door. His jaw dropped. "Tehi," he shouted. He ran over and enveloped me in a great hug. "Thank the gods. I thought..." His nose wrinkled. "What's that awful smell?"

"Makira," Teger and I said as one. I explained it to him and laughed. "Like terbone."

Hyme let go. Hands on my shoulders, he gazed into my eyes. "A celebration is certainly in order, but let's see if we can get your memory back, first."

"Absolutely. Where's the antidote?"

The two men exchanged glances. "There is no antidote," Hyme said.

"But—"

"Trust me, Tehi." He nodded to Teger. "All right. Let's get set up. You sit here," he said, pointing his swivel chair.

Teger helped me out of his vest. Hyme rolled the other chair over, pulling so close our knees were almost touching. Then he drew a beautiful white thalin pendulum from his breast pocket.

Now I was really confused. "Hypnosis?"

"Yes. Let's begin." He held the pendulum at my eye level and began his patter. In moments, my body felt heavy as a rock. The lab disappeared. Still, I heard his voice cutting through the dark, telling me I no longer believed in Astoreth, there was no antidote to my drug, that I remembered the formula and where I'd hidden a copy. Without warning, I was wide awake.

Teger looked at me expectantly. Hyme looked worried. "Do you remember, Tehi?"

I closed my eyes and then opened them. "I—aaugh!" A searing pain zigzagged through my brain. I clapped my hands to the sides of my head and squeezed my eyes shut.

A pair of hands gripped my shoulders. "Älskling. Are you all right?"

The pain was gone as quickly as it had come. I let my hands fall to my lap and slowly opened my eyes. But there was something new. I bounced in my chair, then shot to my feet. "I remember. I remember!"

Racing to Hyme's apartment, I barreled up the stairs, almost tripping over my dress. I hurried to his overstuffed bookcase. Pulling a sheaf of nupapers from the shelf, I flipped through them until I found a blank sheet between two pieces of nupaper with writing on them. I pulled it out and returned the other nupapers to the shelf.

The two men stood at the top of the stairs, obviously bewildered. I looked at Hyme. "Get one of the burners going. Lowest setting." He ran down the steps. Teger and I were right behind him. Hyme lit the burner, and I held the nupaper over it, low enough to absorb the heat but high enough not to burn. While the three of us watched, black writing appeared. It was the formula for the red fever cure.

Hyme roared with laughter. "Alis sap. I don't believe this. The oldest trick in the book!"

Teger and I laughed, too. Our laughter subsided, and then he frowned. "Why didn't you use a tablet?"

"Because if anyone came looking for the formula, a tablet's the first thing they'd look for. Not a piece of nupaper. Especially not a piece of nupaper in the middle of a pile of other nupapers."

"You're brilliant, älskling." He looked his timepiece. "It's almost time for lunch. We'd better go."

I looked at Hyme. "Do you have an envelope I can use? I promised Astoreth the formula as soon as I got my hands on it. And could I have a small bag of linmen, a bag of mytle, and a bag of helly?"

"Of course, of course." He went to a cabinet and withdrew an envelope. Then he made up the three small bags and labeled them. "Here you are. But they're going to need more if they're going to make the cure in any quantity."

"I know," I said, and slipped the nupaper inside the envelope. "This is just to get them started." I grinned. "We'll sell them the seeds. At an exorbitant price."

Teger laughed, but Hyme didn't. "Tehi—"

"Just joking. I'll trade the seeds for some new equipment."

He looked mollified.

At the dining hall, I started for the main door. Teger grabbed my arm. "You'll sit on the dais. We've two healers now."

My lips curved into a tiny smile. *Everything's going to be all right.* "Thank you, Laerd."

"Don't thank me. It was the Council's idea."

We walked into the dining room. I took my seat next to an astonished-looking Morevi Nareet. "Moreva?" he said, sounding uncertain.

"Not anymore."

Hyme and I chatted while we ate. "The habitat you gave me—the plants are growing strong. You've made a farmer of me, yet."

"Knew I could."

After lunch, Teger and I hurried to the landing pad. The pilot was climbing into the airship. "Greetings, High One," I called. She turned and gave us a haughty look. "Would you see that this gets to the Most Holy One? Tell Her it's from Tehi. It's very important." I handed her the envelope and the three bags.

The pilot's eyes widened. Her jaw went slack, and a look of fear crossed her face. "I-I...of course. I'll give it to Her as soon as we land. You needn't worry."

"Thank you." I wasn't worried. If Astoreth learned I'd sent the formula and She didn't have it in Her hands right away, the pilot might find herself stuck ferrying thalin from the southern mines to one or two of Astoreth's backwater towns in Kherah.

Back in the lab, Hyme looked up and smiled. "Would you like some ale? It's a little early for me, but now we can celebrate Tehi's return to Mjor, getting her memory back, and finding the formula...what a glorious day it's been."

Teger gave my hair a single stroke. "Just one. We have to get her fitted for clothes. Much as I like to see her in it, she can't go running around in that dress all the time."

We stayed at Hyme's for about an hour. On the street, Mjorans waved at us. Stopping at the tailor's, the young woman took my measurements and promised she'd have an outfit ready tomorrow with more in a few days. Our next stop was the furrier and then the quilter. "Might as well get them now," Teger said. The shoemaker was last. By the time we'd finished, it was time for dinner.

After eating, we hurried to Teger's tower. He fairly dragged me up the steps. Inside his apartment, he set my harp next to his desk and sighed. "Alone at last." He sank into a fireplace chair.

I had barely settled in his lap when I gave him an expectant look. "So why aren't we swinging from the battlement right now?"

His face turned serious. "I called an emergency meeting and told everyone everything." His brow quirked. "Well, not everything. I didn't tell them about your research or my setting Prag up. But I told them what he'd said was true. I told them about you breaking your vows, and what might happen when you returned to Uruk." His star-colored gaze bored into mine. "And I told them I loved you more than my own life."

He let out a breath. "I told the Council if they sentenced me to swing, I was ready. They voted to spare me, and well, I'm still here."

I snuggled against him. "I'm glad you're still here, too."

We fell silent. The he stirred. "I'll sure be glad when that smell goes away."

I laughed. "I can't smell it anymore. But I know exactly what I smell like."

His look turned mischievous. "Smell or no smell, it's not going to stop me from ravishing you."

I matched his look. "Ravish away."

He pushed me off his lap. Leading me to the bed, he slowly peeled off my dress. Then he laid me on the furs. He took off his clothes, joined me, and then turned out the light.

I smiled in the darkness. A third piece of my new life had fallen into place.

It felt good to be home.

Author's Note

Hello, and thank you for reading *The Moreva of Astoreth!* I hope you enjoyed it.

I've been asked where the idea for this story came from. Well, its roots date back to my college days. A friend and I collaborated on a tale about a princess exiled by her father. Living in a faraway village, she fell in love with a man very much like Laerd Teger. Unfortunately for them, the story didn't have a happy ending. I've long since lost touch with my friend, but that little tale stuck with me. One day, I decided it deserved to be written. I think she'd be happy with the result.

Want to come along with me on my literary travels? Join my email list at https://www.roxannebland.rocks! You can stay updated on my works-in-progress and much more. And by signing up, you'll receive a FREE ebook! *The Final Victim* is the companion novella to my dark, dark paranormal urban fantasy/science fiction/romance mashup series The Underground—available in ebook and print from bookstores everywhere.

Two more things. First, please consider leaving a review of *The Moreva of Astoreth* on the site where you purchased it, on your favorite readers' website(s), or recommending it to a friend. It's much appreciated. Second, I love connecting with readers—feel free to drop me a note at roxanne@roxannebland.rocks!

Roxanne Bland